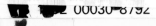
Jones, Tristan
Dutch treat.

DISCARDED

DATE DUE

Ja 9 '80	Dec 22 '80	
Ja 31 '80	May 26 '81	
	Jul 6 '81	
Feb 6 '80	Aug 18 '81	
Fe 23 '80	Apr 28 '82	
	Aug 10 '82	
Mar 5 '80	Jan 23 84	
Mr 18 '80		
	Feb 8 '85	
Aug 6 '80		
Sep 15 '80		
Sep 27 '80		

* DUTCH TREAT *

DUTCH TREAT

9.95

DUTCH TREAT

A Novel of World War II

TRISTAN JONES

ANDREWS AND McMEEL, INC.
A Universal Press Syndicate Company
KANSAS CITY • NEW YORK • WASHINGTON

Library of Congress Cataloging in Publication Data

Jones, Tristan, 1924–
    Dutch treat.

    1. World War, 1939–1945—Fiction. I. Title.
PZ4.J796Du 1979 [PR6060.059] 823'.9'14 79-18856
ISBN 0-8362-6107-0

Some of the events recounted in this book are based on fact. Some of the characters are based on real people who took part in those events. Others are completely fictional. I have tried to do justice to the former and to my readers with the latter.

Dedication: *To Mademoiselle Beatrice Maud Heron, the daughter of a courageous soldier of France and to all who resisted Hitler before and after the Nazi invasion of the Soviet Union.*

In memory of H.M. destroyer *Glowworm,* 1,300 tons, which, on April 8, 1940, emerging from a fog in the Norwegian Sea, found herself under the sights of the 10,000-ton German cruiser *Admiral Hipper.* Vastly outgunned, *Glowworm* turned her puny hull toward the Nazi vessel and rammed her at full speed. *Glowworm* sank within minutes with great loss of life, but she put a crack ship of the Nazi Navy out of action for the most crucial months of the sea war, and she taught the Nazi Navy a lesson that they never forgot: that British *decadence* is a guise worn only before *friends*.

New Year's Eve, 1978
Manhattan, New York

Acknowledgments

Contents

Nid oes ar uffern ond eisau ei threfnu.
(All hell needs is organization.)
The White Book of Rhydderch, A.D. 1308
Gwyddfarch Gyfarwydd (Welsh author and bard)

* *

What they could do with around here is a good war. What else can you expect with peace running wild all over the place? You know what the trouble with peace is? No organization.
Mother Courage, Act I
Bertholdt Brecht

* *

No organization—that's their problem—what they could do with is six months in the peacetime British Army—that would smarten them up.
A very senior British Army officer, as he watched exhausted French troops, after fifteen days of continuous battle on the beaches of Dunkirk, May 1940.

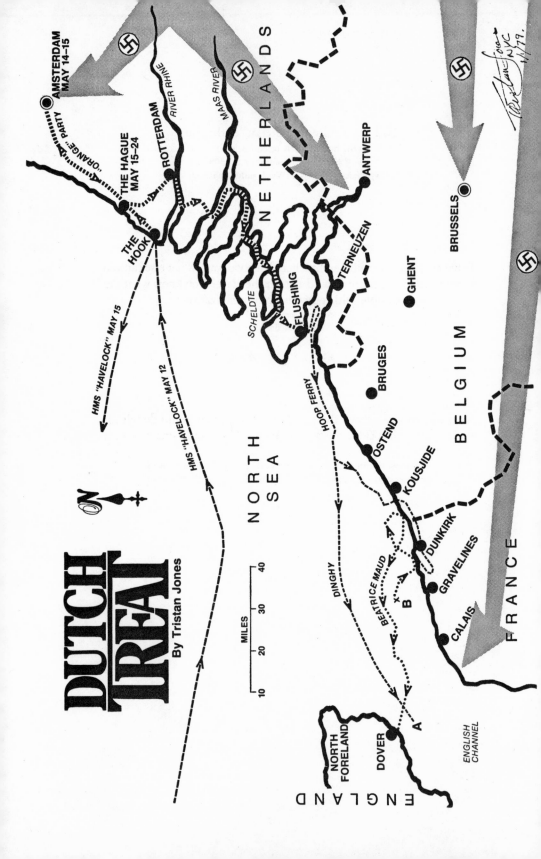

DUTCH TREAT

By Tristan Jones

ENGLAND

NORTH FORELAND

DOVER

NORTH SEA

ENGLISH CHANNEL

HMS "HAVELOCK" MAY 15

HMS "HAVELOCK" MAY 12

DINGHY

BEATRICE MAUD

HOOP FERRY

A

B

X

CALAIS

GRAVELINES

DUNKIRK

KOUSJIDE

OSTEND

BRUGES

GHENT

BRUSSELS

FRANCE

BELGIUM

NETHERLANDS

ANTWERP

TERNEUZEN

FLUSHING

SCHELDTE

THE HOOK

ROTTERDAM

THE HAGUE
MAY 15–24

"ORANGE" PARTY

AMSTERDAM
MAY 14–15

RIVER RHINE

MAAS RIVER

MILES

10 20 30 40

N

Chapter 1

*   *

Have You Any Dirty Washing, Mother Dear?

We're gonna hang out the washing on the Siegfried Line,
Have you any dirty washing, Mother dear?
We're gonna hang out the washing on the Siegfried Line,
If the Siegfried Line's still there;
Whether the weather may be wet or fine,
We'll just rub along without a care,
We're gonna hang out the washing on the Siegfried Line . . .
If the Siegfried Line's still there!

This gem was highly popular in Britain,
late 1939 to May 1940.

1.

"Have You Any Dirty Washing, Mother Dear?"

10th May 1940. 7:45 A.M.
Corner of the Strand and Charing Cross, London

'C' had a face that always looked like it needed assistance. Hunched against the cold morning drizzle, he alighted from the taxi, his raincoat buttoned at the neck, his umbrella held aloft. He thought, *Funny how fewer and fewer people are carrying gas masks.* He passed, limping slightly, through Trafalgar Square, with the stream of clerks and typists hurrying from Charing Cross Station. The wet weather made his leg ache. The pain reminded him, *Pity about that bullet at the Somme, should have kept my head down.* He paused to pick up a *Daily Telegraph*, as he'd done every morning for ten years.

"Mornin' sir," Old Charlie mumbled. He was muffled up to the ears, looking as if he'd been carved into the newstand, a chubby seventy-year-old grinning cockney Buddha smoking a damp Woodbine cigarette. 'C' wondered if he ever went home. He handed over twopence.

"Morning, Charlie, how's the world today?" 'C' grinned.

"Wet." Charlie slipped the twopence into a greasy bag tied around his middle. His left hand had no thumb; it didn't look odd to 'C', but he often wondered of which war it was a reminder.

"Might clear up a bit later, eh?" 'C' glanced up at the clouds—so low they were scraping the statue of Lord Nelson atop its column, making it appear to move to the southwest, as if the little admiral were trying to beat to windward, back to Portsmouth . . . or Trafalgar.

"Then again, it might not," grunted Charlie. "Looks like we're gettin' a right bashin' in Norway . . . bloke in the *Daily 'Erald* says we'll be pullin' out any day now."

"Well, got to look on the bright side, Charlie, the Navy's given Hitler's fleet a hammering in Norway, too."

'C' stuffed the *Daily Telegraph* into his small, battered attaché case. "See you Charlie." He moved on as Charlie passed a *Times* to a bowler-hatted gent. 'C' wiped his damp mustache. He was glad to turn into the small door under the Admiralty Arch, out of the knifing damp. *Like a rat up a drainpipe,* he thought, grinning to himself. He entered the warm corridor, painted standard glossy government green to the shoulder, then off-white, with hazy light cast by bulbs always twenty watts below the need. 'C' passed along the long underground corridor, also green and white. The day shift was not due for another hour yet. The night guards, one at each door, were packing their empty sandwich bags and thermos bottles away, itching to get out into the street and onto transport home. All except Peabody, still wide awake on his chair. *Room 604. First Lord of the Admiralty*.

"Morning, sir," Peabody grinned at 'C', eyeing the wet raincoat. Peabody always looked as if he'd just had a bath.

"Morning, Albert," 'C' nodded towards the door. "The First Lord in yet?"

"Mmm, been in since five o'clock, sir. I don't know 'ow he keeps it up. Left 'ere at midnight, back at five."

"What's going on?"

"The usual crowd's in there. They've been in since six. No one allowed in, no tea girls, no one. Orders, sir, except yourself o'course, naturally, sir."

"Right, Albert. How're things going?" *He must be the same age as me*, 'C' thought, *sixty-two, sixty-three?*

"Pretty fair, sir."

Strange chap, living on his own like that, contemplated 'C' as he opened the door and slid, as quietly as he could, inside the room.

"And so gentlemen, although we are not yet ready to roll up the map of Europe, we shall, however . . . " the First Lord of the Admiralty gestured toward the Women's Royal Naval Service (WRNS) attendant, a neat, pretty young woman with auburn hair. She moved toward the map as First Lord chomped on his cigar.

"We shall, however, move the map of Scandinavia temporarily to one side." The young woman did this, all the while gazing at the cherubic face, which seemed to scowl and snarl at the same time.

" . . . And we shall bring our immediate and undivided attention . . . " The young woman slid the new map of the Low Countries, Holland and Belgium, along the overhead track.

"To this . . . this . . . this pistol pointed at the heart of England." First Lord flung his cigar hand toward the map, then brought it back to take another puff, cigar ash falling onto his blue serge collar.

Two of the four men sitting around the red-baize-topped table did not show any reaction to the spate of hyberbole. They were well accustomed to First Lord's rhetoric by now. He'd been in office for eight months and had quoted every politician, general, and admiral of

note in the past twenty centuries. Only two men grinned: the air chief
marshall and 'C'. The general who was the chief of the Imperial
General Staff turned around and glared at them frostily. First Lord
raised one eyebrow a thousandth-of-an-inch and, in turn, glared at the
general.

"And that, gentlemen, is that, but before we part . . . " The red
telephone rasped in. First Lord removed his spectacles and reached for
the phone. As he listened, puffing on his cigar, his face cemented.
Around the table there was silence.

"C" glanced at his watch—eight-thirty-two.

First Lord dropped the phone onto its rest. He replaced his spectacles low on his stubby nose and slowly raised his head. He beamed.
Everyone waited.

"Gentlemen, the first good news of the day." First Lord cleared his
throat. "In consideration of the serious turn of events that has taken
place, consequent to the Nazi" (he pronounced it "naawzi," with a
feline curling snarl of his upper lip) "incursion into the Netherlands,
Belgium, and Luxembourg early this morning, His Majesty has seen
fit to invite me to form a new government, and I shall proceed to do so
with enthusiastic, if not precipitous, haste." First Lord dumped his
cigar and pressed the "clear" bell push.

'C' grinned to himself. *Now the fireworks will start*, he thought as
everyone made for the door.

Even as 'C' passed Peabody, he heard First Lord's urgent call. "Oh,
'C', one moment before you depart." First Lord caught up with 'C'
and put one hand on his shoulder, speaking quietly. "You no doubt
recall Case Orange? . . . Oh, Good day, Sergeant." First Lord had
noticed Peabody.

" 'Day, Sir." Peabody, flattered, acknowledged the greeting.

'C' thought for a second. "Case Orange? What . . . ? Oh yes,
indeed, Case Orange."

"Put it into effect, please, 'C'," said First Lord.

"You think . . . ?"

First Lord puffed at a new cigar, the shadow of a frown creasing his
broad face.

"Yes, 'C', I most certainly do think, and, in fact, as you may recall,
I have been thinking for some time, so much so that we discussed the
matter, and we both agreed on the action to be taken should certain
circumstances arise. . . . "

"Of course, immediately." 'C' was silent for a minute as he and
First Lord walked to the elevator. They were accompanied at a
distance by Geary, the Scotland Yard man, who had just broken off an

interesting conversation with Peabody about soccer cup finals. 'C'
turned to First Lord, "By the way, let me congratulate you."

First Lord smiled. "Thank you, indeed, 'C'. I don't know what the
chances of beating these Nazi scoundrels are, but at least we have the
opportunity now to try."

"Goodbye, sir, you know you have my fullest support."

"I shall need to see you again at four of the afternoon clock," said
First Lord, as he stepped back under Geary's proffered umbrella to
make his way to the waiting Daimler. 'C' moved out into the drizzle.

That was quick, 'C' mused. *He was asked to the Palace only eight
minutes ago and already they have a second detective in the Daimler . . . I
must give the chief commissioner a pat on the back.* 'C' checked his watch.
As he stepped into his regular cab, he thought, *Well, so it's come to that*,
Operation Orange. He settled back.

"Where to, guv?" the driver asked.

"Cambridge Circus, please."

Operation Orange, he reflected, as the cab moved through the honk-
ing traffic. *Purpose: to secure the rights and titles to all resources in the Dutch
East Indies. Oil, rubber, hemp, copper, iron, gold, silver, etcetera, etcetera.*
'C' lit his pipe. *Operation Orange. Action: to bring the Netherlands Royal
Family, by invitation, persuasion, coercion, or, if necessary, force, to British
territory and to secure the Netherlands Royal Treasure by any means. The
thinking,* 'C' ruminated, *is typical of him. Simple but audacious. Secure the
Dutch Royal Family and government. Prevent the Germans from forcing
Queen Wilhelmina to form a new, Nazi-controlled government in Holland. A
government that would rightfully control the rich resources of the vast Dutch
Empire in the East Indies and that would, under German direction, hand over
control of these resources to Japan, the third partner in the Axis. If this move is
blocked off, Japan may be forced into military action to seize the East Indies to
secure her war materials. And Japan may not make that military move
without first attempting to neutralize or destroy the American Pacific
Fleet . . . and that move will . . .*

But the thought was unthinkable, too much to hope for. 'C' shifted
his mental gears back to Operation Orange. *By any means. Plan One: to
persuade and assist the Dutch Government to bring the treasure over themselves. Plan Two: to coerce the Dutch into voluntarily handing over the
treasure. Plan Three: to seize the treasure and bring it over ourselves with or
without Dutch Government permission. With the speed of the Nazi advance . . . it looks like Plan Three. Simple*, thought 'C', *all we have to do
is burgle the Royal Palace and come back with the loot. Burglary in a good
cause. Must get those two chaps . . . what're their names, Michael?
Mitchum? No, Mitchell, and that ruffian, the other one . . . well, it's all*

5

on file. . . .

As the taxi squished through Leicester Square, 'C' caught a glimpse of a barrage balloon rising slowly, slowly up into the low gray clouds. *Very fitting*, he thought, *a balloon going up. If only we can avoid bloody trench warfare . . . anything rather than that.*

'C' paid off the taxi and wished the driver good day.

The building was small and unostentatious. There were, of course, no sandbags, no indication of the beehives of activity with which it was connected by every possible means of communication, from shortwave radio to underground tunnels. The only sign of the office's previous occupant was a Bertram Mill's Circus poster on the stair wall.

Must get that taken down one day, 'C' reminded himself. *All the same . . .* he nodded to Lawson as he doffed his coat. *All the same, we did get a few damned good men from that outfit; know every nook and cranny of Europe.*

"Morning Lawson, Margot in yet?"

"Yes, sir, in fact she's just brought me down a cuppa'." Lawson grinned and shifted his big body awkwardly, but 'C' knew this was merely an act—Lawson was probably one of the fittest men in the kingdom; an expert killer with fist, foot, elbow, knife or revolver, despite his gentle voice and his approaching half-century.

"Good, good. Send Lieutenant Dennis up to me as soon as he arrives." *Pity about that mess in Finland blowing Lawson's cover*, 'C' pondered, *just the man for this Orange job.* He mounted the stairs, noting the frayed carpet that would now remain frayed for the duration of the war.

"Morning . . . tea?" Margot was always a half-hour early.

"Good morning, mmm, that's very acceptable." 'C' settled down in his chair. He had purposely chosen an inside office with no windows through which the sane world of London could intrude.

Margot said, "DI has an urgent message, and Ultra is kicking up about your . . . well, they call it your impatience. Jamieson's threatening to walk off the job."

Margot was forty-five, the mirror image, outside the Circus, of a vinegary spinster, with a sharp face, thick-lensed spectacles, graying hair, low-heeled shoes, and a collection of frocks that all looked as if they had been picked up at a Hampstead jumble sale. But this was deceptive, because when she removed her glasses, which was not often, the gray eyes betrayed her keen intelligence. Her caustic wit was famed throughout the Circus. She had been with the firm for so long now that the whole show seemed to revolve around her. Only 'C' and Canning had been around before Margot, and together, during the early thirties, they had seen the Circus wither away to almost nothing but a few university dons. Together they had scrimped and cajoled their way through the lean years, until the writing was on the wall by the mid-thirties. Now they controlled a worldwide staff of several hundred agents in the most unlikely lairs and on the most obvious promenades.

"I'll deal with Jamieson a little later," 'C' said, returning the code wizard's cable back to the "in" tray. "Margot, be a dear and dig out for me the file on . . . er, what's the name?" He thought for a moment, sipping the hot tea. "Er . . . let me see . . . you know, the one on experts under surveillance, section not under control, subsection . . . er, what the dickens?"

"APG, criminals, incarcerated?" Margot prompted.

"Quite," 'C' stared at Margot for a moment. She smiled at him. "How did you know?" he asked her. He was always amazed at her seemingly miraculous knowledge of the file system. Thousands and thousands of files.

"I heard the news this morning." She poured him out another tea. "And I thought of Operation Orange," she said, quietly smiling.

"Just like that?" 'C' smiled back. *Good woman*, he thought to himself. *Hope Lieutenant Dennis, the boy wonder of Bloomsbury, is half as bright.*

"Just like that." She walked out of the office like a battleship under full steam.

'C' shook his head in grinning disbelief. *Makes good tea*, he reflected.

Margot returned with a flat, thin file and set it out in front of 'C'. He opened the file and flicked through it, almost carelessly. Then he stopped and picked up the phone. "Get me the governor of Dartmoor Prison," he asked the operator in a low, doubtful voice, as if he didn't believe it was himself speaking.

10th May 1940. 9:15 A.M.
Dartmoor Prison, Devon

There are few buildings on this earth that really live up to their sinister legend in appearance. Of these few, probably the greatest number are prisons. By no means are all prisons sinister looking, despite their history. The Tower of London, for example, could conjure up fairy tales of princes and dragons. Seen from a distance, it seems innocuous, like the backdrop of a pantomime.

"The Moor" had a reputation as ugly as it looked. Built by French prisoners of war during the struggle against Napoleon, it lurked behind squat, long gray thirty-foot-high walls, in a hollow in the bleak, mist-shrouded hills of Dartmoor. Behind the walls were blocks of dingy rust-colored brick cell buildings, with row upon row of tiny barred windows. Only the top two floors of cells had windows from which a view could be had over the tops of the walls. These were reserved for the privileged "good conduct" prisoners. The star-men, those considered or known to be bad risks, were housed in the bottom floors, and their place of work was, in most cases, the mailbag workshop. Here a close eye could be kept on them.

As the star-men trooped into Workshop C, there was a muttering among those passing through the door; it was difficult for the warders to enforce the rule of silence until all the gray-uniformed lags were seated at their places in the whitewashed hall. Paul Mitchell, as he had managed to do once a week for the past year, shuffled and sidled just before the doorway, until he was shoulder to shoulder with Ginger Bannion, the IRA man who was now the tobacco baron of Hall C. In the prisoner's way, they talked through the sides of their mouths, trying to prevent their lips from moving, shuffling their feet, marking time.

"Who's carrying, Ginger?" asked Mitchell, his eyes fixed on the nearest screw just inside the workshop.

"Queenie," murmured Bannion, jerking his head slightly backwards.

"Jesus Christ." Mitchell glanced quickly backward at Queenie, who had his hair somehow peroxided, even here in the Moor. "Can't you get somebody less conspicuous, Ginger? Every screw in the nick watches *her* all the time."

"Right, but not for passing *snout*. He'll be up with yer at break, I've told him to put it in yer left-hand *sky*." Ginger tailed off as the logjam in the door, on rhythmic purpose dictated by the 120 years of Moor custom, cleared slightly, to let the next couple or trio of conspirators-for-small-comfort into the doorway.

In ten minutes all the C block men were sitting at their tables, hand-sewing away at the strictly ordained rate of four stitches per inch, two inches to the minute.

Mitchell had managed to gain his usual place between Carney, a big, quiet, soft, friendly mug in for his third stretch of bird— GBH—"Grievous Bodily Harm," and Brigham Young, who'd drawn fifteen years for stuffing the dismembered body of his mother-in-law, bit by bit, into a meat-grinding machine at the dog food factory that in 1932 had seen fit to employ ex-convicts for a pittance. The law had no body to produce for evidence, of course, so Brigham had been arraigned for manslaughter and only just missed getting topped (hanged).

Let's see, where are we now, Mitchell thought, *six years, three months, and four days . . . two years, one month in the bag room. Eight hours a day, that's* . . . he did his reckoning every day at the same time, at the start of the working day, the hardest time, except at eight at night when they turned off the day-lights and switched on the dim cell night-lights . . . *six days a week . . . 650 days; 39,000 minutes, 156,000 stitches . . . and eight years to go . . . Think of something else, anything else . . . Rosie, a good'un that one. Didn't think much of her at first, a bit of the old grumble now and again, that's all, but she does come down every two months. Can't see what the hell she sees in me, except for little Billy. . . .* Mitchell turned his head slightly to spot Queenie, to make sure of his week's supply of tobacco.

"Right, pay attention!" A leading screw rapped on the doorframe with his swagger stick; a big, burly middle-aged man. Mitchell looked up. *Tug Wilson*, he thought, as the other prisoners brought themselves to sitting attention. *Old Tug, good bloke for a screw. Funny how the older screws are much more human than some of these young bastards. Shouldn't recruit 'em until they're at least thirty.*

Tug Wilson rapped again on the doorpost. "660680, Mitchell, P., rise and step forward!" Mitchell stood up, thinking, *Christ, what now?*

"Governor's office, come with me! All right Chief?" Tug turned to the screw in charge.

"Very good, sir," said the screw.

"You in the rattle?" Brigham Young hissed under his breath.

"Fuck knows . . . " murmured Mitchell, stepping over the bench.

"An' he ain't telling," giggled Carney, softly.

Mitchell made his way down the side aisle and stood at attention before the leading screw.

"Follow me, Mitchell. Carry on, Chief." Tug rapped the doorpost once more with his cane as he marched through, Mitchell close on his heels. Once outside in the whitewashed passage, with the walls scuffed and grimy up to shoulder height, the air permeated with the smell of urine and porridge, Tug dropped back alongside Mitchell.

"Got any snout on you, son?" he asked Mitchell.

"You must be joking, Chief."

"Right, we'll nip into my office first, so you can square yourself up, before we see the governor."

"What's it all about, Chief?" Mitchell asked.

"Search me, but I don't think it's a charge, so cheer up, son."

"I did apply for a review of the remission withdrawal."

"It's not that; the magistrates aren't due for another six weeks . . . let's see, you're an old soldier, right?"

"Sort of, France and Russia."

"Good, well, give him the old military one-two when you go in, son, he loves a bit of bullshit."

"Don't they all?" observed the convict.

Minutes later Tug tapped on the governor's door and immediately transformed himself into Leading Warder Wilson, B.E.M.

"Enter," came a voice at conversational level.

"Wait 'til I call your name and number," Tug said throatily under his breath.

"It's okay, been here before," replied Mitchell.

"Yes, Wilson?" inquired the sepulchral voice of Sir Mortimer Bartley, K.C.B.

"Prisoner 660680, Mitchell, P., sah!" bawled Leading Warder Wilson.

Mitchell stepped forward into the governor's office, his forage cap held in both hands as the regulations commanded, and stood, feet together, at attention. Sir Mortimer looked him over for a second or two, in an absentminded way. He was accustomed to seeing far beyond rough gray serge uniforms or eyes defiant or repentant. He saw before him a man of *What was it?* He tried to remember. He glanced down at the record sheet. *Forty-three years old, born Putney, 1897. Father unknown, mother kitchen maid.* Fairly average history until, *Army service in the Duke of Wellington's Own Durham Light Infantry, France 1916 to 1918, Russia 1918–1920. Mentioned in dispatches November 1917 for gallantry under heavy enemy fire and in hand-to-hand combat. . . .* And the criminal record of twenty-eight known offenses. Only one of those had been proven. Mitchell had admitted to the remainder, falsely or not, in the hopes of a lighter sentence. A hung-over Lord Chief Justice had *really* taken all the crimes into account, adding three months for each plea of guilty. A total of seven extra years to the normal five years. *A professional, clever criminal, a menace to society, you must be kept in custody for the maximum period allowed by the law*, the lord chief justice had ruled.

Sir Mortimer conferred with himself, *A good man for this type of work, under close surveillance. Excellent military record. Good prospects. Yes, must be susceptible to a call to his patriotism. Sound him out, first, no need to let him think there's any urgency. Good health, strong body, pity to see that go to waste here.*

The governor glanced at the medical report. *Height—five feet eleven inches, Weight—twenty-four stones five pounds, Eyes—gray, Hair—Light brown, Nose slightly irregular, broken as an army amateur boxer. Distinguishing marks—no scars, tattoo on left forearm—Union Jack with, below, the words "true to the last" and below "Mum R.I.P. 1922."*

For the seconds he gazed at Mitchell, the governor's nose seemed to sniff the air. "Ah . . . yes, Mitchell . . . er, at ease." He nodded to the leading warder. "Very good, Wilson, wait outside please."

The governor's complexion reminded Mitchell of well-boiled ham. He stared for a moment at the ginger hairs sticking out of the governor's ears.

"Sir?" Tug was nonplused. This had never happened before in his fifteen years at the Moor.

"Wait outside, please. I want to talk to Mitchell privately."

"Sah!" Tug turned on his heels and stepped smartly outside, closing the door softly behind him.

The governor motioned with one hand toward the single chair in front of his desk. "Please take a seat."

"Is this about Miss Leighton, sir?" Mitchell felt a sudden pain in his chest.

"No, Mitchell, now do please take a seat. I want to talk with you about something that has cropped up." Mitchell sat down on the edge of the chair, his hands still holding his cap on his lap.

The governor picked up his notes on the telephone conversation and scanned it again, then laid it, face down on the desk top. He looked directly at Mitchell and gave a fleeting smile.

"Now Mitchell, I want to discuss an important matter with you, one that could involve your early release." He paused for a moment, then, folding his arms in front of him, carried on. "But before I do, I must have your word—and I've studied your record, Mitchell, and I shall willingly accept your word—that not one syllable of what we discuss in this office will be repeated outside this office."

"If it's about narking, sir, count me out."

"I give you my word it's not. It has nothing whatever to do with what goes on, or what has gone on, within the confines of this . . . establishment. It has only to do with you and you alone."

"Right, sir, you have my solemn word."

"Good, then please allow me to put all the facts before you. Then I shall hear your statement on the matter and pass it on to the appropriate authorities." The governor passed over a cigarette box. "Smoke?"

Mitchell looked puzzled as he took a Player and accepted a light from the governor, who also lighted up a cigarette.

"As you know, Mitchell, the outside situation since you joined us has changed somewhat for the worse. Our country is now at war once again with a ruthless enemy." The governor noticed Mitchell's reaction, a slight shifting back of his shoulders and torso, as if awaiting a blow.

The governor studied Mitchell's face for a moment. He sighed, unfolded his arms, and leaned back. "Anyway, to cut a rather long story short, the Home Office is looking for men like yourself, with experience in clockwork mechanisms and such, to form a team of . . . well, let's say expert technicians. Your name has been mentioned to them, and the Home Secretary has decided to offer you immediate remission of your sentence, should you decide to volunteer." The governor blew smoke at the ceiling. "Now I don't want you to make an immediate decision, take your time, but if there are any questions about this, please ask me now, and I will attempt to satisfy them, to the best of my knowledge."

Mitchell's brows knitted in concentration. Then he raised his head and looked at the governor's collar. *What's the catch? What's this about clockwork mechanisms, sir?* "You know I'm a peter-man; my trade is opening safes." There was pride in his voice.

"Quite." The governor tapped the desk top with a pencil. "But as I understand it, the enemy is dropping delayed-action-mechanism bombs and mines, and the Home Office is recruiting a sort of disposal team, to . . . er . . . analyze these infernal machines. . . . " He trailed off weakly into silence.

Mitchell was thinking hard. *Home Office? Delayed action bombs and mines? Who's he think he's kidding . . . that's the army and navy's job . . . Watch yourself, there's probably someone else listening!* "I don't know, sir, got to think," he said.

The governor droned on, "Of course, there'll be a period of probation, but not for the full extent of your present sentence. The Home Secretary is thinking in terms of four years. . . . "

Mitchell started. *Four years' probation; four years! I can be outside!* his mind raced.

Seeing this sink in visibly, Sir Mortimer went on. "On condition, of course. . . . "

Four years in the last bloody lot; four years sloshing around in trenches; a million British dead, three million total British casualties; God knows how many of the others, poor sods.

". . . that you commit your services, whenever required . . ."

The Somme, the Aisne, the Marne, my mates; heads missing, lungs gassed, legs off, four bloody years . . . Mitchell kept his face calm as his brain seethed.

". . . for the duration of the war, and of course . . . "

And Russia, shooting away . . . freezin', couldn't move, all that winter, and five mates castrated and sent back over the lines to us, just to cheer us up . . .

". . . on condition that you give your parole to be of good . . . "

And coming back to what? Thirty bob a week for four years, and six years on the dole . . .

". . . behavior for that period. It's up to you . . . " The governor's voice droned on.

Mitchell's eyes narrowed, *And these sods in their bloody mansions looking down their toffee noses at anyone who ain't been to their schools, who don't talk the way they talk, who make the bloody fortunes that they . . .*

". . . to think about this, there's very much in it to your advantage . . ."

Spend. Well, I took a bit . . . an' if I've got to pay for it. . . .

"What do you say, Mitchell? You've nothing to lose and everything to gain; freedom, self-respect, and you'll be serving your country in the bargain."

I'm the best cracksman in Britain; how would he know I clobbered the Glasgow Ranger on purpose to get into the bag room? Have to look after my hands . . . my sense of touch . . . don't want to lose it digging gardens with shovels. . . . Mitchell kept a poker face.

A minute of silence had passed. "And also . . . " the governor had a thought, " . . . there might be a chance of travel abroad."

More silence. *Abroad? He must be joking!* thought Mitchell.

"And there's Miss Leighton to think of, too. I must say, she seems quite fond of you. Pays you regular visits." The governor smiled.

So they've thought of that, too, eh?

"Now then, Mitchell, what about it?"

"No, sir."

"But dammit, man, the country . . . " Sir Mortimer's voice rose.

"I'll sit this one out, if you don't mind, beggin' your pardon, sir."

"That's your final word?"

"Yes, sir, 'fraid it is."

"Then there's nothing more for me to say, is there?"

"No sir."

The governor pressed his buzzer button. Tug Wilson entered and came to stiff attention. He looked at Sir Mortimer, who nodded.

Tug bawled, "Prisoner rise!"

Mitchell stood up at attention, concentrating on a spot just above the governor's left shoulder.

"Don't forget your word, Mitchell," said the governor, in low tones.

"No, sir."

"Very good . . . dismissed!" The governor gave the curt order. Mitchell turned and followed Leading Warder Wilson out of the room, then waited for Tug to close the door.

"What was all that about?" asked Tug, as they marched back to Workshop C and the mailbags.

"He wants me to play outside-right instead of fullback," said Mitchell, quietly.

"No joking? He must be blind when it comes to soccer, son."

"Yeah, and other things as well," said Mitchell as he stepped into the bag room and stuffed his cap into his left jacket pocket. *Where the snout should have been if it hadn't been for that silly old geezer*, he thought as he sat down to the curious glances of Carney and Brigham. He imagined Queenie three rows behind him wondering what to do with the snout. *I'd tell her, too!* he said to himself ruefully. Then he caught sight of the little screwed-up package of tobacco under his mailbag. *Well, good for Queenie!*

"Mitchell seems to be one of the awkward squad, sir," said Simmons, the governor's secretary, as he reopened the curtain behind which he had taken note of everything said. He had a face as blank as a milk bottle and he had shoulders to match.

"Yes, and a bit Bolshie, too. I'm afraid that spell in Russis was a mistake. I sense a whiff of contamination there, for some reason. . . . "

"There is that, sir. A cagey bird, if you ask me." Simmons sat his skinny frame down on the seat Mitchell had vacated moments before. He passed his hand through his thinning hair, thinking, *God, of all the thankless jobs . . . thank goodness he didn't know I was skulking there.*

The governor said, "Strange; all that unschooled intelligence. Rather frightening in a way. Best safecracker in the business. We'd never have nabbed him if he hadn't made the one mistake."

"Mistake, sir?"

"Yes, he did only one job, out of all of them, with some other villains, and, of course, no honor among thieves and all that . . . he was ratted on, and here he is."

"But that wasn't very intelligent, was it, sir?" Simmons tried to gain a point.

"No, that's true, but attacking one of our men in my *gar-*

den . . . now that was a brilliant move, don't you think? Pity he slipped and hit the warder."

"Brilliant? But how, sir?"

"Saved his hands, didn't it?" The governor shook his head slightly and slowly reached for the phone. "They don't call him 'Feather Fingers' for nothing, you know."

10th May, 1940. 9:30 A.M.
Foyle's Wharf, Faversham, Kent, England
Onboard the sailing barge Beatrice Maud

"Mornin' Tansy . . . mornin' Bert."

Knocker White scrambled onto the bulwark nimbly for a man of his years. He wore a derby hat, a walrus mustache, a stiff white collar, a blue serge suit, and calf-length rubber boots. He carried in one hand a black shiny oilskin jacket and a small battered leather attaché case. His face was ruddy and weatherworn, and as he mounted the cap-rail of the ship's side he peered aloft. It was not only a sailor's peer, it was a skipper's, taking in everything. As they followed the line of the mainmast, up eighty-feet, his light-blue eyes danced.

Beatrice Maud, a thirty-year-old spritsail barge, leaned against the jetty as if she wanted to make the most of every moment of blessed rest before the tide, now slowly creeping up her eighty-ton capacity hull, beckoned her once more to toil.

"Josh!" Knocker shouted in a surprisingly virile voice.

"Comin' up, Knocker!" a muffled voice called from down the hold.

"Bound for Southend to load bricks, mate!" Knocker jumped off the caprail, landing on the balls of his feet like a ballet dancer.

Josh emerged from the hold, clambered over the top of the ladder, and picked up Knocker's oilskin jacket from the deck with a hand like a side of beef. Josh was a big man, dressed in a dirty boilersuit and once-white tennis shoes. He was about thirty-five and almost completely bald except for a fringe of hair around his ears. He looked, claimed Knocker, like "Friar bloomin' Tuck." Because of his flat feet, Josh had not been called up. His voice was soft and gentle, giving the lie to his rough appearance. Anyone could be forgiven for thinking that, except for his complexion, which was almost as sunburned as Knocker's, Josh would be more at home in a factory than onboard a sailing vessel.

"Bloody bricks?" said Josh, but Knocker knew by his smile that he was pleased at the prospect of visiting Southend, despite the thought of the seventy thousand bricks to be loaded all by hand—back-breaking labor for one man and a boy.

Knocker half-grinned back at him, thinking, *Josh's bit of fluff's over at Southend—no wonder he's smiling.*

"Young-Mike onboard yet?" he asked Josh.

"Over 'ere, Knocker!" a voice chanted from the far side of the cargo-hatch and a lad of seventeen stood up from his painting job on the deck. He wore only a pair of moleskin trousers and about a pint of red-lead paint on his upper torso. Under the grime his hair was tow and tousled, and his grin was as mobile as a London sparrow's hop, as it flittered around his blue-green eyes.

"Heard about *Susan May*, Knocker?" asked Josh, his face fallen into concern. "Got shot up by a Jerry fighter. She was headin' round the North Foreland with coal for Dover."

"Anybody hurt?" Knocker had friends onboard *Susan May*, as indeed he did onboard at least two hundred of the five hundred sailing barges then plying the British coast.

"No, but she had to pump her way into Whitstable under tow."

"What happened to the Jerry?" Knocker asked, relieved.

"Nothin'. They reckon he waggled his wings at 'em when he'd finished shootin' and flew off toward the east." Josh waggled one of his hands, the muscle on the exposed forearm weaving like a dragged steel cable, the bottom of his "Death before Dishonour" tattoo, fuzzy with age, just showing.

"Well. We shouldn't get too much trouble in the estuary, eh, Josh, not now they've finished arming those bloomin' forts out there?" Knocker said.

"S'pose not" said Josh, doubtfully. Josh threw away his dog-end, dead again, over the side. "They reckon the Jerry fighters can't reach further than Harwich." He delved for another Woodbine cigarette in his breast pocket. "And them's the buggers what causes the trouble."

"That's what they say . . ." said Knocker, leaning over the side to see how the tide was. "No, Josh mate, it looks like a nice quiet war for us, this time, not like the last blinkin' lot, eh?" Both he and Josh grinned and their eyes twinkled as they studied each other.

"Couldn't be like the last lot," said Josh. "Touch wood."

"Yes, touch wood," said Knocker as he laid his hand, gently on the oak side rail of *Beatrice Maud*.

"Don't hold with bloomin' superstitions," said Young-Mike, as he passed them, making his way forward to light the donkey boiler, a bunch of fire-lighting faggots clutched tightly in his fists.

Thirty minutes later, *Beatrice Maud*'s mooring lines were cast off, the topsail was unrucked, the sprit mainsail unbrailed, and, like a great ugly-footed goose, she unfolded her wings, and slid, silently and gracefully, away down the river, with Captain George Edward White, sixty-seven years of age, fifty-four years' continuous service at sea, in command.

Chapter 2

*   *

Beer Barrel Polka

May 10th–11th 1940

Roll out the barrel, we'll have a barrel of fun,
Roll out the barrel, we've got the blues on the run;
Zing! Boom! Ta-rar-rel—Ring out a song of good cheer,
Now's the time to roll the barrel,
For the gang's all here!

Chorus, "Beer Barrel Polka"
Czechoslovakian song
English words by Lew Brown
Popular in Britain, 1939–40

2.

"Beer Barrel Polka"

10th May, 1940. 9:18 A.M.
HQ Intelligence (The Circus) London

". . . Ah, Colonel Canning, good." 'C' turned his head to greet Canning's companion. "Morning, Lieutenant Dennis," he said.

"Morning, sir," said Dennis. Canning grunted as he removed his British-warmer overcoat to hang it on the rickety ash willow coat stand, his eyes on 'C' as he sat down. Canning thought, *He's aged in the last three months.*

Canning was the sort of man who always appeared to be slightly sunburned in the tropics and heavily sunburned in the more temperate zones. He looked ten years younger than his forty-eight years. Lean and spare, graying round the ears with a regulation toothbrush mustache and a strong square jaw. The most striking feature about him (apart from his elegant Gieves Brothers khaki uniform, the jacket, *à la mode*, of a slightly darker hue than the trousers) were his eyes. Gray-green-blue under a high forehead. In repose they seemed to be pained, but the laughter lines above his slightly burned cheeks were a contradiction to the rest of his features. The high bridge of his nose was a sign of his descent from a long-past prime minister, and his languid movements betrayed his aristocratic upbringing.

At Harrow a decade behind 'C,' they had first joined forces in India on Canning's completion of three years' junior service with the North West Frontier Force. They had knocked around together in the Middle East for some months and in East Africa on the Somali exercise. During World War I, they'd parted for a few years, until 'C' had started to carve his little empire from part of the old Naval Intelligence Service in the mid-1920s. In the interim, Canning slogged away in Flanders, one of the two surviving officers of his battalion. Carrying out 'C's' sometimes bizarre assignments had been a pleasant relief from trench warfare and grubbing around for a civilian job. Slowly it had become a crusade against the forces threatening all Canning held dear. Since 1932, Canning had given the job his mind, his soul, and his body. *Just like 'C', in fact*, was Canning's thought, as he watched his chief sorting out a rather starved-looking file. Canning's heart was for Susan, Richard, and little Elizabeth. He looked at 'C' again. *I wonder whom his heart's for?* he asked himself, but found no answer. 'C' showed no sign, ever.

Lieutenant Dennis took the second chair, placing it deferentially a little further away from 'C's' desk than Canning's. He contemplated the two other men. *So here they are, the two top men, together. How odd it is that my being at old Henchley's archaeological dig in Silesia has brought me here. I'd only gone along for a skylark. Cambridge could be so wearing. Funny how I picked up German as easily as putting on my shirt, but the Army saw fit to appoint me to the Royal Engineers. . . . I imagined I would spend the war on the administrative side of bridge building, but like an idiot (but perhaps not), I entered "French, Spanish, and German fluent" on that "languages spoken" line of my qualifications form. It took six months for Captain Cowley to turn up. My God, billeted in Nissen huts stuck in the middle of Stafford-shire. . . . And that was that. I jumped at it. Anything but checking blueprints outside Stoke-on-Trent. And here I am. Twenty-three years of age, and already getting on well. . .*

Dennis was stocky, thick-set, with a square face, his nose a little flattened. He felt somewhat overwhelmed by the present company and a little lost. *Mustn't show it*, he reminded himself.

'C' passed the cigarette box. Canning accepted one and took a light from 'C's' lighter. Dennis declined with a slight feeling of embarrassment. "Now, gentlemen," 'C' said, "you both know the rough sketch of Operation Orange, and you both know that under certain conditions, it's on. Time here is of the essence, so we won't bother with preliminaries. I've feelers out . . . " He paused as Margot hurried into the room with three signal flimsies in her hand.

"Here it is, sir."

'C' gave a slight squint of annoyance at the intrusion and took the yellow signal sheets out of their envelopes.

"Have you seen them, Margot?" 'C' asked.

"Couldn't resist it, sir." She waited, expressionless.

'C' laid the telegrams out, in numerical, chronological order, side by side and studied them.

FIRST LORD, ADMIRALTY TO CAPTAIN IN CHARGE, H.M. DOCKYARD, CHATHAM. COMMANDING OFFICER, H.M.S. HAVELOCK; C-IN-C, THE NORE. TIME 0810. 10–5–40. 04985832. WHAT IS THE STATE OF READINESS OF H.M.S. HAVELOCK? IF SHE BE NOT READY FOR IMMEDIATE SEA SERVICE PRAY REMEDY HER CONDITION WITHIN TWENTY-FOUR HOURS. H.M.S. HAVELOCK IS TO BE DETACHED FOR SERVICE UNDER THE DIRECTION OF THE PRIME MINISTER AND THE MINISTER OF DEFENSE UPON RECEIPT OF A CONCURRING SIGNAL FROM THE AFORESAID MINISTERS. ACKNOWLEDGE.

"What time did he get to the palace, Margot?" 'C' murmured. "Eight-thirty, sir."

'C' turned the first signal face down on the table as his eyes turned to the second.

DEFENSE MINISTER TO C-IN-C. THE NORE. CAPTAIN OF H.M. DOCKYARD, CHATHAM. COMMANDING OFFICER, H.M.S. HAVELOCK. TIME 0900. 10–5–40. 04985833. PRAY ACCEPT PRESENT AS SIGNAL OF MY CONCURRENCE WITH THE FIRST LORD'S 04985832. TIME 0810. 10–5–40. H.M.S. HAVELOCK TO BE ON ONE HOUR'S NOTICE FOR SEA COMMENCING 0600 HOURS. 11–5–40. ACKNOWLEDGE.

'C' grinned, laid cable number two face down, and read the third note.

PRIME MINISTER TO C-IN-C. THE NORE. CAPTAIN OF H.M. DOCKYARD, CHATHAM. COMMANDING OFFICER H.M.S. HAVELOCK. TIME 0903. 10–5–40. 04985834. CONCUR WITH FIRST LORD, ADMIRALTY'S 04985832. TIME 0810. 10–5–40. AND DEFENSE MINISTER'S 04985833. TIME 0900. 10–5–40. BUT PRAY AMEND THE LATTER SIGNAL TO READ QUOTE H.M.S. HAVELOCK TO BE UNDER IMMEDIATE NOTICE FOR SEA COMMENCING 0400 HOURS. 11–5–40. UNQUOTE. ACKNOWLEDGE.

All three cables had exactly the same signature.

'C' chuckled aloud as he thought, *Just like him . . . He can't bring the other services in, no hope for a RAF transport without involving the air people in this game. He took a Daimler to the palace and came out with a destroyer! Talk about containment!*

Margot asked, "Do you think he'll get away with it, sir?"

'C' smiled widely and thought for a moment. "I don't see why not, who's to know?" His teeth were obviously his own, gleaming in his cadaverlike face.

"If it gets out there'll be a rumpus; the House will have his neck!" she said.

'C' looked at Margot for a moment, his smile fading. "Some neck," he said, not dreaming that he was paraphrasing almost exactly the prime minister's snarl two years later. "Thank you, Margot," he said, as she turned to leave the room, closing the door softly behind her.

"Now gentlemen, let us continue. Our friend Van Velzor in Amsterdam knows where the stuff is. The combination's a different matter. Only Kramp knows that, and he's on the other side." 'C' sniffed, then went on, "Transport for the operation will be by sea. The P.M.'s laying on a destroyer. She's under orders from early tomorrow.

As I was saying earlier, I have feelers out for our two experts. One of them, Mitchell, has already been informed of our desire for his services. The other one, Lynch, has yet to be approached. Mitchell is the key man, Lynch is the back-up. It mainly hinges on Mitchell—if we are to undertake this task with a minimum of fuss. I have high hopes for Mitchell. He is the gentleman who perpetrated and carried off the single-handed entry into the strong room of the Amsterdam Diamond Bureau in 1933. He was never brought to trial for that escapade, but the Yard assures me that there is no doubt, not a single shard of doubt, that it was Mitchell. For the simple reason that there is no one, *no one*, alive today who could possibly have executed the deed with such consummate skill."

'C' lit another cigarette. "No one, that is, except an American gentleman, let's see . . . " 'C' checked his notes. "Yes, Corrigan."

"Why not Corrigan, sir?" Dennis asked. "I mean at the Diamond Bureau job?"

"Good question, Lieutenant." 'C' exhaled. "For the simple reason that Corrigan was, at the time, incarcerated in his native country. In Alcatraz, to be precise." 'C' thought for a minute. "No, Mitchell's our man. We even checked with Chubb's, and they tell us that their own master locksmith could not open the Amsterdam vault. Not after two whole days of, I'm told, rather sweaty effort."

"What's his background, sir?" It was the first time Canning had spoken since he had entered the room. His accent was more clipped than Dennis', his vowels slightly narrower. As Canning spoke, it flashed through 'C's' mind that while all three men present were speaking King's English, there were yet slight differences in their dialects. His own was mid-Victorian, clear and precise, Canning's more clipped, more affected; Dennis' slurred, lazier.

"Mitchell?" 'C' said, rousing from his brief reverie.

"Yes, sir."

"Interesting. Lockmaker's apprentice at the start. Volunteered for Army 1916. Four years' service. France and Russia, intervention and all that, came out with good discharge, mentioned in dispatches, and from there seems to have gradually drifted into crime. Skilled crime, I would call it. Very much a loner. The one time he was nabbed was the only occasion when he, when he . . . worked . . . with three other chaps on the Southminster Bank in Leadenhall Street. . . . " 'C' glanced down again. "1934. It seemed to be another solutionless crime, except that one of the accomplices left a fingerprint some-where. Of course, the Yard nabbed that one and he . . . I believe the term is . . . *squealed* on the other three. Bad luck, really, for Mitchell. But other than his propensity for obtaining other people's money by stealth, craft, and guile, he seems to be a steady sort of chap. I have high hopes for him. I think our cover story will appeal to the old soldier in Mitchell." There was silence for a few moments.

Canning asked, "What about the other chappie?"

"Yes, Colonel," 'C' replied. "Mister Lynch. He'll bear watching, that one . . . known in the underworld as Banger Lynch. Peculiar fellow. The number-one explosives man in the villian's *Who's Who*. The only one known to have used the new plastiques. That's pretty good going, seeing that they were only invented . . . developed four years ago and, except for this one leak, were kept top secret. And to successfully blast open the strong room in the liner *Mauretania*, down in the bowels of the ship as she sat in New York Harbor, without blowing a hole in the ship's bottom . . . well, gentlemen, you must admit it does show a certain finesse? A certain delicacy of touch, a modicum of skill?"

"Yes, sir, very curious. How was he caught?" Dennis asked, fascinated. His Bloomsbury drawl was, now that he was off-guard, more pronounced.

"Bad luck again." 'C' smiled. "One of his suitcases fell open as he boarded a taxicab, right in front of the ship's gangway. That must have been a strange sight; thousands and thousands of pound notes being blown by the wind off Pier 92 into the river Hudson." All three smiled at the thought. "They recovered the bullion bars he'd lowered over the side in a sack, with the idea of later recovering them. I must say it shows a spirit of . . . ingenuity?"

"But he's an out and out thief, sir?" exclaimed Dennis.

"Seems to be . . . we've checked his record as far as we're able . . . " 'C' frowned. "There was one affair, a murder, in Rio that he *may* have been involved in."

"A murder?" interjected Canning.

"Yes, a matter involving a woman. There seems to have been a sort of love triangle . . . a man and the woman were found with their throats cut. Ghastly affair. Lynch was in Rio at the time, but the police report that he had a satisfactory alibi—another woman it seems. It's not very clear, but I would advise you to keep a close eye on him."

"Seems to be something of a desperado?" observed Canning.

"It's all very vague," 'C' continued. "There's certainly nothing in his record in *this* country to indicate any blood-thirsty . . . ah . . . propensities, and anyway beggars can't be choosers, and this is a job that needs desperados. It will take weeks to train anyone else to the standard of Lynch's expertise."

"But he didn't kill on the *Mauretania* job, sir?" asked Dennis.

"We're not sure . . . a fireman was missing . . . lost overboard on the voyage to New York. He was a friend of Lynch, but there was no evidence, of course." 'C' waited. Everyone was silent for a moment.

"Where's Lynch now, sir?" asked Dennis.

"Wormwood Scrubs. He drew seven years. Four to do. I . . . I'm glad you asked me that, Dennis. You will suggest to him that he serves that four years with us . . . better make it the duration."

"Me, sir?" said Dennis, surprised.

"This very day." 'C' grimaced. "Margot has all his details, address, and all that."

"Very good, sir," said Dennis.

The black phone intervened. "Yes," said 'C'. A minute passed. "Very good, Sir Mortimer." 'C' thought for a second, his eyes screwed up against his cigarette smoke. "Look, do you mind awfully if I send one of our people down to see him?" 'C' listened for ten seconds. "Today, this . . . no, we can't manage that. It will have to be later today. Yes. Yes . . . Colonel Canning . . . Yes, I'll confirm it in writing . . . certainly there can be no error . . . Good, good . . . right, thank you, Sir Mortimer, and good day to you." 'C' replaced the phone, sighed, then picked it up again. "Margot, contact Miss Leighton."

Canning grinned at 'C' as he slammed down the phone. "Mitchell turned us down," he said.

"Spot on, old chap. You gather what I've proposed?" 'C' asked.

"Certainly, I'm to go down to Dartmoor today," replied Canning.

'C' explained, "We . . . you will talk with a Miss Rose Leighton first. Margot is arranging it now. Take her down with you if necessary. With Mitchell's type we need levers. She's our only lever, she and North Kensington, the boy. Sorry, Canning."

Canning groaned under his breath, thinking, *Next of kin job, another one.*

'C' glanced at the wall clock. "Now gentlemen, we have thirty minutes in which to discuss tactics. The strategy is clear enough. First, we'll deal with Lynch so you can get away," he glanced quickly at Dennis, who nodded. "And then, Colonel Canning, you and I will discuss our fine-feathered friend Mitchell and his lady . . . and their . . . offspring."

10th May, 1940. 10:30 A.M.
Wormwood Scrubs Prison, London

Prisoner Lynch 853610 and his attendant warder were waiting in the interview cell when Dennis arrived, both half-sitting on the one heavy table, silent, smoking. At the knock on the door, the warder stubbed out his cigarette and hurriedly stood by the wall as the door opened. Lynch in his gray serge prison clouts left his Gold Flake dangling and slouched around to the side of the table nearest the door.

"Morning." Dennis beamed at the warder, then at Lynch. "Ah, you must be Mister Lynch," he said. His accent was easier now. With the lower orders, "Mister" sounded more like "Mister" than "Mistah."

"That's right, sir, how did you guess?" Lynch strained at the aitch.

Dennis said, "Do please take a seat, Lynch." There were only two chairs in the cell. "Heard the news? Arsenal four, Wanderers two." He looked at Lynch and thought, *Must try to cheer him a little. What is he . . . oh yes, thirty-two. Five-nine, ginger hair, blue eyes, sprightly little chap by the look of him.*

Dennis turned to the warder. "Step outside please, officer."

The warder glanced at Lynch, then did as he was bid.

"Good team, Arsenal, sir. Have you heard anything about Everton yet?" Lynch sized up Dennis. *Stocky little bugger, this. Good bloke in a barney, been in a few scraps, pity he talks so bloody nancy.*

"No, 'fraid not." Dennis cleared his throat. The air in the cell was smoky, and there was no ventilation. He said, "Now Lynch, I want to put a proposition to you. We at the Ministry of Defense," he coughed quietly, "are establishing an experimental laboratory down in Kent. To put it bluntly, we thought that with your experience with the new plastiques, you might be able to help us."

Lynch started to speak. Dennis held up his hand slightly. "Now please let me go on for a moment, Mr. Lynch. In return for your services for the duration of the hostilities, the Home Office has agreed to your conditional release. Of course you'll be on your own recognizance for good behavior and while working with us, you'll come under army rules. If you agree, your release will be immediate, on parole, once the necessary formalities have been gone through here. Now, what do you say?"

"What's the pay?" Lynch asked.

Dennis looked at his notes for a few seconds. "Corporal's pay and emoluments. Not bad, about a fiver a week."

"Right, sir, I'm on. Will I be leaving with you?"

"What? Oh, yes, yes . . . we'll ask the officer to escort us to the governor's office so we can get the paper work done." He stood up.

"Just a minute, what about time off?" demanded Lynch.

"You'll have the rest of today to yourself, and our unit meets early tomorrow, quite close by, in fact."

"We wear uniforms?"

"No. Some of us do, some of us don't," Dennis replied.

"Sounds good. Any chance of a couple of quid in advance?" said Lynch.

Dennis searched his trouser pocket. "Er . . . I can give you ten shillings now and thirty shillings when we get to the office."

"Right, sir, count me in," Lynch laughed. "Cor, what a skylark—pay, time off, and bangers! Legal bangers!"

Dennis said, "Yes, quite." He followed Lynch at the heels of the warder, out and along the passage, glossy government green up to shoulder height, dimly lit whitewash above. He felt a little taken aback by the ease of Lynch's agreement to go along. He thought about Lynch. *Enthusiasm, just what we need. Holds himself well, too. Can't quite make out his accent . . . North Country? Square peg in a round hole, here, it seems. God, what a place. Imagine three years of it. Poor devil. Looks a decent sort . . . that murder in Rio . . . what nonsense. Unoffensive chappie . . . can't possibly be true. Probably a false charge.*

Lynch put on a little swagger, thinking, *Experiment . . . plastiques? Christ, I'd shovel shit for nothing as long as I could get to a bit of kyfer now and then. Keep this bloke sweet. Just get out of this sodding hole.*

10th May, 1940. 12:15 P.M.
J. Lyons Cafeteria, Coventry Street, London

At St. John's Wood, Canning had changed into his city gent's blue pinstripe suit and bowler, doffing his air of languor along with the uniform. He had eyed himself in the looking glass and let the muscles of his face relax, the military tension dissipate. Hurriedly, he had walked to the underground station and took the train to Piccadilly. By the time he reached Lyons', he was convinced he blended in unobtrusively with the lunchtime crowd of office workers, typists, salesmen, and small-time entrepreneurs, a few hundred of them, who entered and left the noisy, crowded cafeteria. Now he took a seat by the wall mirror that rose from shoulder height to ceiling and waited.

He heard a voice, "Mr. Canning?" He looked up. She was not at all what he had expected from the telephone conversation. Slight, rather shapeless at first glance. Medium-brown hair, mousy, drawn face.

"Miss Leighton? Do please sit down." He rose, noticing that she had dyed her hair slightly where it was drawn back over her ears into a bun.

"I was rather concerned that you would not recognize me." Canning smiled as he reached for her tray, but she had already laid it down.

"You're the only gentleman in here with a buttonhole," she commented as she glanced fleetingly at his white carnation. Her hand fussed quickly over her hairbun.

Canning felt a little surprised. *Well, at least she pronounces her aitches.* He caught himself. "Really? It didn't occur to me . . . " He looked around the room. "Yes, you're right, of course."

"And the only one with a copy of the *Financial Times* under your arm." She smiled as Canning, somewhat abashed, laid the paper down.

"I wanted to talk with you personally, Miss Leighton," Canning said.

"About Mitch." She sized him up in quick glances. *This is a real toff. Wonder what he is—Major? Must be married, couple of kids, a boy and a girl. Nice cottage in Surrey, a horse for the kids, probably. A sheep dog. What a suit—it doesn't suit him at all.*

"Yes, about . . . er . . . Mitch." Canning avoided her eyes for a moment.

Miss Leighton said, "He knows I'm waiting for him. It's not easy. I can only afford to get down to see him every two months." She pushed a wisp of hair back into place. "Oh, Mr. Canning, do you think the Remissions Board will review his case? I mean that extra two years. I don't know . . . " she trailed off. She thought anxiously, *And little Mitch . . . with Mum in North Kensington . . . almost six now, and never seen his Dad. But Mum looks after him well. I give him everything. I wonder if he knows?* She looked for a sign from Canning. *No, 'course not, silly, how could he? Only Mum and Mitch know.*

"I can't tell you about that, Miss Leighton, but what I can tell you may hold out some hope of an early release for . . . er . . . Mitch."

"Please call me Rose, Mr. Canning."

"Yes, of course, Rose. An early release. In fact, a very early release."

"Release?" Rose's eyes brightened. She stopped eating, fork suspended. "What are the conditions?"

"A government department wishes to employ Mr. Mitchell. They have some highly specialized work on which they think that he can be of great assistance."

"War work, Mr. Canning?"

"War work, Miss Leighton . . . Rose." Canning smiled.

"Is it dangerous?"

"No more so than many other jobs that must be done." He checked himself.

"Does Mitch know about this?"

"Yes and no."

"What does that mean?" she insisted.

"It means, Rose, that he has been approached, but that the exact nature of the task has not been explained to him . . . though he has been told that he can be released . . . on probation, but he has refused."

"Refused . . . Mitch? You must be having me on, Mr. Canning."

"No. The whole thing has been handled . . . wrongly, and that's why I have asked you to meet me."

"Why, what can I do?"

"I'm asking you to come down to . . . " Canning looked at the diners nearby " . . . the place he's stationed and talk with him. Get him to see that it's to his advantage, and to yours, too."

"What do you people get out of it?" she demanded.

"His expertise . . . and perhaps the opportunity of seeing a good man out of a bad situation." Canning hoped he looked sincere.

"How do we know that the situation he would be going into wouldn't be worse than the one he's already in?"

"Because, Miss Leighton, I intend to lay the truth of our intentions before him. I can't tell you what they are. It is entirely up to Mitch."

She looked at Canning, studying him, gazing into his eyes for several seconds. *He's sincere. He's being straight with me . . . I have to trust him . . . I can't go on . . . six years . . . and little Mitch . . . and big Mitch. Oh Mitch.* "Will I see much of him?" she asked.

"Far more . . . much more than you do now."

"You mean he'll be able to be with me?" She almost choked.

"Certainly, on his off-duty periods. I can assure you that leave will be . . . generous . . . frequent."

"Then I'll come, Mr. Canning. When are we going? I have to let the office manager know." She buttoned her dowdy brownish wool coat.

"That's already been taken care of."

She stared at him in doubt.

"But if it will set your mind at rest, by all means telephone Mr. Fleming."

She smiled, showing good teeth. "You've thought of everything, haven't you?" *They even know my boss's name*, she thought.

He returned her smile. "It's our job, Rose."

Outside, Canning hailed a taxi. Rose remembered that this was the first taxi she'd ridden in since she'd been hurriedly rushed to Praed St. Hospital to have little Mitch. *When was it? Five years and seven months ago?* She tried to remember. *Oh Mitch . . . I'll do my hair on the train.* Her heart was pounding.

They were silent all the way to Paddington Station. Canning thought, as they pulled in, *God, I wish this were Victoria Station. I'd be heading for Dorking, and Susan, Richard, and Elizabeth . . . and the sheepdog Rover and Jock the pony. Elizabeth is managing Jock quite well, now.* He handed Rose out of the cab and felt for the rail tickets already in his pocket. He stiffened his jaw. *It's our job to think of everything*, he reminded himself.

10th May, 1940. 2:30 P.M.
No. 154 Langley Rd., St. John's Wood, London

Lynch's mind raced. *Fair suit they gave me, gray pinstripe, very nice, too. The brown shoes go well.*

"Here, sign for this, please, Mister Lynch." Edwards, the caretaker, handed over two notes. "One pound, ten shillings." Lynch put the notes in his inside pocket and signed a scrawling scratch.

"Ta, guv." He grinned at Edwards, whose face was bleak.

"All all right, Lynch?" Dennis came bounding into the room. It was a very Victorian room, a legacy of 'C''s aunt, who had bequeathed the house complete with furnishings to her favorite nephew. *That sly rascal*, she had chuckled affectionately. The aunt had passed away in 1919, at the age of 93. Except for cleaning and dusting, nothing had been touched since in the downstairs rooms. *Upstairs is another story*, old Edwards was apt to pun. There the five bedrooms had been converted into a barracks for ten persons, sleeping in three-tiered bunk beds, a kitchen, four lavatories, three baths, and access to the most powerful shortwave radio and the most efficient code-breaking system on earth.

"Fine sir. What time do you want me back?" Lynch grinned.

"Midnight, no later. Orders."

"How do you know I'll be here?"

"Oh, you'll be here, Lynch, no doubt of it," said Dennis firmly.

"Yes, I suppose so. Well, thank you, sir . . . until midnight."

Lynch stepped out of the door—a free man for the first time in three years. He had walked a hundred yards towards the tube station before he was certain of the man following him. He grinned as he thought to himself, *Oh well, bugger it, Soho, here we come, tail and all!*

10th May, 1940. 7:30 P.M.
The Courteney Club, St. James', London

"Pardon me, telephone call for you, sir, in cabinet number five."

"Thank you, Higgins . . . er . . . while I take it, ask the steward to bring me another drink, will you? He knows what it is." 'C' reflected, *Good chap, Higgins. Joined the club same time as I . . . what, thirty years ago?*

"Of course, sir." Higgins gave a slight bow, creaking at seventy-nine. Higgins, even alongside 'C,' looked antediluvian.

'C' closed the door of the cabinet and, perched on the arm of the chair, reached for the phone. "Yes?" he said.

" 'C'?" a voice inquired.

"Yes." *Canning . . . of course it is; no one else knows I'm here.*

"What's L's second child's name?" Canning asked.

"Christopher." 'C' felt embarrassed, *Sounds damned stupid, this childish rigmarole, but you can never tell.*

"Mitchell's come over. She did it. She was in with him for five minutes alone. When she came out he was ready to listen." Canning sounded pleased.

"Good, *good*! Did you tell him the score?"

"Yes, I had to. All except the location, of course. There's no chance of him falling for anything else."

"What was his reaction?"

"He stonewalled a bit at first, until I mentioned our cousin in California, you know, on the island. That got to his pride. He swears that our American friend couldn't get near you-know-what in a month of Sundays, as he put it."

'C' laughed. "Where are they now?"

"He's completing the formalities in the governor's office. She's waiting outside. I must say she looks awfully happy.

"Not surprising after all that time." 'C' thought for two seconds, "Damned glad we didn't have to use the little boy in North Kensington. Bad enough for her as it is. You didn't say anything?"

"Not a word, sir. They've no idea at all that we know about him."

"Good, we'll keep it that way, makes for better relations all round."

"Yes, sir. They're coming up to Paddington with me, and I'll arrange for him to be at St. John's a couple of hours later," said Canning.

"No, make it in the morning. Eight A.M. Coming up to town right away?" 'C' asked.

"Yes, sir, be there at 2 A.M. They'll appreciate the five hours."

"Yes, and, of course, the usual precautions, as discussed?"

"Of course, sir."

"And from now on no contact apart from the laid-down schedule."

"No contact," Canning agreed.

"Good luck," 'C' said.

"Thank you, sir. We'll do our best!" promised Canning.

"I'm sure you will. Good night."

"Good night, sir."

'C' pressed the hang-up lever, then asked for a Whitehall number. He said three words, *"Orange is on."* He put the phone down and went back to his own easy chair in the senior members' corner by the big fireplace with the logs blazing away. He picked up his copy of the *Times* and settled down to sip his Scotch and soda. *I'll get a nice toy to little Billy tomorrow, through that gal who plays health visitor for us*, he thought as he opened the paper.

10th May, 1940. 11:38 P.M.
St. John's Wood, London

Lynch staggered slightly, his ginger hair was sticking out at all angles. "Where'm I goin' sleep?"

Half-crocked, thought Edwards.

"Edwards, show Mister Lynch to his bed, please," Dennis ordered. He had already given instructions for Number Three Barrack Room door to be locked. Dennis half-smiled at Lynch. *No chance of escape through the windows with their small iron frames.*

"Had a good time," Lynch hiccupped and lurched toward the stairs.

"Fine. Glad you enjoyed it. Good night," said the lieutenant.

"G'night, chief." Lynch disappeared up the stairs. Dennis went to the window and signaled all clear to Myers, the agent who had been tailing Lynch all evening. *Poor Chap*, Dennis thought, as he waved, *must be tired out, nine hours on duty.*

Myers returned the signal. *What a lad!* he thought. He was glad to be on his way home to Golder's Green at last, back to Rachel and the cats, out of the rain. *What a lad, how many young ladies was it? Four? Five? And all that booze; glad I'm not on his case tomorrow . . . the pace would kill me.*

11th May, 1940. 8:00 A.M.
St. John's Wood, London. Room Number One

"Good morning, all here?" Canning asked. He was back in uniform.

"All present and correct, sir. This is Mister Lynch," replied Dennis, who had been up since six, arranging, with Edwards' help, the display models. Some additional information had come in from Briggs in the Hague during the night.

"Pleased to meet you, Lynch," said the colonel. *I'll watch you, Mister Lynch*, he thought.

"Sir." Lynch felt tired, though he tried not to show it. He stared at Canning for a moment. *Have to watch my P's and Q's with this one*, he thought.

"You've met Mister Mitchell, I see, Lieutenant?" asked Canning.

"Yes, sir."

"Lynch? Mitchell?" The colonel looked sharply at each one as he spoke.

"Yes, sir, we've met," they chorused.

"All signed in?" the colonel asked Dennis.

"Yes, sir, but there's a problem. Braithwaite's wife has phoned in. She says he's gone to hospital, acute appendicitis."

The colonel frowned. "Dash it, damned inconvenient," he said. Then his face brightened. "Oh well, we shall just have to recruit a body off the ship, you know—muddle through?"

"Yes, sir."

"Might be quite useful, having a naval type with us, eh?"

"Might be, sir; they're usually quite good on lines and that sort of thing."

"Good, then without further ado we'll get down to business. You can draw the curtain now, Lieutenant, please."

Dennis grabbed the edge of a roomwide curtain and drew it to one side. Revealed behind it was a model. At first, it looked like a child's toy soldier fort, except for its size, almost half the area of the room, and for the replica of several streets and canals around it. Lynch and Mitchell stared in wonder at the quality of the workmanship bestowed on the model.

"Nice job, eh?" Canning smiled. "This, gentlemen, is an exact replica in miniature of a building we shall hopefully be visiting very shortly. In a moment we will take the roof off to inspect the interior."

Take the roof off. Both Mitchell and Lynch caught that one, both grinned as they listened carefully, more carefully than they had listened in years. They stood side by side, like a set of jugs, the lieutenant, the two criminals, and the colonel, tallest, on the right.

Mitchell stared at the model, his mind struggling for a moment. Then he remembered. *Canals? I know that building . . . it's the Palace in Amsterdam. That gray box over there is the Diamond Bureau . . . 1930 . . . pity they'd just cleared the safe out!*

But he didn't say a word.

Chapter 3

*   *

The Sailor with the Navy Blue Eyes

11th May, 1940

Who's got girls in every port,
Hanging around like flies?
Yo ho ho ho ho, ho!
The sailor with Navy blue eyes.

When the boat comes home,
After crossing the foam—
He's still at sea;
Thinking—wond'ring
Who he's going to take
Rowing on the lake.

Who's the guy they love to buy
Dozens of socks and ties?
Yo ho ho ho ho ho, ho!
The sailor with Navy blue eyes.

This masterpiece was current in 1940

3.

"The Sailor with the Navy Blue Eyes"

11th May, 1940. 8:15 A.M.
89 Stanton Road, North Kensington, London

Little Billy's red Mickey Mouse gas mask, one of the straps broken and dangling, was slung over the back of his chair.

"Put some milk on for 'im, Rosie." Mrs. Leighton's comfortable body belied the anxious look on her chubby face. There were streaks of gray in her hair, which, like Rose's, was tied in a bun, but at this time in the morning, loosely. She sat down to pour her second cup of tea, then looked at Rose for a moment. "You're sure it's all . . . straight, Rosie? I mean, you did meet this bloke from the 'Ome Office, Mr. Canning?"

"I've told you, Mum, it's the feller what was in the taxi last night. Oh Mum, we wouldn't muck you around, not after all you've done for Billy." She poured some milk onto Billy's cornflakes.

Mrs. Leighton nodded towards the boy, who slurped and grinned, milk running down his chin. "Eat proper, Tichie Mitchie, for Gawd's sake!" She wiped his face quickly with the edge of her apron. She looked back at Rose. "Did Big Mitch wake him up . . . say anything to him?"

"No, he just looked at him for a minute or two, that's all."

"I s'pose he was too eager for summink else, eh, Rosie?"

"Not surprising after six years inside, is it?"

"I s'pose not. Gawd, when your Dad came home from Egypt, an' that was only after two years. . . . " She giggled, jiggling her well-upholstered breasts. Then her face quickly saddened, "But I do wish your Dad 'ad seen the little 'un. They'd 'ave got on like a 'ouse on fire. Loved kids . . . pity we never 'ad a boy. . . . "

Rose sidled her eyes at Billy, then back to Mrs. Leighton. "Watch it Mum, he can U-N-D-E-R-S-T-A-N-D now."

"No 'arm in that. He has to know some time."

"Not yet. Now . . . " Rose stood up and reached for her coat, which was hanging on the back of the kitchen door. As she did so, she checked the alarm clock on the mantelpiece above the firegrate. "What do you want me to pick up? Couple of lamb chops?"

"And this week's three eggs, Rosie love." Mrs. Leighton delved into the Peake Frean's biscuit tin standing on the sideboard, *Silver Jubilee—1935 Peake Frean's Assorted*. She took out their ration books. "Don't forget these; won't get far without 'em."

"Oh, yes." Rose searched her handbag. "Mum . . . Mitch gave me this last night. It's an application form for his civilian rationbook. I've filled it in. Be a good Mum and take it down to the Labor Exchange; they'll fix it up."

Mrs. Leighton took the form, frowning. "How's this come about?" she asked. "He's not staying here, is he? You said he was . . . "

"Yes, but he won't need it 'til he gets back from wherever he's going. Mr. Canning said we might as well use it. It was all arranged," Rose explained.

"Very thoughtful of Mr. Canning, I'm sure." Mrs. Leighton looked doubtful.

"Yes, he thinks of everything." Rose pecked her mother's cheek hurriedly. "Bye, Mum . . . " She leaned over Billy, straightening his jersey collar. "Now be a good boy for your Gran." She opened the door, which led directly into the street. "See you usual time."

Mr. Mitchell, you're a lucky man, Mrs. Leighton thought. *A very lucky man indeed.* She wiped Billy's chin again, bent down, and kissed him, hugging him to her breast.

11th May, 1940. 9:05 A.M.
The Circus, London

"*Ultra*'s quieted down somewhat," Margot said chirpily.

She must have been out with that damned poodle-faker Ffoulkes again—but he seems to be good for her, thought 'C.' "Good . . . er, is there anything on our two *Monte Cristos*, Margot?" He had been called—a sign of things to come for the foreseeable future—to the war room at five-forty A.M.

"Yes, came in at eight-forty." She placed two envelopes before him. "Canning's with them now," she said.

"Good. Make sure Orange gets down to Sheerness as soon as the briefing's completed." 'C' tapped his teeth with a gold pencil—a sure sign that at least one thing was going well. "Canning to take all necessary precautions, of course."

"Of course." Margot cleared out the out-tray and left the room. 'C' turned to the reports, thinking as he slipped them out of their envelopes, *Filthy business this.* He contemplated, *But Myers is good. Philips, well, at his age not surprising; must find him an assistant, someone younger, to take over.* He started to read.

Mr. Lynch left Langley Rd., took tube Leicester Square. Entered King's Head on Coventry St. Was refused service as time had been called. Subject walked to Wardour St. via Shaftesbury Ave. Entered Green Cockatoo club at 3:33 P.M. Emerged at 4:46 P.M. Walked to No. 18 Croft's Alley, entered doorway marked "Birgitte, French Model," at 5:01 P.M. Emerged at 5:04 P.M. To Cavalier Club, Berners St. Entered at 5:08 P.M. stayed until 5:46 . . . and so on, until . . . *11 P.M. subject emerged from Anchor public house. Walked Piccadilly tube station, returned to Langley Rd., St. John's Wood, which entered 11:38 P.M. 11:42 P.M. surveillance ceased on receipt prearranged signal. As far as could be seen, subject did not encounter anyone out of the normal run. Expenses: seven shillings and fourpence. Myers.*

'C' checked the list of addresses Lynch had visited. He hurrumphed. "Mmm . . . " he ruminated, *Anyone out of the normal run . . . my God, what a life!* 'C' tapped his gold pen on his teeth, half-smiling and thought, *Five whores in as many hours? Where the dickens can five whores be had for two pounds? Well, at least it shows a certain stamina, and probably some skill and ingenuity . . . just what we need. Have to watch. . . .* He turned to read the report from Philips.

Contacted Mr. Mitchell Platform 3, Paddington Station. In company with male in camel hair coat, bowler and military mustache, about forty-eight years. Six-feet one inch. Military appearance. Female was thirtyish, brown coat, flat-heeled shoes, light brown hair in bun. Trio took taxi to 89 Stanton Road, North Ken. Subject and female alighted and entered aforesaid premises. 'C' winced. *Aforesaid . . . God, these ex-policemen!* He read on. *. . . At 2:32 A.M. man in bowler hat stayed in taxi, left in direction of Notting Hill Gate. Maintained surveillance on 89 Stanton Rd., until 7:30 A.M.* 'C' smiled to himself. *I'll bet he reads Eric Ambler!* he thought. *11th May, when subject emerged from 89 Stanton Rd. alone, walked Notting Hill Gate tube station. Subject then proceeded . . .* 'C' winced again. *Why do policemen proceed, when ordinary mortals go?* he asked himself. . . *to Langley Rd., St. John's Wood, where entered at 7:53 A.M. Expenses: One pound fifteen shilling and fourpence half-penny, including puncture repair and parking fine (Notting Hill Gate).*

'C's' brows knitted. *Puncture? Parking? Those damned motorcars. Philips is getting too expensive. I wonder how the little chap took to his father?* 'C' initialled the expense sheets, tore them off the report forms, and placed the forms in the Orange file. *That's that, at least for the moment.* He thought fondly of the good old days when agents moved about London by bicycle—the minor agents—and horse-drawn cab.

11th May, 1940. 9:15 A.M.
H.M.S. HAVELOCK, Chatham, Kent

The duty yeoman of signals was waiting outside Lieutenant Commander Euan Cameron's door. "Signal, sir, immediate priority," he said.

"Thank you, Yeoman," the destroyer's captain said. His mind was still dwelling on the First Lieutenant's defaulter's list. Able Seaman Goffin had been fighting ashore again. Almost absentmindedly he read:

DEFENSE MINISTER TO CAPTAIN OF H.M. DOCKYARD, SHEERNESS, REPEAT TO COMMANDING OFFICER, H.M.S. HAVELOCK. PROCURE AND SUPPLY MATERIALS NECESSARY FOR COMPLETE REFURBISHING OF CAPTAIN'S CABIN AND HEAD. H.M.S. HAVELOCK. PRAY REQUIRE THE SAILMAKER TO EXERCISE HIS CRAFT, PADDING HEAD SEAT. CAPTAIN'S STEWARD, H.M.S. HAVELOCK, TO DRAW NEW SLOPS. H.M.S. HAVELOCK TO BE UNDER NOTICE FOR SEA AND IN ROYAL REVIEW ORDER NOT LATER THAN NOON TOMORROW, TWELFTH. ACKNOWLEDGE.

The captain stared at the cable as if he were inspecting the contents of an uncooked haggis; then he shook his head slightly and reread the signal. *Head . . . head?* he puzzled to himself *What the devil?* And then it dawned on him. *So that's the game! Well, well, he"s certainly a laddie. Even now, with all hell let loose, he can think about bloody toilet seats*! He tried to suppress a groan and grin at the same time.

"Any reply sir?" asked the yeoman.

"What? . . . No . . . no. Just acknowledge please, Yeoman," Cameron said as he stuffed the signal into his pocket. He made for his settee. He felt suddenly weary. "Steward . . . bring me a really strong coffee, will you?" he called. His dark Hebridean eyes stared grimly at the first lieutenant's report as he wondered how soon the Good Lord would allow him to rid himself and his ship of Able Seaman Goffin. After a minute, he picked up the ship's telephone and rang the First Lieutenant. "Hullo Number One? Er, look considering the effort we need, issue double rum today."

"Aye aye, sir, splice the main brace . . . that'll shift them!" replied Lieutenant Bates.

11th May, 1940. 9:45 A.M.
No. 18 Crofts Alley, Soho, London, "Birgitte, French Model," Room 4

Florence "Effie" Smith sniffed as she rubbed her bruised shoulder. She sat on the floor, where Nobby had just flung her. "I couldn't 'elp it, Nobby!" she wailed. " 'E looked all right to me, sort of, you know . . . like one o' the boys." At this early hour, she looked like a skinned rabbit; she knew it and she didn't care.

Nobby, whose face and gestures betrayed him for what he was, a wily, oily, sadistic sprucer of a ponce, in an incongruous Shetland Island jersey, corduroys, and suede shoes, kicked her other shoulder. "You . . . silly . . . cow!" He sat down on the unmade bed and ran a hand through his off-blond curly hair. "You stupid bitch . . . wot cher go an' leave a bloody fiver under th' fuckin' flower vase for? An' then goin' out to change a quid for 'im!" He lashed out with his foot again.

Effie dodged the blow. "For fuck's sake, Nobby, 'e looked all bloomin' right!" She pulled her chemise up around one exposed thin breast.

"Wot's this geezer look like . . . wot *are* you . . . barmy or summink? Wot's he look like?"

"Ginger 'air, wide blue eyes . . . a sort of gray pinstripe suit . . . an . . . " Effie wiped her wrist across her nose, " . . . an' brown levver shoes." She sobbed again.

"I'll clobber the bastard . . . cor, fuckalittleduck . . . a fiver!" He leaned back on the bed and glowered at the ceiling. "What else?"

" 'ad a scar on his nose," she wailed. " . . . about thirty, five-foot-five. 'E looked all right, Nobby." She leaned over and grabbed his leg. "Said 'is name was Banger . . . "

He flung her off with a kick. "I'll scar the fucker! I'll bang the barsted!"

"An . . . Nobby . . . 'e'd been in the nick . . . recently I fink. I could tell by the way he 'eld 'is fag in the palm of 'is 'and . . ."

"I'll nick the bleeder," Nobby growled as he charged through the door and slammed it behind him. Effie flung herself on the bed and sobbed. " 'E looked all right, Nobby!" She heard the front door slam. She sat up and reached for a brush to tend her hair and stuck her tongue out at the door, with its sacred heart picture still swinging violently from the coat hook.

11th May, 1940. 10:00 A.M.
H.M. Destroyer Havelock, *underway on the River Medway*

"Head oh-nine-five-and-a-half," the navigation officer sang out down to the wheelhouse, his left hand resting on top of the bronze voicepipe lip.

"Oh-nine-five an' a 'alf it is, sir!" came the faint reply, back up the tube.

"Like Chiefy says, Number One," Cameron sucked on his pipe.

"Sir?" asked Lieutenant Bates, the first lieutenant.

"Lovely day for duck shooting," Cameron said.

"Yes, sir," Bates agreed.

"Oh-nine-eight and a quarter," the pilot chanted, leaning low over the forward windbreak to get an eyesight on a distant mark with the bow-jack-staff.

"Bit late, now, though, I suppose." Cameron's voice was low, regretful.

"Get a few sitters, sir." Bates thought it his duty to be optimistic, besides, he always felt better when the ship was moving.

"Unsporting, old chap. Never do," said Cameron as yet another body joined the group around him.

"Signal, sir, immediate, urgent." The yeoman handed it over, thinking, *The skipper must be going' crackers, they're comin' in like bloody confetti*.

Cameron accepted it. "Thank you, Yeoman; I'll send any reply down with the bridgehand, if there is one." He tore the signal open.

TOP SECRET. DEFENSE MINISTER TO COMMANDING OFFICER, H.M.S. HAVELOCK. PASSENGERS FOR SEA BOARDING AT 1500 TODAY, ELEVENTH, ORANGE TECHNICAL STAFF, DIPLOMATIC MISSION, ADD TO VICTUALING LIST CANNING, COL.; DENNIS, LIEUT.; MITCHELL, FOREMAN; LYNCH, CHARGEHAND. DO NOT ACKNOWLEDGE.

Cameron turned to the bridge messenger. "Give my compliments to the supply officer and ask him to contact me, will you?" he ordered. The ship's siren belched out, high-pitched and sharp, and, this close, ear-piercing.

"Aye aye, sir," said Able Seaman Goffin, as he dashed for the ladder, knowing he'd get a quick cup of stand-easy tea in the mess before he returned. The starboard lookout pulled his mouth slightly. He knew, too.

"Goffin!" Bates called to the seaman as he slid down the ladder.

"Sir?" Goffin kept a straight face, his Navy-blue eyes looking over Bates' shoulder.

"There's a line trailing over the starboard side amidships. Tell the Buffer his slip is showing!" Bates shouted.

"Aye aye, sir." *Jimmy's showing off again,* he thought, as the quartermaster piped over the Tannoy, "D'ye hear, there? Up spirits! Splice the mainbrace!" The quartermaster's voice boomed, metallic and authoritative, and to Goffin it sounded like Jehovah commanding, *"Let there be light!"*

11th May, 1940. 11:00 A.M.
Langley Road, St. John's Wood, London

The colonel was saying, "Good, then it's the roof first, the wall second, and as Mr. Lynch so delightfully put it, the bloody sewers last. I think we're agreed on that." The phone brought their thoughts back to St. John's Wood.

Canning picked it up. "Yes, sir? . . . good . . . right . . . 1500 at the latest. I'll pick up a three-tonner. What about a driver? I see. Right, we'll leave it there for the returning passengers, then, shall we? Yes sir. Thank you." He jotted down some numbers on his pocket pad, then looked at the others. "Well, chaps, climb all over this . . . " he gestured at the model, "as much as you like. It's our final look at it."

"Where're we goin', sir?" Lynch was still dozy.

"Can't say yet, but we move off at noon. The necessary supplies will be on the transport." He stroked his mustache. "So . . . gentlemen . . . dismissed for the time being. We'll take lunch at 11:15."

Mitchell said to Canning, "Can I see you for a minute alone, sir?"

"Not allowed I'm afraid, Mitchell. Lieutenant Dennis is responsible. He should be here." The colonel looked at Dennis.

"If it's personal, sir . . . " Dennis said.

"Is it?" Canning turned to Mitchell.

"Sort of," said Mitchell in a low voice.

"Then I'll leave," said Dennis. He stood up and made for the door, leaving it open behind him.

Canning looked at Mitchell.

"I just wanted to say, sir . . . well, thanks a lot for the time off last night," Mitchell stuttered.

"Oh, think nothing of it, old chap."

"Well, sir, that was very decent, and I think I ought to tell you, sir," Mitchell gestured at the model. "I know where that place is. I was around there some years ago, but . . . er . . . well, it's a bit embarrassing like . . . women and all that, you know, sir, but I do know the area well. It's Amsterdam. It's the Palaas-plaas . . . and I think you ought to know that I've been there."

Canning stood for a moment in silence looking Mitchell straight in the eye. "Really? I'd no idea . . . well, that's a help, eh? what?" He picked up his swagger stick off the desk and put it under his arm, slowly moving to the door. Mitchell followed three steps behind. Suddenly the colonel turned. "Look here, Mitchell," he said, "I think it would be a good idea to keep this to ourselves, what?"

"Of course, sir, that's why I asked to see you."

"Wouldn't do for that kind of thing to get out, would it, I mean . . . never know where it might leak." Canning grinned. "By the way, Miss Leighton, such a delightful person."

"Yes, sir." *I get it, I do indeed get it*, Mitchell pondered as he made his way to the tea urn. *They've even got her number*.

"Nice little chat?" asked Lynch, stirring a mug of tea.

"Oh . . . yeah . . . 'e's fixing us up with ration books," explained Mitchell.

Lynch leered. "Good . . . won't get far without 'em, will we, leastways not when we're away from the site?"

11th May, 1940. 11:05 A.M.
Onboard the sailing barge Beatrice Maud, *Marlow's Wharf, Southend-on-sea, Essex*

"Let's go, Josh. Young-Mike, unruck the top's'l as soon as she slides off!" Knocker was on the wheel, fondling it at first with his calloused hands, then hefting it over slightly to port. Big Josh threw the mooring lines off the two bollards. He ran the hundred feet between them much faster than his bulk would allow a landsman to guess. As *Beatrice Maud* slowly edged away from the jetty on the tide, he flung himself onto the portwale and down on deck, heading for the dolly winch, picking up the main halyard on the way. He made four turns of the halyard on the winch drum, then turned to await Knocker's command. *Thank Gawd that's the last load o' bricks for a while*, he thought.

Knocker scrutinized the top's'l, as it flogged itself for a moment before Young-Mike brought in the sheet; then, as the wind filled the sail, he shifted his gaze forward, ahead of the bow, to get a line-of-sight on the outer buoy with the forestay. He felt pleased. The wind had shifted during the night, veering to the west-northwest. That gave him a reach leaving Marlow's, and he needn't pay for a short tow out.

Big Josh was reading his thoughts. "Save a few bob, eh, Knocker?"

Knocker grinned. *Josh was at it last night*, he thought. "Yes," he said, "lovely job; we'll be at the buoy in no time." He cupped his left hand around his mouth, first wiping his mustache. "Young-Mike!" he yelled, "let's 'ave the stay'sl!"

Young-Mike, a hard-muscled, slim lad of seventeen, with tow hair, a bit long around the ears for those days, grabbed the stay'sl halyard and heaved. The shackle on the stay'sl head scraped as it slid up the forestay wire, a crying screech, as if the sail were protesting, reluctant to give up its rest. The block on the mainmasthead groaned and wheezed, insisting on its need of the sail, and *Beatrice Maud*, a great oblong wooden box with masts—when she was alongside—came to life and became a thing of surprising beauty. As she lifted, slightly, with each sea, she seemed, to Knocker, to carry with her against the slight rising tide, the dreams and love of the twenty men who had built her, back in 1910, on the muddy foreshore at Sittingbourne. They had launched her, he recalled, with cheers, ale, roast beef, and beer as twenty Union Jacks had whipped bravely in the wind, and the seabirds had cried a welcome to her and drawn her to the full-tide waters.

Beatrice Maud reached the outer buoy. Knocker, with one elbow wrapped around a wheel spoke, had lit his pipe, face turned to port, away from the wind. Once he'd a good draw on the Erinmore tobacco, he nodded at Josh. Josh knocked the wedges onto the dolly winch gypsy, then he kicked at the steam-valve lever with one tennis shoe. Slowly the mainsail unbrailed, its parrels scraping, the leech flapping, the sprit thudding against the shrouds at first until the sail filled. Knocker hauled in, delicately, it seemed, on the great mainsheet. The sheet blocks protested, grumbled; the wind shaped the ochre-colored eighth of an acre of canvas; and, a young girl again, *Beatrice Maud* picked up her skirts and gently danced to the May breezes.

After Young-Mike had hoisted the foresail he strode aft, tow hair awry, ribs like a starved whippet, swaggering. "Want a cuppa, Knocker?" Young-Mike's hands were a mass of cuts and scars from the bricks. His movements were jerky and shy, with the angularity of adolescence.

"Ah . . . that'll be nice, my son," Knocker said.

"When d'ye reckon we'll fetch Gillingham?" asked Josh as he swigged the mainsheet.

"Oh, 'bout dusk. Got to wait for the tide in Sheerness Roads." With his hands on the wheel and his head tilted to one side, so he could watch the sails, Knocker, a shabby little old man, and clumsy *Beatrice Maud*, together as one, made caressing love to the sea and the sky and the crying gulls.

11th May, 1940. 1:30 P.M.
H.M.S. Havelock, *Buoy No. 28, Sheerness*

The launch came gently alongside the refit barge. Canning and Dennis scrambled onto the great splintered, oily timbers, trying to guard their uniforms from the creosote. The launch-cox'n smartly saluted. Two army officers climbed up the ship's side ladder. Mitchell and Lynch, with the aid of the launch bowman, unloaded the baggage off the launch, passing it by hand, one to the other, across the pipe and cable-strewn barge, to the bottom of the ladder.

Colonel Canning reached His Majesty's Ship *Havelock*'s deck as the quartermaster piped him onboard. The Officer of the Day, Sub-Lieutenant Wilkins, saluted. The colonel faced aft, almost bumping into a *very young, very extraordinary seaman looking*, he thought, *a bit Dickensian in that long coat*, and gave a military salute, palm out, the hand reverberating slightly as it came swiftly to the peak of his cap.

"Colonel Canning?" Wilkins' voice was almost broken now.

The colonel asked, "Permission to come aboard?" Canning knew the ropes.

Wilkins replied, "Glad to have you, sir . . . er . . ." He gazed at Dennis as Canning stepped to one side.

Dennis spoke, "Lieutenant Dennis—permission . . . ?"

"Certainly, Lieutenant . . . er . . . sir," Wilkins said. He looked again at Canning. "The captain's holding defaulters now, and the first lieutenant is with him, of course," Wilkins' voice faltered.

"Fine." Canning smiled. "I can wait."

" . . . But if you'd care to step this way, sir, I can take you to the wardroom." Wilkins gestured across his chest with one hand.

The colonel said, "Good, good. Ask your man to check the baggage, will you? Should be eight pieces." He turned to Dennis. "Eight, that's right?" he asked.

"Yes, sir, eight." Dennis was relieved that there were officers even younger than himself on this ship.

They all three meandered forward, Wilkins leading the way, scrambling over snaking hoses and electric leads, dodging busy sailors and workmen. As they reached the starboard break ladder, Dennis wondered to himself about the lack of formality on the part of the crew, who carried on working, ignoring the new arrivals. This was his first visit to a Royal Navy vessel. *Not like the Army*, he thought. *God, if a ranking naval officer visited an army depot, everyone would be saluting or standing to attention*. Then he realized that in a ship this size, the whole spit-and-polish thing would be impossible if anything were to get done. He was astonished that as they passed the men talked just as they would have done, he imagined, had they not been there. " 'Ere, pass us that bloody chisel, Bert." "So I told 'im I'd have 'is bleedin' guts for garters . . . " Dennis looked at Wilkins' face as they passed a line of men standing, smartly dressed, at ease, outside the wardroom screen door. Wilkins seemed to hear nothing from the deck crew. Absolutely nothing. It was as if they were earth visitors to a far planet, as if the sounds from the natives were unintelligible, unimportant, and irrelevant.

They passed through the wardroom door into another world, although the outside racket, muted, could still be heard. The wardroom was about as big as his parent's sitting room in the Georgian house back in Bloomsbury. It was fully carpeted, wall to wall. Under the portholes, with the white-painted steel deadlights dropped down to screen out the noise, was a line of settees. To one side was a small bar, behind which a white-jacketed steward stood. In the center of the room were four very comfortable-looking easy chairs and a table, with eight dining chairs around it. On the walls (as Dennis thought of them) were several pictures of hunting scenes and a couple of yachts under full sail. *Bit like a club lounge*, he thought.

There was one other person in the wardroom beside the steward. He was sitting on the settee and rose to meet them, saying, "Ah . . . you must be the passengers. Lieutenant Commander Brown. Call me Doc. I'm the quack . . . drink?" He shook hands with both the officers and nodded to the steward, who turned to lift a bottle of Booth's Dry Gin.

Two yards and three worlds away, on the other side of the one-eighth-of-an-inch of steel plate that surrounded the wardroom, Able Seaman Goffin (Goff to everyone onboard below the rating of chief petty officer) rigged in his number-one blue serge suit with gold badges, waited with the patience of resignation to hear his fate. He stood at ease to which the cox'n, Soapy Hudson had called him five minutes ago, just before the two army officers had climbed the ladder and passed him. Nolan, the buntings killick, who was up for promotion to petty officer, stood between him and the flat door. "Wonder who they are?" said Nolan, a slight, pointy-nosed Irishman from Cork, who reminded Goffin of a bookie's runner.

"Skipper's chums?" suggested Goffin, quietly.

"No . . . passengers. It's a ride they're after," Nolan spoke out of the side of his mouth.

"Pity it's not my bloody relief!" said Goffin. Nolan grinned as the cox'n popped his head around the screen door opening.

"Quiet, Goffin!"

Goffin let his clean-shaven, handsome face relax, wondering how Soapy had overheard him. He could just see the two civilians bringing their baggage up the side ladder, both trying to keep their suits from soiling. He could tell, from the way they moved themselves, that they weren't sailors. *Couldn't be matelots. That big one, could be a squaddie*, he reflected. *He looks like a soldier . . . getting on a bit, though. The little ginger 'un looks more like a bloomin' jockey.*

Soapy yelled out, trying to sound officious, "Leading Signalman Nolan!" Paddy disappeared at as smart a trot as the screen doorsill would allow.

Goffin lost interest in the civilians and daydreamed, gazing out across the anchorage, not seeing the craft lying at anchor. He remembered the two occasions when he had been promoted to the dizzy heights of petty officer, and the two occasions when he had been, inevitably, it seemed to him, disrated again. Always the same trouble, he thought, *Always bloody booze.* That's why they'd drafted him from the submarine service. The only times he'd been in the rattle, in all the thirteen years, had been ashore, and always because of booze. *Ah well, all in a day's work*, he mused, as the quack breezed out of the screen door and passed him, with the two army officers in tow. Directly behind the army lieutenant, a brand-new Petty Officer Nolan emerged beaming. He winked at Goffin, who thought, *Snivelling Irish get! Still, not a bad lad, old Paddy*.

His reverie broke off as the cox'n, pad in hand, stepped out of the screen door, did an about-face, pointed toward the door, and hollered, "Able Seaman Goffin!"

Goffin trotted in the prescribed manner, moving his trim, shipshape, six-foot frame in tiny shuffling steps because of the confined spaces, over the screen door sill. Soapy was only a foot behind him by some miracle, and he found himself staring, over a lecturn-type desk, at the stern, angry eyes of Skipper "Jock" Cameron. He stood at rigid attention and found a spot, just over the skipper's right shoulder—a rivet on the far portside bulkhead, and held it in his stare, concentrating on that one rivet.

"Defaulter . . . off . . . cap!" The cox'n snapped out the order.

Goffin smartly passed his right hand across his body, brought it up to the rim of his cap, and whipped the cap off his head, bringing it down to his right side in a flash.

Cameron frowned at Goffin for a moment. "Read the charge, Cox'n," he said.

The first lieutenant, as his divisional officer, although by the rules there to defend him, was also frowning.

Soapy bawled, "Sir! Able Seaman Goffin, William. Official number C stroke K 586340 *did*, on the evening of the 10th May 1940 break out of ship. Charge 2 . . ." Soapy spoke in a singsong, "*did*, on the same evening as aforesaid, outside the *Army and Navy* public house, High Street, Chatham, strike Corporal Fleming, Henry, P stroke M 634987, this being his superior officer, said action being in contravention of the King's Rules and Admiralty Instructions and the Articles of War. Such an offense being repeated and aggravated and in direct contravention to naval discipline and good order. Charge 3, *did* break into ship on the aforementioned evening. Charge 4, *did* return onboard improperly dressed. Charge 5, *that*, being intoxicated he *did* use threatening and obscene language against Petty Officer Brookes, Petty Officer of the Day, this being . . . " The Cox'n droned on, stumbling over some of the longer words.

At the end of the charges, Cameron was silent for a few seconds. Then he turned to the cox'n.

"Witnesses?" asked the captain.

"Corporal Fleming is in Chatham, sir," the cox'n said as he checked his pad.

"Others . . . naval policemen?"

"They're in Chatham, too, sir."

"Petty Officer Brookes?" Cameron insisted.

"Drafted yesterday, sir, fire-control course at *Royal Arthur*."

"Then . . . " Cameron spoke to Goffin. "What do you have to say Goffin? Of course, you realize that if the witnesses to these accusations can't be here, I'll have to stand you over. Quite possibly until we return to Chatham, but if you admit to the charges . . . well . . . it's possible you might come off lighter." He jerked his head up as a sign that Goffin could speak.

"He was with my party, my girl, sir," Goffin said.

"Who was?" Cameron leaned forward, slightly, over the lectern.

"The bootneck, I mean Corporal Fleming. And he called me a bloody bastard, sir. I just got mad," explained Goffin.

"Then you feel that the charge is unjustified?" asked the captain.

"Yes, sir," mumbled Goffin, thinking that to call a British sailor a bastard is the ultimate insult. Call him *anything* but bastard.

"I mean charge number two. That's a serious charge, Goffin."

"Yes, sir."

"What about the other charges?" Cameron gazed at the charge sheet, then looked up again at Goffin. "Breaking out of ship, improperly dressed, and breaking back into ship. What about them?" he demanded.

"Guilty, sir," Goffin said.

Cameron said, "Right, then I'll deal with the minor charges first. Breaking out of ship; seven days' stoppage, seven days' number tens. Being out of the rig of the day; three days' stoppage, for breaking into ship; seven days' stoppage, seven days' number elevens. Using threatening gestures and obscene language to Petty Officer Brookes; case dismissed in the absence of the witness."

Goffin reckoned, *Not too bad*. His leave was stopped for seventeen days, also his rum ration; but the other was a bit much, he thought. Number tens meant two hours extra work each day, usually mucky, dreary work, and number elevens meant disciplinary drill—running round and round the quarterdeck with a heavy Lee-Enfield rifle held above the head, at full arm's length for an hour at a time, two hours a day.

The captain tapped the charge sheet with a pen. "All three sentences to run concurrently. As for the major, more serious charge. This could very likely be a court martial case. In the absence of witnesses, I must bind you over until the witnesses can be brought before me. Charge number two stood over indefinitely!" He looked again at the charge sheet, then back at Goffin. "You're determined to be a skate. Twice a petty officer, six years in submarines, conduct 'excellent,' excellent seamanship, good work record, what the . . . what's got into you? You can't resent being kept on for the duration. You'd have been called up anyway, even if you'd gone outside after your twelve years were completed. Every one of these past offenses . . . ashore." The captain waited for a reply.

"He was with my girl, sir, and he called me a bloody bastard."

"Right. Cox'n, dismiss defaulters, please!" the captain ordered.

"Defaulter, about turn, quick march!" Soapy bawled out.

Goffin did another turkey trot over the door sill, out on deck, turned aft, and shuffled out of sight. There he broke into his normal walk. As he passed his killick, his leading hand, and his watchmates, clearing up around B turret, someone asked him, quietly, "Howdja get on, Goff?"

He grinned. "Okay. One case dismissed, one stood over, and three weeks' stoppage." He thought, as he swung around to the port foc'sle break, *Don't mind the leave. It's the bloody rum that I'll miss*! Then he cheered up slightly, as he remembered that Rattler Morgan owed him two tots for standing in for him on a weekend duty. He thought he'd take his time going down below. It was quiet on the portside. As he lit a tickler, ready-rolled, he gazed out to the estuary. He watched a sailing boat beating in against the tide, her red sails fluttering at the leech momentarily every minute or so. As she drew nearer, he saw that she was one of the local sailing barges. He leaned over the guardrail, watching her, recalling the sampans in Hong Kong, the junks up the Yangtze, and the feluccas on the Nile. He turned to go below, and as he passed through the breakdoor, he noticed the name on the sailing boat. She was well astern now—*Beatrice Maud* and below, *London*.

He gazed after her for a moment longer. He watched her slight list, her gentle lift, her great shapely mainsail, half as big as a football field, the sprit moving gently with each lift, and then he walked forward, feeling, for some reason, better.

Further aft along the upper deck, Mitchell and Lynch had completed stowing the baggage in the sick bay. They were now idling, waiting for someone to show them to their places.

"France, that's where we're goin', Mitch," said Lynch.

Mitchell dragged on his cigarette, which he held in the fingers of his left hand. He didn't want to make the mistake of holding it in his palm, like Lynch, it was too much of a giveaway. " 'Spect so," was all he said. Mitchell crossed to the rail and looked forward along the ship's side. Then he saw the sailing boat, her great sail, red, orange and brown streaks, lifting, shivering and waving slightly, curved like the heart-rending sweep of the roof of a cathedral, and the white bow wave as the boat, lightly loaded it seemed to him, moved against the wind. She was close enough now for him to hear the groaning of her blocks and the scraping of her parrels on her mast.

Lynch joined him at the rail. "Cor . . . look at that!" he cried out.

"She's a beauty, ain't she?" said Mitchell. "Must be some kind of a yacht or something, I suppose. But no, look at the bloke on the front, and for crying out loud, look at the old geezer who's driving her!"

The old geezer, as they watched, eyes wide, looked up at the bridge of the destroyer and saluted, one hand to his bowler. Both Mitch and Lynch waved back, shyly, at first, then wildly, excited by the strange sight and by their own new freedom of which the old sailing boat now passing them only twenty yards off reminded them.

"I'd love to know what her cargo is. Think it'd be worth nicking?" Lynch lit another Senior Service cigarette as he spoke out of the side of his mouth.

Beatrice Maud with a coquettish lift of her stern, her foresail fluttering as if she were sniffing, passed on upstream, in her majestic style. The young tow-haired lad onboard her stern hauled up her ensign again. The barge moved as if all else but the sea and the sky were beneath her notice.

"What was its name, did you read it?" asked Mitchell.

"No, didn't think of it," replied Lynch.

"I think it was Beatrice Something," murmured Mitchell as he turned away, leaving Lynch to contemplate the prospect of being once more out of Britain, where even the most hardened criminals would turn in a murderer to the police. *Funny thing*, he said to himself, as he watched *Beatrice*'s ensign hauled up, *the only times I ever felt really comfortable was in places where the bloody Union Jack doesn't fly.*

Knocker hummed softly to *Beatrice Maud* as he sat on the barrel that Josh had strapped to the deck especially for this very purpose. He steered *Beatrice* with one hand, now that she was close on the wind. He could have steered with one finger, her helm was so light. As he hummed, his glance shifted continually from the topsail, down to the luff of the foresail, and onto his eyeline mark, buoy No. 28. But he laid her off the mark a touch. There was a destroyer laying to the buoy, and she might swing out into the fairway.

He sang, *If I should plant a tiny seed of love*
   In the corner of your heart,
   Would it grow to be a great big love some day?
   Or would it die and fade away . . . ?

He sang the lilting melody from the days of old Queen Victoria, and remembered, fleetingly, how he had brought his bride on this very same passage in 1897. He'd been a brand new skipper then, and they'd been married in Whitstable Church. Elsie had taken passage with him the thirty-odd miles to Gillingham. That had been their honeymoon. She'd been in her white dress and holding a bunch of flowers, laughing. He had handed her ashore on Gillingham pier, with his sister, Maggie, to see Elsie to their new home, the new house he'd just rigged up, by the church on the hill. Before he'd gone to her he'd set to, loading a cargo of 70,000 bricks, just him and the lad, by hand, so he could be off to The Isle of Dogs next day on the tide. He shook himself out of his memories and looked before him, standing up, feet apart, to see ahead of the boat.

Beatrice was almost level with the bows of the destroyer and only about twenty yards off. Knocker looked up to the destroyer's bridge and noticed the heads and shoulders of some figures. As *Beatrice* drew slowly closer, he saw that two of them were wearing naval officers' caps. *One o' them must be the skipper*, he thought. He hollered to Young-Mike, who was washing the straw off the decks. "Hey, Young-Mike!"

Mike looked up from his task. "Wot's up, Knocker?"

"Come back aft 'ere and lower the bloomin' flag." He nodded his head astern. Young-Mike came running, looking quizzically at Knocker as he passed.

Knocker looked up at the naval officers and saluted, forefinger on the brim of his bowler. When one of the officers saluted briefly back, Knocker shut one eye in a broad wink and grinned up at everyone in sight, showing them all his five teeth. He remained so, a little old man, with a gray mustache, standing at the salute, for no more than a minute or so, until *Beatrice* was abreast the midships part of the destroyer. Then Knocker turned, glanced forward, heard and saw the foresail luffing, and eased her gently a little off the wind.

While Cameron was holding defaulters, he had caught a glimpse of the two army officers as they passed into the wardroom. Now that defaulters was over, he had a chance to speak with them. As he stepped out on deck, he spoke over his shoulder. "Where are they, Number One?"

Lieutenant Bates announced, "Doc's on the bridge with them, showing them around, sir."

Cameron bounded up the bridge, Bates close behind him. He stretched out his hand to Canning. They shook hands. "Glad to have you onboard, Colonel," Cameron said.

Canning gestured to Dennis. "This is Lieutenant Dennis." Dennis saluted. The other three officers and the four ratings on the bridge all noticed, but no one minded. Dennis was still young and obviously had never been on a naval ship before. Cameron, kindly, saluted back, feeling a little embarrassed, yet knowing that Bates and the others would understand. He turned to Canning. "All fixed up? You're in Number One's cabin, Colonel. The lieutenant is in . . . er . . . " he looked at Bates.

"In the cox'n's office, sir. It's the only cabin spare," Bates said.

Cameron continued, "Yes, in the cox'n's office, unless you are onboard a few days. Then we can perhaps fix up something a little more comfortable for the lieutenant. The two civilians will be berthed in the sick bay, and you can use that as your operations HQ; plenty of room."

Canning smiled and brushed his mustache. "Just been admiring the view up here," he said. "The doctor tells me you're interested in duck hunting? I was looking at the flats over yonder. Ideal, I should think, what?"

The captain said, "Oh, very much so. We might get a chance, if there's any delay. We can be back onboard in five minutes or so if the balloon goes up, Colonel. Perhaps in the morning."

"Quite. And that sailing vessel," Canning turned and pointed ahead, downstream, about a hundred yards away, to where red sails shimmered and glistened in the light of the westerly sun that was behind their backs. "What is she, Captain?"

"Oh, one of the local spritsail barges. They knock around here quite a bit. Do any sailing yourself, sir?" Cameron asked. He himself did not sail.

Canning grinned apologetically. "A little, from the Hamble, you know, I keep a small twenty-foot sloop down there; take the family down on weekends. At least used to." He stared at the sailing barge, beating against wind and tide, now almost abreast of the destroyer. "She . . . they certainly are beautiful, aren't they?"

"Beautiful and inefficient. Not many of them left now," Cameron said, quietly. "About 140, I believe, around the estuary, quite a few more around the coast."

The barge was passing them. The officers watched her as she lifted and fell, lifted and fell. They stared at the sprit as it rose and fell with the lift, and at the mainsail as it filled its lovely curved shape and backed slightly with each rise; and its leech, all of sixty feet long, the afterend of the orange-ochre, rust-colored mainsail, how it fluttered as she nosed periodically into the wind, then steadied again as she shuddered, sighed, and fell off. They could plainly see the crew now, and the gulls wheeling, crying, around her wake, as if they were following her eagerly home.

An old man, with a gray mustache, dressed in a shabby blue suit, his bowler hat set forward on his head, his pipe upside down, peering aloft now and then, gave slight pushes on the great wooden wheel. Standing by the mainmast step, a bucket in hand, scooping water from the river, casually, was a young tow-haired lad, bare-chested, dusty, and bronzed, and up forward, working on a line, a big, bald-headed man in a dirty boiler suit and tennis shoes. They watched the lad as he put down the bucket and raced aft to haul down the dirty ensign, very nearly black, with an almost indiscernable Union Jack in the upper fly.

Lieutenant-Commander Cameron turned to his duty yeoman. "Yeoman, phone the afterguard. Tell them to dip the ensign!" he commanded.

"Aye aye, sir." The yeoman grabbed the phone handle and whizzed it around. "Dip the ensign!" he hollered into the mouthpiece.

Cameron strolled to the afterend of the bridge to watch as *Havelock*'s white ensign was slowly lowered. Then he gazed back at the barge. The old helmsman was saluting, his forefinger on the brim of his bowler. Cameron felt touched. He saluted and waved quickly, then stood back, feeling slightly embarrassed.

The other officers were too fascinated by the barge to notice Cameron's wave. The colonel was moved. He said, "It's like watching something out of the past—from the seventeenth century." He almost gushed, "And the contrasts in color—the sails and the sky."

"We get them past here quite often, sir," murmured Bates.

"Too often," Cameron told him.

They stood watching for the three minutes it took for the sailing boat to pass the destroyer, noticing, she was so close, the name on her stern. "What an old-fashioned Victorian name," Canning muttered. *Beatrice Maud* . . . how very delightful." Then he turned to Cameron. "Look, Captain, I'm in a sort of bind. It's a bit awkward."

"Anything I can do, Colonel?" Cameron smiled at Canning as he made the offer.

The colonel said, "One of my chaps is missing. Got a case of acute appendicitis this morning."

"I see, and you want me to . . . " Cameron trailed off.

"Quite. I'm wondering if you have a spare chap around here that you can loan to me for . . . say a week or so." He thought for a minute, while Cameron looked at him, the smile gone now. "But we need someone who's good at lines . . . a sort of rigger would be just the ticket. And that reminds me, another thing. I want to have a chat with you about methods of passing lines to other ships at sea . . . the watchamacallit?" He gestured as if firing a rifle.

"Costain gun?" suggested the captain.

"Absolutely. If you can do anything about setting up a chappie I'd be more than . . . " Canning got no further.

"I've just the man for you. Expert line handler, a good chap with any kind of wire and splices, and the best Costain shot onboard." Cameron passed a quick, stern look at Bates, who was trying to keep a straight face.

"Steady?" The colonel murmured as he peered astern again at the sailing barge.

"Reasonably so. About average for his group, I'd say. Good patches and bad, you know," Cameron said quietly. He looked around at the sky, as if gauging the weather.

Colonel Canning laughed. "Sounds ideal, old chap. When can I have him?"

"Immediately," replied Cameron, thinking, *if not sooner*. He turned to the duty bridge lookout. "Lookout," he ordered, "I want Able Seaman Goffin outside my cabin in ten minutes' time. Go down and let him know, will you, please?"

The colonel brushed his mustache with the back of his gloved hand again. "Goffin, eh? Let's see, Cornish, isn't it?" he inquired.

"I believe so. Somewhere out in the West Country." Cameron had no idea where Goffin was from.

"Mmm . . . make good sailors?" asked the colonel.

"Among the best," Cameron said.

"And miners?"

"I wouldnae ken about that." Cameron fell into Scots dialect whenever a subject was tiring.

"Mind if I wander around a bit, Captain?" the colonel asked.

"No sir, by all means. It's a bit of a mess onboard right now, but we have high hopes of having everything cleared and shipshape by early tomorrow morning." As Cameron said this, he glared at Bates, who excused himself quietly to climb down the ladder.

The colonel said, "Good, then I'll take Lieutenant Dennis with me." They separated, the two army officers to explore the hardly comprehensible world of a ship completing a rush refit, and Cameron to get down to his cabin before the bridge lookout had time to say too much to Goffin.

Five minutes later, there was a muffled knock on his cabin door.

Cameron snapped, "Enter." The stocky figure of Able Seaman Goffin stood in the open door, his eyes fixed again at a point somewhere over Cameron's right shoulder. Cameron beckoned him, "Come in and stand easy, Goffin." Goffin advanced two paces and stood at ease. "Shut the door. Oh, Steward, step outside a moment, will you?" the captain called.

The leading steward, a great source of buzzes and rumors for his mates on the lower deck, left his pantry, where he had been hoping to stay. He stepped outside, closing the door silently.

"Goffin." Cameron kept his voice low.

"Sir?" the seaman acknowledged.

"I'm not a fool. I know that you already know something of what this *is* about."

Goffin grinned slightly. "Yes, sir, of course, sir."

"Good man; nothing like a bit of honesty."

"Yes, sir."

"Well, do you want the job or not?" Cameron demanded.

"Do I get my jankers scrubbed—my punishment cancelled, sir?"

"No, Goffin. You know damned well I can't do that, once it's on record, but it's going to be difficult for you to do it if you're on duty ashore, isn't it?" Cameron smiled.

Goffin laughed, quietly. "Yes, sir. I s'pose so."

"Good. Well, Goffin, here's the deal. You go with Colonel Canning and the others. They tell me that the job will be for about a week. When it's completed, you return to the ship, and I shall send you on special leave for a week or so. By that time your punishment will have expired. How's that?"

"What about the serious charge, sir?"

"Nothing I can do about that, I'm afraid. But, of course, I can put an extra-specially good word in for you in view of your cooperation in volunteering for this . . . er . . . enterprise. Perhaps I can get you back into submarines. I know that's what you want."

"What's the job, sir?"

"Believe it or not, I don't know. But if you give me your word you won't repeat what I tell you, I can give you what I think is an idea."

"You have my word, sir. Mum's the word."

"Well, I believe that they're going to land in France or another Allied country to assist in repairing a bit of broken-down technical equipment." Cameron noticed the unusual color of Goffin's eyes. Dark, dark blue. *Navy blue*, he thought.

"What they want *me* for, sir?"

"Oh . . . hoists, slings, tackles, lines. You know how these shoreside types are."

"I see . . . well, sir . . . I'm on. I'll go along."

"Good man!" Canning stood up. "They're meeting in the sickbay at eight this evening, after supper. A sort of get-together; I think it might be better if you don't mention your spot of bother."

"Aye aye, sir." They both knew now that an order had been given.

"Good, Goffin . . . dismissed."

Goffin opened the door. Cameron called him again.

"Oh Goffin, did the first lieutenant mention the head seat?"

"Yes, sir, he did, and I'm going to start padding it tomorrow. Couldn't do it today, 'cos it was early closing day, and we didn't have no material with roses on it. Postie says he'll pick up some in the morning, sir."

"Very good, Goffin; you may leave." Cameron did his best to hide his smile until the door closed.

11th May, 1940. 5:00 P.M.
The Hague, Holland

The slightly Welsh voice said, "London? Miss Camperdown? Yes . . . ah, Margot . . . give me the managing director, please." The voice hummed to itself, tunelessly for a few seconds. "Ah," it said, "What . . . oh, yes, Christopher . . . yes. We're not quite sure. The daughter seems eager to take the holiday, it's her mother who's reluctant. No, the board members—six for, four against, but, of course, our district manager is working on them." Silence for a full minute. "Yes, Briggs is in Amsterdam with Van Velzor now. They were in touch with me minutes ago. No, they insist on our own mechanics coming over. Briggs? No . . . he is setting up in Apeldoorn, tomorrow. Early warning, you know. There seems to be some doubt as to the whereabouts of the blueprints, but Briggs thinks Vee might work that out.

Silence.

"*Over*, I think, first, but if not then *through*, but my memory's a bit hazy on that; haven't been there for over a year."

He listened for the space of two minutes.

"Right . . . yes, foreman, charge-hand, welder, mechanic, and laborer. Yes, very good sir, I'll meet them myself. No, I'll ask Van Velzor to come up, and it'll look better if they trot along with one of their men, don't you think, sir? Yes, sir. Goodbye."

The phone clicked. The Welsh voice hummed again, the tune only just recognizable. *Guide me oh, thou great Jehovah . . . Bread of heaven, bread of heaven . . . feed me 'til I want no more . . .* The voice dropped into bass, too low, *want no more . . .*

Captain Llewellyn Daffyd ap-Rhys Morgan, D.S.O., O.B.E., Royal Naval Attaché to the British Ambassador to the Court of the Hague flicked a spot of dust off one of his four gold rings, cocked one black-browed eye and stared through the French windows for a minute at the sunshine patches passing over the flower beds. He drummed his fingers on the desk, then stood up. "Damn" he said aloud to himself and grabbed his cap off the hat stand. As he passed through the great oaken double doors, he thought, *Got to give it to 'C'. He's let the Huns blow Walcheren. No, take it over. Old Canaris gets all the duff-stuff, and we use the bloody public telephone system*.

Captain Morgan smiled at Jenkins as he passed him in the hall. Jenkins saluted, one finger to his forelock, and smiled back.

Oh where are the yeomen . . . the yeomen of England? Captain Morgan hummed to himself as he ascended the stairs, thinking what a stout chap Jenkins was, as the porter passed out of the front door.

Jenkins walked down the driveway and entered the gatehouse.

"Cup o' tea, Jenkins?" Beasley the guard asked as he lit the tiny stove.

"Thankss, Beass, don't mind if I do." Jenkins lisped his s's.

There was silence for a minute until the kettle boiled. The two men studied each other. Beasley was reminded of a rabbit as he stared at Jenkins.

"Any new orders from Kiel?" asked Beasley.

"Yess. Captain Morgan's using the public telephone system to talk with the Circuss in London. I've been listening in on the switch-board . . . like they requested."

"What about the radio?" Beasley poured a cup.

"Barton's reporting the messages to Kiel, direct, but it'ss all a load of old codswallop . . . all false information . . . and the Jerries know it."

"They must be doing their nuts in Kiel?" said Beasley as he passed the cup.

"No. They know that there's a party bein' sent over for a special job. They've been monitoring Morgan's house phone for a month now. Only snag is they don't know when, or where, or how."

"Or who?" said Beasley.

"Right . . . and that'ss our job. To find out the *'ssix sstalwart sserving men who taught me all they knew.' "* Jenkins misquoted, *"Their namess are What and Why and When and How and Where and Who."*

Beasley grinned. "And report them to Kiel?"

Jenkins nodded. "The Germanss seem to be doin' well . . . Po-land . . . Denmark, Norway. They'll be through thiss little lot like a hot knife through butter . . . in what, a week?"

"About that. Then it's England, home and beauty. For us, well, for me at least, seein' as how you prefer the boys."

"Yess" said Jenkins, "Berlin for me. Yesss, oh yesss, I should ssay sso . . . yess." He thought of his blond Nazi lover in Berlin.

"Yes." Beasley stared out of the window, across the tulip beds and rose gardens, thinking of money and power, and how it had taken seven very dangerous years of patient treachery for him, Jenkins, and Barton to bring those elusive prizes within their reach.

11th May, 1940. 5:50 P.M.
War Room, London

The P.M. picked up the phone from its red base, holding it firmly against his ear with one hand. The other hand placed a large, partly smoked cigar in the shell-base ashtray. "What?" he said, "Oh, good . . . so now all the birds are in one coop. Who's the fifth man? Good, they're usually dependable types . . . good." Silence for a minute. "I don't know about that. You'll have to wait for news of a voluntary move from our lady friends. Oh, I'm certain it is worth the risk. Wouldn't have started it otherwise." A longer wait, "Ha, ha, yes, very good, except that it should now be rephrased, *Cry HAVELOCK and let slip the dogs of war!*"

He replaced the phone, picked up his cigar, and grinned to himself.

Chapter 4

*   *

Wish Me Luck . . .

11th–12th May, 1940

Wish me luck as you wave me goodbye,
Cheerio, here I go, on my way.
Wish me luck as you wave me goodbye,
Not a tear, only cheers, make it gay.
Give me a smile I can keep for a while
In my heart while I'm away,
'Til we meet, once again, you and I,
Wish me luck as you wave me goodbye!

Song popular in Britain 1939–40.

4.

"Wish Me Luck . . ."

11th May, 1940. 6:00 P.M.
H.M.S. HAVELOCK at Sheerness

The captain's cabin, despite its comparative roominess compared with any other living space in the ship, was crowded when the engineer officer, McAllister, arrived. Cameron, the Owner to his officers (out of his hearing), the Skipper to his ship's company, was perched on a corner of his desk. The first lieutenant, Number One to the officers, Jimmy to the ratings, was leaning against the steward's pantry hatch. The navigation officer, Lieutenant O'Connell, known to all as The Navvy, was contemplating the brass port. On the settee sat Colonel Canning and Lieutenant Dennis. McAllister took in the scene with one swift glance. This was a "ship's business" occasion. No one was smoking or holding a glass. He laid his cap, gloves, and torch on a small table by the door.

"Come in, Chief, make yourself at home." Cameron gestured toward an armchair. He nodded to the steward in the direction of the door. Leading Steward Deighton, regretfully yet smartly, stepped outside. Cameron looked at Lieutenant Bates for a moment, then spoke in a low voice. "Now we all know each other we can get down to brass rags." He held a signal form up for a moment. "This has just arrived by hand. I'll read it out to you."

TOP SECRET—PRIME MINISTER TO COMMANDING OFFICER H.M.S. HAVELOCK. BEING IN ALL RESPECTS READY FOR SEA, H.M.S. HAVELOCK WILL PROCEED TO THE HOOK OF HOLLAND, TO AWAIT ORDERS TO ESCORT OR TRANSPORT ROYAL PERSONAGES, TOGETHER WITH THEIR ENTOURAGE AND MEMBERS OF THE NETHERLANDS GOVERNMENT, TO A DESTINATION LATER TO BE DESIGNATED. COMMANDER, H.M.S. HAVELOCK, WILL REPORT ON ARRIVAL TO L.D.R. MORGAN, CAPTAIN, R.N., BRITISH MISSION, THE HAGUE, TOGETHER WITH TECHNICAL ADVISORY PARTY "ORANGE" AND WITH "ORANGE" PARAPHERNALIA. ACTION WITH ENEMY UNITS TO BE AVOIDED EXCEPT FOR DEFENSE. MAXIMUM SPEED TO BE MAINTAINED WHERE THIS IS PRACTICAL. ACTION IMMEDIATE. ACKNOWLEDGE.

There was silence in the cabin, until Cameron continued, "Well, gentlemen, there it is. I've acknowledged. We will now take the immediate action. I want all ship's officers and ship's company one hundred percent on their stations at all times. I want maximum alertness in every department. Colonel Canning . . . Lieutenant Dennis."

He looked at the two army officers, each in turn. "You are to stay within the confines of the bridge superstructure and B gundeck for the whole passage, except for your visit to the sick bay this evening. Your two civilian members are to confine themselves to the sick bay and to Y gundeck, immediately above the sick bay. In the event of an enemy attack, action stations will be sounded on the klaxon. In that event, you yourselves will come in here, in my cabin, and your men will remain under cover in the sick bay, ready to assist with stretcher parties if necessary. Is that clear?"

"Quite clear, Captain," murmured Canning, while Dennis nodded.

"Good." He looked at Bates. "Clear, Number One?"

"Clear, sir," replied Bates.

Cameron turned to the navigation officer. "Well?"

"All set, sir . . . all correct," the Navvy responded.

"Chief?"

"Straining at the leash," retorted the engineer.

Everyone smiled as the tension eased.

"Number One, 'Y' gun crew will set a standing sentry watch over the two civilian . . . er . . . technicians to make sure my orders are carried out." Cameron gave the order quietly.

"Aye aye, sir," said Bates.

"Colonel, in consideration of what you have told me, I have ordered my gunnery officer to place the Orange wooden cases in B magazine. And Goffin has been ordered not to contact your people until you give the word."

The colonel nodded. *Good thinking*, he mused.

The captain looked around at everyone in turn. "Any questions?" There was a ten-second pause, then he said, "Good. We weigh anchor in fifteen minutes."

As he passed out of the door, into the wardroom flat, McAllister said a private prayer to himself. *And may the Lord have mercy on our souls!* He headed aft for the engine room. As he passed down the hatch he heard the pipe, *"Pheew . . . pheeeeeew. D'ye hear there? Hands to stations for leaving harbor! Foc'sle-men close-up!"* But McAllister knew that the news was already around the ship by the urgency in the movements of the men he had passed on the upper deck and the rising whine of the machinery.

H.M.S. *Havelock* slid out of Sheerness Roads, into the broad Thames estuary on her way out to the North Sea on a winding, twisting course caused not only by the sandbanks, but also by lain minefields and sunken ships in the channels.

Colonel Canning and Lieutenant Dennis dined in the wardroom with the doctor informally, simply, but well. All the other officers were at their stations.

The doctor, the oldest man onboard at fifty-two, amused them with tales of his peacetime voyages in the West Indies and the Mediterranean. Like most older Royal Naval officers, he was an articulate raconteur.

At 7:40, as the officer's steward cleared the dining table, after Brown had recounted (for the fiftieth time) the climax of an hilarious yarn of his early days, Colonel Canning turned to Dennis. "Look here, Dennis. I'm postponing the briefing tonight. Go back there, will you, and inform the men? Might as well wait until we're in our base in Holland before letting our fifth man . . . what's his name?"

"Able Seaman Goffin, sir."

"Yes. Before letting him in too much."

"Very good, sir." Dennis stood up to leave and reached for his cap. The doctor moved away from the table and picked a book from the small library of paperbacks.

"Make sure they're comfortable, food all right, you know." The colonel spoke now as if he was talking about horses.

"Yes, sir." Dennis left, pleased at the prospect of being alone for a short while.

Colonel Canning finished his cigarette and wandered off to the bridge, being careful, on the way up, not to obstruct people passing to and fro. On the bridge, in darkness now, except for the luminous glow of the captain's compass, over which Cameron, in his dufflecoat, was hunched, Canning moved to one side. His eyes regained their night vision, staring into the slowly brightening gloom. The ship was starting to rise to the sea, slowly, up and down, up and down, juddering as the speed increased. He wondered if he would be seasick. He had no further thought for the others in his party. He knew they were housed and fed, and as he had learned in the Indian Army, that was all that mattered at such moments. To him, Lieutenant Dennis was an instrument, to be used circumspectly and with precision. Mitchell and Lynch and Goffin were tools. Calculate how to employ them (for the greater good, of course) with the maximum accuracy, with the maximum dexterity and effect; and when the work was finished, put them away again in their racks; and if they could be of further use, see that they were kept well oiled and free from rust. If they should be damaged on the job, "fall by the wayside," he called it, well, that was bad luck. There were always others to do other jobs.

It was not that Canning was not mindful of the well-being of these lesser people of the lower orders, but first his nanny, then his aged grandmother and then Rugby and Harrow, Sandhurst and the North West Frontier Force, all the influences of his childhood and adolescence, had instilled in him the certain knowledge of the inherent inequality of men. His whole life, his work, his particular brand of patriotism, with its near-worship of the Crown, was founded on this fundamental bedrock of the natural order. Any suggestion that this scheme of things might not be correct was to him anathema ("a bad show"). Anyone who might question the possibility that perhaps there were not essential natural God-bestowed differences among men he labeled "Bolshie" (the severest epithet in his repertoire). There was the monarchy; there was the club—officers, the aristocracy, "ladies," gentlemen (including now, British colonials, of course; well, at least *some* of them)—and there were "outsiders." "Cads" were in limbo. Beyond the outsiders there were foreigners in their various layers, and in the dim distant mists of his far horizon, "natives." Not that he didn't *get on* with foreigners and natives—some of his most fondly thought of acquaintances were Indian officers and subhadars. But these British outsiders, they were another kettle of fish altogether. He had been taught by suggestion and innuendo all his youth that "they have their place and are content with it; you have your place; maintain it, untarnished, and pass it on."

He sometimes wondered if his grandmother had not been right when she insisted that Darwin was mistaken in his theories on the origins of the species. *The reason the dinosaurs are extinct, my dear, is simply that they were too large to enter the doors of the Ark.* He smiled slightly at the memory of his grandmother, peering through the misty windless offing. *Dieu et mon Droit.* It was inscribed on his buttons.

Now that he could see more clearly out into the night, he observed that *Havelock* was steaming through the two lines of a convoy heading westward, into the Thames estuary. He gazed at the dark, ghostly bulks of the cargo ships and made out three of their escorts, low and slender. One of the escorts was signaling with an Aldis lamp, very rapidly, at *Havelock*. Even as he saw the blinking light, a dark shape passed by, brushing his shoulder. It was the duty-bridge-yeoman. In a minute the yeoman had his own Aldis lamp uncovered and ready to reply. As Canning moved away to the other side of the bridge, he sighted a fountain of faint, glowing sparks shooting up from one of the merchant ship's funnels. He started to recite to himself a poem he had once memorized, long before:

The strength of twice three thousand horse
That seeks the single goal;
The line that holds the rending course,
The hate that swings the whole;
The stripped hulls, slinking through the gloom,
At gaze and gone again—
The Brides of Death that wait the groom—
The choosers of the Slain!

Canning, try as he might, frowning to himself in the dark, could not recall the rest of the poem. Only a single couplet

Quiet, and count our laden prey,
The convoy and her guard.

At last, standing silently, he recalled the name of the poem. "The Destroyers," it came to him suddenly. He knew it must be by Kipling, who was the only poet he had ever bothered to read—much less remember. *Good chap, Kipling . . . The Brides of Death . . . The Choosers of the Slain!* he concluded to himself, as he gazed astern at the hazy disappearing shadows of the symbols of ten thousand dreams and a billion man-hours of human effort and toil.

Canning was aroused from his thoughts by the sing-song voice of the officer-of-the-watch calling a change of heading down the voice pipe. Then he realized that they were clear of the convoy, out in the open sea, and that the captain had gone below to dine, as captains do, alone in his cabin.

Lieutenant Dennis waited for a moment outside the screen door on deck for his eyesight to become accustomed to the darkness. He felt the breeze on his cheek, caused by the ship's fast forward charge, and, looking downwards, caught, dimly at first, the sight of the silver-white water rushing past. As his eyes joined the night he stared at the lines of froth and the bubbles in the bow wave. He deliberated for a space. *I have ploughed the seas; who was it?* he asked himself, *Yes, Bolivar, Simón Bolivar.* Then he shivered and climbed down the break ladder to walk aft to the sick bay, slowly, enjoying the night air and the sensation of movement in a seeming void.

Dennis did not like his Christian names—Aubrey Fowler. He had been pleased when at his Bloomsbury prep school his companions had decided to use the diminutive derivative, "Denny"—and this had carried on through Noneaton and Cambridge. He'd scored many a touchdown to the yell of, *"Come on, Denny!"* A more suitable name was not all that he acquired at Noneaton. He had also picked up the seed of the idea of "collective responsibility." ("Am I my brother's keeper? Yes, I am!" the Quaker headmaster had roared.) Cambridge had reinforced his mother's teaching, while Dad was away in Burma, that man is a creature of circumstance. ("You must always think, Aubrey, 'there, but for the Grace of God, go I.' ") Marx, he thought, had paraphrased it—"man is a product of his environment."

These were the ideas held by many of Dennis' contemporaries, at least most of those not involved in the Young Conservatives or Oswald Mosley's British Union of Fascists. They were ideas, in Britain, almost exclusive to Dennis' class, the middle class, except for a minority of more radical socialists whom the workers, the rank-and-file Labor Party members, looked upon, but not unkindly, as strange highbrow freaks, or, from the point of view of the more elemental manual laborers, "big-mouthed agitators, and if they like Russia why the 'ell don't they go an' live there?"

Dennis considered himself, politically, a Liberal. In any other country on earth that would mean something else, but in Britain it meant treading the left-hand side of the white line down the center of the road. It meant holding humanist ideals *and respectability*. If Mitchell and Lynch had been in prison, it must be because their circumstances had dictated that it should be so. Basically, he believed they were decent chaps. Everyone he had known at school and university, even, thinking back, even Mr. Yates, the games master at Noneaton. He admitted to himself that Mr. Yates did rather puzzle most of the boys, giving some favored ones extra marks for no apparent reason. It was strange too, how Mr. Yates had left the school, suddenly and mysteriously, under a vague cloud. But all things considered, even Mr. Yates was a decent chap—almost like one of the boys himself.

Honi soit qui mal y pense could very well have been Dennis' own motto. He sincerely thought of himself as a decent chap, and so he was, by the lights of all who knew him. To his few young female friends he was, perhaps, a little "too decent," at least so most of them thought.

Now, vaguely lost on the poop deck, at the very afterend of the ship, he heard a voice. The stern of the ship shivered, rattled and trembled noisily.

"Evenin' sir." Dennis saw a dark shadowy figure. It shone a torch at his feet. "Torpedoman Griffiths, sir," the figure introduced himself in a sing-song South Welsh dialect.

"Good evening. I say, can you show me the way to the . . . er . . . hospital quarters, please?" Dennis grabbed at a nearby rail.

"Sick bay? Yes, sir, this way. Mind the sill." The torpedoman knocked the clips off the after-deckhouse screen door and they passed into a passage, dimly, eerily lit by a dull red lamp. At the fourth door the torpedoman halted and turned to Dennis. " 'Ere you are, sir, 'ome and dry!"

"Thank you." Dennis grinned good-naturedly at the seaman, opened the door, and stepped into the brightly lit sick bay. He screwed up his eyes for a moment against the brightness of the light reflecting from the snow-white painted bulkheads and deckhead.

"Hello, chaps!" he greeted.

Mitchell was sitting on the chair behind the sick-berth attendant's small desk, while Lynch was sprawled out on the lower of two gimballed iron cots, one below the other.

"Evening Lieutenant," Mitchell said as he looked up from a *Picture Post* magazine he was reading. He was in his shirt sleeves, tieless.

"All right, Chief?" asked Lynch, tapping the end of a cigarette over an ashtray precariously perched on the edge of the clean gray cot cover. Lynch had one foot on the deck and was pushing the swinging cot to and fro lackadaisically. He was down to his undervest and shorts. Dennis noticed the tattoo on Lynch's left upper arm, a bluebird with a scroll in its beak, and in the scroll the words "Rio De Jan. 1935."

Dennis grinned apologetically as they looked at him. He said, quietly, "Sorry, but the colonel has decided to postpone the briefing until we arrive."

"Arrive where?" asked Lynch.

"Can't tell you that, chaps, not yet. But the colonel . . . well, I've come to see that you're all right, anyway. Eaten yet?"

"Yes, okay, we're muckin' in with the steward's mess, downstairs . . . down the ladder outside. Grub's good. Shepherd's pie," Mitchell said in a flat voice.

Dennis tested the top bed mattress, bouncing his hand on it. "Beds all right? Seem to be."

"Fair," approved Lynch, winking at Mitchell.

Dennis studied the cot cover pattern for a moment, blue and white, like a willow leaf pattern. It reminded him of his mother's best china. Then he remembered something else suddenly. "How are you men getting your food? Who's bringing it to you?"

Lynch replied, beating Mitchell to it, "One of the blokes on the

gun crew upstairs brought it. Funny little cove; wouldn't say anything to us. Just brought the grub in and cleared off. Then he came
back with a mess fanny full of tea."

Dennis felt relieved. "Good. Then you're all right. The captain
wants us to stay in our . . . er . . . quarters. It won't be a long run,
so be good chaps and don't wander around . . . er, anywhere."

"I'm going to turn in shortly, how about you, Mitch?" demanded
Lynch.

"Yes, I'm ready for a kip." Mitchell stood up.

"Then I'll say good night, chaps . . . until tomorrow," announced
Dennis.

"Right, until tomorrow" said Mitchell.

" 'Night," Lynch grunted.

Dennis walked out, softly closing the door behind him onto its
gently swaying jamb, and groped his way out to the upper deck,
where he stood for a minute, watching the stars shining on a smooth
sea. After he had accustomed his eyes again to the darkness of the
night, he walked forward to find his way to the cox'n's office. There he
spent a much less comfortable night than either Mitchell or Lynch, or
for that matter anyone else onboard, stretched out on a very hard
mattress on the heaving deck.

Lynch was already in his berth when Mitchell clambered up to the
top cot. "Best job in a ship . . . steward," he observed.

"How do you know that?"

"Did it myself for a spell," Lynch replied. "On the old
Mauretania." He grinned at the underside of Mitchell's berth. "Cushy
number, it is. 'Course, you got to work at it, running up and down
from the cabins to the kitchen and the bar, but, blimey . . . some of
those old girls!"

"What old girls?" asked Mitchell, intrigued.

"The lady passengers. A bloke would have to be a blind eunuch not
to have his end away every night with some of 'em."

"How long were you doing that, Banger?"

"What, in the Merch? First time three years; second time only
three months," Lynch asserted.

"Couldn't get your end away the second time, then?"

"No, Mitch, it wasn't that. I had my eye on somethin' else. You
know the story. Old Carney must 'ave told you down in the Moor,
didn't he? How I blew the bloody door of the ship's strong room and
nearly 'ad it away on me toes to Rio with fifty-eight thousand quid
and another two-'undred thousand in gold bars?"

"Yeah, he told me. He used to tell everyone in the Moor."

Lynch exploded, "What a skylark! Cor, you should have seen those New York coppers' faces. Not bad blokes though, once you get to know 'em. Leastways not with me. All carry shooters."

"Good job you didn't have one, they'd have blown your bloody head off," Mitch said, sleepily.

"But fancy being here, going on a job with you. Blimey, it seems incredible. Banger Lynch and Featherfingers," Lynch chortled, as he leaned up to light another cigarette. "Here, we ought to get together when we get back. I've a lovely job just aching for a team like us . . . up in Manchester."

"Count me out, Banger. I'm goin' straight, after this little tickle."

"Ah well . . . pity. 'Ere, I wonder what this bloomin' caper is, you got any ideas?"

"I'll tell you what," Mitchell offered, "I'll tell you what my idea is, if you'll tell me exactly how you got hold of that new secret government explosive."

"Not me, mate . . . more than my life's worth."

"Okay, well, good night, tosh." Mitchell reached for the light switch, turned it off, and settled back, remembering Rosie, and how he had, it seemed a century ago, lost himself in her.

"Night chum," replied Lynch.

Lynch smoked his cigarette, grinning into the smoke, remembering how he had kept the woman in Rio terrified and used her in front of the corpse of her man until he had done with her; and how she had gurgled as he slowly sliced the razor over her throat. Then he carefully stubbed out his cigarette in the ashtray that he placed gently on deck, despite his slightly trembling hand and closed his eyes, content to be leaving the oppressive air of England, hopeful at the thought of freedom in the chaos ahead.

At the other end of the ship, in the foc'sle, in the starboard-watch-of-foc'slemen's mess (to be as precise as mariners are in these matters), Able Seaman Goffin stood on the table unlashing his hammock. It was slung from the forward bulkhead to a rail that crossed over the ship from side to side. In the foc'sle mess deck, about thirty-five feet by twenty feet in area, there were almost eighty other hammocks slung. They all swung gently from side to side, in time with the ship's movements as the destroyer's fore-foot, just ten feet ahead of them, plunged and rose in the sea.

Goffin was dressed only in his underwear and a pair of socks. When things were rough at sea, or if there were a chance of Action Stations being sounded, the sailors slept fully clothed, but it was so warm and stuffy in the seamen's mess, even with the punka louvres of the ventilation system open and blowing at full blast, that whenever they had the chance, all the seamen slept unclothed. The killick of Goffin's mess, Leading Seaman Slinger Woods, hailed him, quietly, so as not to wake the off-duty watchmen snoring in the hammocks. "Hey, Goff. How d'ye get on at Skipper's, mate?".

"All right, got off light. One case dismissed, one belayed," replied Goffin. He and Slinger were friends, *oppos*, and often went ashore together. They had both, as boy seamen, endured the Invergordon Mutiny.

"Heard you was detailed off for a special shore party," Slinger allowed.

"Yes, I got to 'elp those army blokes off with their gear when we get in," said Goffin.

"What they pick on you for, Goff?" asked Slinger.

"Dunno," he beamed at Slinger. "Maybe they fancies me," he said jovially.

Slinger chuckled. " 'Ow about that head seat?" he asked.

Goffin wondered how Slinger knew about it, but he was not oversurprised. The way news and gossip traveled around a warship was no more a wonder to him, after thirteen years in the *Andrew*.

"Got it arranged, mate. The officer's flunky is lettin' me have a spare armchair cover. It's got roses on it," asserted Goffin.

"D'ye know what I reckon, Goff?" asked Slinger, after he had clambered into his hammock, next to Goffin's. He took off his socks sitting up, and poked them among the clews, the strings that suspended the hammock to its rope.

"What's that?" demanded Goffin.

Slinger spoke very low, close to Goffin's ear. "I reckon we're off to the Hook to pick up Queen bloomin' Wilhemina!" Slinger grinned as he whispered.

"Garn . . . for crissakes Slinger . . . tell us another one!" Goffin declared as he grabbed the hammock bar, slung his legs up and over, and settled down to sleep.

By the time the morning watch took over from the middle watch at 4:00 A.M. next day, the surmise was raging throughout the ship. By 8:00 A.M., when the ship's company had finished their breakfasts, it was no longer a rumor, it was gospel. It had to be. Ordinary Seaman Coggins had bet Rattler Morgan a whole week of his rum ration that their destination would NOT be the Hook. That news flew around the ship even faster than the original rumor, putting the seal on the

Hook as a 'dead cert' for all the ship's company.

12th May, 1940. 9:15 A.M.
Zliuthaven, Hook van Holland, Netherlands

The Dutch naval sentry saluted and beckoned the shining black car through the gate. It was an Alvis, 1930, Silver Eagle Atlantic, all of fourteen feet long from glistening chrome front bumper to the back edges of the gracefully downward sweeping rear mudguards. It was a half-open landau, with a white canvas convertible top folded down over the back of the oxhide leather passenger seats. In front of the rear seats, on the floor of the passenger section, another seat was folded down into a well in the floor. This seat could be raised to accommodate yet another two passengers in Edwardian comfort, making a total of eight seats for riders, together with the driver.

Behind the driver's seat there was a fixed Plexiglas screen, separating the front and rear sections of the car. Beneath this, in the rear compartment, there were three walnut cabinets with brass handles. The center one contained three small square spirit bottles and three glasses cushioned in green baize padded racks. There were two magazines, *The London Illustrated News* and *Punch* in the left-hand cupboard. There was a miniature dressing table for ladies that unfolded out of the right-hand compartment. All the contents were held securely in padded sky-blue silk.

Behind the six-foot-long hood, the top edge of the car body followed a slight, gently sweeping upward curve, finally complemented by the flourish of the folded canvas top. Under the hood was an eight-cylinder, 1.5 liter, front-wheel drive, supercharged engine, which, at the present necessary eight miles per hour, ticked. The wire spokes on the wheels shot slivers of reflected sunshine into the sentry's eyes. The driver, humming to himself, wore the uniform of a Royal Naval Captain.

Captain Llewellyn Morgan tooled the car over the macadamized cobblestones of the quay, almost to the very seaward end and stopped. He pulled the softly clicking hand brake, and, with his silver lighter, lit a Benson and Hedges cigarette. He checked his Omega watch, then looked around the harbor.

Apart from a half-dozen barrage balloons floating overhead, there was hardly any sign that a full-scale Blitzkrieg was raging only fifty miles away. The Harwich ferry, just across the basin, was a little more crowded than usual, and there were a few more Dutch military and naval personnel about than usual. The two Royal Netherlands Navy destroyers that were normally based in the Hook had slipped their moorings and left for sea. Otherwise, everything else looked the same as it had when he had driven down two days previously to say goodbye to his wife and son, off on the ferry to England. He mused to himself that the ferries were lucky. There had been very little enemy air activity over the North Sea since the tenth, just a few nuisance shoot-ups of coastal traffic around the Frisian Islands, Walcheren and the Kentish North Foreland. He concluded that it must be because the Nazis were concentrating every available plane on the front (wherever *that* was), and in attacking communications centers behind that nebulous demarcation.

He climbed out of the Alvis. The small door clicked gently behind him as he stepped off the high running board. A Dutch army truck rumbled past him. In a long sweep, it stopped. He saw it was pulling a mobile Bofors antiaircraft gun. The soldiers clambered out of the truck and set to, folding down the legs of the gun support frame. He was impressed with the lack of shouting and bawling, and how each man seemed to know exactly what to do without any fuss being made.

Captain Morgan strolled to the edge of the quay and gazed out into the seaward end of the River Rhine. He sighed, as he watched the small coasters heading out. He knew that the prospects for the Dutch Army holding out against the Germans until Allied reinforcements arrived were practically nil. Against the full thrust of the Nazi panzers of the Wehrmacht, with the Luftwaffe in complete control of the skies, the Dutch Army of eight divisions had no more than a few days to exist. Then, trapped in Northern Netherlands, north of the destroyed Rhine bridges, they would either be compressed into a pocket, to await, helplessly, rapid and absolute destruction, or they would surrender. With the speed of the German advance to the sea toward Antwerp, there was no chance for the Dutch Army retreating south into Belgium to join up with the British and French who were already, but slowly, advancing into that country. There was not sufficient time, given the speed of the Blitzkrieg, for the Dutch Army to transport any sort of an effective force, with all its necessary equipment and arms, by sea. Holland, he concluded, was going to fall like a ripe plum.

In the distance, Captain Morgan heard the sound of a siren, and a minute later the pop-pop-pop of a lone antiaircraft gun. He looked over to the northwest, towards Gravenzande and Schveningen, and saw, in the far distance, low, the black blossoms of ack-ack explosions in the blue sky. He knew that the Germans must be after the great radio installations at Schveningen. They wouldn't bomb, he guessed. It was just a nuisance raid, to disturb activity. With things going so well for them they would avoid destroying anything that they knew would be important to them later. They would bomb civilian centers and shoot up roads choked with civilians, yes, but they would be damned careful not to damage valuable installations too much.

Captain Morgan comforted himself that, standing where he was, on the last seaward maritime facility on the Rhine, the key that would unlock the direct access to the oceans for all the hellish resources of the Ruhr, he was probably in the safest place in Holland. Then he saw the ship. She was merely a bright gray smudge, at first, but as she steamed closer, a "white bone in her teeth," he recognized the outline, by the two funnels. Even at this distance he could see her rapid signal flashes and tried to read them, but they were in a special code and too fast for him. He was a bit rusty on Morse, now, after six years of shore duty, first three miserable years at the embassy in Madrid, and the three happier years here, within sight, sound, and smell of salt water, in the midst of a people who loved the sea.

By now the soldiers had set up the Bofors and were operating the aiming mechanism of the gun. Round and round it went, up and down, the crew grimly serious. Morgan thought it a waste of time. The Nazis would prefer this jetty to remain intact. It would be one of their launching sites for the invasion of England. That's mostly what Holland meant to them—airfields, the Rhine, and ports. And they'd get them—soon. The Dutch could open all the dikes they wished; it wouldn't affect the outcome one iota. It was a grand gesture, this sinking of land so hard-won over the past thousand years, but it wasn't land the Nazis were after. He knew they were more interested in bombs than in butter.

Something was happening in modern warfare, he reflected, this kind of warfare aimed at keeping military and politically important facilities, even the enemy's, if possible, intact but neutralized, while the civilian population was terrorized on *both sides*. Except, of course, for those civilians who were engaged in producing offensive weaponry, and they could be counted as a part of the military. *A sort of military-industrial . . . er . . . complexity* were the words he used to himself. *Self-generating, self-preserving*, he frowned slightly, *and, God help me; I'm part of it*.

The destroyer was close now. Lines of seamen stood at attention on deck fore and aft. Puffs of smoke rose from her funnel at intervals. A white wisp of steam feathered from her bright brass siren. He watched with more than professional interest as she came alongside the quay.

The Royal Netherlands Navy line party, a petty officer and seven sailors, caught the heaving lines, dragged ashore four yellow manila mooring ropes, and cast them over the great iron bollards. The lines of seamen broke up; there was a scramble here and there, with each man going, despite the seeming chaos, to his own particular task. Within a minute the gangway was rigged and Captain Llewellyn Daffyd ap-Rhys Morgan, D.S.O., R.N. was piped onboard by the side party, a chubby quartermaster, looking pleased with himself, a rather downcast ordinary seaman, and a sub-lieutenant whose voice was just breaking.

Captain Morgan snapped a salute aft and, without further ado, made for the bridge, briefcase in hand. Lieutenant Commander Cameron was waiting for him, still in his duffle watchcoat.

"Euan . . . long time no see!" Morgan exclaimed as he shook Cameron's hand.

"Good morning, sir. Welcome aboard!" Cameron replied. He was delighted. His rugged Hebridean face broke into a smile.

"When was it . . . Martinique?" asked Morgan.

"Hong Kong, sir, '32 . . . no . . . no . . . it wasn't. Shanghai, '32."

"Yes, I suppose the old club's looking a bit sorry for itself now?" Morgan spoke low as he stepped to one side while Cameron passed him to lead the way to his cabin.

"This way, sir," Cameron announced.

"Yes, I suppose we ought to get down to things right away. Time for a chat later on, perhaps?"

As they passed down the bridge ladder, Morgan noticed, with approval, that the gun crews were at their stations, all in flashproof hoods, with steel helmets, and that the oil and water hoses were even then being passed onto the jetty. He also caught a glimpse of a young army officer, a lieutenant, and two men in civilian clothes. With the help of a naval rating they were carrying kit bags and cases down the gangway. Morgan beamed as they passed into the wardroom flat. "She does look shipshape."

"Thank you, sir. I'm afraid it was a pierhead jump." Cameron flung his cap onto the settee. "Colonel Canning . . . Captain Morgan," he introduced them. Cameron told the army officer, "Captain Morgan and I last met in Shanghai, 1932."

"Ah, Captain Morgan. At last . . . pleased to meet you."

There was no sign, nothing in the subsequent conversation to indicate that Canning and Morgan had been in irregular contact, both personal and official, with each other since they had first met, five years before, in the British Embassy, Madrid.

12th May 1940. 3:00 P.M.
The Hague, Holland

The Alvis horn was a four-inch disc bolted to the front bumper. "Er . . . ooh . . . ah! Er . . . ooh . . . ah!" Morgan pressed the ivory button with a gloved hand. Beasley, the guard, peered through the little gatehouse window and pulled a lever. The great wrought iron gates opened slowly. The Alvis moved silently forward and cruised away, up the wide pebble path between the tulip beds, as Beasley stared after them. He shook his head slightly as he returned to the gatehouse.

The three officers were in the front seat, Morgan driving, Lieutenant Dennis next to him and Colonel Canning, swagger stick held over the door, sitting on the offside. The shape of the seat backs molded their spines into an upright stance. In the rear compartment Goffin sat with Lynch and Mitchell. All three were smoking, Lynch making a great show of waving his cigarette and gently tapping it into the silver ashtray. "This is the way to travel, eh, mates? This is the car old Royce was tryin' to build for Rolls!" he chortled. They all laughed, including the colonel.

The baggage was piled in front of their knees. Five suitcases, a wooden box, and five kit bags. They gazed ahead curiously, up the drive. The Alvis coursed its stately way up to the front door of the great house. They stared at the cream-colored walls and white-painted window frames.

"Just like Chatham barracks," commented Goffin, emotionlessly.

"Or the Moor," suggested Mitchell.

The car had come to a smooth halt. "I ain't sayin' nothin'," Lynch mumbled as he climbed out. They set to, unloading the car, without speaking.

"She's a beauty, Captain." Colonel Canning tapped the Alvis' hood gently with his swagger stick. "Yours?" he asked Morgan as they alighted.

"Yes, had her since new. Didn't take her to . . . " Captain Morgan caught himself in time, " . . . to . . . my other stations, of course, but over here the roads are so good . . . seems a great pity."

"Pity?" queried Canning.

Captain Morgan replied, "Yes, with things moving as they are. Doesn't seem any chance of taking . . . " Morgan remembered Dennis, who was close behind, "of sending her back home. And, of course, they'll . . . " He trailed off for a second, regretfully. Then, as they reached the bottom step of the great staircase he stopped. "I say, I've just had an idea; you're leaving by . . . further down the coast. Why don't you use the old flivver for your transport? Chances are the front may have firmed up by then, and you can bring her back with you."

"Splendid. I shall be more than happy to . . . " the colonel averred. He tapped the knee of his jodhpurs with his swagger stick. As he climbed the stairs, one step behind Captain Morgan, his Sam Browne belt clip jingled.

"Good," said Morgan, "good, then that's settled. Otherwise it would have meant your using the gardener's van. Not quite suitable really. Trojan, chain-driven, you know. But apart from the Rolls and my flivver . . . er . . . it's all we have. Here we are!" Morgan opened a pair of ceiling-high white doors with brass handles. He ushered them into His Britannic Majesty's Ambassador's anteroom.

In a few moments a gentle buzzer sounded. Colonel Canning and Captain Morgan disappeared through another pair of white doors. Lieutenant Dennis, seated on a cane chair, waited.

Perkins the butler, and Jenkins the house porter, gazed through the front door glass at the scene below. The butler, a tall stout man of fifty-three, had a fringe of graying hair around his ears. Another asset was his snub nose. the tip of which he held at his accustomed angle of twenty degrees from the horizontal.

"Looks like another one of Captain Morgan's special parties, Jenkins," he complained, without turning his head.

"They don't look like navy, not the civilians," replied Jenkins. He was wearing a bright green waistcoat. It was the only remarkable thing about him. Four inches shorter than Perkins' six feet, he could have been picked out by some celestial hand from the most crowded stands at any Saturday soccer match in England.

"I wonder . . . " Perkins said as he took hold of the door handle and turned it, pulled open the door, and glided through. "Excuse me, gentlemen," he said. He looked like a trout that had somehow strayed into an industrial waste outlet.

The three men below, sitting on the kit bags, looked up and grinned.

"Wotcher, mate," ejaculated Lynch cheerfully. Goffin stood up and looked away across the hood of the Alvis, trying hard to stop himself from laughing. Mitchell, too, found it hard not to laugh.

Perkins stood on his dignity. "Has Captain Morgan said anything about allocating you . . . gentlemen your accommodations?"

"No, we're kippin' in the car," replied Lynch. "Matey 'ere . . . " he nudged Mitchell, who was smiling at Perkins, " 'e's takin' the arse-end, I'm in the front, and Jolly Jack the sailor," he pointed with his thumb over his shoulder at Goffin, " 'e's dossing down with a tart in the rumble seat . . . she's a dwarf, see?"

By now Jenkins had descended the front steps and was standing just behind the butler, to one side, poker-faced.

"Thank you, sir," Perkins intoned, reddening. He turned to Mitchell, raising one eyebrow as he did so.

Mitchell said, "No, we're waiting for the boss to come out and tell us . . . "

"I see," Perkins declared, and he turned to climb the front steps. "Thank you, gentlemen." Jenkins followed him up the steps, trying to keep his face straight, and they both disappeared indoors.

"Marks and Spencer," sniggered Lynch.

"Laurel and Hardy," said Goffin, chuckling.

"Mutt and Jeff," Mitchell had just said this when they heard the sound of a car approaching through the gate.

The car, a small blue French Citroën, dusty, with a slight rust spot on the right front fender, came to a halt. A Dutch army officer emerged. When he unfolded himself, he was tall and lanky, over six feet, with a pointed nose and slightly protruding teeth. His hair was so blond it was almost white, and at first Mitchell thought he was an albino. Under his blond brows his eyes were a startling blue. He smiled at the group, jerking his head to look at each in turn.

"Orange?" he asked.

"No—green!" Lynch replied. "Up the Republic!"

"Shurrup, Lynch," Mitchell snorted as he grabbed Lynch's elbow. He looked at the officer. "We don't know about that. You'd better ask inside," he said.

The Dutchman stared at Lynch for a moment, then marched purposefully up the steps, where Perkins was waiting to let him into the door. Mitchell guessed the Dutchman's age at about thirty.

Goffin said to Lynch, when the front door had closed, "Steady on, Banger. In these places you don't know who you're talking to."

"Yeah, it might be the bloody Prince of Wales!" said Mitchell, "But Goff's right. Come on; we're only here for a few days."

"Okay, okay. Just slipped out," explained Lynch, kicking a pebble and remembering how *he'd heaved the fireman* over the side of the *Mauretania*. He started to perspire as Lieutenant Dennis emerged from the front door.

The lieutenant gazed at the unloaded baggage for a minute. "Sorry, chaps. There's been a bit of a . . . misunderstanding. We're off to our . . . er . . . base. Right away. Have to reload the baggage, I'm afraid," he ordered, apologetically.

Mitchell asked, "What transport do we have?"

Dennis explained "Why, the Alvis, of course." He waited.

"What, this one?" demanded Lynch, rubbing his hands on his trousers.

"The very same. Of course, you didn't know," Dennis declared.

Goffin picked up a kit bag and threw it into the car. "No, we didn't sir, but now we do. Here goes nothin'!" he exclaimed.

As the gear was being loaded back into the passenger section, a thought struck Dennis.

"Any drivers here?" he demanded.

"That's me," Lynch shouted from the other side of the Alvis. Then, in a low voice to Mitchell, who was helping him to load the wooden box, "Best tear-away blag man in the Smoke, that's me! A ton or nothin'! Never rounded a corner on four wheels in me life, 'cept at me christenin' and me old Mum's funeral!"

Mitchell couldn't help laughing. It was true. Banger Lynch was not only a legend among the lags and rozzers of Britain for his explosive expertise, he was renowned as a number-one driver. Mitch had heard in the Moor that Banger could command one-third of the take from any smash-and-grab team in the kingdom.

"Lynch?" Dennis called out.

"Sir?"

"Was that you . . . you're volunteering?" Dennis queried.

"I wouldn't normally," Lynch replied, as he patted the mudguard of the Alvis, "but with this one, she's a beauty, ain't she?"

Dennis said, "Good, then you are appointed the company driver, among your other duties, of course."

"Of course, sir," Lynch agreed. *Make myself indispensable.*

The Alvis reached the safe house, the apartment above the Three Horses bar in Schliegerstraat, Amsterdam, in four hours, just in time for six hot lunches to be sent up the tiny meals elevator.

"Good show," said the colonel. Then, turning to Lynch, "You manage the Alvis extremely well, Mister Lynch; top-hole, my man."

"All part of the Cooks . . . crooks . . . service, sir," replied Lynch. "Wouldn't think there was a war on hardly, would you, sir, I mean no bombing, well, not much. The only thing was the number of squad . . . soldiers about, and them civilians with their beds all shoved in vans."

The colonel picked up his lunch tray. "Oh, I think you'll find we're quite out of it all here," he pontificated. The Boche are more than sixty miles away. The front's jelling up. You can think of it as a sort of Paris 1916 affair, if you like." Canning marched across the room and into his own private suite, taking Lieutenant Dennis and Captain Van Velzor, of the Queen of the Netherland's personal staff, with him.

"Come to think of it," cracked Lynch, in a low voice to Goffin, "I wouldn't 'ave minded an affair in Paris in 1916."

Captain Morgan sighed as he lifted the phone. He had just been looking through the window, thinking, *what a spiffing day it would be for sailing.* "Yes, Miss Camperdown, please." He waited. "Yes. Good morning Margot . . . Christopher . . . Helen . . . Martin . . . Orange in the box, sir. Left here four hours ago. Canning's just sent me a signal. No . . . no problems at all . . . my car . . . oh, tip-top condition, I can assure you. None at all . . . if worse comes to worst, at least it will be of some use to us before they . . . good . . . yes, she's agreed. And we have her agreement on our requisition for the material. It depends on how long it takes . . . if the ship's still here. Yes . . . good day, sir."

Morgan sighed again. Now he'd have to use the Trojan van.

The house porter, Jenkins, used the local baker's telephone. It was set in a little cabinet in the wall. *Safer that way*, he thought as he made the connection. "Hello, Kiel?"

"Yes, Feigler here. Are they there yet? What do you have for us? Be quick."

"Their code name is Orange," Jenkins spoke softly, "a colonel, a lieutenant, and two civilians . . . and a sailor . . . no, they don't seem to be . . . too sort of . . . rough. They've gone to Amsterdam. One of the civilians was driving. They had a lot of baggage and a wooden box. No, I don't know their names. The car? A big one, it had a . . . " and then the line went dead. Jenkins shook the phone, then guessing that the line had been cut, put the phone on its hook. He bought a loaf of bread, then walked back to the big house comforting himself that he would have only a few more days to wait until *they* arrived, and then he'd be safe for the first time in seven years. *That sailor was nice. Pity they hadn't stayed*, he reflected. He pursed his mouth and a pained look crossed his face. He stepped into the guard house to report to Beasley. "Got through okay, but the line was disconnected. I managed to tell 'em the important stuff though."

Beasley grinned as he put the kettle on the stove. "Well done, Jenkins."

12th May, 1940. 4:00 P.M.
German Abwehr Intelligence Headquarters

"They're in Amsterdam, Herr Admiral." Oberleutnant Feigler placed a sheet of paper on the admiral's desk. "Their code name is Orange. Just got word from one of our agents in the Hague."

"So, Orange? . . . Original . . . How many?" Admiral Canaris asked.

"Five and the Dutchman. Two British officers, two civilians, and a sailor."

"Where?"

"We don't know yet. Our local men are looking around."

"Inform our advance unit going in with the Werhmacht. What's his name?" the admiral asked, frowning.

"Von Bhielsdorf, Major . . . group Amt Z-342."

"Yes, that's the fellow. Ask him to locate them as soon as they go in. Tell him to pick up . . . what's the man's name . . . the British agent in Apeldoorn?"

"Briggs?"

"That's him. He'll know where these Orange people are."

"Jawohl, Herr Admiral."

"What transport are they using, the English?"

"A big car, but we don't know what make."

"Mmm . . . " the admiral thought for a few seconds, before he dismissed the oberleutnant. "Right, Feigler, thank you. . . . "

"Herr Admiral!" Feigler gave the German naval salute. He did a smart about-turn and marched out of the door, closing it softly behind him.

Admiral Canaris stood up, frowning slightly. He asked himself, *Now why should they send these people to Amsterdam in such a hurry?* He turned around to look through the window at the naval dockyard below. As he did so he met *that army corporal's* eyes glaring down from the large picture on the wall behind the desk. *I wonder why he never had a picture taken in naval uniform?* A sardonic smile flittered, hardly disturbing his tightly pressed lips. *It would be funny, with that mustache, I suppose.* He narrowed his eyes, gauging how much he detested that *noncommissioned upstart!*

Chapter 5

*   *

Pack up Your Troubles in Your Old Kit Bag

12th–13th May, 1940

Pack up your troubles in your old kit bag
And smile, smile, smile—
While you've a lucifer to light your fag—
Smile boys—that's the style!

What's the use of worrying?
It never was worth while, so—
Pack up your troubles in your old kit bag—
And smile, smile, smile!

Over a million Britons went to their deaths in World
War I to this sprightly lyric. Lucifer was a match. Fag
was a cigarette. It was written in 1915 by Felix Powell
and George Asaf.

5.

"Pack up Your Troubles in Your Old Kit Bag"

12th May 1940, 5:00 P.M.
Schliegerstraat, Amsterdam

Goffin lifted a meatball with his fork. He held it in mid-air and chanted, to the tune of "Colonel Bogey":

Hitler . . . has only got one ball . . .
Goering . . . has got a pair, but small,
Himmler . . . has something sim'lar—
But poor old Goebbels—has no balls—at all!

Mitchell grinned between mouthfuls of potato.

"Tucker's all right," Goffin pronounced between mouthfuls of meatball, peas, and potatoes, "and this beer's just the job!" He took another swig from a pot beer mug. It had, he saw, a coat of arms on the side. He turned it around. "Hmmm, Heineken's—sounds like a Jerry aircraft factory."

Lynch picked up his plate and took it over to the service hatch. "Hey, below!" he shouted, cupping one hand over his mouth. He turned to wink at Goffin, who raised an eyebrow at him. He heard a woman's voice, muffled, reply in Dutch.

"How 'bout some more grub, then?" demanded Lynch.

The woman's voice shouted, "Ja . . . ja!" The little wooden trolley arrived at the top of the shaft with a clunk.

Goffin grinned. "Them what asks don't get, and them what don't ask don't want," he pronounced, remembering his father's rough, kind, Cornish miner's ways at the table. A vision of his father, with his head bent, saying grace at the scrubbed kitchen table, passed through his mind.

Mitchell finished his plate and joined Lynch at the serving hatch. "And them what don't ask get knackered," he intoned quietly, as he placed his plate alongside Lynch's on the wooden tray.

"Wonder what she's like?" asked Lynch, jabbing his forefinger, pointing repeatedly down the trolley shaft.

"Party down there?" asked Goffin, leaning back on his chair.

"Yeah, sounds all right," Lynch leered.

"Ask her to come up with the grub . . . nothin' like a bit of the other after each meal," Goffin grinned.

"Probably old enough to be your bloomin' grannie," Mitchell retorted.

"Hulloooo, Tommiiieee!" A female voice called up the shaft.

"Right my love, my rose, my petal, my pearl, send her up, darlin'!" Lynch chortled. The tray arrived, with the two plates piled with food, and two more steins of beer. Lynch handed the plates and pots to Mitchell and, pulling one of the trolley hoists, sent the tray down again, first planting a big noisy kiss on the tray. As it went down he shouted, "Big fat kiss coming down, my flower!" They all listened and smiled when they heard the sound of a woman's laugh down below. They were pleased that she understood. Not the subject of the remark; that was only part of an elaborate verbal ritual, almost traditional. Their pleasure stemmed more from the fact that she understood English.

When Mitchell had finished his second helping, he looked around the room. It was quite large, running, it seemed, the whole depth of the building, from front to back. It was about forty feet long and twenty-five feet wide. It had two full-length windows at each end. The front overlooked the narrow, quiet Schliegerstraat; the rear was two stories above the flower-planted courtyard, completely surrounded by the backs of other tall houses that they had glimpsed when they had parked the Alvis in the archway. The floor of the room was tiled in black and white squares. Mitchell was reminded of a Dutch painting that he and Rose had once stared at in the National Gallery. They'd gone in to shelter from a September rainstorm. Arm in arm, they had wandered around the long halls all afternoon. He was so taken up with Rose that he had even forgotten to keep his eye out for the alarms and wiring. He smiled to himself, remembering. The picture had been of a girl sitting at a table in front of a window, and the room could very well have been this one, except, he thought as he stared at a calendar, the room in the painting had been a lot narrower, and it hadn't had three mattresses in it.

Mitchell turned from the rear windows as Lieutenant Dennis and Captain Van Velzor came out of the officer's rooms.

"All satisfactory, chaps?" Dennis called, his hands clasped behind his back.

"Top-hole," replied Lynch, sarcastically, finishing his plate with a flourish, wiping the gravy with a slice of bread and stuffing it into his mouth.

Mitchell glanced at Dennis, then at Goffin. Their eyes met for a flash. They both knew that the other was wondering how long Lynch would get away with taking the mickey out of Dennis. Dennis, who seemed to notice nothing, spoke again.

"As soon as lunch is over, the colonel wants a meeting, out here. He asks that you bring the baggage up before six . . . eighteen-hundred hours."

"No problem," acknowledged Mitchell. Goffin moved toward the stair door with him.

"D'you mind if I'm excused, sir?" asked Lynch, taking his empty plate over to the hatch, limping slightly. "I strained me shoulder this morning and it's beginning to hurt." He rubbed his shoulder.

Dennis looked at Lynch, "No, certainly not, Mister Lynch. You must be careful here." Dennis moved over to the table. "Here, I'll clear these things away. You sit down and rest, there's a good chap."

Lynch sat down and lighted a cigarette. Van Velzor, for a moment, stared at him. Lynch held the Dutchman's eyes for ten seconds then dropped his and whistled quietly to himself. Van Velzor, with an almost indiscernible shake of his head, took out his checklist and studied it.

Minutes later, with all the kit bags and suitcases and the wooden crate lined up on the floor, under the service hatch, and the dining table cleared to the other side of the room, Colonel Canning breezed in.

"All correct, Lieutenant?" Canning glanced at Lynch, then turned to Dennis, tapping his swagger stick on the tabletop.

"Just arranging the chairs, sir," reported Dennis.

"Top-hole," said the colonel.

Mitchell and Goffin were lining the five dining chairs into position, three for the nonofficers, and then a space, then two chairs for Dennis and Van Velzor. Dennis had already marked, with chalk, a little cross at the place where each chair should be placed.

On the wall opposite the chairs a large sheet of paper was pinned. It was a large street map of Amsterdam, turned back to front.

"Good, good, then we'll begin right away," asserted Colonel Canning. He laid down his swagger stick. He drew a large square on the paper, using a short piece of charcoal.

The officers and men took their seats. "Smoke, sir?" asked Lynch, standing up to reach for an ashtray from the window sill.

"Certainly, gentlemen, by all means," said the colonel. He was too preoccupied to express his annoyance. He drew more lines on the paper.

He turned to face his audience. "This is the Royal Palace, here in Amsterdam," he commenced, and, picking up his swagger stick, pointed at the square.

Lynch gasped. *So that's it*, he thought, as he settled down to listen carefully. *Blimey, this'll be something to write home about*!

"Pardon me," the colonel carried on, "I should say this is the basement of the Royal Palace here in Amsterdam. And we are here, gentlemen, *to burgle the vault*." He tapped his swagger stick at a small square within the larger square. He reached up with a piece of chalk and scrawled a little x inside the small square.

"I suppose you're all wondering *why*?" asked Colonel Canning. He brushed his chalk hand over his mustache. He was enjoying the drama, the looks of disbelief on the faces of Goffin and Lynch. He studied them, each in turn, then took in Mitchell, sitting with his eyes almost closed, slumped in his chair, expressionlessly. He then looked quickly at the two officers. Dennis was smiling. Van Velzor looked anxious. The colonel continued, "I won't go into it very far, here and now. Just suffice it to say that there are . . . " he hesitated for a second, " . . . certain materials in that vault that are of the most vital importance to the Dutch Government." He glanced at Van Velzor, who nodded approvingly, imperceptibly, " . . . And to our own."

Lynch held up his hand. The colonel frowned slightly. "Well, Mister Lynch, what is it?" His voice betrayed a slight impatience.

"Why don't the Dutch Government just move the stuff themselves, sir? I mean, if it belongs to them?"

"Good question, but one thing at a time. Captain Van Velzor," Canning waved his stick towards the Dutch officer, "will deal with that when I've finished."

"Right, Colonel." Lynch crossed his arms and leaned back, his face a little flushed.

"Theirs is not to reason why, and all that, you know," the colonel addressed the meeting in general again. Everybody except Van Velzor smiled. Canning tapped the paper with his stick again. "Now, our immediate job is to consider how to do this, and so far as we can tell at the moment," he glanced at Van Velzor again, "there are two ways in which we can penetrate into this . . . er . . . establishment with a minimal risk of detection. *Perhaps* with a minimal risk of detection," he corrected himself. "First by the upper floors, as some of us discussed in London . . . and that is where Mist . . . Able Seaman Goffin comes into the picture."

And the Costain gun, thought Goffin. *Now I see*.

"We'll get together on that after the . . . discussion's over, Goffin."

"Aye aye, sir." Goffin shifted his legs into a more comfortable position.

" . . . and the second way, which we won't discuss yet," the colonel continued. "There is a third way, by bluffing or forcing our way in through the one main entrance, past the guards and perhaps penetrating the building through a secondary entrance. Any questions so far?" asked Canning. Mitchell raised a finger.

"Mister Mitchell?" the colonel said, cheerily.

"What about getting under? I mean through the drainage system?" asked Mitchell.

Canning replied, "We don't know too much about that yet. The captain is investigating. It seems that a new, small bore pipe system was installed a few years ago; six-inch—a foot, right, Captain?"

"Thirty centimeters . . . roughly a foot, sir," replied Van Velzor.

"Yes," *damned metric system*, Canning cursed to himself, "yes . . . though there is an old underground canal that meanders somewhere through this area," he tapped the paper again with his stick, "but we don't as yet, have much info on it. So, for the time being, the situation being as it is, and time being of the essence, we're concentrating on our "over" attack solution."

Over or through . . . back to the trenches, lads, the thought flashed through Mitchell's mind.

Canning continued, "This evening we'll change into *mufti* . . . er, civilian clothes, all except the captain here, of course, and reconnoiter the . . . er . . . scene of the crime." Everybody, including the Dutchman laughed. "Lieutenant Dennis will arrange the recce parties, and then, well chaps, a sort of spot of the good old British muddling through, what . . . eh?" He smiled widely at the five listeners, who all, except for the officers, gazed at him with the fascinated stare of lunatics peering over an asylum wall. "And now gentlemen, I'll hand you over to the good offices of our host here, Captain Van Velzor." The colonel smiled again, then he remembered, "But before I do, let me warn you men not to leave the company at any time, while we're operational, for more than is necessary . . . for ablutions. I want you all to stay here in these quarters while you're off-duty. The less people know we're here, the better. The hostelry people downstairs are all right, of course." Canning looked at Lynch, who had held his hand up. "Yes, Lynch?"

"Supposing the Germans arrive quickly?" argued Lynch. "Us civvies'd be . . . I mean we're working for you, aren't we?"

"Then, Mister Lynch, the sooner we get this job done, and trot off out of here, back to the coast, the better, don't you think?" The colonel, one eye almost closed, pinned Lynch down. Everyone tittered. Lynch slouched in his chair even further. The colonel said, "Now, Captain Van Velzor, please." The colonel exchanged places with the Dutchman, sitting in Van Velzor's chair at attention, arms crossed, holding his swagger stick.

"Gentlemen," greeted Van Velzor. He had a way of snapping his head from one direction to another. It was as if a key was turning in a lock. Goffin strained his ears for the click. The Dutchman's English was excellent. There was only a slight guttural distortion of the hard consonants. Except for this, like many highly educated, nonnative English speakers, his vocabulary and pronunciation were as accurate as an Oxford don. "First, I'd like to take this opportunity to welcome you as allies and as friends to Holland. Now, having said that I'll get right down to brass tacks, as you say. Mister Lynch here . . . " he turned his head toward Lynch, "asked a pertinent question earlier on. He wanted to know why the Dutch Government cannot 'just move the stuff themselves. The answer is quite simple." Van Velzor stiffened his shoulders and continued. "Amsterdam cannot be defended. Our main army is confined to . . . split into two halves. One of them is isolated in the northeast of the country, on the other side of the Ijsselmeer. I believe your name for it is Zuider Zee. And the other half is to the south of the Rhine, the Maas. There's a great gap between the two halves, and through that gap the Germans are approaching the city—Amsterdam—as fast as they can. The only things slowing them are the bridges that our people have been able to destroy and the *polders*—the low, reclaimed sections of the country that we have been able to flood."

The silence in the room was funereal.

Van Velzor, choking down his inner emotions, continued. "As in Norway, gentlemen, we, too, have our Quislings. The chief of the palace staff is one. He has arranged that all the palace servants and guards who are not sympathetic to the Nazis be discharged. Our army people can do nothing. Mynheer Captain Kramp, the chief of the palace staff, has seen to it that he is the only person who has the combination to the door of the vault. The security . . . the construction of the vault is such that, even if our men were to force an entry, it would take them several days to break their way into the vault . . . even if they should use high explosives."

"Sir," Goffin spoke. "Surely if your army blokes . . . soldiers capture the palace they can force Kramp, or whatever his name is, to give them the combination?"

"Maybe, my fine sailor, but the problem is that Kramp is in hiding. One of his henchmen is left in charge, with twelve of their men who are Nazi sympathizers. At least they think they are, but one of the servants is working for me. And that is the man who will be on the receiving end of our sailor friend's line. He will keep lookout for us when our safe-opening friend arrives and escort us down to the basement. That, gentlemen, is the overall sketch of our intentions. The details will be finalized later, when we have looked over the palace grounds. As for the getaway, I will be waiting in the car . . . the . . . " He looked at Dennis.

"Alvis," prompted Dennis, unsmiling.

"Yes, the Alvis," said Van Velzor.

"How heavy are these . . . materials?" asked Lynch.

"There are two boxes, both steel, both heavy, both about the size of a sewing machine case," replied the Dutchman.

"How heavy, sir?" Mitchell insisted.

"About thirty kilos . . . say sixty pounds each," Van Velzor replied.

"The upper floor will never work," claimed Mitchell, "not undetected."

"We'll have to decide that when we've seen the locale," Colonel Canning announced in a measured voice.

"You're flogging a dead horse," asserted Lynch. "With that weight, it's going to take two men to lift each box."

Canning countered, "We'll deal with that problem later. For now, let Captain Van Velzor tell us what the situation is on the ground . . . in the field."

"I don't have anything else to say, for now," Van Velzor said. He had lost the thread of his speech. "I think the thing for us to do now is muster our equipment and plan the reconnoiter this evening."

Colonel Canning stood. He spoke softly to Dennis. "Good, that's that. Muster the equipment, please, Lieutenant."

In five minutes all the kit bags and suitcases had been unpacked. The room now looked like an attic sale, with different groups of clothing and gear in neat batches all around the floor. The colonel walked to each section, listening carefully as Lynch checked off a written list, and Goffin called out the name of each article.

"Boiler suit, six in number," Goffin droned.

"Good, always wanted a romper suit, save the soup stains," quipped Lynch.

"Balaclava helmets, blue, six in number," Goffin sing sang.

"Charge for the guns, they said."

"Gloves, navy blue, six pairs."

"Your tiny 'and is frozen, let me warm it into mine," Lynch softly sang

the first few bars of the aria from *La Boheme*.

"Shoes, gym, assorted sizes, blue, six pairs."

"To the wall bars . . . go!"

"Belts, webbing, with pockets, four."

"Four belts!" Lynch snapped.

"Sea boots, black, admiralty issue, six pairs."

Lynch chortled, "If the ship sails we can walk back, eh, Goff?" Goffin looked up and grinned at him.

They slowly made their way through all the kit bag contents and then came to the wooden crate. Mitchell handed out the contents as Goffin called out the item.

"Five jackets, gray."

"Straight from Bertram Mill's Circus." Lynch had no idea how he had hit the mark exactly. The colonel, startled, looked at Lynch, then down again.

"Torches, rubber, waterproof, admiralty pattern, five in number."

"Lead kindly light," Lynch crowed.

"Trousers, gray, five pairs."

Lynch lisped, *"So* much better than khaki . . . it's the in color for the 1940 season, ducky." He held one hand out, wrist limp.

"One canvas bag . . . contents," Goffin, grinning, read the stencilled markings on the bag, "Costain line launching gun and line."

"Poor sailor that can't shoot a line, eh, Jack?"

"Enfield revolvers, .32, army issue, three in number, together with ammunition, 300 rounds.

"Stranger, where ah come from," Lynch mimicked an American western drawl, "they smile when they say that." Everyone except Canning guffawed.

"One steel box, army issue, containing hand grenades, Mills, twelve in number."

"There'll be a hot time in the old town . . . tonight," Lynch did a little jig.

"One small box, four-inch nails."

"Right, where's the cross?" Lynch glanced mockingly around.

"Boxes, Bakelite, eight in number, contents," Goffin looked at the colonel and shrugged. The small black Bakelite containers were still in the bottom of the wooden crate, packed tightly between chipped straw.

Colonel Canning spoke. "All right, don't move those yet. I think Mister Lynch knows what the contents are . . . correct, Lynch?"

"Bang on with Banger, sir!" Lynch's face beamed.

"Quite," declared the colonel. "Good, that seems to be everything.

Nothing missing? Top-hole!" he turned to Dennis. "Get the stuff stored away, will you Dennis? Bring the side weapons into my room."

The three troops were already picking up the gear, stowing it in a large cupboard neatly on the shelves.

"Careful with the thermos, mate," said Goffin to Mitchell. "That's the most useful thing we got with us on this job, so far."

Lieutenant Dennis called to Goffin, "Better come with me, Able Seaman Goffin, I have a civilian suit for you, I hope it fits, blue pinstripe, all right?"

Goffin turned and followed Dennis into the officers' rooms, saying as he did so, eyes turned upwards towards the ceiling, "At last, oh Lord, at last!" Both Mitchell and Lynch broke up laughing.

After tea, which they all took together, standing around a big chromium tea urn, they sallied forth for the reconnaissance. They were in two groups, all in civilian clothes, except for Van Velzor, who was in the first trio with Colonel Canning and Goffin. The others, chatting amiably, followed at a distance of twenty yards. They headed for the Palace Square, just around the corner, at the end of Schliegerstraat.

The streets showed few signs of war. There were some pedestrians looking perhaps a little more anxious than usual, but otherwise there were few signs that this was a city about to fall to an invading army. Some of the shops in the street were open, although their blinds were drawn, and the cars drove along the darkened street with only sidelights. There was a nip in the air, which only Goffin felt. He had, as yet, no overcoat.

They turned the corner, the first trio, and walked across the wide expanse of the Palace Square. On the far side they saw the Royal Palace. It was surrounded by a wall, twenty feet high. Behind the wall they could see the Palace itself, four stories higher than the wall. There was an ornate main entrance in the middle of the wall facing the square. Two guards, in blue overcoats, with rifles slung across their shoulders, stood at ease inside the gate. As they drew closer to the gate, Van Velzor pulled up his mackintosh collar, to obscure his features. They passed the gate at a moderate pace, neither slow nor fast. Both Canning and Goffin glanced quickly around, past the soldiers. They walked along the pavement under the wall, until they came to the corner.

Past the corner they found themselves in a wide boulevard. This they crossed over, turning their heads now and again in the direction of the Palace, inspecting the lie of the upper stories and the roof.

At the next corner they turned right. They walked down the

narrow street a couple of hundred yards, until the way was blocked by a canal. All this was done in silence. At the canal, the three leaned on the verge rail. Canning took out a cigarette and lit it. "Well, Goffin, how does it look to you?" he asked.

"Pretty hopeless, sir," Goffin murmured as he also lit a cigarette. "That space between the wall and the Palace is at least forty yards."

"But your Costain gun can reach two hundred yards?" the colonel countered.

Goffin replied, "Yes, but it's not that, sir. It's when you've got the line over, into the Palace. Of course, it will be tautened at the inboard . . . at our end . . . but the snag is that as soon as you get any weight on it, it's going to sag, and a weight like Mitchell . . . and the boxes . . . "

"But surely it sags at sea, doesn't it?" Canning demanded.

"Oh, sure, sir, but when you hits salt water it don't feel as 'ard as concrete, and it don't stop you being dragged to the other ship anyway. Anyone what's on that line is going to be dragging the ground. The sentries'll see him and collar him."

"Yes . . . quite . . . " Canning muttered as he turned to Van Velzor. "Hopeless with the line. Have to think of something else. Unless your friend Van Alten comes up with something. Well, it means we'll have to go in for a spot of gate-crashing."

Van Velzor thought for a moment, his brows knitted, as he watched a motor barge, huge and slow, with her exhaust puffing diesel fumes above her wheelhouse. "I'll go and see him right away, Colonel," he announced. "He may have turned something up, please God."

The three stared silently as a motor barge passed them. She was almost as wide as the Kappel canal itself, pushing a foot-high bow wave before her. Goffin was surprised to see flowers in a window box below the wheelhouse door, and the faces of a woman and two children looking up at them from behind the windows. One of the children, a little fat boy of about two years, smiled and waved at Goffin. All three men, despite their long, serious faces, waved back. Goffin was the only one to break into a wide smile and wink at the child.

Then, as previously arranged, Canning took out his white handkerchief, blew his nose twice, and the two trios returned to Schliegerstraat. Except for Van Velzor, who sloped off as they crossed the Palace Square and headed in the direction of city engineer Van Alten's house in Beurenstraat, on the other side of the Kappel canal. The first drops of rain spattered down as the Dutchman silently took his leave.

They got to No. 69 just in time for supper. Trailing along in the second trio, Mitchell racked his brain for the answer to a question. A question he had almost blurted out when Van Velzor was speaking at the meeting. *Why the hell can't I go into the Palace with the Dutch Army?* But he kept silent about it, knowing that he would not get a straight answer. In the army they had drilled into him, *Never rock the boat.* Now he was back again, in the army.

Lynch thought the same question over, too. He kept quiet, because if there were anything crooked going on, *Mister Lynch is in for a slice of the pie.* He had a good idea what the pie was, too, *so better a slice of pie than nothing*, he thought. *Even if it is a stolen pie. Better if it is a stolen pie and better the whole pie . . . even if it means killing for it.* Again he remembered how he'd heaved the fireman over the stern of the *Mauretania*.

The three officers knew the reason why Mitchell would not be helped by the Dutch Army. The treasure was not the property of the Queen, nor of the government, but of Parliament.

The Socialists in Parliament would never allow it out of the country. Not if there were any hope of it being used as a lever to persuade the Germans to modify the methods by which their military governments in occupied territories were known to dragoon the local inhabitants. Not, for example if it might avoid the persecution of the hundreds of thousands of Jews in Holland . . . they were, after all, Dutch nationals. The Conservatives in Parliament would never allow it to be removed as long as it might be fed to the Germans, bit by bit, over as long a period as possible, in return for the right to continue business as usual and to retain Dutch-grown food to feed their own people. The Nationalist members, many of whom were ready to welcome the Nazis anyway, had a vested interest in handing over the treasure as soon as possible to the Reich. It would put them in good standing with their masters for the foreseeable future. There was, they imagined, an important part for Holland to play in the New European Order. They would rather play that part in the role of a trusted ally. An ally that had provided the means for Japan to attack the true enemy of Europe, the USSR. To attack Russia away on the eastern side of the vast sprawling Communist empire, while the Führer's European armies with its Dutch contingent mopped up the red virus in the western steppes, assuring Holland's place in the sun.

But the officers, all three of them, held their counsel together on these matters. The troops would not understand. *Keep it simple, chaps*, 'C' had said, as if anything in life could be simple.

It was eleven o'clock when Van Velzor returned to Schliegerstraat. His mackintosh dripped rainwater over Lynch's mattress as he leaned over to unpin the reversed map on the wall. Lynch, in his underwear, dragged the mattress away from under the Dutchman.

"So sorry, sir, I'm in a terrific hurry," Van Velzor said, as he rushed over, map in hand, and knocked on the officer's door. It opened and he went in, closing the door with a slam behind him.

"Bleedin' foreigners!" Lynch complained as he replaced the mattress. "All wogs start at fuckin' Calais!"

"Did call you *sir* though, didn't he?" jested Goffin, as he pulled his blanket up around his ears.

"I think I've found something, sir . . . good evening." Van Velzor was excited as he spread the map, reversed again, on the coffee table that stood in the center of the carpet. His cap fell on the floor as he bent over.

The colonel looked up. "Captain . . . please remove your raincoat. Here, let me help you." Canning made to stand up, but Dennis was at Van Velzor's side, helping him to shuck off the dripping coat. Dennis hung it on the back of the door.

Van Velzor retrieved his cap, which had rolled under the small table. He unfolded himself, and mopped his face with his handkerchief. "It's . . . how do you put it?" he queried the Englishmen.

"Raining cats and dogs?" suggested the colonel, who was now at Van Velzor's side.

"Exactly." The Dutchman took a pencil from his breast pocket.

"Gentlemen, I think we have another means of getting into the Palace basement . . . as you call it. Actually, it is a subbasement, half above the ground. He knelt down and carefully drew a line on the paper. The coffee table was too small, so as he drew the line, he moved the map to provide the pencil with a firm base.

"City Engineer Van Alten's found an old man who remembers when the new . . . " he faltered, " . . . when the old sewage canal was sealed off. It passed quite close to the Palace basement, to service the kitchens, of course."

"Or perhaps," suggested the colonel, "they built the Palace there to service the canal?" All three officers smiled.

"Yes, indeed, Colonel, that's exactly it," said Van Velzor, who was then silent until he finished his sketch. Then he stood, stretching himself.

The colonel and the lieutenant both studied the new lines on the paper, their eyes almost closed. Canning looked expectantly at Van

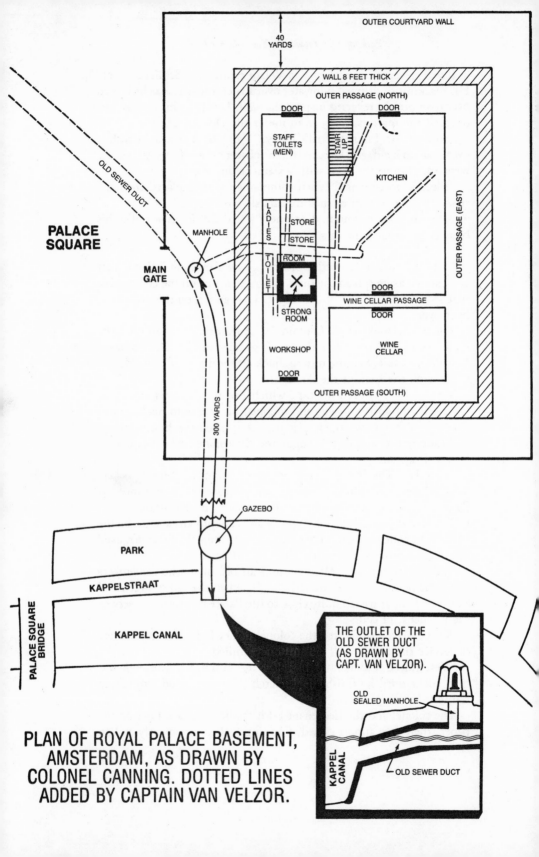

OUTER COURTYARD WALL

40 YARDS

WALL 8 FEET THICK

OUTER PASSAGE (NORTH)

DOOR   DOOR

STAFF TOILETS (MEN)

STAIR UP

KITCHEN

OLD SEWER DUCT

PALACE SQUARE

MANHOLE

LADIES TOILET

STORE

STORE

ROOM

OUTER PASSAGE (EAST)

MAIN GATE

STRONG ROOM

DOOR

WINE CELLAR PASSAGE

DOOR

300 YARDS

WORKSHOP

WINE CELLAR

DOOR

OUTER PASSAGE (SOUTH)

GAZEBO

PARK

KAPPELSTRAAT

PALACE SQUARE BRIDGE

KAPPEL CANAL

THE OUTLET OF THE OLD SEWER DUCT (AS DRAWN BY CAPT. VAN VELZOR).

OLD SEALED MANHOLE

OLD SEWER DUCT

KAPPEL CANAL

PLAN OF ROYAL PALACE BASEMENT, AMSTERDAM, AS DRAWN BY COLONEL CANNING. DOTTED LINES ADDED BY CAPTAIN VAN VELZOR.

Velzor.

"I'll start at the beginning, sir," explained the Dutchman. "As you know, Amsterdam is built on ground that is just above sea level. "Now . . ."

The colonel went back down to his chair, first turning the map so he could study it sitting down.

" . . . Now, when the old drainage system was constructed, back in the seventeenth century, they merely dug canals, ditches all over the place, smaller than the barge canals, of course, and built . . . " He made an up and over sweep with one hand.

"Arches?" Dennis suggested.

Van Velzor smiled a thanks. "Right, arches, vaulting, that's the word, to turn the small canals into underground tunnels . . . " He was stuck for a word again.

"Ducts?" gently prompted Dennis.

Van Velzor nodded. "Ducts. And the one that feeds the Palace passes out into the Kappel canal."

"Where we were earlier this evening," Canning said, quietly.

"Yes," Van Velzor replied as he looked at the drawing again, then he knelt. In one corner of the paper he quickly drew another sketch. "And when they built the ducts, they arranged it so the lower side of the roof—the vaulting—would be four feet *above* the level of the water in the main canals, to . . . " he paused again, searching for English words.

Dennis spoke for him, remembering his basic Royal Engineer's training, "To allow extra capacity for floodwaters."

"Yes, that's it!" Van Velzor exulted.

"Then we can just jolly-well walk into the . . . er . . . tunnel?" asked the colonel.

Van Velzor smiled, apologetically. He replied, "It's not quite as easy as that, sir. You see . . . " He gestured at the latest drawing. "Here I have drawn the . . . er . . . outlet of the tunnel. Where it joins the canal. According to Van Alten's informant, it . . . "

"Dips downward," Dennis interjected.

"But not too far." Van Velzor was silent for a moment. "If your men can swim, they can dive into the outlet to the Kappel and with a bit of luck be through to the . . . "

"Surface-free section of the tunnel." It was the colonel who spoke this time, rising as he did so. "What's the diameter of the old main duct, the distance across it?"

"The old man says two meters," Van Velzor replied.

"Then once we're under the . . . sill," the colonel murmured as he dropped into a crouching position, studying the drawing as he spoke, "we can stand or crouch in the damned thing with our heads above water?"

"Exactly," Van Velzor agreed.

"How near does the tunnel come to the strong room?" Canning demanded.

The Dutchman said, "Very close. There's a smaller pipe, about a meter wide, that runs from under the kitchen, and joins the old big duct . . . here." Van Velzor pointed with his pencil tip to a bend in the line 200 yards from the Kappel. "And to get from the kitchen to the main duct it passes under a storeroom . . . right bang-slap." He hesitated for a moment.

"Slap-bang," corrected Dennis.

"Thank you . . . slap-bang next to the vault."

"But there must be a ground-surface access to this system some-where," the colonel said. "I mean manholes, that sort of thing?"

"There are, but one is inside the Palace grounds, right in the parade ground, here." Van Velzor pointed to a spot close to the main gate. "And the other one, near the outlet to the Kappel, was sealed over with cement and a stone dais. Van Alten informs me they built a sort of pagoda on top of it, with a statue inside."

"Of whom?" demanded the colonel.

"Schopenhauer," replied Van Velzor.

"God, it would be a blasted Boche!" snorted the colonel.

The colonel continued, "Seriously, though, is there any chance of getting a drawing of the old tunnel-canal outlet?"

Van Velzor grinned wanly. "Van Alten tells me that he's having two trusted men search the files and drawings archives of every museum in Amsterdam, as well as his own city engineer's racks."

"Good," said the colonel. "Well, in the meantime, we'll survey the site of the outlet first thing tomorrow. But before we go to bed, gentlemen, I want a word with the troops."

He opened the door and marched out, followed by both Van Velzor and Dennis. The light had been switched off, and all three troops were half-asleep. Canning searched for the light switch, fumbling around the doorframe.

"It's by the outside door, sir," called Goffin sleepily.

Canning switched on the light. "Attention, men!" he called sharply.

Mitchell and Goffin sat up. Lynch pretended to sleep. Canning walked over and gently tapped Lynch's shoulder with his boot. "Mister Lynch," he called in a conversational tone.

"Eh, wazzat?" Lynch looked up at the colonel. "Coo . . . blimey!" he exclaimed. He sat up. Both Mitchell and Goffin were grinning. The officers kept straight faces. The colonel moved back from Lynch three paces and addressed the room.

"Any nonswimmers?" the colonel demanded, brusquely.

Only Lynch spoke. "Here, sir."

"You're a fibber, Lynch," Canning retorted.

"Sir?"

"I've seen your Merchant Navy papers." The colonel, reddening with anger, turned to the others. "Good!" he announced. "All volunteers. Quite. Good." He cleared his throat and continued, "Now, anyone good at underwater swimming?" He looked directly at Goffin. Goffin stayed mute.

"Goffin, good," the colonel exclaimed, "with your experience in submarines. I need your advice on a little matter. How can a man breathe underwater long enough to swim a distance of thirty feet at a depth of three feet?"

"Davis escape apparatus, sir," replied Goffin.

"Can we get one?" Canning turned to Van Velzor.

The Dutchman shook his head. "I don't know that the Netherlands Navy uses it, sir . . . in any case, the time element . . ."

"Damn!" The colonel looked at Goffin again. "Anything else?" he asked.

Goffin said, "I could try and make one, or something like it, sir, only take a few hours or so."

"How?" Canning turned to Dennis. "Write down what Goffin needs."

Dennis dashed into the officer's room for a pad and pencil. He ran back to stand by Goffin's bed. Goffin sat silent, his arms clutched around his knees under the blanket, frowning.

"Well, man, speak up, what d'you need?" the colonel demanded of him.

" . . . Er, five feet of rubber tubing, inner diameter 'alf-an-inch . . . a brass petcock, with two male outlets, outside diameter 'alf-an-inch, a bicycle tire valve . . . that's inner tube valve . . . make it two of those . . . a bicycle pump to . . . with an outlet to fit the valves . . . two ¾-inch pipe clamps . . . a screwdriver, medium size . . . a set o' drill bits, a 'and drill . . . no, electric'd be quicker . . . two clothes pegs, the ones with wire on 'em . . . a four-pound scales weight . . . " Goffin frowned, racking his brain, gazing at the colonel's swagger stick.

"Yes, yes, come on, man . . . what else . . . anything else?" the colonel tapped his jodhpurs excitedly with his stick.

" . . . and . . . a rubber 'ot-water bottle, with a screw top," Goffin said.

For a moment the colonel wondered if Goffin was joking, but he saw that the seaman's face was serious. "That's all?" he asked.

"That's all, sir."

"Got that . . . everything?" Canning demanded of the lieutenant. Dennis read the list back to the colonel.

Canning turned to Van Velzor. "Captain," he asked, "how soon can you obtain these materials? The sooner the better, of course."

"Of course, Colonel," the Dutchman said. He walked to the officer's door, took down his still dripping mackintosh, accepted the written list from Dennis, and with a muffled "thank you" he went through the outside door.

So it was, that as the full force of the right wing of the German army rapidly descended on the commercial capital of his country, the military aide-de-camp to the Queen of the Netherlands went searching the rainy streets of Amsterdam at midnight—for two clothes pegs and a hot-water bottle, among other things.

"It's a pity we don't know which box is which, sir," reflected Dennis.

The colonel replied, "Well, we don't; they're both identical; their fastenings are so intricate and solid it would take at least an hour to open either box. There just isn't time for Mitchell to waste finding out which is which. No, we must bring them both out. We can't risk discovery. We don't have an hour to spare."

"What about weight, sir, couldn't we tell by the weight difference?" asked Dennis.

"No. The one with the Crown Jewels also contains enough diamonds in the bottom to make it weigh exactly the same as the one containing the securities."

"Quite a responsibility, sir. Must be a fortune?"

"Agreed. Of course, it'll all be returned when the hostilities are over."

"Of course, sir."

The colonel went on, "Over half-a-billion pounds sterling in precious stones and metals. The securities and titles . . . monetary value inestimable . . . and politically, possibly the future of the world for the next twenty centuries . . . the future of the whole damned galactic system . . . You know, Dennis, when Goffin was telling us his list of things, I thought of . . . what was it? *For the want*

"Pack up Your Troubles in Your Old Kit Bag"

of a nail . . . ?"

"A *kingdom was lost*, sir," prompted the young man.

"Quite. Good night, Dennis. Look after Van whatsisname when he returns," said Canning.

"Good night, sir."

They had no idea that Lynch, standing on the troop's toilet seat, listening through the grill, had heard every word through the open door of the officer's bathroom.

Goffin woke with a start. A hand lamp was shining in his face.

"We have your . . . er . . . bits and pieces here, Goffin," Dennis whispered hoarsely. "The captain has had . . . difficulty finding . . ."

"Okay, sir." Goffin was wide awake. He clambered out of his blankets. He wriggled into his trousers. The officers looked away, into the darkness of the ceiling.

Van Velzor spoke first. "There's a workshop downstairs, under the arch where we left the car." He pressed the palms of his two hands together as if in prayer. Goffin looked at him drowsily. "There's a . . . a . . ."

"Vice," prompted Dennis. He glanced at his watch. It was three-twenty.

"Quite," Van Velzor repeated one of the colonel's favorite phrases.

Dennis opened the outside door, lighting the stairs with the hand lamp, and they all passed through, Van Velzor leading the way.

The workshop was through a small door that led off from the archway into the area under the officer's quarters. It was tidy, clean and well equipped, with a large carpenter's bench, a big fixed electric drill, and tools stowed in wooden battens over the table. Goffin looked around. He touched a small electric stove on the bench, and picked up a coffee jug. "Home from home," he grinned.

Van Velzor laid the package on the bench and opened it.

"I'll help Goffin," Dennis murmured.

"Fine, sir, and the captain can make the tea, okay?" Goffin jested.

Van Velzor laughed quietly. "Top-hole sailorman!" he said as he laid the little parade of banality on the bench, each item at the side of the next, all in line, like a small boy would muster his toy soldiers. Then he crept back upstairs for the tea, thinking, *Verdommd Englanders with their tea*!

They woke Lynch and Mitchell with an intentional clatter. "Wakey, wakey, rise and shine, the mornin's fine, you've had your time!" Goffin strode over to the two ex-convicts' beds. He lashed at them lightly with a rope lanyard tied to the contraption he was wearing on his chest. "Come along, me lucky lads, rise and shine . . . 'ands off cocks and onto socks!" He sang out the traditional Royal Naval lower-deck reveille, as the two officers stood, smiling, tired.

Mitchell, half-awake already, sat up. He reached for his trousers, which he had folded over a dining chair the previous night.

Lynch was wide awake, his top blanket pulled up over his face, lying there like a corpse. His muffled voice recited,

The first awake was Bollocky Bill . . .
The Stoker on a lugger . . .
It wasn't coal 'e shoveled . . .
It was shit—the rotten bugger!

Then Lynch flung the blanket up and away from him and sprang out of bed. He stood, in his underpants, for a moment, then, catching a glimpse of the officers, he bellowed to Goffin, "What are you, Goff, a bleedin' Christmas tree?"

Mitchell turned to look at Goffin and burst out laughing. The seaman was shuffling his feet, softly. He wore his blue pinstriped trousers and collarless shirt, his naval boots, with their square toes peeping out from his trouser cuffs. His hair was disheveled and on his chest he wore the hot-water bottle, inflated, tied with a rope around his neck. In his mouth he had stuck a rubber hose that led from the screw lid of the rubber pouch. The bottom of the hot-water bottle was tied with yet another rope around his waist. The rag-ends of a big knot dangled over his rear end. From the rope, where it passed over his midriff, was suspended a two-kilo weight that banged his knees as he danced a little jig. Over his nose he wore a clothes peg.

"What's that, mate?" shouted Mitchell. "The latest thing in the Riviera? Mae West will scratch your eyes out."

Goffin stopped jigging on his toes. He removed the tube from his mouth and pointed it at Mitchell. He put one hand under the hot water bottle and placed one foot in front of the other. He dropped his chin over his chest and pronounced, in a deep voice, "M'sieurs, zey weel nevair keep me on St. Helenaire!" He opened the petcock. There was a sound as if he'd passed wind as the air rushed out and the rubber bottle collapsed.

Everyone in the room burst with laughter, just as Colonel Canning entered the room. For one frozen moment he stared at Goffin, like a boy who has found a bird's nest, then at Van Velzor and Dennis. He took in the sight of Lynch still in his underwear, then the colonel, too, guffawed, slapping his knee with one hand. "Good show, Goffin!

Top-hole, man!"

13th May, 1940. 6:00 P.M.
The House of Commons, London

" . . . I have nothing to offer but blood, toil, tears and sweat . . . " The P.M.'s eyes glistened under his half-frame spectacles. He peered gloomily about him, over the heads of the somberly silent, packed chamber. Every eye in the house was on his face, waiting for a sign. He glanced down and saw the Secretary of State for War, poker-faced as usual, lips pressed together. He bent down and in a stage whisper said, "And of course, some good old-fashioned British muddling through."

The Cabinet ministers, a black-striped phalanx all around him, overheard and broke out into involuntary smiles. Little by little, in the moments of silence that followed the P.M.'s quiet outburst, the tension dissolved, slowly at first, until the ninety-two-year-old Member for Codchester-on-Wye, straining at his ear trumpet, boomed out, "Hear! hear!." Soon the call was echoing throughout the Chamber, so loudly from the back benches on both sides of the House that even the Secretary for War was constrained to raise his eyebrows at this uncustomary display of enthusiasm.

13th May, 1940. 7:00 P.M.
3rd (Death's Head) Panzer Division, 4th Section

"Walkyrie . . . Walkyrie," Hauptsturmführer Shrenke shouted into the mouthpiece of his radio. He listened, straining his ears against the roar of the panzer tanks following. His face was pointed—as arrogant and threatening as a flame-thrower nozzle.

There was a painful howl over the transmitter for a few seconds, then a voice, calm and monotonous replied, "Lentz here, Blue Danube, what is your position?"

"We are in the eastern suburbs of Amsterdam—no resistance—no resistance. It's just a straight drive through. Over."

"Good. Hauptsturmführer Shrenke, take your whole unit directly to the south side of the Kappel Canal. Cover the Royal Palace Square bridge, then wait for further orders. Is that clear? Wait for further orders!"

"*Jawohl*, Oberführer Lentz. Heil Hitler!" Shrenke bawled.

"Heil Hitler! And congratulations. I shall see that the Führer is informed."

The seventy-five m.m. guns of the *Mark IV Panzerkampfwagens* of the elite number four section of the crack Totenkopf S.S. Panzer Division swung from side to side as the tanks clanked and roared at a steady six miles per hour along the deserted, dark streets toward the Royal Palace. Shrenke pounded his fist on the turret coaming, mentally roaring the Nazi fighting hymn to himself, "*Die Fahne Hoch! Die Reihen fest geschlossen . . . !*"

Chapter 6

*   *

Side by Side

13th May, 1940

Oh we ain't got a barrel of money,
Maybe we're ragged and funny,
But we'll travel along, singing a song,
Side by side.

Don't know what's coming tomorrow,
Maybe it's trouble and sorrow,
But we'll travel the road, sharin' our load,
Side by side.

Chorus:
Thru all kinds of weather,
What if the skies should fall?
As long as we're together,
It doesn't matter at all!

When they've all had their quarrels and parted,
We'll be the same as we started,
Just travelin' along, singing a song,
Side by side!

Popular British Song, World War II
Words and music by Harry Woods, 1927

6.

"Side by Side"

13th May, 1940. 9:15 P.M. Amsterdam

The Alvis was parked under a plane tree in Corlandstraat. The street lamps were not lit. They had passed only three pedestrians and one or two civilian cars on the way from Schliegerstraat. In the distance, as the Alvis pulled up, they heard the sounds of sirens, and shortly after, the crash of gunfire. To the east and south the sky lit up in bright flashes like lightning.

Except for Van Velzor, they were dressed in new blue, almost black, naval boiler suits. They wore balaclava helmets, blue gloves, and tennis shoes. Lynch was at the wheel.

Canning clambered out first. Van Velzor, in civilian clothes, followed him, carrying a fishing rod, and Goffin, with the inflated hot-water bottle worn under his boiler suit, followed Van Velzor. Goffin carried the weight in one hand, a rubber waterproof lamp in the other, and the bicycle pump in his ruler pocket.

The colonel leaned over and spoke to Dennis. "Ten minutes," he said. He turned and spoke to Van Velzor. "Right, off we go."

They ambled down the street, towards the Kappel Canal, a short distance down the slope, Goffin trailing slightly behind the others. As they started off, Goffin turned around quickly and winked at Lynch as he put one hand on a hip and swayed his hips slightly. Then he straightened up, and they all three faded into the dark under a plane tree.

"He's a lad," commented Mitchell, quietly.

"Good bloke," Lynch replied from the back of the Alvis.

As the trio walked down Cortlandstraat, Van Velzor gestured to a grassy knoll on the opposite side of the street. "That's where the old . . . er, access . . . the . . . what do you call it?"

"Manhole, old chap," the colonel told him.

"Yes, it's under that bandstand, there, on the rise," the Dutchman said.

The colonel looked, saying, "Pagoda, Chinese-style, belvedere . . . no . . . gazebo. That's it. Very popular at the turn of the century."

"You see, it's standing on many stones," Van Velzor murmured.

"Mmm," the colonel glanced at the ornate structure. It was well lit in the moonlight. "Who's the chappie up there? I mean the statue?" he asked. "You did tell me, but I've forgotten."

"Schopenhauer, German philosopher."

"Yes, quite." The colonel pondered. *What was it he had said? War . . . was it war? . . . no . . . life, that was it . . .* "Life swings like a pendulum backward and forward between pain and boredom." Canning struggled with the thought in his mind as they came to the bottom of the street. *But he's wrong of course. Should have said war . . . not life,* he told himself. *Life is Susan and Richard and little Elizabeth . . . very little pain there . . . and not much boredom either. God, what gloomy chaps these Boche philosophers.*

They crossed over Kappelstraat and glanced around. Then, seeing no one about, they quickly climbed the railings. Van Velzor and the colonel pulled down their balaclavas. Crouching low they made for the shade of a bankside linden tree.

"Goffin?" the colonel whispered, a little breathless.

"Sir?" Goffin spoke up. He felt silly, out at night, with two "toffs," under the trees.

"All set? Pull down your balaclava, man," Canning hissed.

Goffin did so, muttering, "There's a bit of a leak in the screw top, sir. Better give her a couple more strokes with the pump." Goffin took the bicycle pump out of his ruler pocket and handed it to the colonel. Then he opened his boiler suit front and produced the offending hot-water bottle lid, as if he were holding a fluttering pigeon's head, with one hand, and reached down the the other hand inside the suit to bring out the mouth tube.

The colonel unscrewed the small tube from the top of the pump handle and twisted it onto the business end of the pump. Then he screwed the free end onto the bicycle inner-tube valve that Goffin had threaded into the bottle top, and gave three or four slow strokes. Goffin's chest swelled visibly.

The sailor gasped, "Right, sir. I think that's it." Goffin patted the lump on his chest.

"Let's hope so. Here, let me help you with the weight," the colonel whispered. He secured the weight to a line that he tied around Goffin's waist, bringing the free end of the line up and over the seaman's shoulder, tying it again to the waist rope. "There, that'll keep it from slipping," he said.

"Think I should take me gym shoes off, sir?" asked Goffin.

"I don't . . . what do you think, Captain?" the colonel turned to Van Velzor.

"No, there will be broken bottles, and iron spikes," Van Velzor muttered.

The colonel held Goffin's elbow. "Now don't forget," he whispered, "the tunnel comes into the canal ten or twelve yards that way," he pointed down the canal, in the direction of the Palace Square embankment. "The upper sill is about three feet under water. Tread water along the canal bank until you are in line with Schop . . . with the statue, then feel around for it with your foot. You'll have about twelve to thirteen feet of tunnel absolutely full of water, then, where it rises there should be a space between the water level and the roof. Pop in there, check the air space, and come on back and report. Understood?"

"Aye aye, sir." Goffin bent down to pick up his rubber torch lamp.

"Good, then off you go, and good hunting!"

"Good luck, Goffin," murmured Van Velzor.

Goffin crouched down and at walking pace headed for the canal bank. He lay down at the edge of the stone embankment and lowered his legs over and was gone.

They waited, under the linden tree in the dark, the Dutchman anxiously, the colonel patiently. He knew his man. Canning thought of what Schopenhaur had said about people like Goffin. *There is no absurdity so palpable but that it may be firmly planted in the human head if only you begin to inculcate it before the age of five, by constantly repeating it with an air of great solemnity.* "Quite," he said to himself, aloud.

"What, sir?" asked Van Velzor.

"Oh, nothing, just thinking, old man."

"What about?" asked Van Velzor.

"Oh, the war, you know," replied Canning, thinking to himself, *In war there are only victims. There are unlucky victims and there are lucky victims, but they're all bally victims. The lucky ones are called heroes. Goffin might be a lucky victim.*

The water bubbles on the surface diminished as Goffin reached the excrement-laden sewer outlet, but all he said to himself, as he tripped over an old cast-iron bedstead half-sunk in the muddy bottom, was, *Sod it.*

13th May, 1940. 9:40 P.M.
Apeldoorn, Holland. Geheime-Feldpolizei Head-quarters, Holland
(The Town Hall Mayor's Parlor)

"It's unfortunate for you, Mr. Briggs." Looking almost academic, like a senior professor, Major Von Biehlsdorf picked a cigarette box off the desk. "Cigarette?" He offered the box, open, to Briggs, whose expression reminded the German of a worried spaniel.

"Thanks Major." Briggs took it, trembling slightly as he accepted the proffered flame. "How did you know?" Briggs murmured, "but of course, it's useless to ask, isn't it?"

The German officer felt, for a moment, genuine sympathy with this elderly man sitting in the chair in front of the desk. *A real English gentleman*, he pondered as he watched Briggs' finely wrought features, the, to him, handsome hawk nose, the intelligent blue eyes. The major thought, *Pity we're on opposite sides. What we couldn't do together . . . our army . . . and Luftwaffe . . . our navy alongside theirs.* Von Biehlsdorf laid his cigarette down on the Dutch Mayor's ashtray. He sighed and continued speaking.

"You might as well tell us. We know about Orange." Von Biehlsdorf watched for a sign in Briggs' eyes. There was none. *Well trained*, he reflected. He shuffled the sheaf of papers in front of him. There was only one page concerned with the scrappy information they had garnished about Orange.

"We know your code name, Keystone. We know about Colonel Canning. We know he's in Amsterdam. We know about the others—all four of them, and, of course, Van Velzor." Von Biehlsdorf scribbled a note on the sheet of paper in front of him, "But what we don't know is their . . . their base." He stood up and sat on the corner of the desk, one foot swinging. He looked down at the British agent. "Now be a good chap and tell me exactly where the base is. We shall be in the city within hours . . . we shall find it anyway."

Briggs silently looked up at Von Biehlsdorf and shrugged.

"Very well, Mr. Briggs. In that case I shall be obliged to hand you over to the Sicherheitsdienst." He paused, then said quietly, "Klug's methods are much more . . . crude than mine. He made your fellow agent Lewis . . . spill the beans. Is that the phrase?" He thought for a second. "Yes, spill the beans, last night. They drove a twenty-five-ton tank over his left leg." He frowned, staring at the top of Briggs' head. "And his left arm, too. He's in the Deventer hospital. Shall we show him to you?"

Briggs' face showed no expression. He said nothing.

"All right, Mr. Briggs. Then I shall send for Klug." Von Biehlsdorf placed a finger on the mayor's bell-push. He waited five seconds.

"Schliegerstraat . . . " Perspiration started from Briggs' forehead. " . . . Number 69, the Three Horses."

Von Biehlsdorf stood up, went back around the desk, leaned over, and scribbled the address on his sheet of paper. His eyes gleamed as he unbent himself. He placed his hands in his uniform jacket pocket. He walked around to place himself behind Briggs. He took one hand out of his pocket and placed it on Briggs' shoulder. "Good man," he said, "You'll be kept here with us, of course, until we confirm the address, and then I shall see that you travel comfortably to Kiel." The German paused for a moment, then he smiled down at Briggs, "And I shall recommend that you be treated with . . . how does it go? . . . the utmost leniency."

"No tank tracks over the legs?" asked Briggs.

"Certainly not. Let's just say we shall hold out certain . . . inducements . . . for whatever else you can tell us."

"Thank you, Major." Briggs laid his head on his arm, resting it on the desk, and waited for the young S.S. stormtrooper to escort him back to his cell in the basement.

13th May, 1940. 10:05 P.M.
German Abwehr Headquarters, Kiel

Admiral Canaris felt chipper as he hoisted the phone to his port ear. "Yes, Admiral here . . . good . . . well done. Get round there as soon as you go in. Oh, at least ten men. Yes, Kapitan Ludwig, just the man. Congratulations, Major Von Biehlsdorf. Well done again." He thought for a moment as Von Biehlsdorf, on the other end of the line, thanked him. "Yes, and before I forget it, as soon as that's done, get some of your men around to the Royal Palace. Yes, I've had Schliegerstraat located; it's just around the corner. Double up with the Dutch guard. Check them first, of course. I've been considering the matter, it might just be . . . " He listened. "Exactly. We don't want those clumsy oafs from the Reichsmarshall's Berlin zoo clomping around collecting all the choicest pieces, do we?" He listened again for ten seconds. "Good. Thank you, Major." Admiral Canaris replaced the telephone. He grimaced as he placed his hand over his forehead. *That great fat . . .* he searched for a word, *drug addict*! He was angry as he thought of the Reichsmarshall mainly because Goering was the only real officer in the whole of that corporal's gang.

Admiral Canaris turned to the wall to study the street map of Amsterdam. It was an exact replica of the one Van Velzor had used in Schliegerstraat. He stooped and stared at the printer's name in small print on the bottom margin, Stanford and Co. Ltd., London WC2. The admiral laughed aloud. "A nation of shopkeepers—it's true!" he said to the window.

13th May, 1940. 10:06 P.M.
Kappelstraat, Amsterdam

Captain Van Velzor started as he heard a clinking noise in the direction of the tunnel outlet. He nudged Colonel Canning and gestured with one finger towards the noise. They waited, staring.

"Pss, sir . . . over here!" Goffin hissed as he clambered, a dark shadow, over the embankment edge. He ran over to them, half-crouching, dripping wet.

"All clear, Goffin? Any trouble?" asked the colonel, anxiously.

"Clear as a bell, sir," Goffin replied, breathlessly. He breathed deeply for a couple of long gasps, then continued. "No problem . . . it's like you said, about thirty feet from the outlet to the inside air surface. Got to watch your step, though, there's a lot of junk on the bottom of the tunnel."

"What about the air space inside, Goffin?" asked Van Velzor.

"A good foot and a half . . . " Goffin spluttered, "maybe two feet."

"Over a third of a meter," said Van Velzor, quietly.

"Yes, sir, you could say that, I s'pose. The water's pretty shi . . . " Goffin caught himself, " . . . pretty dirty, but there ain't no dead dogs in it, s'far as I could see."

Both the officers grinned.

"Could you see very far with the lamp?" asked the colonel.

"What, underwater, sir?" Goffin coughed quietly. "Hardly a thing."

"No, in the duct."

"Yes, very well, in fact, about twenty yards, I'd say, sir."

"How's the air in there?"

Goffin replied, "It's not exactly fresh as a daisy, sir, but it's not too bad . . . about the same as a sub's engine room when she's been submerged for a pair of 'ours."

The colonel tried to see his watch. "Sit down here and wait," he said. "I'm going to brief the others. As soon as you hear me coming back, in you go again. Don't forget to take the Costain line with you this time, and tie it, midway, onto the breathing apparatus when you divest yourself. Leave the pump behind and keep your torch with you, of course. Captain Van Velzor will haul the apparatus back here, ready for the next man to go through."

"Aye aye, sir."

"And be ready to help them through," the colonel added.

" 'Course, sir."

"Good man . . . top-hole." The colonel glanced at Goffin, then turned to the Dutchman. "All clear?"

"Yes, sir. I see the last man through, then return to the car and wait."

"Correct." The colonel crouched and half-ran to the railings. He leaned over the low iron railing bars and stopped. He looked both ways along Kappelstraat, then ran over the road and up Cortlandstraat.

Canning was almost out of breath by the time he reached the car. He dodged around the front of the car to the offside driver's seat and clambered in. He intoned in a low voice, "Right, chaps. All set. You will all three come down to the linden tree on the canal embankment, the third one on the right from the bottom of this street. Got that?"

There was a murmur of assent from Dennis, Mitchell, and Lynch.

Canning continued, "Good, you will come in this order, at intervals of ten minutes. Lynch, you first, with me."

"Right, Colonel," murmured Lynch.

"Next Mitchell."

"Yes, sir," Mitchell agreed.

"Lieutenant Dennis—rear guard. Check your side arm is wrapped up well before you dive.

"Yes, sir," muttered Dennis.

The colonel waited a moment, then continued, "You will all bring with you, as I shall, two of the Bakelite boxes. As you know, they have been sewn up in the webbing belts around our waists. You will also each bring a waterproof torch. Check that you have them now."

There was another murmur as the check was made.

Canning's voice droned on, "Now we've all gone through the drill with the breathing apparatus, and the petcock . . . er, handle has been fixed so that it will only allow a rather slow flow of air to pass. Take your time when you go down underwater. Breathe slow and easily, breathe out through one side of your mouth, then close it and breathe in through the tube. The weight will counter the floating tendency of the bottle. Just put your feet on the bottom of the tunnel, crouch down, and in you go. Then walk forward. Goffin will be pulling steadily on the guideline, and if you get into any difficulty give it a jerk. He's waiting to come and give you a hand. But if you go carefully that shouldn't be necessary. Now, all right, everybody? Any questions?"

"Do we get danger money, sir?" Lynch grinned at the colonel.

Canning smiled as he turned to Lynch. "Only if you get the loot back home."

"Well, better late than never," chuckled Lynch, climbing out of his seat. Once out on the sidewalk he bent over and spoke softly to Mitchell. "Here goes 'is Majesty's 'eavy brigade."

Mitchell laughed quietly, as he watched the tall man and the short man, wearing their boiler suits, stroll down the deserted street as if they were out for a pleasant Sunday evening promenade.

As the colonel and Lynch climbed over the railings, they saw the shadowy form of Goffin slide away and drop over the embankment.

They waited, in silence, for five minutes, the colonel in the shade of the linden tree, Van Velzor, with his flat cap pulled down low over his eyes, his collar turned up and his fishing rod held out over the canal. Suddenly the rod jerked. The Dutchman reeled in the thin, strong Costain line. Soon, dangling on the end of his bent rod, was the hot water bottle and the weight, together with the two harness lines.

As Lynch took in the sight of the captain walking back to the tree with his catch, he burst out laughing. "Where's the old boot, then?" he scoffed quietly.

"Ssshh Lynch!" ordered the colonel, as he reached for the harness. "Here put this on. We'll blow up the bottle when it's in position, as per the drill."

Soon Lynch was in the breathing apparatus, the inflated bottle on his chest. The colonel patted his shoulder. "Good man, Lynch; off you go. Don't forget, take your time, within reason, of course."

Lynch crouched, as the colonel had instructed him during the (to him) hilarious drill they had practiced that morning and ran for the stone edge of the embankment. He lay down, then, with both hands holding onto the sharp angle of the stones, he swung his legs down into the cold water of the Kappel Canal. One by one, he shifted his hands along the coping, away from the linden tree, until he came to the cigarette packet, empty, that Goffin had staked into the grass.

He felt with his left foot, for the upper sill of the tunnel, then having located it by running the instep of his gym shoes along the angle of the stone, he took a deep breath, opened the petcock as far as it would go, with one hand stuck the peg on his nose, grabbed the upper sill, and dived.

As he descended into the water, the cold almost made him expel all his breath, but he remembered what Goffin had told them at the drill. He forced himself to breathe out slowly. He couldn't see a thing. He felt for the slimy sides of the tunnel, his feet, his legs in the fetal position, and touched bottom. He started to crawl. He ran out of breath and remembered to keep his mouth closed as he sucked in through the tube, and to keep moving forward the whole while, slowly. He breathed out again. In again, out, in, out; then the fourth time he breathed in he forgot to keep his mouth closed, and took a mouthful of water. He panicked for a moment, jerking the line. Then he felt a hand grabbing his weight rope, dragging him. The next thing he knew his head was above the surface inside the tunnel. He was kneeling on the bottom of the sewer, and Goffin was grinning at him in the light of his flashlight.

"Hello, mate, welcome to Brighton Beach!" Goffin laughed.

Lynch spluttered for a minute, spitting out the filthy sewer fluid. "Blimey!" he gasped, standing up. "Didn't think I'd—Talk about the bloody tunnel of love!"

"Let's untie you." Goffin said as he undid the knots of the harness. He then took the thin trail line and gave it a hearty jerk. " 'Nother big bloomin' 'addock for you, Captain Van Felt 'er," he shouted.

Even as Goffin shouted, the ridiculous-looking apparatus, as if it were alive, jumped out of his fingers and seemed to drag itself into the sewer water, out of sight.

Goffin turned to Lynch. "Welcome, Mr. Lynch," he intoned in a deep bass voice, "to the 'appy 'unting grounds of the lesser spotted underground Cornish pheasant."

"Yeah, a right bloody underground peasant I am, cock!" replied Lynch, at ease now, even though he was up to his waist in the effluvia of a thousand Amsterdam households. "Cor, get a whiff 'o that!"

Goffin commented, "Salubrious, ain't it?" He felt the leading line jerk in his hands. "Here comes the next one," he shouted. "All aboard for the skylark!" His voice boomed into the dark, dripping roof arch between him and the canal.

The next one through was Mitchell. He, too, splashed and floundered around for a few seconds before he was steadied onto his knees and calmed down under the combined banter of Goffin and Lynch. "Christ," spluttered Mitchell, when he'd recovered his breath, as Goffin removed his harness. "We ain't going back out that way, are we?"

"No, the big white chief's got other plans," pronounced Lynch, darkly.

"Thank Gawd for that," Mitchell gasped as he undid the weight.

"Anyone who breathes more than one breath at a time down here is a greedy bastard," Goffin told Mitchell, who shook his head.

Goffin held the neck line of the hot-water bottle in one finger and thumb, waiting for the line to jerk. With his other hand he held his nose, turning his head away from the outstretched apparatus arm. "Colonel, darling, I never knew you cared!" Then the line jerked and the gear shot away again, out of Goffin's hand.

Lieutenant Dennis was next. He was steady when he emerged from the sewer water. He'd been a first-class blue at Cambridge. "Well done, Goffin," he blurted, when they pulled him up from the water-logged passage.

Above them, as Colonel Canning waited under the linden tree, and Captain Van Velzor, his coat collar turned up, held out his fishing rod, waiting, in the slight rain, for the line to jerk, an air-raid siren suddenly commenced howling. Over to the southeast, the sky was rent with gun flashes and the roar of heavy bombing was loud in the distance.

"Must be the RAF bombing the panzers," Van Velzor suggested in a speaking voice to the colonel behind him.

"Who're you talking to?" demanded a strange voice behind him, in Dutch.

Van Velzor almost jumped into the canal. He turned around, startled, to see a city policeman sitting on his immobile bicycle, one foot on the railing.

His voice switched to Dutch, "Oh, Officer, why, no one. I usually talk to myself when I'm fishing," he explained to the policeman.

"There's an air raid on, haven't you noticed?" the policeman asked.

"I don't think the Germans are out to bomb me, do you?" Van Velzor jested.

The policeman, a man of fifty, pushed his cycle off, shaking his head from side to side, wondering how the Germans would deal with his pension.

Colonel Canning breathed again. He had stood stock-still under the shade of the linden tree, hardly breathing, from the second he had seen the policeman approach, the moment after Dennis had disappeared over the bank. "God," he said to no one in particular as he replaced the Walther in its waterproof pouch.

"Yes, close, wasn't it, sir," Van Velzor agreed, and started reeling in the Costain line again.

Within two minutes, Colonel Canning was searching with his foot for the upper ledge of the tunnel, and Captain Van Velzor, rod under his arm, was heading back for the Alvis.

As the Dutchman crossed the road, he saw the first German tank wheel at almost full speed on its tracks, on the other side of the Canal, opposite the Palace Square. *So they're here*, he thought, and glanced in the direction of Schopenhauer's statue. Then he climbed into the car and waited.

The colonel had more difficulty than the others. The extra weight of two Enfield revolvers and a Walther PPK, wrapped in waterproof canvas, slowed him down. The first words he said, when he'd finished spluttering and spitting were, "Well done Goffin, well done indeed! absolutely top-hole!"

"All in a day's work, sir," replied Goffin. Everyone except the colonel tittered, but it was only Dennis who was amused by Goffin's remark.

They looked around them, keeping their voices low. The noise they made was greatly increased by the echoes. Their voices sounded eerie. They were all on their knees, the water up to mid-chest level. The colonel reached in his pocket and took out a four-inch nail. He delved into his jacket and brought out one of the Enfields, still wrapped in its green waterproof canvas. With the handle of the Enfield revolver he knocked the nail into a space between two of the great granite stone blocks over his head. On this he hung the breathing gear, with its harness ropes, the bicycle pump jammed in, coiled over the top of the bottle. "We'll leave this here," he said. "Doubt if we'll need it again, but one never knows." He looked at Goffin and beamed. "Don't mind if we leave your apparatus here, Goffin? Right, men." The colonel held up a dripping hand. "Now we'll get down to business. This sewer obviously hasn't been sealed off . . . only from the Palace."

Goffin held up one finger.

"Yes, what is it?" The colonel's voice was sepulchral.

"Can I keep my peg, sir?" Lynch and Mitchell burst out laughing, Goffin had one of the pegs on his nose.

The colonel snorted, "God, yes, man. I say, what a topping idea. Lieutenant Dennis, you take the other peg. We'll take turns wearing them!"

For a moment everyone thought the colonel was joking. Then they saw, in the dim glow of the flashlights that the expression on his face was dead serious. Lieutenant Dennis pinched the second green peg over his nose.

The colonel said to Dennis, "Five minutes each man. Troop's peg the red one, right?"

"Nyess, sir, nofficers ngreen peg," Dennis replied.

"Top-hole, I'll lead the way. Dennis, rear guard!" the colonel ordered.

"Nyess, sir."

The party formed up Indian file, all standing on the tunnel bottom, stooped under the low roof. Canning first, then Goffin, with his nose pegged, then Lynch, Mitchell and Dennis, who by this time had removed his nose peg in embarrassment. They moved forward, with the colonel calling out as he felt for obstructions on the slimy bottom of the sewer. "Lump here, some wire, watch the tangles, muddy here, chaps."

The walls of the sewer were dirty green, and they shined glossy in the flashlight glare. The water was almost as thick as soup, a deep brown color, they decided, although by the light of the colonel's torch it was not easy to tell. A steady flow of human excrement, rubbish, and offal slowly drifted past them. As the colonel pushed forward he disturbed the slimy skin on top of the water, and pushed it back in little folds, fish-belly white in 'the glare of the lamp. The scum hovered, thickening, as the colonel waded forward, then it broke and drifted, obscenely, past the four men behind the colonel. Far ahead in the gloom, they saw the wakes of a hundred swimming rats.

As they slowly moved ahead, the tunnel described a gentle curve to the left. They passed many small outlets set in the sides, sometimes dodging forward or holding back to avoid a spurt of water or excrement from the outlets. As they moved inland, the tunnel rose very lightly, and soon the liquid was down to their knees.

At one point Goffin was passing a street sewer outlet when a great gush of liquid hit him, splashing all over his head, and onto Lynch, behind him, who cursed.

Goffin blew out a great breath of tunnel air, and violently shook his head. He stood, dripping sewage. He put both hands on hips. He looked straight at the offending outlet. "Now, now Gertie," he said in an effeminate voice, "I'm only here for the fun!" Everybody laughed, including the colonel.

Canning called, "Watch out for the large one-meter Palace pipe, coming up on that bend. We can't mistake it, there's a manhole entrance practically over the top of it." The colonel's voice sounded as if it were coming from the grave.

"Why didn't we come in through that, sir?" demanded Lynch.

"Because it's directly in front of the main gate," explained Dennis.

Lynch said, "Oh, I see. Wouldn't do to come in there, would it? Disturb their tea break?"

Dennis tapped Mitchell on the back. "How're you feeling, Mitchell?" he asked.

"All right, Lieutenant," Mitchell spoke without turning, as he moved forward behind Lynch. "A bit like old times in the Somme trenches. 'Fact I'm enjoyin' myself. Can't wait to get into the dry though, out of this bloody stinkin' muck."

"Me, too," agreed Dennis.

"Old Goff's all right, ain't you mate?" shouted Lynch, tapping Goffin's shoulder. "Me and Goff's quite at 'ome down here, ain't we?"

"Just like the old 'S' class boats," observed Goffin.

Dennis tapped Mitchell on the shoulder again. "Mitchell, I say, Mitchell," he hissed.

"Sir?"

"Pass the . . . er . . . officers' nose peg on up to the colonel, will you, please?"

Mitchell took the peg from Dennis and passed it to Lynch, who glanced back to see if Dennis were watching. Lynch dipped the peg in the sewer water, rubbing the liquid all over it. "One officers' nose peg coming up for the boss, Goff!" He passed the peg to Goffin, who handed it to the colonel.

Canning took it with a muffled, "Thank you, Goffin, well done!" and stuck the green officers' peg on his nose. "Nthant's nbetter!" he snorted. He set to pressing on again. "Ncome non, nchaps!" Canning slipped on some slime, recovered his balance, "Not nfar nto ngo now!" The colonel shone his torch along the sewer roof and caught sight of the manhole entrance, a dark shadow, only thirty yards ahead. "Nthere nit nis, nchaps! . . . nup nthere!"

All three of the troops cheered, sarcastically.

"Oooh bloomin' ray!" Lynch cried.

"Thank Gawd for that," said Mitchell.

"Nanyone nchecked nthe meter?" snorted Goffin, and all behind him smiled.

"Yes, my turn for the peg, Goff," replied Lynch.

"Goff's turn in the barrel," said Mitchell.

Goffin passed the red peg to Lynch, who fastened it on his nose, winking back at Mitchell, tilting his head at the colonel.

It took them almost an hour to reach the one-meter outlet from the palace. It entered the bigger duct about half-way up the side. It was comparatively dry, with merely a trickle of slowly moving urine sliding down its lower surface. Over the curved surface dozens of spiders scampered away into the dark.

The colonel removed his peg. "Here we are chaps. Right, let's sort the equipment out here." The colonel climbed up into the smaller pipe. He called to Lynch to accompany him. Lynch, too, hopped up. Canning moved forward ten, fifteen yards, counting the outlets in the meter pipe. At last his flashlight shone upwards. There was an iron manhole cover, dry and rusty, covering the concrete opening ascending from the roof. A spider dropped onto his face. He brushed it off, shuddering.

The colonel whispered, "There . . . see it, Lynch?" He stood up in the manhole shaft and tapped the iron cover. His voice boomed down on Lynch. "A foot of concrete over that." He tapped it again, with his mittened hand. "A foot of concrete. Shift that and we're into the storeroom next to the vault."

Lynch was lying along the old main Palace sewer outlet. His head was by Canning's feet. He looked upwards, past the colonel's torso. Lynch nodded. The colonel tapped him, and Lynch moved out of the way, sliding down the pipe, back to the main sewer. The colonel followed quickly and sat on the lip of the Palace sewer, his rear end in an inch of foul liquid.

"Well Lynch, think you can do it?" Canning asked.

"A walkover . . . easy as pie."

"Without making too much disturbance up there? We only need a hole big enough for a man to slide through, at first, eh?"

"No problem, sir, don't you fret."

"Good. We'll divest ourselves of the plastique now, chaps. Lieutenant, go back down the main duct." He felt in his pocket for another four-inch nail that he handed to Dennis. "Knock this in with your side-arm, and hang the three spare belts on it. Mitchell, give your belt to Lieutenant Dennis, please."

Dennis retreated in the direction they had come, the webbing belts draped over his arm.

"As soon as Lynch is ready, we'll rejoin you," the colonel told him.

"Very good, sir," replied Dennis.

Colonel Canning turned to Lynch, "Good, now let's get this thing moving."

"Don't you fret, Colonel," said Lynch. "Move on back down the tunnel please."

"I'd rather wait until . . . " the colonel trailed off.

"Who's doing this tickle, you or . . . me?" Lynch asked. He stood still, looking into the colonel's eyes, a Bakelite box in each hand.

"Oh, all right, Lynch!" The colonel looked at Mitchell and Goffin. "Come on chaps," he told them, "let's move off down the tunnel." He hesitated a second then looked at Lynch again. "Good luck, Lynch, eighteen-inch caliber, right?"

"Right, guv."

The three moved away. Lynch disappeared into the old Palace sewer. Five minutes later he emerged again, humming to himself. Now he had only one plastic box under his arm. With his hands he was carefully feeding back two thin loose wires. Soon he had joined the rest of the party, the long wires trailing behind him in the water.

Silently they watched as Lynch connected the two wires onto two contacts in the plastic box. Then they saw him break the seal off a tiny switch, and they heard the noise . . . BANG! It was sharp and sudden, like a huge firecracker. A great spurt of smoky dust shot out of the Palace sewer.

When the dust had cleared, Colonel Canning jumped up into the Palace sewer and disappeared. He emerged smiling all over his perspiring, filthy face. "Perfect, Lynch . . . absolutely perfect!" he cried. "Top-hole indeed, excellent performance!"

"Quarter of a box, that's all I used," said Lynch modestly.

"We're through, sir?" asked Dennis.

"Good old Banger," Goffin murmured as he patted Lynch's shoulder.

Canning said, "Through, home and dry . . . an eighteen-inch diameter hole, straight into the jolly old storeroom!" He looked at Mitchell, "Now, Mr. Mitchell, let's see what you can do!"

Mitchell rubbed his hands, winked at Goffin, and followed the colonel into the Palace sewer.

Hauptsturmführer Schrenke was elated, but, in the best tradition of the Totenkopf Division, he did not allow it to go to his head for more than a brief moment. He had sent panzer tank TK-Z 043 ahead, over the Kappel Canal bridge fifty minutes before. He had radioed the group commander for permission to occupy the Palace Square. Oberführer Lentz had almost cheered when he had learned of Schrenke's location—that his five tanks and three half-tracks had reached the south bank of the Canal.

"Good, very good, Schrenke. My recommendation to Brigadeführer Becker for your Knight's Cross is already in the works," Lentz had shouted into his radio. "Send one heavy unit across the Palast-platz-brugge, into the middle of the Square, facing the main Palace gate. Then wait for further orders. Tell the tank commander not, repeat not, to open fire unless there are obviously hostile elements over there. Tell him to cover all the approach roads to the Palace entrance. You can follow him when you receive my order, and surround the Palace grounds. *Verstehen?*"

"*Verstehen*, Herr Oberführer!" Schrenke had replied.

"Good—Heil Hitler!"

"Heil Hitler!"

After this exchange Schrenke had given the abrupt order to Untersturmführer Miehl. He was a fellow Nuremburger. Miehl had smiled widely as he heard the shouted command from Schrenke. He had shot his arm out and mouthed the Hitler salute, but it could not, of course, be heard over the roar of the tank engines.

Schrenke had followed closely, through his night glasses, as Miehl's TK-Z 043 had moved off, clanking its way over the bridge, up the slight rise past the grassy knoll with the strange little bandstand. He watched it as Miehl's tank swung into the Palace Square, describing a wide flourish as it came to rest. He saw its turret gun pointed for a minute directly at the shut Palace gates, straight at the wide entrance doorway. Then he observed that Miehl, inside the shut tank, was revolving the turret slowly, round and round, first one way, then the other, threatening, with its 35-m.m. cannon, any possible resistance.

Now, fifty minutes later, Haupsturmführer Schrenke led the rest of the section to join Miehl. He had left one tank and one half-track, with its complement of twelve stormtroopers, to cover the southern approaches to the bridge. The remaining three tanks had now crossed the canal, one at a time, in case the bridge should collapse under the weight of more than twenty-five tons. The three panzers paused at the bottom of the Palace Square slope and waited for the two half-tracks to take up position behind them.

Perched on top of tank TK-Z 041, half out of the turret, Schrenke swept the square with his night binoculars. Nothing moved. He waited, until the first two-man stormtrooper patrols alighted from the rear half-track; then the whole section, at a wave of his hand, roared into life and clanked up the slope. At the first corner of the Palace wall, the second two-man patrol was dropped off quickly. Schrenke watched the evolution through the corner of his eye, as he maintained surveillance of the Palace Square. The three tanks quickly took position by Miehl's, all facing the Palace, Schrenke to one side of Miehl, Berger and Schmidt on the other. When they were in perfect line, Schrenke used hand signs to order the two center tanks to revolve their turrets slowly, while the two outside turrets pointed their guns directly at the main door of the Palace. Then Schrenke reported by radio to his Oberführer, who told him there were three more Iron Crosses in the works, but for the time being to do nothing.

"Stay put, Schrenke. Wait for orders. Make sure the sentries are posted around the walls, of course. I'll be back to you as soon as I know what Divisional Command says," Lentz said.

"Understood sir!" he replied.

"Heil Hitler!"

"Heil Hitler!" When he snapped this out, Schrenke's arm involuntarily started to rise, then it dropped again when it hit the underside of the turret coaming. Schrenke peered through his binoculars at the Palace gatehouse. There was a light on. He could see, through the unshielded windows, four blue uniformed men inside, waiting.

"Message, Haupsturmführer!" A hand tapped his knee. He stretched his hand down inside the turret. The gun layer, Schmelling, handed up the radio telephone.

"TK-Z 041," Schrenke said into the mouthpiece.

"Lentz here, Blue Danube," Lentz gave the night's code words.

"Walkyrie . . . Schrenke."

"Good. Look, contact the Palace guard and order them to light up the Palace. All windows to be illuminated, including the skylights, immediately . . . move on this, it's come directly from the Reichsmarshall. Fat Herman wants a beacon for the Luftwaffe." Lentz's voice was cheerful.

Schrenke repeated the order, then clambered out of the turret. He checked his Mauser, then strolled at a casual walk to the gatehouse. He knocked on the door. "Hello Kamerad!" He heard the shout from inside. The door opened. The four guards stared at him, smiling but nervous. He introduced himself, clicking his heels and bowing slightly. The Dutch guards effusively gave their names, calling him "Captain." He ignored this, excusing their ignorance, and gave them the order to light up the Palace. Two of the surprised Dutchmen eagerly turned tail and ran to the great door of the Palace.

"Captain," the Dutch sergeant said, when the two runners had left.

Schrenke replied "Yes, Sergeant?" The Germans were under orders to be polite to Dutch officials.

"Our chief of the Palace Guard has been on the telephone."

"Where is he?" Schrenke snapped the question at the Dutchman.

"It's Captain Kramp. He's inside the Palace main foyer waiting for you . . . for a ranking German officer, so he can surrender the Palace, officially."

"Tell him to come out to the lefthand tank," he grunted.

"I've already suggested that he come out, but he insists on waiting inside. He's talking about protocol."

"Well," Schrenke smiled at the Dutchman, a fat man of forty or so, obviously trying to be friendly. "You'll have to tell him to wait; we've no orders yet to take over the building."

"Very well, Captain," the Dutchman acquiesced.

"Haupsturmführer!" Schrenke snarled back, quietly, as he turned to leave.

"Certainly, Mynheer . . . Hauptsturmführer," answered the guard, apologetically.

Schrenke returned to his tank. As he clambered up into the turret, he waved and winked at Schmidt, in the righthand tank. Schmidt grinned back, pointing his chin at the Palace, raising his eyebrows, as if asking a question. Schrenke nodded violently, then grinned back at Schmidt, who threw back his head and laughed.

The two stormtroopers waited at attention on the curbside.

"Got your orders correct? Gluckman, Brandt?" Untersturmführer Dorfer, sitting beside the driver of the half-track, glared down at them. The tanks were moving off. Schrenke had told him to keep closed up. *Schrenke can be a bastard*, he remembered.

"Yes, Untersturmführer," Gluckman pulled himself to attention. His machine pistol fell down to his left elbow as he did so. His chubby face reddened. He recovered the pistol shoulder band with his right hand.

"Well, man, repeat the order!" Dorfer shouted, impatiently. *God in heaven . . . these Dresdener fools*! he thought angrily.

"Patrol the western edge of the Palace Square, between the canal and the southwest corner of the Palace grounds wall. Herr Untersturmführer," Gluckman droned. Then he hesitated for a second and went on, "Observe for suspicious activity along the canal bank, both ways. Watch the bridge, and blow the alarm whistle . . . " Gluckman tailed off.

"In the direction of the next patrol, Trooper Gluckman!" shouted Dorfer above the half-track and tank engine noise. "And where will the next patrol be, Trooper Gluckman?"

"At the southwest corner of the Palace wall," the trooper replied.

"Good. You've got it. Your relief is at one o'clock," Dorfer told him.

"Very good, Untersturmführer," said the fat man.

"Heil Hitler!" Dorfer raised his arm, and tapped the driver.

"Heil Hitler!" replied troopers Gluckman and Brandt. They waited, their right arms stretched out, unil the half-track gave a lurch and pulled away. Then the two sentries looked at each other.

Gluckman puckered his lips and raised his eyebrows as he faced Brandt, but Brandt's face was still and firm, under the shadow of his steel helmet. He waited for a command from his elder, Gluckman.

"We'll head this way first," Gluckman said, turning to face the Palace. He started moving at a steady pace. Brandt fell into step. He felt relieved that he was with old Gluckman and so had less responsibility on his shoulders.

Van Velzor hunched down low in the Alvis as he watched the four Nazi tanks, one at a time, cross the bridge. Following them the two half-tracks moved over, slowly, while the tanks waited at the bottom of the slope. Van Velzor stared as the last half-track dropped a two-man patrol on the far side of the park knoll. He watched the tanks move off, followed by the two half-tracks. He gazed at the two-man patrol left behind, as they slowly marched back and forth along the park edge of the Palace Square. They seemed to be talking to one another. There was a fattish man and a thin man. From his movements, Van Velzor guessed that the thin stormtrooper was younger than the fat one. Sitting in the shadow of the Alvis canvas top, the Dutchman eased himself up, as he listened to the roar and clank of the tanks occupying the Palace Square. Then he saw the increasingly brilliant glare in the sky as the Palace lights were switched on, one by one.

"The German tank commander orders that all the Palace lights must go on, with all the curtains and blinds open," the guard spoke to Captain Kramp in an easy tone. Kramp detected in the guard's casualness that his authority was already diminishing. He sat behind the desk, an ornate Louis XVI piece he had, an hour before, ordered to be carried into the entrance hall. He was in full dress uniform, blue with silver facings. He tapped his fingers on the desk for a moment. "Right away?" he asked the guard.

"Immediately, sir," was the guard's reply.

Kramp stood up. "Right; you'd better round up everyone. Leave two men at the gate. The reliefs will be here at midnight. That makes how many?" he asked.

"Eight men and the duty kitchen staff."

"Get them on the job, too—everybody!" Kramp ordered brusquely.

"Yes, sir." The guard saluted and moved off hurriedly, along the carpeted hall. As he passed through the inner double doors, with their glass windows and intricate scrollwork, he switched on the hall chandeliers. There was a brilliant blaze of light, all 300 bulbs cast a bright glare on the carved vaulted ceiling, the delicate tracery of the sixteen delicate columns, the eight old masters' paintings hung under the side alcoves, and on Kramp's face.

Kramp removed his cap. He wiped his bald head with his handkerchief. It was not going to plan, but perhaps it would be even better like this. There would certainly be no mistake by the Germans as to who had received them with all honors. Who had passed over to them the information. Who had told them the strong room combination numbers they would, surely, be so delighted to hear. It was possible, he thought to himself, that they might even install their military governor here. *No reason why not. There's certainly room enough for them.*

He looked at the hall curtains at the sides of the door, and hurried over to open them, his scalp gleaming under the chandeliers. *God,* he frowned as he remembered, *three days in that stuffy storeroom next to the vault.* He tugged at the curtain cord. The curtains opened. Kramp stood in the window, watching the increasing brilliance in the Palace yard. Now the upstairs lights went on one by one. His attention was caught by the two tanks as he could see on the other side of the gate. *The New European Order is with us,* he silently rejoiced. *And I shall be in a position to ensure Holland's place in that Order.*

He walked back to the desk and sat down to wait.

Colonel Canning was the first to pass up through the hole blown in the concrete. Mitchell followed him. It was a tight squeeze. The colonel had been forced to take off his pistol belt from under his boiler suit before he could ascend. Mitchell had handed him up the heavy belt before he joined the colonel. Then Dennis squeezed himself up through the hole, tearing his boiler suit on one of the broken reinforcing rods.

For a moment the filthy black trio, excrement stuck to their gym shoes, stinking of urine, gazed around them.

"Lovely job," exulted the colonel brightly. "Hardly scratched the ceiling. Right men, you remember the form from the rehearsal?"

Dennis and Mitchell nodded.

Dennis felt a tap on his foot. He moved to one side. Lynch clambered out of the hole. "Glad you like it, sir, all part of the Cunard Line service!" Lynch joked, as he placed his short jemmy on the storeroom floor with one hand, and two Bakelite boxes with the other.

The colonel took his Walther from its waterproof holster. He placed it, gleaming blue in the torchlight, on a nearby box. From the bottom of the holster, he took a scrap of paper and unfolded it.

"Mitchell, Dennis; come over into the light a moment will you," Canning ordered. He shone his flashlight on the paper as the trio studied it, heads all bent down together.

Canning spoke, after a minute. "Obviously, we have to secure both the kitchen doors—the one on the north side, and the one on the south. I'll take the north, Dennis take the south, and don't forget the wine cellar door. Might be someone in there."

"Right, sir," mumbled Dennis.

The colonel continued, "Mitchell will wait in the storeroom until we give him the all clear, right, Mitchell?"

"Right," Mitchell murmured as he dried his hands again on a rag he'd found.

"Lynch, Goffin?"

"Goffin's not through yet, sir," Lynch said, bent down over the hole. "Hey, Goff!" he hissed.

"Just dryin' off me hair, darlin'," joked Goffin from below, "Be right with you!"

"He's on his way, Colonel," said Lynch.

"Right," the colonel acknowledged. "You and Goffin widen the hole as far as you can within reason. We need twenty inches diameter." Canning handed Mitchell an Enfield revolver. "Careful, Mitchell, it's loaded," he murmured.

The colonel turned again to Lynch. "You'll have to work fast. With luck it'll be over in half an hour."

"Eight minutes, sir," retorted Mitchell. "Timed it this afternoon at rehearsal."

The colonel grinned. "Got the cord?" he asked Dennis.

"Yes, sir," Dennis brought out two twenty-yard lengths of Costain gunline and handed one to the colonel.

"All set, Mitchell?" the colonel demanded.

"In the slips, sir," Mitchell replied.

"Right. Good hunting all of you chaps. Right, Mitchell. *Open the door!*" The colonel nudged his Walther in the direction of the storeroom door.

Mitchell stuck the Enfield in his side pocket, took a piece of box wire out of his ruler pocket, and knelt down by the door. After a half-minute of fiddling around, there was a click. "Right. She's ready," said Mitchell, as if to himself.

"Good show. Now, after me, Lieutenant Dennis rear guard." The colonel walked over to the door and turned the knob. He and Dennis passed out into the brightly lit corridor. Dennis closed the storeroom door quietly behind him. He turned right, then left, and tied the Costain line silently onto the kitchen door handle. He pulled the line tightly as he crossed the passage and tied it onto the wine cellar door. The colonel did the same thing to the north kitchen door, tying it, as taut as he could, to the door of the men's toilet.

Mitchell did not wait. It would make no difference. He left the storeroom.

While the two officers were securing the four doors in as many minutes, Mitchell had picked the strong room outer wooden door lock. He swung it back on its hinges. Dennis rejoined him. Mitchell stood in front of the great steel strong door for the space of a minute, until the colonel was back in their passage, Walther in hand, pressed against the wall, guarding the north passage. Dennis, seeing the colonel thus, stood against the wall by the side of the storeroom door. He pointed his Enfield in the direction of the south passage.

"Mmm . . ." Mitchell murmured, "Chadburn XE 745 . . . 1908," his voice echoed off the walls of the narrow passageway. "No trouble at all . . . just up my alley . . . must be a twin to the Leadenhall Street job."

"Ssshh!" the colonel hissed. He jerked his Walther toward the end of his section of the corridor. Nobody moved for a minute. They all listened, stock-still. Then from behind the storeroom door came the muffled sound of concrete being chipped to the softly sung tune of "I've been working on the railroad."

The colonel gestured at the storeroom with his Walther. Dennis sprang for the storeroom door. He opened it softly. "Sssh! chaps!" he whispered loudly. The humming ceased.

Mitchell was on his knees before the combination disc. He turned it slowly, this way and that, softly murmuring to himself.

Dennis felt the sweat break out on his brow. His pistol trembled slightly. He pressed his lips together.

The colonel was still as a rock, on the opposite side of the passage.

"Got the bastard," Mitchell exclaimed in a whisper as he stood up. Both the officers heard him distinctly. As they looked around they saw Mitchell grab hold of the great brass handle of the strong room door. He pulled it gently upwards. The door opened. The colonel beamed at Mitchell, who stood there, smiling at Dennis, who grinned at them both.

The colonel tiptoed along the corridor. "Good man," he said quietly to Mitchell, as he passed through the strong room door.

Dennis opened the storeroom door. Both Lynch and Goffin ran out, silently, and into the strong room. They emerged carrying a gray metal box. They rushed, staggering under the weight of the box, back into the storeroom. Mitchell and Dennis carried the second box as far as the storeroom door, then Lynch and Goffin took it over from them. Dennis took up his place again by the wall, as the colonel had taken his.

Mitchell softly closed the outer door. He bent down to lock it with the box wire. He stood, up, flicked the rag at the door, winked at Dennis and strolled into the storeroom. The officers ran softly in their gym shoes and untied all four doors. Dennis was first into the storeroom, poker-faced, the colonel last, breathing heavily.

Mitchell relocked the storeroom door, then stood up. The colonel checked his watch. "Seven and three-quarter minutes, Mitchell," he said. He watched Dennis pass the boxes down to Lynch and Goffin, already waiting below in the sewer. "Went like clockwork—just like the rehearsal, really top-hole."

"Message sir," Schmelling called and passed the radio telephone handpiece to Hauptsturmführer Schrenke.

"Schrenke here."

"Lentz, Blue Danube," the radio squawked. It was Totenkopf Division Hq.

"Walkyrie," Schrenke replied.

"Listen Schrenke. Order's come through from Brigadeführer Becker himself." Lentz sounded as if he were trying to keep the excitement in his voice down. "You are to send one heavy panzer into the Palace grounds. It is to be placed just inside the main gate, with its attack piece directed out towards the Palace Square. Is that clear?"

"Understood, Oberführer," said Schrenke. Had he been on the ground, he would have clicked his heels.

"Good. Take immediate action. Heil Hitler!"

"Heil Hitler," Schrenke pushed the telephone handpiece down onto the top of Schmelling's head. *Now* he thought, *A moment in history*. A scene flashed through his head as he gave the orders to the driver. He saw himself, as an old man, on the family estate in . . . France? Ukraine? With a dozen little children, all good Aryan stock, standing, gazing adoringly at him, Gauleiter Ritter Von Schrenke, as he told them, in his kindly old voice, how he had once captured the Palace of a queen. TK-Z 401 started to move forward, toward the Palace gate. The two guards at the gate watched for a moment as the panzer approached, then, both heaving at one ornately wrought iron frame, they pushed the gates open.

Down in the main duct now, the Orange team, up to their thighs in sewer water, started to carry the heavy boxes 200 yards, towards the sealed manhole cover, near the duct outlet. The boxes were known to be absolutely watertight, so the men rested them now and again on the sewer bottom.

Dennis and Goffin were in the lead, with the first box. Lynch and Mitchell followed. The colonel trailed behind, looking backward, holding his Walther clear of the water.

The colonel waited. He heard something. There was now silence between the men. He stood, for a moment, then heard it again. The men were a good fifty yards down the main duct. He waited. He heard a rumbling. Something plopped down from the gatehouse manhole cover shaft. *"God . . . they're opening it!"* he said, almost aloud. He moved back, toward the manhole shaft. He aimed his Walther directly at the shaft. He waded closer, stepping up his forward motion. He reached the manhole shaft and looked up. There was a shower of dust falling, and he closed his eyes.

The five-ton block of granite that fell onto Colonel Canning killed him instantly, squashing his body flat on the floor of the sewer.

The Dutch Army working party that uncovered him two weeks later found the green peg three meters away. They thought it had come from a house drain and threw it away.

Chapter 7

*　　*

Run, Rabbit, Run

13th–14th May, 1940

Run rabbit, run rabbit, run, run, run.
Don't give the farmer his fun, fun, fun.
He'll get by without his rabbit pie,
So run rabbit, run rabbit, run, run, run.

Chorus, British Pop Song, 1939–40
from Musical *The Little Dog Laughed*, 1939
Words by Noel Gay and Ralph Butler; music by Noel Gay

7.

"Run, Rabbit, Run"

13th May, 1940. 11:50 P.M.
The Royal Palace Square, Amsterdam

Hauptsturmführer Schrenke stood as high as he might in the turret hatch. The Dutch Palace guards saluted as Panzer tank TK-Z 401 trundled noisily past them. Schrenke returned their courtesy with a Nazi salute.

Schrenke had not felt so pleased with himself, nor as proud, since the Führer, the physical, spiritual embodiment of the German nation, had paused, for three celestial seconds, to inquire his name, at the Nuremburg Party Rally in 1934. True, Schrenke remembered, his sixteen-year-old voice had failed him when he tried to reply. Nothing had come out. The Party leaders surrounding the Führer had all smirked at his awkwardness. Schrenke gazed at the great Palace ahead of him. *Let them smirk now*, he reflected.

TK-Z 401, as Schrenke had ordered, passed close by the right-hand gatehouse. Making a wide sweeping turn, Schrenke's tank passed arrogantly only a yard away from the bottom step of the wide stone stairway that led up to the main Palace door. TK-Z 401 ground on its way, roaring, tearing up the gravel of the driveway. It kept turning, right, and headed back towards the gateway. Then the driver skillfully steered a little left, the right track spun for two seconds, and the tank was again facing the gate, but from inside the Palace grounds.

There was a moment's hesitation as the driver revved the twelve-cylinder Mercedes engine. Hauptsturmführer Schrenke was now, he thought sternly, in possession of the Palace of the Royal House of Orange and Nassau. The tank lurched forward to take up the position ordered between the gateposts.

Suddenly, the tank's rear end dropped into the ground. The tank lurched. The forward end flew upwards into an angle of fifty degrees from the vertical, and Schrenke was flung backwards from the turret hatch. He just managed to save himself from falling off the tank by grabbing the radio aerial with one hand and the hatch lid with the other. Then the aerial broke off, and Schrenke, for two seconds, hung in space, holding the lid. The tank engine slowed down, then stopped.

Recovering his wits, Schrenke jumped to the ground. He surveyed the scene for a moment, cursing. Then he heard muffled shouting from inside the tank. He swiftly realized what had happened and scrambled back onto the turret.

Looking down inside the tank, Schrenke saw that Schmelling's head had been thrown backward. It had hit the rear of the inner turret track. Schmelling was unconscious. The Hauptsturmführer quickly gazed around him, saw that there was no smoke, no flames, and that six men of the other tank crews were running over to assist. Schrenke reached inside the turret. He started to try to drag Schmelling out. "Pull his legs out straight, first, man!" he shouted to the driver and ammunition passer.

It was hopeless, Schrenke decided. He turned and shouted to Schmidt, who was the first to arrive from the other tanks. "Go inside. Get some brandy, smelling salts! Schmelling has been injured; we can't get him out!"

Schmidt turned and ran to the gatehouse. There was no brandy or smelling salts there. The guard and Schmidt, both together, headed for the main door of the Palace at a fast run.

Schrenke thought fast. "You!" he ordered Berger, his second-in-command, "Don't stand there shaking, *Dummkopf*! Get your tank in here and hook your damn towing cable onto this one!"

Berger raised his arm. "Heil Hitler!" he shouted and ran off.

"And be quick about it Berger, or I'll have your damned stripes, you *Scheissenkopf*!"

Schrenke, still shaken, paced up and down beside the capsized tank. He heard Berger's tank start to move. He glared at it. He beckoned it on, towards him, violently, stamping one jackboot on the gravel.

Schmidt returned breathlessly with a bottle in his hand. He stood trembling in front of Schrenke. They had been guards together at Buchenwald.

"Pass it inside, you idiot!" Schrenke bawled at Schmidt, who had jumped at the first word and was even now handing the bottle into the turret. There was a sound of tinkling glass. Schmidt turned and looked fearfully down at Schrenke.

"It's broken . . . Hauptsturmführer!" Schmidt stuttered.

Schrenke, feet planted apart, hands on hips, one fumbling for his holster, screamed, "Get another one, you *Scheissehund*!"

Schmidt stumbled down off the tank and fell flat on his face. Schrenke kicked him, hard. "Be back in one minute, or I'll stand you up against that *gott-verdammte* wall and shoot you! . . . MYSELF!"

Schmidt scrambled up, rubbing his grazed hands on the sides of his trousers. "Hauptsturmführer!" he whined, quietly, and took off at a run.

Schrenke yelled after him. "Schmidt!"

"Hauptsturmführer!" Schmidt halted and turned to look at Schrenke.

"Give me your pistol."

Schmidt ran back, unbuckling his holster belt. He offered the belt to Schrenke, who was, by this time, pointing his own gun at him.

"Drop it there, you swine," Schrenke ordered. The pistol clattered to the ground. Schrenke pointed his pistol toward the Palace door. "Now, if you value your life, Schmidt . . . get!"

Even as Schrenke said this, Berger's tank rumbled through the gates. It stopped ten feet away from Schrenke's capsized panzer. The sight calmed Schrenke down. He was cheered to see Berger's crew jump out with alacrity and start to secure their towing cable on his tank.

As the roof of the tunnel collapsed around the manhole, the two box-carrying pairs both dropped their loads into the sewage. They cowered, crouching beside the wall of the sewer, holding their arms over their heads.

Suddenly all was quiet again. Dennis was the first to shine his flash lamp up the duct. "Oh bloody hell!" he murmured. Then he started to wade back quickly, splashing, calling for the colonel. The other three splashed after him.

They were silent, except for plaintive calls of "Colonel Canning!" from Dennis. They came to the fallen roof blocks. Dennis scrambled over the top of them, to look for the colonel on the other side of the jumbled heap.

Mitchell was the first one to see it.

"The bastard . . . look lads," he pointed up at the roof. There, poking through the roof, was the rear end of one side of a tank. They could see slivers of light from the brightly lit courtyard. They stared at it for a moment or so. Lynch moved to search around the bottom of the piled blocks of granite. Goffin cleared some of the smaller blocks from the top of the pile, uncovering stencilled printing on the tank body, above the track treads.

"He's down here," they heard Lynch say, quietly.

"Alive?" Dennis asked, almost sobbing. He had climbed back between the rear of the tank and the side of the sewer.

" 'Fraid not, sir. He's . . . crushed . . . flat as a pancake," Lynch replied.

There was silence for a moment; then they heard plainly someone cursing in German. "*Dummkopf!* . . . *Scheissenkopf!*"

Goffin stared at the tank track. "Fucking Nazi bastards."

Mitchell grabbed Goffin, and drew him down the rock pile. "Steady on, Jack," he said to the seaman, quietly.

"See if you can find anything down there, Lynch," Dennis ordered. "I've got to think a minute."

Goffin exploded. "Think . . . think? Look there's a bleedin' Jerry tank there, and the colonel's as dead as a bloody dodo. Let's get out of here," his voice dropped; then he said, "sir."

"Nothing down here." Lynch sloshed about, his hands in the sewer water around the five-ton block of stone sitting on the colonel's body. Then he stood up. All four men looked at one another in a short silence, broken by Goffin. "Bloody barsterds!" he muttered, glowering at the tank track. "Bleedin' fuck-pigs."

"Let's move out, men," exhorted Dennis, clambering down to water level.

Lynch exploded, "Move out, bollox! What about another bloody bang, eh?" He caught hold of Dennis' boiler suit, his teeth bared, as he glowered up at the tank track. "Let's kill the bleeders! Kill them, *sir*!" Lynch's face was twisted into homicidal fury.

"We'll need all the plastique for the manhole cover. There's fifty tons of stone over it," Dennis retorted.

"I still got three-quarters of the first box left. Look," Lynch pleaded as he drew from his boiler suit pocket a cellophane bag, tightly closed, his hands trembling. "Look at it . . . loverly grub . . . kill the bastards!" His eyes bulged, his lips trembled, frothing, as he glared at Dennis.

Mitchell exclaimed loudly, "Best bleedin' idea I've heard yet."

Goffin slapped Lynch's back. "Good old Banger!" he said enthusiastically.

Dennis pulled his face into a grimace. "I don't know. Are you sure you'll have enough explosive for the other end?"

"Listen mate," Lynch was shaking with excitement. "I've got enough explosive down here to blow up London soddin' Bridge!"

"It's too dangerous. We'll be right in the middle."

"Keep yer bloody 'ead down, you'll be all right," Lynch grunted.

Mitchell started off down the duct, taking Goffin by the sleeve. As he waded away he shouted, "Right, Lynchey boy. Set this end up. Dennis will run your wire as far this way as he can. Then you come on and set up the manhole end. Goff'll run the wires back for you. Then we meet in the middle and blow the bleedin' lot up. Right, mate?"

"Bloody all right, we'll kill 'em . . . blow 'em to smithereens!" asserted Lynch. He was already climbing up to the tank. "Let's have them wires out, Denny, mate. String 'em out as you walk up the sewer. Take it easy, don't pull 'em too 'ard."

Dennis took the proffered wires. They were almost too thin to see. He started to slosh backwards, down the tunnel.

Within ten minutes they had both ends of both wires running from the explosive charges, one on the tank and one on the gazebo manhole cover. The wires were not quite long enough to meet in the middle of the distance between the two targets. Dennis was in control of the tank charge, Mitchell at his side, while ten yards away Lynch held the gazebo charge switch box, with Goffin standing by.

"All set here Mitch," shouted Lynch.

"Don't fire until you've counted to thirty after our tickle . . . like I said, we wants a diversion, right?" Mitchell called as he and Dennis crouched, heads together.

"Spot on, Mitchy boy," called Lynch. "Keep your heads between your knees!"

"Okay . . . 'ere goes, this is for the colonel," Mitchell stared at the collapsed stones. "For a decent old stick," he said quietly, as he released the switch.

This chap Brandt is a clod, brooded Trooper Gluckman, as they strolled together on the downhill part of their patrol. *Not a Dresdener nor a schoolteacher. A Wurtemburger, so not too bright*. Gluckman decided he wanted to urinate. He was also curious about the little bandstand up there on top of the grass knoll. It would be quite dark enough up there, he thought, *and I can kill two birds with one stone. Find out who the statue is erected to and relieve myself*. Gluckman turned his big bulk in the direction of the knoll, and stepped his heavy feet, in their field boots, onto the grass. "Just going up there a minute, Brandt," he said to the young potato-faced blond peasant at his side.

"But where are you going, Trooper Gluckman?" Brandt asked.

"I need to relieve myself," Gluckman muttered, embarrassed.

"But the Untersturmführer . . . it's against orders. If he comes by, we'll be in the *Scheisse*," complained Brandt.

Gluckman hesitated for a minute. *Damned orders!* Then he said to Brandt, "Oh, all right, then. Come up with me. You can stand in the shadow of the bandstand—the gazebo, and keep an eye out for me."

"Of course, Gluckman, my friend," said the Wurtemburger.

The two men plodded up the slight grassy rise, side by side. Gluckman felt a little ridiculous in his coal-scuttle *Stahlhelm*. *My friend . . . damned impudence*! he thought.

As they reached the mid-point between the sidewalk and the statue, they were startled by a series of tremendous explosions over by the Palace. They stared at the sky. They couldn't see the Palace, of course, because of the intervening houses, but they could see a great ball of scarlet and gold fire shoot up into the sky, then another explosion, and another, in quick succession, then one more. They stared for two seconds, speechless, then Brandt was the first to say anything. *"Verdammte* RAF."

Gluckman felt a trickle running down his left leg. *Gott* . . . He cursed to himself and, fumbling with his fly, he turned to urinate on the base of the small statue.

The tank charge exploded directly under Schrenke's tank's gasoline. The now-conscious Schmelling, clumsily, dizzily, was clambering out of the turret hatch. Within one-hundredth of a second after Mitchell pulled the switch, he was burnt to a cinder below the waist, along with two other men trapped behind him. Schrenke, who had been angrily dragging Schmelling out of the tank, was bodily shot, still conscious, eighty feet into the luridly lit night sky. He described a gently curving arc as he flew through the sky for five seconds. He saw the brightly lit conservatory Palace roof rise to meet him. He hit the closely criss-crossed iron pane frames. He dangled, face down on top of the iron girders, minus a foot, with all his ribs and his pelvis broken, for what seemed an eternity. Finally, Hauptsturmführer Schrenke grew tired of watching his own blood dripping into the rising sea of flame below. His last thoughts were that Fat Herman now had the beacon for his fly boys, and that, at last, he had received his Knight's Cross of the Iron Cross.

Captain Kramp, sitting at the Louis XVI desk in the Palace foyer almost jumped out of his skin at the first blast. He ascended from his chair, involuntarily, just high enough for a three-foot-square chunk of ⅛-inch plate glass, whizzing horizontally at supersonic speed across the foyer, to encounter his throat. His eyes bulged as, for less than a-third-of-a-second, he saw his dark, almost purple, blood spurt out in a wide warm spray over the glass, which had been stopped dead in its track by his upper spine.

Immediately after Schrenke's fuel ignited, all his tank's ammunition exploded. Fifty rounds of high-penetration armor-piercing shells, liberated violently from their casings, shot out of the panzer at the same time. Some passed through Berger's tank. Some passed through both gatehouses, and some flew through the front wall of the Palace, to thud against the steel casings of the outside Panzers or to pulverize nearby buildings.

They were immediately followed by a thousand rounds of general issue and incendiary bullets. Some of these, in their swift passage from the disintegrating TK-Z 041, annihilated ten of Kramp's relief guard, who were drawn up at attention between the gateposts, the two guards about to be relieved, and their inspecting sergeant. They also either killed or severely wounded six German tank men and four Dutch guards who were assisting in the towing operation. The wounded did not have long to wait.

The shells that passed into Berger's tank at the same time that the first fireball rolled over it, put into progress a chain effect. First one of the shells carried away Berger's driver's head. Other rounds ricochetted around Berger's tank for a split second. Berger's fuel whoofed. Berger's ammunition exploded.

Three of Berger's armor-piercing shells passed through Schmidt's tank, exploding its fuel en route. Schmidt's crew fried half a second after Mitchell pulled the switch. Their commander, sixty yards away, saw nothing of this. He was waiting at the top of the Palace kitchen stairs, for the wine steward to fetch him a bottle of brandy. He was killed by an incendiary bullet that penetrated his skull at about the same time that his men sizzled and disintegrated. Two more of Berger's armor-piercing shells sliced into Miehl's panzer. The fuel explosion in Miehl's tank lifted its turret bodily and threw it over the outside Palace wall. The ton of turret landed on top of the already wholly scorched, but still conscious, gateguard who had run so willingly with Schmidt for brandy.

As Miehl's fireball fell back onto the Palace Square, it roasted alive the eight remaining occupants of Untersturmführer Dorfer's halftrack, which exploded.

To the human senses, all five vehicles would have appeared to have exploded simultaneously.

The armor-piercing shells from the two panzers out on the Square, Miehl's and Schmidt's, mostly found their mark within the Palace. The 2,000 or so bullets that followed the shells scattered through every room in the front section of the Palace, turning them into roaring infernos of flame.

Ten seconds after Mitchell pulled the switch on the little black Bakelite box, there were no sounds within a radius of eighty yards from the site where Schrenke's tank had exploded; no sounds but the echo of the roar of the four collapsing fireballs, the crash of bodies and bits of heavy metal as they fell out of the fire-raging sky, and the low sobbing screams and pleadings of the dying, those who, under their shiny black scorched skins were still alive enough to be conscious of pain. They were conscious of nothing else, only pain; nothing else at all.

There was a ghastly pause of thirty seconds after the the first searing blinding burst of the inferno. Then another ear-shattering report blasted the already glowing hot night sky asunder. By that time, very few souls within the Palace or its grounds, or in the wide Square before the Palace, heard it; and those that did hear it did not care.

Trooper Gluckman peered at the inscription under the statue and decided to change his angle of aim. In the glare of the bombing glow he read, *Arthur Schopenhauer*.

There was more inscribed writing under the name, but ex-schoolmaster Gluckman did not read it. He was too preoccupied recalling his favorite Schopenhauer quotation. It was, he remembered, the one he used to intone sonorously and ponderously to the boys he caught making too much of a commotion in the school classrooms and corridors. He was accustomed to twisting the boys' ears and, as they squirmed in pain, reciting: *The amount of noise which anyone can bear undisturbed stands in direct inverse proportion to his mental capacity, and may, therefore, be regarded as a pretty fair measure of it.* Gluckman tucked away his (he feared, rather small) member. As he buttoned his fly, he completed the quotation to himself, *Noise is a torture to all intellectual people.*

Gluckman turned to repeat the quote aloud to his peasant companion, Trooper Brandt, just as the gazebo, fifteen tons of good Limburg granite, the statue of Schopenhauer, the thin Wurtemburger, *and* Gluckman disintegrated.

The ex-schoolteacher from Dresden felt no torture. There was no time for his intellect to be disturbed, no time at all.

Van Velzor, his head almost sunk below the top edge of the Alvis' front door, stared in hypnotic fascination. First he gazed in apprehension at the approach of the two soldiers, then he spun his head at the sky over the Palace. Four, almost instantaneous fireballs shot up a hundred feet, then collapsed. He focused his horrified eyes back on the two German sentries on the knoll one second before the gazebo, with a bone-jarring roar, disappeared. Van Velzor's eyes had shut and his head had sunk onto his knees involuntarily at the ear-blasting report from the direction of the gazebo.

The Dutchman looked up again. There was simply nothing on top of the grassy knoll; nothing but a gaping crater. He groggily groped for the rope at his feet, fumbled with the car door, opened it, and staggered towards the now subsiding clouds of smoke and granite dust.

South of the Kappel Canal, in tree-lined Boweriestraat, Panzer Tank TK-Z 405 sat in the middle of the street, its gun turret pointed towards the Palaas-plaas-bridge. Obersturmführer Hoffner stood high in the turret, searching the night scene to the north.

Hoffner was an Austrian, from Vienna. He had joyfully joined the Hitler Youth back in 1934, at the age of sixteen, with the enthusiastic approval of his family. His father had been, until the Anchsluss, a cement salesman for a Jewish concern. Hoffner Junior was weaned on the bitter curses of his father's frustration. For Hoffner Senior to traipse the streets of Vienna trying to sell cement owned by Jews to workers' cooperatives whose purchasing commissions were controlled by Jews was bitter fruit indeed to the taste of ex-Cavalry-Sergeant-Major Hoffner. Like most of the Totenkopf Division, Hoffner had served his apprenticeship as a concentration camp guard—in his case at Dachau for eighteen months.

Now, the Obersturmführer reflected, with satisfaction, *this is all changed. Now they'll see who owns and buys the cement and who slugs away pouring the damned stuff*. He saw, enviously, Schrenke's tank enter the Palace gates. He thought, *Lucky stiff, that damned Schrenke, only three months older than I, and a Hauptsturmführer already, with control of the whole section*. Hoffner shifted his gaze down closer to the canal. He saw two sentries pacing down the slope. *Schrenke's efficient, though . . . got everything covered*. Even as this thought passed through his head, the sky over the Palace erupted. He dropped his night glasses and holding the turret rim tightly, gazed horrified at the fireballs exploding in the sky.

Hoffner kicked his gun layer below the turret. "Get the Group!" he screamed. He felt the gun layer radio operator's elbow moving against his knee as the radio was switched on.

"Walkyrie here, Hoffner . . . Walkyrie here; red alarm, red alarm!"

"Lentz here," came the reply, steady and calm, "Blue Danube."

"The Palace is being bombed!" shouted Hoffner.

"Impossible; the city's been declared open!" replied Lentz.

"But it is, Oberführer, or it could be mines!"

"Steady Hoffner. Where are you now?"

"Boweriestraat, a hundred meters south of the Palace Bridge."

"How many units?"

"One panzer, one half-track," Hoffner recited, automatically.

"Wait a minute. Do nothing, wait."

Hoffner waited. He stared through his binoculars, over to the north. He beheld, fascinated, the black blobs of metal and masonry, bodies and limbs, flying through the blood-red sky.

"Lentz here," he heard the quaking voice even as the top of the knoll, on the other side of the bridge, exploded.

"It's . . . mined . . . all over the place, Lentz. There's another one gone up."

"Obersturmführer Hoffner, get a goddamned hold on yourself!" shouted Lentz. "Here are your orders! Are you ready?"

"Yes sir!" Hoffner muttered, his hands shaking with excitement.

"Good. Leave your half-track to guard the southern side of the canal and move your tank right onto the bridge. Immediately. Hold the bridge. Do you hear me? Hold the bridge at all costs!"

"Yes, sir. At all costs hold the bridge," Hoffner repeated the order.

"Correct. Execute the order. Heil Hitler!" Lentz bawled.

"Heil Hitler!" cried Hoffner. He crouched into the turret to shout his orders to his crew.

On the north side of the Kappel Canal the two dark gray Volkswagens rattled east along Schliegerstraat and stopped at No. 69. The window of the Three Horses bar was dark. Ludwig clambered out of the first car, casually. He stretched himself for a moment. He felt for the Mauser in his black leather overcoat pocket. As his two companions disgorged out of the back of the Volkswagen, he held his hand, palm outwards, over his mouth for a second to signify silence. The three men in the second car were disembarking.

He stood to one side of the street door beside the bar entrance. He gestured to the big man at his side. "Ready Hartmann?" he murmured. He turned to the smaller man, who was holding a Schmeisser submachine gun at his side. "Zeigler?" he whispered. The small man nodded.

"Now!" Ludwig grunted. He slapped Hartmann's shoulder. Hartmann raised a boot and kicked the door. It sprang open at the same time that the whole sky to the east burst into flames. Ludwig looked over his shoulder toward the source of the tremendous explosion.

Hartmann had charged through the door. He was now at the bottom of the stairs aiming his Mauser up into the darkness. Zeigler also stared at the sky in the east, over Ludwig's shoulder.

"Goddamned Luftwaffe!" Ludwig cursed.

"Could be the RAF, Captain," said Zeigler.

Ludwig grabbed hold of Zeigler and pushed him into the door. Ludwig followed. They had just smashed in the stairtop door, Hartmann falling face down into the room, when they heard the dull thud of another explosion. Zeigler rushed over Hartmann's prone body and kicked open the inner door. Ludwig stood at the head of the stairway, waiting.

"The bastards have scrammed, sir," Zeigler called.

"Son-of-a-bitch," muttered Hartmann as he recovered his feet.

Ludwig strolled into the room, his emaciated face strained. He planted his feet slightly apart, looked around and ordered, "Right . . . all right. Open all the closets and drawers, carefully, look for any wiring, and bring all the contents out here, into the middle of the floor."

Petty Officer Hartmann and Leading Seaman Zeigler, of the Deutscher Kriegsmarine Friesland-Section Intelligence Unit of the Abwehr moved to do as they were bid.

Kapitan-Corvetten Wolfgang Ludwig stared, for a moment, at the tea urn standing by the service hatch. He lifted the lid and sniffed. "Earl Grey Breakfast," he said aloud to himself. He smirked, replaced the lid, and waited to see what his companions would discover.

Downstairs, Unterleutnant Martin Fliescher and his two men, also of the Abwehr, had the bar owner and his wife already in handcuffs. They, too, were busy, emptying every cupboard, drawer, closet and laundry bag in the house and throwing the contents on the floors.

The blast of searing hot air rushing through the tunnel knocked Mitchell and Dennis down into the liquid slime. Goffin was holding tightly onto Lynch as the heat whooshed over them, pushing him hard against the sewer side. Lynch was holding his switch box tightly against his chest, when the first explosion almost shattered his ear-drums. There was a split-second pause, then the whole of the tunnel for thirty yards either side of the spot where Schrenke's tank had capsized, collapsed in a deafening roar. Hot air whooshed in the section where Mitchell and Dennis were coughing and spluttering on their hands and knees in the sewer muck, and where Lynch gasped out to Goffin, who was writhing his face at the pain in his left ear, "Darling, I never knew you cared!"

Goffin stood back, half-crying, half-laughing as Lynch counted. "Cowson ten . . . and bastard eleven . . . and shit-face twelve . . . "

Mitchell and Dennis now staggered, dragging their box, to join the other pair, "Bleedin' eighteen . . . and poxed-up nineteen . . . " They crowded around Lynch, all the four bodies pressed together, "And soddin' twenty-eight . . . and bloody twenty-nine . . . and . . . " Lynch hesitated, leering through the filth and sweat on his face. "There you are, my love, another one of Doctor Lynch's Little Liver Pills." He lowered his head down between his knees, gritted his teeth and released the switch. The Walther Lynch had stolen from Colonel Canning's corpse, which he had hidden, belted, under his boiler suit, gouged his stomach.

The backfire, from the detonation that sent troopers Gluckman and Brandt into kingdom come, threw all four of them into the slime. The tunnel between the gazebo manhole shaft and the canal outlet crashed down. The temperature in the tunnel rose another twenty degrees. The air was thick with evaporated sewer water and disintegrated granite, and as the four men, spluttering, staggering, dragged the two boxes toward the manhole shaft, a cold blast of air swept over them. Ten feet before the spot where the manhole should have been, there was only the night sky glowing a dull red, and Van Velzor's face staring down at them in awe.

"Chuck us the bloody line!" Goffin was the first to recover his voice. The Dutchman hurriedly threw down one end of his twenty-foot manila rope. Goffin bent over, delved for the rope in the sewer and lashed it around the first box. Goffin then grabbed hold of Lynch and pushed him toward the crater side. "Up first, give 'im a 'and!" he ordered. Lynch scrambled up, dripping slime onto Goffin. Wordlessly, he hauled on the rope with the Dutchman. By this time Mitchell, too, had scrambled out of the hole, helped by Lieutenant Dennis.

Dennis dragged the second box over to Goffin and waited.

As the first box reached ground level, Lynch and Mitchell picked it up and hefted it, in a crouching stagger, down the slope and into the Alvis. There they slumped down on the back seat.

Goffin shoved Dennis up the hole, lashed the second box and followed it to ground level. As soon as the box was on the ground, Van Velzor grabbed one handle, Dennis the other, and they too, followed by Goffin, rushed, heads down, for the car.

By the time they reached the Alvis, Lynch was in the driver's seat with the motor running. As soon as the second box, dripping sewage, was on the floor of the Alvis he declutched. The car shot away. Van Velzor jumped into the front passenger seat. Dennis was half-way into the rear compartment, Goffin was hanging on for his life, crouched on the running board, when the car had accelerated to forty miles an hour. As Lynch took the right-hand turn onto Kappelstraat, Goffin threw himself head-first over the rear door and landed in a heap on top of the boxes. "Jesus Christ, Banger!" he screamed.

Both Mitchell and Dennis grabbed Goffin and pulled him prone onto their knees, rolling him over so his face was upturned.

As the Alvis reached the north end of the Palace Bridge on the corner of Kappelstraat and the Palace Square, its speedometer indicated eighty-five miles an hour, but no one was watching it.

Van Velzor hung onto his seat beside Lynch, directing him with his left hand. Goffin had managed to swing himself so that he was sitting now in the middle of the rear passenger seat. Mitchell was on Goffin's right, trying to take in the chaotic scene around the Palace gates. Dennis was staring over the canal bridge, where he imagined he could see a tank moving toward the bridge. Lynch, shoulders hunched, grasped the steering wheel at the "ten to two" position, a maniacal grin on his face, as he gritted his teeth and swung the Alvis half right. By the time they reached the little square of flower beds in the middle of Palace Square, they were doing eighty miles an hour. All they felt, as the tires hit the flower-bed curb and rolled over the beds, were a couple of slight bumps.

Lynch missed William of Orange's statue, at the center of the flower beds, by inches. He eased the car down to sixty miles an hour as they approached Schliegerstraat, on the northwest corner of Palace Square. By the time the entrance to Schliegerstraat had been reached, he was down to forty.

The Alvis shot into the street. Both Van Velzor and Lynch, at the same time, sighted the Volkswagens parked outside the Three Horses. For a hundredth of a second they thought there was only one. Then they saw the other car.

"Germans!" gasped the Dutchman.

"Rozzers . . . fuck!" Lynch murmured. "Rammin' . . . 'old onto your 'ats boys!" Lynch hunched down further. "Swipin'!" he shouted.

The rear-left mudguard of the Alvis caught the right front mudguard of Captain Ludwig's Volkswagen such a blow that the squashed mudguard tore into the front tire and pushed the right front wheel over so hard that the steering rod parted from the axle. The first Volkswagen rammed into the second, its front end caved in. The rebound of the second Volkswagen hurled Unterleutnant Fleischer against the bar front wall, leaving him a burden on the German state for the next few years.

The Alvis, all three tons of it, felt only a slight shudder. As Lynch picked up speed again, Dennis, who was hanging out of the left rear, glanced back. He saw and heard three pistol shots from the windows above the Three Horses bar. As they reached the first turning off Schliegerstraat and swung left on two wheels, Dennis saw the rapid flashes of submachine gun fire. By the time they hit Kappelstraat again, the car was doing sixty miles an hour. Everyone in the Alvis cursed as Lynch took the corner, ramming over the wide offside pavement, missing the canal embankment railings by two inches. The car in five diminishing jolts steadied itself. It roared away, along the side of the canal, as both Dennis and Goffin looked through the canvas top rear window. They both saw and heard the bark of the tank gun, coming from the Palace bridge.

"Christ, now we're in for it," cried Goffin, "they got the bloody artillery on the job."

"Sod 'em!" shouted Lynch and increased speed to eighty-five miles an hour. "Sod'em . . . kill 'em . . . *kill* 'em all!"

Kapitan Ludwig didn't smoke. He passed the carton of Senior Service cigarettes to Hartmann. "You want these P.O.?" he asked.

Hartmann clicked his heels "Thank you, sir," he said. He passed the package to Zeigler. "Put it on the shelf over there, by the door," he told the leading seaman. Zeigler laid his schmeisser down and did as the P.O. ordered.

Ludwig then told Hartmann to take the two packets of Earl Grey tea to the car. "Tell Fleischer to shift his car out of sight, too." He said. "You drive ours. Back them down the street and park in the first turning left. Then get back here, fast."

Hartmann saluted and left the apartment.

Kapitan Ludwig studied the laid out pieces of gear on the floor.

He stood still in his open leather overcoat, and stared down as he considered, *Amateurish crowd. Gray uniforms, incorrect badges, and that damned rifle with the oversized bore. No ammunition, one colonel's uniform, Indian North West Frontier Force, an able seaman's uniform, six pairs of seaboots . . . seaboots?* Ludwig frowned as he asked himself again, *seaboots . . . now what?*

The crashing noise jolted him. Fleischer's scream, from the street, shook him.

Ludwig dashed to the front window. Zeigler was close behind him. "Smash the glass out!" he shouted at Zeigler. The leading seaman raised the butt of his schmeisser and thrust it through the plate glass. He pulled it back, gashing his hand badly, and crashed the gun butt against the latch. The window frames flew open. Ludwig, his Walther already in hand, leaned out and fired. Zeigler crouched low, thrust the gun and his head through the window and, his cut hand bleeding onto the wrecked Volkswagen below, fired a burst after the long black car disappearing around the corner up the street.

"Goddamn it!" cried Ludwig. "Hold your fire. He's gone." He looked down at Zeigler, then at the blood all over the bottom of his leather overcoat. He took his handkerchief out of his jacket pocket and passed it to Zeigler. "Better tie that tight around your wrist," he said. Zeigler nodded and laid his schmeisser down on the floor. Then Hartmann walked into the room, pale and shaken.

"Steady yourself up, Hartmann," ordered Ludwig. "Give Zeigler a hand . . . tie his wrist up." He looked at Zeigler, who was trembling.

After Hartmann had tied up the leading seaman's wrist, he bandaged his hand with a piece of torn bedsheet from the colonel's room. He remembered the cigarettes. He took them down from the shelf. As he was about to open the carton, the captain called him over to the window. Hartmann passed the carton to Zeigler, who grinned in thanks. The P.O. marched over to the window. Zeigler tore open the carton.

BANG!

The bandaged hand was blown straight through the open window.

All three men stared horrified at the bloody stump for half a second, then Zeigler dropped to the floor in a dead faint. Hartmann jumped to the leading seaman's collapsed body. He grabbed the blood-pumping wrist, squeezing it tightly with both hands. The petty officer looked at Ludwig appealingly. The kapitan ran into the bedroom for more strips of bedsheet.

"Not so amateurish, after all, the bastards!" Ludwig shouted as he ran, half-sliding, over Zeigler's blood.

As Panzer tank TK-Z 405 rumbled down to the hump-backed bridge, Obersturmführer Hoffner suddenly caught sight of a black shadow swiftly turning onto the canal embankment, on the far side, to his right. He quickly raised his night glasses. He focused on the dark, gleaming object. As the Alvis passed the other side of the twenty-yard-long humped bridge, it was out of sight for a second. Hoffner raised himself up as high as he could. He saw that it was a long, black car, now speeding at an angle across the Palace Square.

Hoffner watched the Alvis disappear into the comparative gloom in the center of the wide square. He dived down into the turret.

"Main gun loaded?" he shouted to the gun layer.

"*Jawhol*, Obersturmführer," was the muffled reply.

"Radio operator, inform Group that a suspicious car has passed over the square and entered the street on the northwest corner."

Hoffner stretched himself so he was half out of the turret again. "Turret left," he ordered the gunner. The turret turned gently left, so that the gun covered the far canal bank to Hoffner's left.

By now the panzer, its engine stopped, was sitting right on the center of the humped bridge.

In city street fighting with tanks always gain maximum visibility, they had taught him at the panzer school. Hoffner waited, hearing nothing for a few seconds except the faint screams and moans of the dying in the square, and the crackling of the burning Palace. Suddenly, around the first turning of the canal bank he heard car tires screeching.

Hoffner shouted into the mouthpiece of his head phone set, "Left-left-left-fire!" The turret, with its death's-head emblem, moved left.

The gun fired. The gun recoiled. The recoil lurched the tank backward. TK-Z 405 rocked forward on its center of gravity. The bridge collapsed. The panzer, upside down, Hoffner still clinging to the skull-bedecked turret coaming, fell into the Kappel Canal. As the tank capsized, a split second before he hit the water, Hoffner heard the first sound of the *rat-tat-tat* of his half-track's machine gun firing on the late Hauptsturmführer Schrenke's remaining half-track, as the latter clattered its way into the Palace Square over on the northeast side.

Hoffner did not hear the noise as Schrenke's half-track, firing back along the street it had been following, obliterated an Amsterdam city fire brigade engine.

Schrenke's half-track crew, in pure panic, set up a mortar. They started lobbing bombs at the late Obersturmführer Hoffner's half-track and reached it with the fourth bomb.

As the Alvis raced along the whole three-mile length of Kappelstraat, away from the blood-red glare, no one spoke. They had guessed, after the car had torn through the square, that Lynch's Little Liver Pills had caused a great deal of damage. They would never know until years after, from those who survived, that the total toll, as Hoffner's half-track flashed up in the sky behind them, was forty-one German dead and dying, and eighteen crippled for life. There were dozens of Dutch dead, including all but one of Kramp's guards, and almost a hundred Dutch civilians injured and wounded, most of them in houses near the Palace.

They did not realize, either, as they bounced over the approaches to fifteen bridges that led over the canal, that they had annihilated all but one half-track and eight storm troopers of the only Nazi forward unit that had, so far, entered the city, the crack Totenkopf Division's finest men. Nor did they realize that within one hour the beautiful, ancient Royal Palace would be a black smoking shambles.

Of the five people in the car, only two of them half-knew of the true value of the treasure they had looted. Two of the others only thought of getting back safely to England. In the mind of the fifth, as he clamped his teeth and concentrated on the road thirty yards away, a vague plot was already forming: *to get rid of this lot, nick the loot, and 'ave it away on me toes to Spain.*

Even as the phrase flashed through Lynch's mind, he felt Van Velzor tapping his right arm. "Haarlem . . . take the Haarlem turn . . . there . . . " gasped the Dutchman. Mitchell hung onto the roof support, his elbow dripping over the side.

Lynch saw the main road ahead. There was no traffic on it. He thumbed the horn button. "Er . . . oh . . . ah! Er . . . ooh . . . ah!"

Lynch kept his thumb on the mid-wheel button as the Alvis listed over to the right, ten degrees from the vertical. The two tires still on the road surface screeched at eighty-five miles an hour. Lynch grinned. Everyone else relaxed slightly. Ahead of them was a long, straight, flat road with no traffic on either side. They counted four burning plane wrecks on the road to Haarlem.

In the sky to the south of them, a Luftwaffe transport plane exploded, hit by shells. It fell to earth like a comet, fifty men frying as it plunged.

The only moving vehicle they sighted all the way to the Hague, was the Dutch Army Provost Marshall's Citroën, as it patrolled the long lines of army trucks pulled off the road, parked on the verges on both sides, waiting for the result of the surrender negotiations with the Wehrmacht. There were also a few civilian trucks and cars stopped in their flight by the provost marshall. His men had removed the distributor caps from the offending refugees' engines, while the mobile Dutch Army antiaircraft guns fired away, bringing down 40 percent of all Nazi dive bombers and transports over the land their people had wrought from the sea.

The provost marshall did not even try to stop the Alvis. He merely sat in his car and gaped as the long, black and gleaming silver chassis ripped past at eighty-five miles per hour. He caught only a blurred glimpse of the occupants. The speeding driver was hardly visible above the wheel. The rest were dark, mysterious forms. As the car flashed by, the provost marshall saw something from the car splatter on the road. "It's leaking. Go and see if it's water or oil," he said quietly to his sergeant.

The sergeant alighted, walked over to the long streak of discharge and tested it with his finger. He put his finger to his nose and sniffed. Then he screwed up his face and walked back to the provost marshall, who was waiting, with the Citroën window open. The sergeant composed himself. Another plane exploded on the horizon, lighting up his face.

"Oil?" asked the provost marshall, sticking his head out.

"No, sir. It's . . . well . . . " The sergeant searched for words.

"Come on man! We don't have all night . . . water?" the major roared.

"Excrement . . . sir, excrement . . . liquid excrement . . . " The sergeant bent down and rubbed his finger on the tarmac, while the major hurriedly got out of the car. The provost marshall's eyes followed the direction in which the unlit car had disappeared. He stood staring into the dark for a full minute, hands on hips, riding crop in one hand. "One thing's for sure, Van Erk," he said loudly to the sergeant, "*they're not Hollanders!*"

As the rushing Alvis shot through the deathly quiet, unlit streets of Haarlem, Dennis spoke. "The Hook, Captain?" he asked Van Velzor.

The Dutchman, staring ahead, piloted Lynch with his left hand. He replied without turning around. "The Hague first . . . got to find out the situation . . . only sure way." Then there was no more talk, until twenty minutes later, when they pulled up outside the Hague Army Headquarters.

"I'll be five minutes," Van Velzor said. He looked round at Dennis. "Lieutenant," he tilted his head to one side, toward the Army HQ entrance.

"I'd rather not, Captain . . . not like this," Dennis murmured, holding his torn, stinking, soaking wet boiler suit sleeve up a little.

Van Velzor frowned. "No, I suppose not. Anyway, it's safer all round the less people notice you." The Dutchman alighted, walked around the gleaming radiator grill, crossed the wide pavement and spoke to the sentry. The sentry looked at a pass the captain showed him and saluted as Van Velzor disappeared into the building.

The night was still, except for the dull thump of explosions far away. Moonlight shone on the darkened street. There was no wind.

"Cor, blimey . . . " said Mitchell, quietly, " . . . don't half-pong in here, eh, lads?"

All four, as they shivered in their cold, filthy, dripping tightly clinging boiler suits, nodded in agreement. Lynch searched the glove compartment. He found a half-full packet of Captain Morgan's Benson & Hedges cigarettes and offered them around, asking with a grin as he looked at Lieutenant Dennis, "Don't mind if we smoke, do you, sir?" Toward Schveningen the sky reddened again.

Dennis frowned, but he replied, not realizing that there was anything odd in what he was saying. "No, not at all chaps. Please do. When the air gets too thick, I can move out of the car."

Goffin, Lynch, and Mitchell, all three, spluttered into gusts of suppressed laughter. When Dennis realized the joke, he smiled, shyly, as he mused, *God, they're sharp*!

They remembered the colonel and were quiet for twenty minutes until Van Velzor reappeared, carrying a full kit bag that he threw into the rear compartment of the Alvis.

"Move off . . . straight ahead!" he ordered Lynch, who already had the engine tickling over. The Alvis, as Lynch declutched and accelerated, leaped forward. They headed first west toward the burning glow of Schveningen, then south, to face a darker sky.

14th May, 1940. 2:45 A.M.
Carinhall, on the 100,000-acre estate of the Master of the German Hunt in the Forests north of Berlin, Germany

The forty-seven-year-old Reichsmarshall, his great diamond ring flashing in the pink glow of the bedside lamp, picked up the phone. He was wide awake. Sleep had not come easy to him in all the years since he had, by the strength of his will alone, given up his morphine habit. "Der Eisern (Iron Man) speaking." He waited. "Forty percent of our Stukas and Junker transports? We must accept losses, of course," then he listened for a few minutes. He frowned, his pudgy face growing redder by the second. Then he exploded, "What the devil do you mean, the goddamned fifth Westphalian tank division? What the hell are they doing at the Palace?" He waited another minute, then he spat out, "What, all five of them? What the *scheisse* was Lentz doing? Have him arrested immediately. Have the other . . . what the devil. How many did you say it was?" another half-minute passed, " . . . yes, all eight of the swine . . . up against the wall!" He glared at the bedside lamp." The goddamned Palace wall! Throw them into the sewer!" The Reichsmarshall slammed the phone down, seeing in his mind's eye seventy-four Old Masters' paintings and "God only knows how many priceless Persian carpets, ivory, furniture," he sobbed aloud. He picked up the phone again, the choking master of 4,500 operational war planes.

"Get me Kesselring.. Yes, yes, *Dummkopf* . . . Luftwaffe Air Fleet Two!" He waited for two minutes, impatiently fingering the pink sheet on his stomach. "Yes, General," he said, "Goering here. Start the Rotterdam thing in motion, will you?" He listened again, staring for the time at the reflection of himself in the ornate ceiling mirror above. "Yes, the Amsterdam beacon is all lit up." He sighed. "It's all in operation, as arranged." He waited another moment then he breathed into the telephone and snarled, "The Totenkopf Division, fifth group, fourth section, but don't bother to congratulate anybody!" He slammed the phone down and turned back to his Dashiel Hammett novel. *Now I'll show those Jewish swine*, he glowered to himself, remembering Epenstein, the Jewish lover of his mother, who was buried in Rotterdam. His mother—the wife of the German consul-general in Haiti, *consorting with a Jew*!—he raged to himself until sleep finally overtook him.

14th May, 1940. 3:00 A.M.
Courteney Club, London, Suite 6

'C' was roused from a deep slumber by the jangle of his telephone. He picked it up and listened. Then he sat up in bed wide awake. He spoke in Spanish "*Si, naranja . . . eso es . . . Carlotta Amelia.*" His face folded into a deep frown as he concentrated for five minutes, listening intently. "*Dios mìo!*" he murmured twice, as he heard Dennis recite his story. "*Mierda!*" he interjected at another point. He grimaced, pursing his mouth as the story unfolded. After three more minutes, he broke into the recitation. "Look, the line will go at any minute if they're already in that place. The priority is to get the stuff back here. If you can't, then bury the things. But it seems that the situation to the southwest of you is in flux. With that car . . . " he paused, "Yes, right away, I should think. Certainly, whatever you do, get it from behind their line if there's any chance at all. From what I've been told, I should think Señor Burges will hold . . . hello . . . hello?"

A voice said, *"Verdammt Ausländer!"* quietly. Then the line went dead.

'C' deliberated. He murmured to himself, in English. "The whole lot blown . . . blown!" Who could have tipped them off? His mind ran through the last roll call he had received from the mission in the Hague. His face cleared as he solved the problem in his mind. "So that's who it was!" he said aloud. "The crafty blighters!" He frowned again as he gave his mind to what Dennis had said about Van Velzor's plan.

'C' picked up the phone and dialed the BBC in Portland Square. "Give me Mr. Findlay, please," he asked the operator. He waited, then he said " 'C' here . . . Charlotte Amelia . . . Look, be a good chap and ask your people to listen out for North Pole, will you . . . that's North Pole . . . any wavelength from Holland? Thanks, Findlay, good night." He turned over and tried to sleep, but he couldn't help wondering if that damned Boche who had sworn as he cut the line, had understood. He made a mental note to see Beasley's and Jenkins' files in the morning, early. *Barton we already know about . . . might as well make a clean sweep.*

14th May, 1940. 3:15 A.M.
Middelburg, Holland. 8th Section, Luftwaffe Air Fleet 2, Ground Communications Unit

Corporal Haldemann scribbled for a moment on a pad. He tore off a sheet and took it to Flight Sergeant Ehrlichmann.

"Yes, Haldemann?" the Flight Sergeant looked up from the Netherlands Overseas Telephone Director's desk. Outside the sound of machine gun fire was steady.

"Funny thing, Sergeant," reported Haldemann. "I was breaking that New York line, like you said, and I heard two men speaking in Spanish."

"What did they talk about?" There was the loud bang of a tank gun as the sergeant spoke.

"Sounded like a polar expedition, but they were speaking too fast for me."

"Mmm," Sergeant Ehrlichmann murmured as he thought about it. Then he said, "Where the devil did you learn Spanish, Haldemann?"

"Condor Division, Spain, March to August last year," replied the corporal. As he spoke he heard the grump! of a plane crash somewhere outside.

"How do you know it's a polar expedition . . . did you say?" Erlichmann raised his blond eyebrows as he said this.

"One of them mentioned the North Pole," explained Haldemann.

The sergeant bent his head down to study the diagram on the desk, frowning impatiently as he said, "Oh, well, write it down, might as well report something. Pity, all this damned writing . . . pity we couldn't record it some other way."

14th May, 1940. 3:20 A.M.
The Hague

Lieutenant Dennis, standing on the newspaper in the city transport manager's office, listened for ten seconds, then he replaced the phone on the wall hook and turned to Van Velzor.

"We just made it, thank God," he announced. "Through the New York people—British security coordination."

Van Velzor studied Dennis, still in his smelly half-dried boiler suit. "The men should be finished bathing now, Lieutenant. The dry clothes are in the locker room, on the bench. I'm afraid they're all that will fit you, but they'll do for the time being, at least until we know exactly which way you're going."

"Anything so long as I can get rid of this," Dennis replied, as he followed the Dutchman out of the dimly lit office, through the yard, and into the shower room opposite. Soon Dennis, too, was dressed in Dutch Army fatigues, and he and his men were all in the wooden shed. It was at the very back end of the Hague City Transport Maintenance Depot, hidden from the road by a jumbled squadron of ancient, outworn and junked double-decker buses.

Van Velzor had brought an oil lamp that he lit inside the shed.

"Thank Christ for that," said Lynch, as he felt his new clothing.

"Yeah," said Goffin, "I was beginning to wonder if you always smelled like that."

"Only in the mating season," injected Mitchell, quick as a flash.

They hosed down and broom-scrubbed the floor of the Alvis. They dropped its canvas top, and piled it with four old bus seats from a junk heap close by. Mitchell and Goffin then opened the doors of the wide, almost empty wooden shed. Lynch drove the car in and parked it in the center of the concrete floor. The doors were closed again. The bus seats were off-loaded. They were set up as settee beds, three on the right side of the car, and one on the left, by the driver's door, for Lieutenant Dennis.

While the Britons were so engaged, Captain Van Velzor stepped outside, soon to reappear with a cardboard box, a primus stove, two kettles, and six tin plates and mugs. He set the things down on the solid wooden workbench in front of the car, at the back end of the shed. "There you are, gentlemen!" he announced, "now you are nice and . . . " he stopped.

"Cozy," prompted Dennis, smiling.

"Top-hole," snapped Van Velzor. He then wished he hadn't. It reminded him of the colonel. He was silent, until Lynch demanded, "Where's the tea, then, Captain?"

"I'll bring you some in the morning," Van Velzor promised.

"Don't forget the milk and sugar," said Mitchell, grinning.

"And a teaspoon," added Goffin.

"Make it Mazawatee Home Brew, this time, eh?" Lynch demanded.

"Right, Mazawatee it shall be Mr. Lynch." Van Velzor pointed at the package he had brought in. "There's soup and corned beef, and chocolate there. So now I'll say good night. I shall be back early in the morning. There are some things I must do. Some people to contact . . . " He looked at Dennis and proffered his hand. "Good night, Lieutenant," he said.

Dennis, a little embarrassed at the Dutchman's gesture, took his hand and shook it. "Good night, Captain. Thank you so much for everything."

As soon as they had scoffed down a plate of corned beef and swallowed a mug of soup, they made for their bus-seat beds. Mitchell and Goffin were asleep almost as soon as they lay down.

After he had turned the oil lamp off, Dennis lay down on his side of the car. Wearily, he lay awake considering the situation in the light of what Van Velzor had discovered at the Army HQ.

H.M.S. *Havelock* had sailed for England with the Dutch government onboard. German paratroops had landed at the Hook and occupied the port.

Holland was on the point of collapse. Despite stiff resistance and heavy German losses, all the Dutch ports and almost all the airfields were now in Nazi hands.

A German army of paratroopers and panzers, twenty-nine powerful divisions, was scattered throughout Holland and astride the Dutch-Belgian frontier. Against them the eight Dutch army divisions were hopelessly weak.

German Army Group B, under Von Bock, further south in Belgium, had reached the suburbs of Brussels. Its right flank was wheeling left en masse to hammer down across the French frontier to Lille. Von Kleist's panzer tank armada was already in France at Sedan. The French army was in full retreat. The Allied armies were outnumbered by forty divisions.

Further south there was chaos on the roads, caused not only by German pressure on the Allied armies, but also by Luftwaffe attacks on civilian centers of population and on the roads themselves.

Van Velzor could not accompany them out of Holland or anywhere else. He was under orders by the legal Dutch government of his sovereign to form a Dutch Resistance to the occupying power.

Without Van Velzor that left himself, twenty-four years old, six months in the army, with complete responsibility for the safe delivery to British territory of one billion pounds worth of treasure, two professional criminals, both older than himself, and a dipsomaniac seaman.

The distance between the Hague and the nearest safe territory was approximately a hundred miles. This time on the morrow it would probably be 150 miles and increasing by the hour.

It was an hour before Lieutenant Dennis fell asleep.

Lynch was delayed in falling asleep, too, but his problems were simple in comparison with Dennis'.

How to get rid of Dennis, how to steal the treasure, and how to get away with it to Spain.

Lynch thought of the two Bakelite boxes safely hidden in the belt around his waist. He nestled the Walther under his left armpit—then he retired into his own private dark world. It was a world that only Lynch had inhabited, ever since he was a small boy; a very small boy indeed. Among its scenes were a small room in Rio and the poop deck of the *Mauretania* on a cold, rainy night in mid-Atlantic.

They were up early the next day, despite the shaky sleep. Van Velzor breezed into the shed as Mitchell was putting the kettle on the stove. The Dutchman left the door ajar.

" 'Morning, Lieutenant Dennis, 'morning, men!" Van Velzor said as he held out his hand to Dennis, much to the latter's embarrassment and the troops' amusement.

Mitchell thought, *Funny how these foreigners are always shaking hands.* He remembered when he had walked into his local pub in Lewisham, back in 1919, straight off the boat from Russia. He unshouldered his kit bag and asked for a pint. A dozen of his old mates had nodded to him. The landlord had said, "Wotcher . . . Mitch, see yer back again. What's it been, three years? 'ere, 'ave this one on me." And that had been it.

Mitchell grinned at Van Velzor. "Cup of tea, sir?" he asked.

"Thank you, Mr. Mitchell, that will be very nice . . . er . . . make it six mugs, will you please?" Van Velzor requested.

"Who's the sixth for?" Lynch interjected.

"The sixth is for me, gentlemen," called a female voice from just inside the shed door.

All the men except Van Velzor spun around, startled.

Chapter 8

* *

Let the Rest of the World Go By

14th–24th May, 1940

Is the trouble and strife
That we find in this life
Really worth while after all?
I've been thinking today,
I could just run away,
Out where the west winds call. . . .

With someone like you,
A pal good and true,
I'd like to leave it all behind
And go and find
Some place that's known
To God alone;
Just a spot to call our own;
We'll find peace, perfect peace,
Where joys will never cease,
Out there beneath a kindly sky;
We'll build a sweet little nest,
Somewhere in the West . . .
And let the rest of the world go by!

Lyrics of an Edwardian waltz. It was very
popular in Britain, before, during, and after
World War II. It is still sometimes sung in
the pubs.
Words and music by J. Keirn Brennan, Ernest R. Ball

8.

"Let the Rest of the World Go By"

14th May, 1940. 9:15 A.M.
The Hague

She was a slim, petite brunette. Her brown eyes were at the same height as the shed door latch, five feet above ground level. Her hair framed a serious, dark-complexioned face. She slid sideways to get past Mitchell's bus-seat bed. Her white shirt was open at the neck. Around her neck, under the black coils of her hair, she wore a thin gold chain.

No one spoke as she moved toward them. She had a well-scrubbed look, but she did not smile. Little lines at the corners of her eyes and mouth gave the men the impression that she was much older than her twenty-six years.

"Gentlemen," said Van Velzor, enjoying the sight of the phlegmatic Britons' surprise, "please let me introduce you to your . . . new traveling . . . er . . . "

"Companion?" suggested Dennis, shyly smiling at her.

" . . . guide. Yes, that's it, guide. Fraulein . . . Miss Hannah Bernard."

The woman smiled. Her years dropped away. Dennis was reminded of the Mona Lisa. She held out her hand to all four of the men in fatigues as Van Velzor made the introductions. Her English was excellent, with a mere trace of an accent.

"Pleased to meet you, Miss Bernard," announced Dennis.

"My pleasure, Lieutenant," she smiled and nodded at the others.

"My pleasure, Miss, I'm sure . . . wanna cuppa tea?" asked Lynch, pressing her hand. It was small; he weighed her up. She had a firm grip.

"That will be nice, I'm sure, Mister Lynch," she said.

"Miss Bernard is from Vienna," said Van Velzor, as Lynch poured hot boiling dark-brown tea into the extra cup.

"Please call me Hannah," she interjected.

"Hannah is from Vienna," Van Velzor said. "She is an . . . old friend. We have worked together for some time. She knows the highways and . . . and . . . "

"Byways?" prompted Mitchell.

"Quite." The Dutch captain bit his lip. A shadow of sorrow flitted across his blue eyes. "And she, too, wishes to reach your destination. I have, therefore, asked her to accompany you." Van Velzor looked at his wristwatch, then at Dennis. "I'll leave you in her capable company, Lieutenant. I must make some contacts," he said, moving away to sidle past the Alvis.

"Very good, Captain."

"If there's anything you need," Van Velzor spoke loudly from the shed door, "let me know when I return."

"Will do, sir."

Lynch turned to Hannah and smiled. "Sugar, Miss?"

"No, thank you, Mister . . . Lynch," she said, quietly.

"Milk?"

"No, thank you."

"There you are, Miss. Nice cup of char; warm the cockles of your 'eart, that will," Lynch murmured as he handed her the hot tin mug. "Careful 'ere, take the handle . . . that's right. Don't want you . . . " He noticed the pendant, *a six-pointed star*, on her neckchain and deadened his chatter.

"Thank you, Mister Lynch." She caught his gaze. Lynch's eyes dropped.

Goffin showed Hannah the Alvis, unclicking the spirits cupboard and the make-up table, jesting for ten minutes. After Goffin had completed his tour, Hannah sought out Dennis. They found their way to reminiscing about university days. He about Bloomsbury and Cambridge; Hannah about Vienna, while the other three listened for a while, understanding the language, but finding the subject, in the main, incomprehensible. Their interest lagging, they turned to playing cards.

No one mentioned the war or the way out of the trap.

Van Velzor was back in two hours. He poked his head around the shed door and called, "Hannah, Dennis, come this way please!"

The woman moved as soon as Van Velzor called to them. The lieutenant hesitated a moment, looking at the men. Then he murmured, "See you soon, chaps," and followed the woman outside.

"Not bad, eh?" were Goffin's first words when Dennis had gone.

Lynch snorted as he sat down on the Alvis running board. "Any port in a storm, you blokes. Typical bloody sailor, you are."

"Looks very nice to me," Mitchell observed.

Goffin stared at Lynch. He took a seat on a bus bench opposite him. "What are you up in the air about, anyway, Banger?" he demanded, "She looks to be a pretty fair party to me."

Lynch closed his eyes and put a pained expression on his face. He slowly tilted his head sideways. Then he half-opened his eyes and stared back at Goffin. "She's a bleedin' Yid, mate!" he spat.

"Arr, fer crissakes, Banger," Mitchell spoke up. "Live and let live. Won't do you no harm."

"What are you, a soddin' Ayrab?" demanded Goffin. In a flash of remembrance his days in Palestine were suddenly with him.

Lynch saw that he was outnumbered. "Well, just watch your bloody pockets . . . that's all," he grunted.

They were, all three, quiet until Mitchell picked up a deck of cards and riffled them before Goffin as the pair sat down to a hand of crib.

Lynch stared through the crack in the shed door, biting his lip, wishing he'd kept quiet about Hannah. *Steady on Lynchy*, he said to himself. *Don't upset the applecart, suck up to her. She'll fall for it, she won't be able to turn down all that money. They never do . . . Not them.* He turned to look at the card players. *They'll never go for it, not those two*, he thought as he stared at Goffin and Mitchell. *Goffin's an errand boy, and Mitch*, his eyes deepened into somber respect, *Mitch is a craftsman . . . that's it. He's no tear-away, and anyway, they've got something on him back home. No, it's the girl. No good trying to get her in before the chips are down, and that means getting rid of that nancy ponce Dennis first.* His reverie was broken by Mitchell.

"Put the kettle on, mate," he asked Lynch.

"Right-oh, lads, nice cuppa comin' up!" Lynch replied as he moved to the bench.

Van Velzor, Hannah Bernard, and Dennis gathered together between the wooden shed and the pile of junked buses. On the far side of the junk heap, toward the yard gates, the crane was making a loud racket.

"We can't be overheard here," shouted Van Velzor, almost apologetically. The young woman and the lieutenant did not speak. They crowded closer to the Dutchman to hear him. "I couldn't tell you in there," Van Velzor nodded his head in the direction of the shed. "Hannah worked with us until the Anchsluss in Austria. Ever since then, she's been a main switch in Holland for the Austrian Jewish children's refugee organization. It's a delicate thing. They have to . . . work with the Nazis, deal with them, and at the same time get as many out illegally . . . "

Hannah nodded and frowned. Dennis stared at her in astonishment.

Van Velzor continued shouting against the roar of the crane engine. "Hannah is op . . . *was* operating the illegal side. Since early last year she's taken, how many, Hannah?" he looked down at the girl.

"1,784 illegals," she said.

Dennis said, "1,784 children, but?" The figure staggered him. "But?" He got no further.

Over the pile of twisted metal, the crane's hoist noisily accelerated. Van Velzor raised his voice. "Many of them were brought down the River Rhine. They were hidden in the holds of Swiss, Belgian, and Dutch rivercraft. Some of them stayed here, of course, some were sent on to England with the legals, but others were passed on through Belgium to France, still undercover."

Dennis leaned even closer to the Dutchman. "How?" he shouted.

"Again, by ship, the regular ferry from Rotterdam to Terneuzen. That's about twenty miles west of Antwerp."

Dennis nodded. "But the Germans are already . . . " he shouted.

Van Velzor held up one hand, palm out and went on, "At Terneuzen they were transferred at night to a Belgian river barge, which carried them to France—Lille, along the Upper Schelde River. It has a false double bottom." The Dutchman and the young woman both smiled wanly.

"You think we can use the same route?" Dennis shouted.

"Not quite. As far as Terneuzen, yes, the neutral embassies are under instructions to send their families out, through Antwerp. There's a Swedish ship." Van Velzor held up his hand again as Dennis started to speak. "And the Red Cross have obtained a *laissez passer* from Berlin that allows the exit of the British diplomatic staff from the Hague." Van Velzor waited a moment as a thin cloud of iron dust wafted by from the crash of another chassis dropping on the scrap pile. "But they're already gone, I arranged for Captain Morgan and Wing Commander Davis to leave their credentials behind. They left with the Queen's party. Mitchell will be Captain Morgan, Goffin will be Wing Commander Davis. The Alvis details are already looked after."

"What about the military attaché? It would be simpler," Dennis suggested.

"Colonel Briggs? I'm afraid not. He's otherwise engaged," Van Velzor snapped.

"What about we others . . . Lynch and . . . "

"You'll be Beasley the gardener, and Lynch will be Jenkins, the house porter."

"But . . . Beasley and Jenkins?"

"They've been . . . their security . . . their future . . . has been looked after, Lieutenant Dennis," replied Captain Van Velzor, with a finality in his voice.

Van Velzor moderated his voice and explained, "Lynch will be Jenkins—he's the right height, and you will be Beasley. It's a matter of whose clothing will fit. One of our photographers will be down here this afternoon . . . "

The crane engine slowed and died. The sudden silence was uncomfortable to Dennis. For a moment he felt naked.

Van Velzor dropped his voice to a mutter, " . . . to get your pictures for the diplomatic passports. I'll have the credentials down to you as soon as they're ready, and I'll let you know about the ferry to Terneuzen as soon as my contact at . . . " he paused, " . . . I am informed of the arrangements."

Dennis turned to look questioningly at Hannah.

"If you're wondering about her, Lieutenant," Van Velzor said, "she's accompanying the party as Perkins' wife."

"Perkins?" Dennis asked him, puzzled.

"The butler," explained Van Velzor.

"And Perkins? What does he do?" Dennis almost lost his voice.

Hannah smiled as she told him, "Oh, he's coming along, too."

"But his wife? What . . . " Dennis was feeling slightly dizzy.

"He doesn't have one," she murmured.

Van Velzor hugged Hannah's shoulder. "This young lady is going along for two reasons," he said quietly. "First of all, to advise you of ways in case Belgium has fallen when you get there, and secondly, to set up a new children's center in . . . " the Dutchman trailed off.

Hannah laughed softly as she watched Dennis' puzzlement.

" . . . wherever. Don't worry, Lieutenant," she said, "I'll go through the aliases and the arrangements with you again today . . . slowly."

Van Velzor said, "Perkins will send you suitable clothes today. He'll be with you as soon as the trip gets . . . as soon as we know the program."

The trio was silent until Dennis looked at Van Velzor. "Wouldn't do for us to be at the embassy, I suppose?"

"No, it wouldn't," the captain agreed. "Too many locals who know the staff . . . " Van Velzor took his arm from Hannah's shoulders. He moved to leave.

"Yes, quite," said Dennis. "Shall we see you soon, sir?"

Van Velzor looked over the scrap heap. "If I can get down," he turned and held out his hand to Dennis, "but if not, good luck anyway." They shook hands heartily.

The Dutchman grinned at Hannah. "*Aufweidersehn*, Hannah," he said as he walked away, through the gate to his little blue Citroën. He was already thinking of the two North Pole stations that had been in operation since five o'clock.

Hannah, with Dennis one step behind, headed for the shed door.

Perkins was in shirt-sleeves, collarless, still wearing his butler's waistcoat, when the city corporation cart horse, pulling the rubbish cart, stopped outside the door. The driver dismounted from the cart, tied a nose bag around the horse's head, and put his finger to the peak of his cap.

Perkins' Dutch was elementary; the dustman's English nonexistent. Silently, they hefted the three bedsheet-wrapped suitcases into the back of the cart. This done, Perkins stood back, breathing hard. He watched the little old Hollander shovel half a ton of ashes into the cart, on top of the cases. The dustman threw the shovel on top of the ashes, untied the nose bag from the horse's head, climbed up on top of his perch, flicked the horse's rear end with his reins, and was drawn away, just as a German army car stopped at the gateway.

Perkins walked slowly back up the stone stairway, feeling a little lonely since Beasley and Jenkins had gone away three hours ago with that nice Dutch officer and left him all alone in the otherwise deserted mission. He waited, unperturbed, for the German officer who was walking up the driveway.

Hannah, Mitchell, and Dennis collected the suitcases, a box of food, and an empty drum from the garbage heap behind the shed, shortly after dark. Dennis suggested that they should change into the civilian clothes in the morning, but Hannah replied that the fatigues should be washed right away, and they'd need something to wear while the fatigues were being soaked.

They sat around the Alvis that evening, by the dim light of the oil lamp. Mitchell was dressed in the full-dress uniform of a British Naval Captain. Goffin was resplendent in a Wing Commander's uniform, complete with fifteen medal ribbons and a gold cord around his left shoulder. Lynch and Mitchell were in the best Sunday suits of the late Messrs. Jenkins and Beasley.

"One of the Brylcreem boys now, eh, Goff?" Mitchell had jested, as Goffin slipped on the Air Force officer's jacket.

"Bollox!" said Goffin.

"This way for the sixpenny seats!" Lynch crowed.

Goffin burst into a loud baritone voice, "If I only had wings . . . "

Hannah, who had waited outside the shed while they changed clothes, laughed as she collected the fatigues. She piled them on the bench by the vat. Jackets first, one by one, she dropped them into the bubbling water.

"Phew," commented Goffin, staring down into the bubbling vat, "reminds me of a sewer I was in once . . . " Everyone laughed again.

"Hannah," Dennis told her, as she lifted the jackets, a soggy mass, in and out of the hot water, "I've set you up a bed behind the car, near the door."

Hannah nodded. She said nothing. She kept her eyes firmly on the steaming mass weighing down the end of her stick.

Dennis turned and called to the men, "Council of wer, chaps!"

They all sat, Dennis and Goffin on the left running board of the Alvis, Mitchell and Lynch on the bus seat opposite them.

"We're going to be here a few days," Dennis commenced. "We ought to set out a duty roster. Count me in, will you?"

"Who sets the roster?" asked Goffin.

Dennis looked at Mitchell. "I suggest the oldest man here," he said.

"Why don't you do it, sir?" asked Mitchell.

"Not customary, is it for . . . " he left the unspoken words *officers to participate, except in an advisory capacity* hanging in mid-air.

"Go on, Mitch," urged Lynch.

"Pick up your hook, don't do cook!" Goffin quoted the age-old naval mess-deck rhyme.

"Oh, all right," Mitchell conceded. "Right, we'll start in alphabet-ical order."

Everyone except Dennis grinned as they looked at the lieutenant.

"Dennis, Goffin, Lynch, and Mitchell. Four duty flunkies, okay?" Mitchell reeled off the names.

Hannah, still stirring the jackets in the suds, spoke, looking down at Mitchell. "No, not okay, Mister Mitchell. *Bernard*, Dennis, Gof-fin . . . "

"But you've special . . . duties . . . " Dennis pointed out.

"The only thing special about me is that I know how to wash Dutch army fatigues," she smiled, showing good teeth.

"Good sport, Miss!" shouted Goffin.

"Sport is not the particular preserve of the English," Hannah said in a pedantic voice, then she caught herself. "Please call me Hannah, everyone," she said.

("Cornish," mumbled Goffin, " . . . calling me bloody English.")

"Got 'ya!" Mitchell grinned at Hannah. "Then it's Denny, Goff, Hannah, Lynch, and Mitch. Alphabetical order, see?"

Hannah laughed, "I give in, Mitch," she said, bowing to him. The soggy jacket hanging on her stick slipped off. She turned back to her stirring.

"Then I'll prepare dinner," Dennis stood up, moving off to peel potatoes.

Mitchell looked up at him. "Yes, you look after supper tonight, breakfast and dinner tomorrow, then Goff takes over."

"Right-oh, chaps. Supper it is, then," said Dennis, remembering the abyss that, in Britain, lies between the words *supper* and *dinner*.

15th May, 1940. 7:40 P.M.
The Elephant and Castle Public House, Lambeth, London

"How much we get altogevver, Slinger?" Able Seaman Morgan asked as he laid his pint pot down on the marble-topped table. They were all in their shoregoing uniforms—Leading Seaman Woods, Able Seaman Morgan, and Ordinary Seaman Coggins. They were sat in the jam-packed public bar, at a small round table, now covered with a newspaper over which was set piles of coins—half-crowns, florins, shillings, and sixpences.

"Two pounds, fifteen shillings and sixpence," said Slinger.

"Not bad for a night's work, eh?" said young Coggins. "Almost three nikker."

"They got a flippin' bargain," said Rattler Morgan, lifting his pint again. "Where else could they get a genuwyne, beduwyne royal shithouse seat decorated wiv roses an' all, complete wiv a little brass plate for sixpence?"

A tall skinny man of about fifty pushed through the crowd to their table. He spoke in a cockney accent with Irish undertones. "Got the winnin' raffle ticket, lads!" he said as he handed over a grubby pink slip to Slinger. "Number sixty-nine it is, boyos!"

"Right you are, Mick," Slinger grinned and picked up the toilet seat and started to wrap a newspaper around it before handing it to the Irishman.

"Sure, that's all right, lads, leave it be so. My mates can read the tally-plate," the Irishman said as he picked up the silk-covered seat, white, with pink roses, and read off the inscription on the little brass plate which Slinger, only that afternoon on the ship, had bribed the shipwright's mate with the promise of half a tot of rum, to affix over the flowery patterned silk. He read it aloud *"H.M.S. Havelock—on the occasion of the visit of Her Majesty Queen Wilhelmina of the Netherlands—her throne onboard. May 1940."* The Irishman beamed. "Sure," he went on, " 'twill be somethin' powerful to hang in the hall."

"It will that," said Slinger, "and guaranteed genuine, too." He turned to Morgan and Coggins. "Another pint, lads? Better make the most of tonight. We got an icicle's chance in hell of gettin' anovver bleedin' leave in the next few weeks, and we got to be back onboard tonight under friggin' sailin' orders."

"Right, Slinger, you get 'em in, then. I'll share out the loot," said Rattler Morgan, starting to count out three separate piles of coins. "We can take a crate o' beer on the train with us, long as the soddin' crushers don't spot us."

15th May, 1940
The Hague

That night their sleep was patchy. They were continually awakened by the zoom-drone-crump-zoom-drone-crump as the bomber squadrons of Kesselring's Luftwaffe Air Fleet 2 flattened the working-class areas of Rotterdam, twenty-five miles to the south of them.

The fatigue uniforms, hanging on a line by the wall of the shed, took twenty-four hours to dry properly.

On the next night, the sixteenth of May, their sleep was patchy again, as they heard the steady low roar of RAF bombers flying overhead to wreak vengeance for Rotterdam on the steelworkers' cottages of the German Ruhr—the first big British bombing raid over Germany.

Each morning, as the dawn broke, the fugitives ran one by one to the shower room to ablute in cold water and wash a shirt or pair of socks. Each dusk two of them scooted around to the rubbish dump to collect the next day's food rations.

Each day, in turn, they performed the repetitive little chores that are the stuff of human life—peeled the potatoes, washed the dishes, swept the floor. When these duties were over, they played cards or huddled around the battery-powered radio receiver that Van Velzor had provided for them and listened to the music and news reports, garbled and panicky from Radio Française, studied and overly calm from the BBC, as northwest Europe collapsed into chaos around them.

Each day Hannah and Dennis, on one side of the Alvis, grew closer in their long conversations about archaeology and Cro-Magnon man, boat races at Cambridge, and the future of Europe. Hannah maintained there was none, only an ever-increasing barbarity, while Dennis hoped that the Germans—he had met many level-headed, sensible ones—would, as the war stabilized in France, overthrow Hitler and come to their senses.

Each day Goffin and Mitchell drew closer before, during, and after hands of crib, talking in guarded English-style phrases about Rose and about Goffin's "party."

Each day Lynch drew more and more into himself, plotting a way to use Hannah, waiting to make his move, cracking jokes the while.

By the fifth day in hiding, all they could hear above the noise of the yard crane and at night were the incessant roars and growls of the Luftwaffe bombers as they passed overhead on their way to and from pounding Northern France and the shipping in the Channel.

In all the ten days they waited in hiding in the woodshed at the bottom of the transport department yard, they spoke to no one from outside but Van Velzor. They never set eyes on the little dustman. They never met the transport manager's secretary who left soap and a new candle every day in the shower. They never knew of the Dutch Army cook sergeant who each afternoon, at deadly personal risk, crept through the back fence of army headquarters to pass a box of food to the transport manager's secretary, who, in turn, waited in the little blue Citroën, under the eyes of German army patrols.

24th May, 1940. 7:43 A.M.
War Room, London

"Anything else before we adjourn, gentlemen?" The Prime Minister-cum-Defense Minister seemed, to the other four men around the table, to be enjoying his dual role.

The new first lord spoke up. "Yes, I've brought along your copy of the latest roll call for Dynamo," he said, as he took a file from his briefcase on his knees. He drew out a sheet of paper with one hand. He adjusted his spectacles with the other. He read, "One hundred and forty-three craft with a draft of less than twelve feet have now been inspected. Of these, sixty-eight are seaworthy enough for the operation envisaged . . . "

"The evacuation," the P.M. broke in.

"Yes, sir, the evacuation. Of the sixty-eight considered suitable to our intended purpose . . ." The admiral paused as the P.M. looked at him.

"For the evacuation," the P.M. intoned in a flat voice.

"For the evacuation, twenty are in blue zone, north of the line Mersey-Humber." First Lord paused for a brief moment. "Fifteen are in white zone, north of the line Severn-Harwich, and the remainder . . . thirty-three, are south of that line, in red zone." He handed the paper over to the P.M.

The P.M. studied the paper for a moment. Then he said, "These vessels north of the blue line? Are they on their way south?"

"Yes, I've two minesweepers on the east coast and one on the west, escorting them. They'll be reaching Dover and Newhaven approximately the same time tomorrow."

"And the vessels in the white zone?" asked the P.M., over his spectacles.

"Already moving into the red sector," the admiral replied.

"I see. So we shall have this . . . Armada in place at the latest by . . . ?

"Dusk tomorrow."

"Excellent. The arrangements at Dover Castle are proceeding as we planned?"

"Yes, sir, they are. All Dynamo staff have been operational since the fifteenth. We have high hopes. It all depends on the weather, of course."

"Of course," the P.M. agreed, a little impatiently.

The air minister and the CIGS stiffened a little. The admiral placed the file before the P.M., who opened it with a brief sigh and riffled through the thick sheaf of closely typed sheets. He was closing the cover again, when the toh page caught his eye. He read the heading on the page. "Other Possibles," he growled as he placed a finger on the heading. "What's this?" he asked the admiral. *"Other Possibles?"* he repeated, slowly.

The admiral smiled. "Oh, that's a list of vessels that have been included in the report. Most of them are rather older or smaller than the first-rank sixty-eight, of course. I thought we'd consider them in case an emergency situation . . . "

"Emergency situation?" the prime minister enunciated loudly.

"A sort of desperate last-ditch gamble," the admiral went on, "in case of . . . "

The P.M. ran his hand down the first column of the paper. "There are sixteen craft here, already all in red zone," he said, accusingly.

The admiral said quietly, "Yes, sir." He reddened slightly.

"Include them in the main list. Get them around to the sally ports right away," the P.M. continued. "Operation Dynamo to commence at midnight on the twenty-fifth of May."

The P.M.'s equerry, a young naval lieutenant-commander, entered the room. He coughed and nodded at the uniformed officers. They all three stood up and filed away on their respective appointments with an air of urgency.

'C' remained with the prime minister when the equerry had left the room. As the P.M. glared at the Dynamo file in silence, 'C' pursed his lips.

The P.M. looked at him. 'C' waited for the explosion.

"Emergency situation? Desperate last throw? What the devil does he think this is—*bloody Henley Regatta?*" The P.M.'s voice trembled as he growled.

'C' was surprised. It was the first time he had ever heard the P.M. blaspheme.

'C' said, "Our Ultra people—our code breakers—report something odd, sir, I think you should know about it right away."

The P.M. turned and looked directly into 'C''s eyes.

"It seems that Von Brauchitsch—you remember he's number one at the German High Command—ordered a flat-out attack on our enclave around Dunkirk, but his order was countermanded by Rundstedt—by my judgment, on Hitler's pesonal command. Anyway, Rundstedt has ordered a massive regrouping of the German armored forces to withstand any possible French attempt at relief from the south. This has taken pressure off the British and French within the . . . enclave."

The P.M.'s eyes lit up for a brief moment, then clouded again. "How do we know it's genuine? How can we know the Germans are not aware we have Ultra?"

"We don't and we can't, sir," said 'C'. "We can only hope . . . pray that this miracle is true. It's all we have left. Pray that we can get the army off before the Luftwaffe destroys it."

"Prayer and the RAF," said the P.M., "and our navy . . . and M19."

'C' looked at the P.M. quizzically.

"I've directed Crockett to form a prisoner-of-war escape organization. We might get back some of those people."

The prime minister glanced at the figures and names listed in columns under "Other Possibles." The P.M. ran his finger down and stopped at the bottom of the list. He read out the third line from the bottom. "13 S/B, *Beatrice Maud* . . . machinery nil . . . C. E. White, Captain, G. F. Sully, Owner . . . 1910." He half-turned to 'C', looking over his spectacles.

"1910?" The prime minister repeated, "1910? What's that, her tonnage?"

"No, sir, *it's the year she was built*," replied 'C' quietly.

The P.M. closed the file with an inaudible sigh. Both men silently wondered how many of the half-a-million or so Allied soldiers trapped in the Pas de Calais at that moment could be saved.

The P.M. picked up the list of sixty-eight first-rank vessels. He called out the first name on the main list of vessels. "One, paddle steamer, *Clyde Eagle*." He looked at 'C', his eyes glistening under the spectacles. "God," he whispered, "300,000 British and only He knows how many French and Belgian . . . "

"Yes," replied 'C', also in a whisper, "300,000."

"It's going to be a tight squeeze, 'C', a tight squeeze indeed," the P.M. observed.

"It all depends on the weather," said 'C'.

"And our seamen," the P.M. muttered, adding, "God help them."

"Amen to that," 'C' said, as he turned to leave.

The P.M. called, "At one o'clock then, on the terrace?"

"One o'clock, sir," agreed 'C' as he opened the door.

24th May, 1940. 8:15 A.M.
Kingston-upon-Thames Electricity Generating Station, Wharf No. 2

A hundred yards from the winding drum of Barrage Balloon Number 83, the post office telegraph boy shouted out in a shrill voice, "Captain White! Ahoy! *Beatrice Maud*, Captain White!" He propped his bicycle on a jetty bollard and half-slid, half-walked down the board that served for a gangway. He headed aft, crunching coal dust under his feet.

"Whazzup?" He heard a voice coming from the hold. He leaned over the hold coaming and saw Josh and Young-Mike, both stripped to the waist, covered in fine black dust, their eyes reddened. They were holding big shovels, eighteen inches across the blades. Josh wiped the dusty sweat off his face as he gazed up at the blue-uniformed telegraph boy.

"Telegram for the captain," called the boy.

" 'E's down aft, 'avin' 'is breakfast," Young-Mike sang out.

The pair of shovelers returned to loading their fourth coal skip of the day. The telegraph boy had turned to walk aft when Knocker appeared.

"Mornin' son; you got something for me then?" Knocker queried. He tore open the telegram. He stared at it for a minute. Then he put his hand in his pocket. "There you are," he said as he passed the post office boy a three-penny bit. "There's a joey for you, lad."

"Cor thanks. Any reply, Captain?" the boy asked. He was already on the gangway.

"No. No reply. Watch how you goes up that there plank, son." Knocker leaned over the hold coaming. "How much coal you got left, Josh?" he shouted over the noise of the power station machinery.

Josh stopped shoveling, but made no reply. He stood and waited for Knocker to peer around into the dusty gloom of the hold to see for himself.

"Right. Finish that skip, mate, and then get cleaned up, you and Young-Mike both," Knocker ordered.

"What, we got an 'oliday, Knocker?" Young-Mike interjected.

"No, well maybe no, maybe yes." The two coal heavers looked at Knocker. Then the captain relented his reticence. "We're off to Whitstable as soon as we're ready!" he said, loudly.

"What about this bloomin' lot?" asked Josh. "We got twenty tons left here," he pointed out.

"We'll drop that off onto *Prince Albert*, old Mad Jack's due to be off Galleons Reach this morning. He can bring it up with him on deck. We'll sack it on the other side of Tower Bridge," ordered Knocker. He walked to the gangway board, on his way to explain to the chief engineer of the power plant why he was going to be twenty tons of coal short on his order, at least temporarily.

"Cor, blimey," Josh wailed to Young-Mike, half in jest. "It's all bloody go, innit?"

Young-Mike covered his mouth and nose with a grimy neckerchief, rammed his shovel into a heap of coal dust, and continued loading the skip.

24th May, 1940. 9:15 A.M.
The Circus, London

Margot walked hurriedly into 'C''s office. She placed a message pad before him. "Orange is moving," she said. "Canning is dead."

"I know." 'C' looked at the form. Findlay had done well. The BBC had handed over the North Pole operations to Jamieson for special attention as soon as the first dots and dashes had been picked up, on the fourteenth. This was North Pole's sixteenth signal. He read it.

ORANGE SIX DEPARTS TODAY NORDHOLM STOP HOOP.

"Laconic," he said to Margot.

"There's so much traffic," she replied. She turned and walked out.

Wonder who the sixth is, and Hoop . . . ? 'C' pondered. *I know Perkins is fifth, who the devil . . . ?*

The questions passed to the back of his mind. He reached for the Madagascar file.

24th May, 1940. 12:53 P.M.
Onboard the sailing barge Beatrice Maud *below Putney Bridge*

"How much more ebb we got, Knocker?" Josh asked between hard pushes on the big sculling oar. It was necessary to scull the barge, while she had no sail up, even when the tide carried her. This was to make her go a little bit faster than the tide, so she could be steered.

In the distance an air-raid siren sounded the All Clear.

Knocker took his pipe out. "An hour and a half. We'll be well downstream by then, coming down to Gravesend. Mad Jack'll be at anchor there."

The barge hull was low, stubby, oblong, squat, and ugly looking without the mast and rigging raised to give her grace. She slid out of the shadow of Putney Bridge. Once again Knocker, Josh, Young-Mike and *Beatrice Maud* were bathed in May sunshine.

Knocker watched Young-Mike for a moment, as the lad sloshed river water over the deck to wash away the coal dust. He said, "You know, Josh mate, I've been thinking."

"Whazzat?" said Josh, his chest heaving as he pushed and pulled, pushed and pulled the loom of the scull.

"When I was a boy, with old Dusty Miller in *Plain Truth*, we used to try to beat the other boats going out with the tide, and old Dusty always won a few pints down in the *Prospect of Whitby*!"

"How'd 'e do that?"

"He used to raise the mast below the Albert Bridge and *sail* down to Westminster Bridge, then he'd lower the mast, punt through, and raise sail again on the other side. The others used to punt all the way down, see?"

"Bit chancy, ain't it?" gasped Josh. "Not much room. What is it, half a mile?"

"Bit less. D'you reckon we could do it, Josh?"

"Ain't racing anybody, are we, Knocker?" Josh protested.

"I thought like, as we're on our way to France, to pick up the lads, well, I thought we'd stir things up passing Parliament," Knocker grinned as he left the wheel to knock his pipe out over the side.

"Garn, you'd need ten tons of bloody gunpowder to stir that lot up," Josh rejoined.

"No, I reckon that you and Young-Mike are strong enough to manage it, Josh. You does it in between the bridges at Rochester. That's only a bit longer distance, and anyway, Bert on *Second Apprentice* reckoned he done it with Tansy Lee back in '35." Knocker knocked his pipe out on the portwale. He strolled casually back to the steering wheel. "And *Second Apprentice*'s rig is two feet higher than ours, but then, I s'pose Bert's a handy feller."

"No 'andier than me, Knocker," Josh grimaced as he said, "I'll tell you what. I'll do it if we gets paid early this week, so we can 'ave a few pints in Whitstable."

"Right, Josh, you're on," said Knocker. "Young-Mike!"

"Helllooo."

"We're a-going to raise the mainmast a bit early, ease the main brails!"

Young-Mike stowed his bucket by the mast housing to do as his captain had bidden.

"You get the halyards ready. I'll scull and steer," Knocker said to Josh.

"Right, Skipper," Josh murmured. He handed the sculling oar to the little old man of sixty-seven. "Let's stir the buggers up!" cried Josh.

"That's the style," approved the old man as he laid his wrist over the sculling oar. He glanced aft and saw the blackened ensign. He looked forward. He turned the wheel slightly, then he called, "Young-Mike!"

Young-Mike looked up from unbrailing the main.

"When you've done that go below and get the best ensign. Let's have the bloody Sunday duster up!"

Both Josh and Young-Mike stared at Knocker for a moment. They'd very rarely heard him swear before. They both broke into wide grins and rebent to their tasks.

"Better than shoveling coal, anyway, Young-Mike," commented Josh as the boy passed him on his way aft to Knocker's cabin.

24th May, 1940. 12:57 P.M.
Victoria Embankment, Chelsea, London

In the distance an air-raid siren wailed, All Clear.

"Let me get up on the wall, Mum, to see the river!" shouted Billy.

"Oh, all right then." Rose Leighton handed him up onto the coping of the Victoria Embankment wall, close to an ornamentally twisted iron lamp post. "Only for a minute, though," she said.

"Little Mitchie, don't fall, hang on tight, there's a love!" cried Mrs. Leighton from the pavement.

"Cor, look Mum," the little boy shouted excitedly. "It's a sailing ship." He turned to look at his mother, who was leaning on the wall, holding him around the knees. "Is it a pirate ship, Mum?"

"No, silly, it's only a blessed old coal boat, that's all," she replied, lifting him down. "Look at it, all scruffy and dirty."

All three, the middle-aged woman, the young mother and the boy, walked on under the budding trees.

24th May, 1940. 1:00 P.M.
The Terrace, House of Commons, London

The P.M. and the secretary of state for war were standing by the outer terrace wall, enjoying a rare spell of sunshine and fresh air.

The secretary for war was speaking, " . . . though at ebbing tide the smell from the river can hardly be described as fresh, perhaps *fish and ships*, sir?" he suggested.

The P.M. was in no mood for puns. He frowned as he puffed his cigar. He stared out over the Thames. Occasionally, he muttered to himself. Even as 'C' joined them to discuss the Madagascar matter, the war secretary heard the P.M. murmur, "Such fine weather for such dark days."

'C' said nothing. The P.M. turned back to face upstream, toward Chelsea Reach, in silence, frowning.

Suddenly the two waiting men saw the P.M.'s face clear.

Still the two men waited, watching the prime minister. The P.M. craned over the wall. Something was catching his attention. He leaned further over the wall. He rested both elbows on the coping and his face broke into a broad smile.

The two waiting men stared at the P.M. After a full week of glowering and growling, of moody doubt and uncertainty, the P.M. was grinning impishly again. They turned their gazes upstream, wondering.

They saw a black dumpy barge hull sliding out from under Chelsea Bridge, heading downstream with the outgoing tide. As the stern of the barge came out into the May sunshine, so the great eighty-foot mainmast was being steadily hoisted. As the mast rose higher and higher so the slight southwesterly breeze fluttered the house pennant atop the masthead more gaily.

All three men watched fascinated, as the eighty-foot-long, three-foot-diameter mast rose . . . up . . . up . . . up . . . until it was perpendicular to the barge's hull. Soon they and fifty other members, secretaries, ministers and officers of the Crown gaped in astonishment at the sight of a vessel raising her rig this far upstream, between bridges so close together. Another twenty souls, as they emerged from the terrace doors of the House saw the P.M.'s delight as he watched the barge's mainsail—an eighth of an acre of red-orange-ochre canvas—break out and flap briefly before the breeze filled it and transformed its shape into a cygnet's wing.

There were gasps of wonder and admiration from the throats of a hundred of the nation's rulers as the breath of the breeze shaped the sail and curved it into a visible dream, and as the sunshine caught the brass pennant staff, sending slivers of gold into the blue sky, and casting scimitars of shade over the ochre sail curve.

Steadily, as they watched, the barge picked up speed, sending out a rippling bow wave, an ever-growing white bone from between the teeth of her blunt bows. Faster and faster she sailed, at what seemed to the observers to be break-neck speed toward the low gray arches of Westminster Bridge, immediately downstream from the terrace.

Suddenly the silence in the crowd was broken. "He's going to smash his mast!" shouted a member standing near the P.M.'s party.

The shout was taken up by other people on the terrace. Those inside the corridor rushed out to see the spectacle. The hub-bub on the terrace increased as members and their secretaries pushed forward.

Soon 259 eyes were staring in fascination. The eighty-eight-year-old one-eyed member from East Kiddington regretted missing a quarter of the show.

The barge neared the bridge at four knots.

Disaster became imminent. The shouting on the terrace died to a murmur.

Suddenly, an army captain bellowed, "The damned idiots! Hand your blawsted mainsail, man!" The P.M. glared at him, then turned his gaze back to the barge.

Even as the captain yelled, an admiral, who had joined the P.M.'s party to discuss the Madagascar affair and was standing at 'C' 's side, mumbled, "Think the P.M. should step inside. Lord knows what it might be . . . some kind of plot."

As the admiral spoke, the barge was no more than twenty yards from the Westminster Bridge. Everyone on the terrace craned their heads, anticipating chaos.

Gently, as they gaped in silence, the great eighty-foot mast descended. The sail flapped as it lost its full bellied curve. Lower and lower went the mast. The bow reached the low bridge arches and passed under.

The mast descended still lower. The barge conformed her shape to the arch even as the tide carried her under the bridge.

For a moment there was complete silence on the terrace. Then, as if by signal, almost everyone of the crowd of people who had rushed out to see what the commotion was about broke into a great rousing cheer, the normally cool and reserved war secretary among them.

The P.M. was silent. He watched the barge's maneuvers all the way between the two bridges. When she disappeared under the arches, he still stared at Westminster Bridge. He saw the top of the barge's mast on the bridge's far side, as it was raised again. He saw the pennant wave in the breeze. He grinned broadly.

"Terribly risky, that kind of thing," he heard the army captain say. "The damned fools could have been sunk, not to mention damage to the bridge."

The P.M. turned to the captain. He looked at him in silence for half a minute. He said, "Captain!"

The captain, startled, turned to face the seething eyes of the King's First Minister.

The P.M. glared at the officer. "Damn the bridge!" he snarled.

The P.M. threw his cigar over the terrace. He turned away from the offending officer and stalked off to the nearest door, followed by the war secretary, the admiral, 'C', and three secretaries. As they entered the House, the P.M. turned to the war secretary. "What was the name of that sailing vessel?" he asked.

The war secretary asked the admiral. The admiral asked 'C'. 'C' asked one of the secretaries, who, in turn, asked his two assistants. No one knew. They'd all been too engrossed in watching the near-disaster.

"A magnificent gesture, a truly brave salute," murmured the P.M.

The story of the barge's daring action was all around the House in a matter of an hour or so. When the P.M. entered the Chamber, two hours later, there was not one gloomy or doubtful face to be seen, not even Mr. Bevin, not even in the front Opposition benches. As the P.M. walked through the door, the members searched his face. They remarked on his more cheerful demeanor, his firmer movements, and his more certain mood of determination. They decided that, even though not a single one of them could think *how*, he would bring them through this terrible crisis. To a man they stood and cheered as he rose to address them.

The P.M. grasped his jacket buttonhole and beamed. As the cheering increased he thought, *The odds are impossible—our stake is precious—the prize is infinite. We must jeopardize civilization in order to save it.*

24th May, 1940. 1:40 P.M.
The Pool of London

"Done the bugger!" said Josh, as *Beatrice Maud* slid out from under London Bridge. "Now, one more 'oist and we're 'ome and dry." He and Young-Mike set to, hoisting the massively heavy mainmast yet again.

"All the bridges from Albert to the Tower!" crowed Young-Mike. "What a tale to tell 'em when I'm Knocker's age . . . cor lumme!"

"If you don't keep your hands out from under the blankets you'll never reach Knocker's age," Josh jested as he guided the main forestay pennant onto the dolly winch. Josh kicked the steam valve lever with a plimsolled foot. The dolly-winch drum started to revolve. The mainmast was slowly raised. The blocks protested. The winch screeched and hissed.

"Only once a day and twice on Sundays," panted Young-Mike, running along the bowsprit. He picked up the two-inch diameter forestay bottle screw. He held it pointed out from his groin, laughing.

Josh shouted, "I'll clip your bloody ear for you, Young-Mike, 'ere she comes, soon as the male screw's there, marry 'em!" Josh looked up the mast, until it was perpendicular to the hull. The mastheel clunked into the tabernacle. "That'll give you a bit of practice," shouted Josh.

Young-Mike leered up, grinned, and set to, screwing the forestay home.

"We done it, Josh," said Knocker, when Josh reached the helm.

Josh replied, "We stirred the buggers up anyway. Did you see the crowd out on the side deck there, up at the 'ouse of Lords?"

"They was having their dinner hour," said Knocker.

"Bet we brightened it up, eh?" Josh hauled the mainsheet as he spoke. "They must 'ave shit a brick!"

"Let's hope so," said the old man. Then Knocker looked astern, to see if anyone was following *Beatrice* toward Tower Bridge. He looked ahead again. He saw that the great bascules of Tower Bridge were raising to allow a coastal steamer out of the pool on her way to sea. He steered to follow the steamer. When he was on course, he shouted for Young-Mike.

Young-Mike ran aft. "Wassup Knocker?" he asked.

"Take the Sunday duster down, Young-Mike, we don't want it to wear out too soon, do we?" Knocker asked him.

The best red ensign came down. *Beatrice Maud* under full canvas sailed through Tower Bridge. There were no seabirds around her stern. They were all after better pickings from the merchantman ahead. As she glided out from between the bridge bascules, two jackdaws fluttered across from the Tower of London terrace. They squawked as they circled around *Beatrice Maud*'s masthead, eighty feet above her deck. *Beatrice Maud* heaved a little as she met the first estuarial swells, and the jackdaws flew over the forest of masts and spars, heading back again to the Great Tower.

24th May, 1940. 2:00 P.M.
City Transport Yard, The Hague

Mitchell had finished cleaning up the dinner dishes when Van Velzor arrived. All the men of Orange party wore fatigue trousers and shirts. The fatigue jackets were carefully stowed away in the chest under the Alvis' rear passenger seat.

Van Velzor knocked twice gently, twice hard on the shed door. Dennis, cocked Enfield in hand, peeped through the crack and opened the door.

"Good day Dennis, no time to lose. You're off today, as soon as possible. Hannah, men, good afternoon!" the Dutchman said heartily.

Dennis stood by the door, watching Van Velzor for a moment. "Now Captain? Good, we'll be ready in ten minutes!" he announced.

"Make it five, please, Lieutenant."

"Five it is!" called Lynch, taking his fatigue shirt off.

"Right-oh chaps . . . er Hannah, get ready for the road!" ordered Dennis. He went over to Lynch. "Tank full now?" he asked.

"Full and overflowing," replied Lynch. "I put the fourth can in yesterday, that makes thirty gallons." *Make a nice little bang, that lot*, he thought.

"Goffin," Dennis turned to the seaman. Goffin was already in his braid-bedecked wing commander's jacket, adjusting the uniform cap on his head in front of the tiny mirror that Hannah had hung over the bench.

"Sir?" responded Goffin.

"You'll be in the front with Mitchell and Lynch."

"Aye aye, sir. I can navigate . . . box the compass."

The lieutenant turned to Mitchell. "I want you in the offside front seat." He reached over and unlocked the spirit compartment in the Alvis. He took out two canvas holsters. "Take this," he said. "It's loaded, and Goffin," he held the third Enfield out to Goffin, "put this under your jacket."

Van Velzor spoke up, as Dennis distributed the revolvers. "Be careful with those, men," he said. "Don't let the Swedes see them, or any German officials at the boat or anyone else, not even Dutchmen."

Hannah and Mitchell hurriedly packed the remaining food and the cooking equipment under the rear seat of the car.

Van Velzor turned to Dennis. "I'm going to go outside and drive my car around the block. Be ready, and when you hear four . . . "

"Hoots, sir?" Dennis prompted.

The Dutchman grinned. "Quite," he said, then he continued, "drive out around the scrap heap and wait just inside the gate until you hear another three hoots, and come out into the road, right turn, then follow my car. Understood?"

"Where are we going?" asked Dennis, quietly.

"I'm going to see you safely into the British grounds, then I shall go to the Swedish Red Cross and inform them you are all prepared to depart." Van Velzor opened the door. He turned to the lieutenant. "I will not see you again . . . for a while, Dennis. Good hunting!" The officers shook hands. The Dutchman waved to the other four. "Hannah, Mitchell, Lynch, Seaman Goffin. Good luck and cheerio, have a top-hole trip!"

"Excuse me," murmured Hannah, bumping into Lynch as he climbed to the driver's seat.

"Sorl right darlin' . . . s'long as you don't bang me Little Liver Pills!" he said as she drew quickly away from him. *Stuck-up cow*! he thought, as a flash in his mind's eye saw the room in Rio. Then it was gone.

The Alvis backed out of the open doors. Lynch spun the wheel. The car skirted the scrap heap. It waited at the gate for a moment. Then it swung right and was off, following the little blue Citroën.

Lynch drove, hunched over the wheel. He wore Beasley's blue civilian suit, his Royal Antediluvian Order of Buffaloes badge in the lapel. He had a flashy yellow and black tie. Next to him sat Able Seaman Goffin, wearing the full, splendid regalia of the dress uniform of Royal Air Force wing commander. To Goffin's right sat Mitchell, in Captain Morgan's uniform, a gold cord around his left shoulder, the Enfield revolver around his waist under the jacket. He rested his four-gleaming-gold-ringed arm over the side offside door.

In the back of the car, obscured by the shade of the raised top, Dennis sat wearing Jenkins' blue serge suit, green waistcoat, flat peak cap, and boots. Hannah sat on the offside door.

As they passed a road exit marked Rotterdam, they saw their first Wehrmacht soldiers. A gray-green half-track was parked just off the main road, and the soldiers were standing around it, watching the sparse traffic. They all stared as the black and silver Alvis ticked past at a stately speed of twenty-five miles per hour. They cast admiring glances at the radiator grill, with its angular chrome surround, its enormous polished headlamps, its bleached-white canvas top, its graceful rear end, its wide running boards, and the sweep of its back mudguards; then they turned to comment to one another, under their steel helmets, shifting the weight of their schmeisser submachine gun shoulder straps, kicking their field boots into the gravel of Holland, hard won from the sea.

"Think they noticed us?" asked Lynch quietly, grinning.

"No, not us, mate, we're not conspicuous enough," murmured Mitchell.

"Nothing like traveling incognito!" countered Goffin.

Everyone in the car, except Dennis, who was looking through the rear window, laughed. Then they saw the blue Citroën flash its rear lights as it slowed down. The Alvis turned into the driveway entrance. Lynch met the stare of a German sergeant.

The big wrought-iron gates were shut. The German approached the car. He looked in and said, "Yes?" He saw the uniforms and saluted casually.

Dennis spoke in German. "Just back from the Swedish Embassy, Sergeant," he explained, "their car's following." He kept his voice steady. "We have one more functionary to join us, here."

The sergeant jerked back and saluted Dennis with a quick flick of his hand. He turned to the gatehouse and nodded. There were two privates inside the late Mr. Jenkins' domain. The gates slowly opened. The Alvis ticked past the admiring eyes and stopped at the foot of the great stone stairs. As it did so, Perkins stepped out of the inner front door. He was wearing a well-preserved black jacket, a small carnation in the buttonhole, black trousers with a white stripe, a white shirt with a stiff-wing collar, and a black bow tie. On his head he wore a homburg hat. Over his shiny black boots he wore snow-white spats.

"Blimey, Twinkletoes," said Lynch. Everyone in the Alvis smiled.

Perkins closed the main oaken doors to the big house. He locked them. He put the big brass key in his jacket pocket. He walked slowly down the steps. When he reached the bottom step he turned to inspect that all was in order with the outside of the great yellow house. He turned again in the direction of the Alvis. He gave a slight bow to Mitchell. Realizing his mistake, he walked around the car and repeated the bow to Dennis. He announced, in a deep, sonorous voice, "Good afternoon, sir."

"Afternoon, Perkins, all well, I hope?" greeted Dennis.

Perkins adjusted the tilt of his head. His nose tip returned to its usual angle. "All correct, sir," he announced. "I have instructed the . . . er . . . local domestic staff to reapply for their positions at the moment of my return, sir."

"Splendid, splendid!" cried Dennis.

Perkins continued, "Of course, sir, I have requested Mr. Winkel—he's . . . he was Mr. Jenkins' assistant—to continue to maintain the grounds and the greenhouses in their present condition."

"Good," said Dennis, "but who will pay him?"

"Ah, yes, sir. I have requested Mr. Velesquez, one of my colleagues," he explained "at the Bolivian Legation, to cater to the remuneration of Mr. Winkel, and he has very kindly agreed to do so."

"Well done," said Dennis, smiling. "It will be good to know that the place will be kept in good order."

"Yes, sir. I have also taken the liberty of informing the local cricket team; they are mainly tradesmen and artificers, you know, sir. I may say I have had the great pleasure of introducing the game to them, that our cricket ground is at their occasional disposal on Saturday afternoons." Perkins thought for a fleeting moment. "Subject, of course, to the acquiescence of the . . . er . . . temporary occupying authority." He sniffed and went on, "I have sanguine hopes, sir, that the . . . er . . . our adversary's command here in Holland will bear in mind the beneficial effects accruing from frequent fresh air and habitual exercise."

Dennis smiled. "Splendid, Perkins. Please pass me your valise." Dennis alighted. He waited for Perkins to climb into the Alvis. A white Swedish Volvo, a large red cross painted on its roof, drove up the drive and stopped immediately behind the Alvis. There were three men in the Volvo; a stocky middle-aged man, the driver, and a Wehrmacht Hauptman.

Perkins eyed the Swedish car. "Ah," he intoned, "our guests have arrived, sir." Everyone inside the Alvis turned their faces, the three men's red with suppressed laughter, to see the new arrivals. Perkins eyed the Wehrmacht Hauptman with obvious disapprobation.

The stocky middle-aged man left the Volvo. He was dressed in a gray suit under a white raincoat. He wore good-quality brown shoes. A brown trilby (fedora) hat almost hid his white hair. His face was ruddy and chubby. He wore black horned-rimmed glasses. He smiled as he asked in English, "Mister Jenkins?"

For a split second, Dennis stood quite still. Then he said, "Yes, sir."

They shook hands.

"Bergstrom, at your service. I'm your . . . how do you say . . . go-between." The Swede introduced himself. "Of course," he said, turning to Perkins, "I know Mr. Perkins."

"How do you do, Mr. Bergstrom," intoned Perkins, as his disapproving gaze left the German officer in the Volvo.

Bergstrom looked inside the car, saying, "Captain Morgan, Wing Commander Davis, Mrs. Perkins, Mr. Beasley, all here, I see. By the way, Captain Morgan . . . "

Mitchell looked at Bergstrom, startled.

Bergstrom smiled and said, "Thank you for the party last month. I haven't had the opportunity before today. Please pass Mrs. Morgan my most sincere best wishes." He was enjoying the play-acting.

"Thank you, sir, I will," muttered Mitchell.

Goffin and Lynch both stared at Mitchell. Neither of them spoke.

Bergstrom turned to Dennis. "Well, Mr. Jenkins," he said, "shall we leave?" He turned to climb back into the Volvo. Dennis waited until Perkins had insinuated himself into the Alvis in as dignified a manner as he could, then he climbed in. The Volvo waited until Lynch was moving ahead, slowly, down the pebble drive. The Volvo overtook the Alvis and led it to the gate, which opened as the two cars approached. The German sergeant saluted. Bergstrom, Goffin, and Mitchell all saluted smartly back at the German, and Lynch, whistling softly, turned left, onto the main road.

There was a line of cars waiting on the main road. Mitchell counted twelve. Each one was full of people and baggage. There was first another white Volvo with a red cross on its roof, then two Fords, a Bentley, an Alfa Romeo, a Daimler-Benz, its engine cover hurriedly painted white with an Argentine flag painted on top, an Austin Princess, two Rolls Royces, a Bugatti, a Stutz Bear-cat, and a stately Hispano-Suiza.

"Looks like Derby day!" exclaimed Goffin.

Bergstrom's Volvo honked quietly as it passed each car. The drivers started their engines. The white Volvo accelerated and drove ahead, the Alvis following close behind. As the Alvis passed the last car, a Ford pulled out and followed it. The rest of the cars pulled out in turn and followed each other, and they formed a long convoy of fourteen vehicles, maintaining a steady speed of fifteen miles per hour.

As the convoy leader turned the corner onto the Rotterdam road it passed the German half-track. The Wehrmacht soldiers, seeing the Swedish flag and the red cross on Bergstrom's car, and the Hauptman sitting at attention inside, jumped to rigidity. They all smartly saluted as the leading Volvo, the Alvis, and the twelve other cars trailing behind, slowly passed them.

Mitchell, at Dennis' prompting gave a Royal Navy salute, his right hand held palm down against the peak of Captain Morgan's gold-leafed cap. Dennis, Hannah, and Perkins gazed, expressionless, at the sentries as the Alvis sedately passed them. Goffin jerked two fingers repeatedly up against the peak of his wing commander's cap, as they ticked their way past one danger, toward much greater danger, but only one of them guessed about that, and he, too, remained silent as he steered the car.

Chapter 9

*   *

Ferry-Boat Serenade

24th May–1st June, 1940

I love to ride a ferry,
Where music is so merry;
There's a man who plays the con-cer-tina,
As he moves along the deck-er-ina.
While boys and girls are dancing,
While sweethearts are romancing,
Life is like a mardi-gras,
Funiculee, funicular!
Happy, when we get together
Happy, when we sing together,
Happy is the ferry-boat serenade!

Italian pop song, 1940–41.
English words by Harold Adamson; music by E. Di Lazzaro

9.

"Ferry-Boat Serenade"

Follow Mr. Bergstrom's Volvo at a distance of ten yards and a speed of fifteen miles an hour, in accordance with Captain Van Velzor's last instructions," Dennis ordered.

There were many German and Dutch army vehicles on the road, as they passed through Vorburg and Delft, but they saw few other evidences of war, apart from the strained look of a few civilian pedestrians in the little towns. The townsfolk, as the convoy passed through the cobblestoned streets at a funeral pace, glanced quickly at them, stared for a moment or two, then turned their sad faces away.

It was not until they reached the fork in the road, where they turned off to head for the Schiedam docks, on the outskirts of Rotterdam, that they witnessed the effects of the great Luftwaffe blitz of a few nights before.

The convoy passed acre after acre of rubble. Occasionally, they saw the blackened shell of a burned-out workers' tenement, or the still-burning hulk of a vehicle, or a group of people digging in the ruins.

"Looks like they've been dropping some of Banger's Little Liver Pills!" Goffin said.

"Same old story," Mitchell said bitterly to Goffin and Lynch, as the ruins gave way to the untouched port installations. "Up the workers!"

Dennis, Perkins, and Hannah pretended not to hear.

The Celt in Goffin stirred, and softly he started to sing to the tune of "Tannenbaum" "The Red Flag," the anthem of the British Labor Party:

The people's flag is deepest red,
It floated o'er our martyred dead,
And e'er their limbs grew stiff and cold,
Their life's blood dyed its every fold—
We'll keep the red flag flying high,
Beneath the flag we'll stand and die . . .

He was interrupted by Lynch who broke into loud parody:

The working class can kiss my arse—
I've got the foreman's job at last . . .

"Can it, Banger," said Mitchell, and there was then a strained silence as the convoy pulled up outside the dock gates. Bergstrom and the Hauptman climbed out of the Volvo. There was a five-minute display of papers for the guard captain, a German naval lieutenant, as each car passed him.

When all the convoy cars had been checked, they moved slowly through the docks, coming to rest at last on an empty jetty. Bergstrom alighted from his Volvo and came to each car window with the Hauptman still carrying his briefcase, striding closely after him.

"We have an hour to wait, ladies and gentlemen," he said, in English first to the Alvis and the first Ford passengers, then, to the people in the other cars in French, Portuguese, Italian, Spanish, and French. "The Antwerp ferry is due to arrive at six P.M." He studied his watch. "My orders are," he continued, glancing at the Hauptman, "to request that you remain in your cars unless it is a matter . . . if anyone wishes to . . . relieve themselves, please signify this by placing one hand out of the window. A German sentry will then escort you to the . . . place."

Bergstrom, with the Hauptman at his side, then returned to the white Volvo to scrutinize documents and credentials and check names with pencil ticks. The Swede and the Wehrmacht officer looked up every few minutes as a small arm protruded from the Spanish, Portuguese, and Rumanian cars with, what seemed to the Hauptman, monotonous regularity. Each time a small arm waved, a German Kriegsmarine sailor, fully armed, stepped over to the signaling arm, opened the door, and escorted an (amazingly, it seemed to Bergstrom) different small child, each one under the age of seven, to the lavatory a hundred yards away. All this was observed in silence by the occupants of the Alvis, until, as the first sentry led away his fourth supplicant, Goffin said, "That's the third kid out of the Rumanian Hispano-Suiza."

"Yes," observed Lynch. "It's their secret weapon. If they ever go to war with Germany, they ain't going to fight them. When the Jerries take over, the Rumanians are going to drive their families down to the town squares. It'll need every friggin', sorry Miss, bloomin' one of Hitler's squaddies to escort the little blighters to the bog, see?"

Mitchell interjected, "Then our blokes go into Jerryland from this way, while all that mob is busy in Rumania, eh, Banger?"

"That's right, second front," said Lynch. "Watch out, here comes Herr General Von Bludendorff," he muttered quietly, as the Hauptman strode over to the Alvis.

"*Sprechen Sie Deutsch?*" the Hauptman snapped at Mitchell in his naval captain's uniform.

Mitchell pointed with his thumb to the back of the car and said, "You'll have to speak to the porter, Mr. Jenkins . . . the one in the green waistcoat."

Lynch grinned at the German as he followed the direction of Mitchell's thumb.

"Yes, here, Herr Hauptman," said Dennis, in German.

"You are enemy diplomats. You go on the ferry last. Do not alight from the car without permission, not even on the ferry," the Hauptman ordered. He unbent and strode away.

"Lynch," said Dennis, quietly, "start the car and drive back to the end of the line." The Hauptman beckoned them out of the line of cars.

Lynch gunned the engine. He kept a straight face as the car moved out from the head of the line.

The Alvis slid into the space ahead of the last Red Cross car.

Goffin said, "Oh well, last on, first off."

Dennis repeated the Hauptman's order in English about not leaving the car. Nobody spoke when he had finished.

The Rotterdam-Antwerp ferry *Hoop* arrived on time. It was a squarish, box-shaped boat, with two funnels, one poking up each side of the car deck.

The ferry's hull was very shallow. The car deck was a mere foot above water level. Over the car deck was a bridge for the wheelhouse. At each end of the car deck was a boarding ramp, like the drawbridge of a castle. The ferry moored bows on to the sloping end of the jetty. The bow ramp lowered. Six German army half-tracks disembarked followed by five Volkswagens, all full of Wehrmacht soldiers.

Bergstrom, with the help of his driver, dragged a tarpaulin out of the Volvo trunk and passed it to the ferry sailors, who spread it over the top of the wheelhouse. It was white, with a big red cross painted on it.

Bergstrom's Volvo moved from the head of the convoy and stopped to one side. The first Ford slowly moved out of line and reversed down the ramp onto the ferry car deck. Soon all the cars in the convoy were onboard the ferry, the Alvis being the last to board.

Bergstrom clambered up the boarding ramp, the Hauptman still trailing behind. The siren gave a short toot; the boarding ramp was lifted. *Hoop* moved off into the evening light on a seemingly deserted River Rhine.

The car passengers, all except for those in the Alvis, were out of their cars, standing around on the car deck, by the time they moved off. When the ferry reached midstream, a small German naval gunboat, her deck also covered by a white, red-crossed tarpaulin, fell into line astern. Above the car deck, on the wheelhouse bridge, two German naval sentries, both armed with schmeisser MP38 submachine guns, kept watch on the captain, the crew, and the passengers.

Hoop moved downstream for an hour, before heading south through the Rhine Delta to the Haringvliet arm of the Maas River. The passengers, all of nine different nationalities, were introduced to each other by Bergstrom, who told them that the English car was, by order, out of bounds and its passengers in quarantine. They were, he told them, not to approach the Alvis under any pretext. There was the danger of being shot at by the sentinels who were above their heads. Accordingly, with much chatter from the children, the diplomats' families all moved to the stern end of the car deck, away from the Alvis.

At eight o'clock, the ferry moved out of the delta channel into the Haringvliet. The German gunboat followed closely in her wake. The night sky was athrob with the noise of Heinkels and Dorniers passing overhead on their way to drop their deadly loads over fleeing refugees in Belgium. Above the top of the loading ramp, behind the Alvis, the Orange team craned their heads occasionally to see the loom of searchlights jabbing the night, sweeping their beams in a southerly direction, guiding the bombers on their way.

Bergstrom appeared at the side of the Alvis. In the dim light cast by the moon, his face was pale and eerie. "We have something here for you to eat." He passed three boxes through Lynch's window. The Hauptman, saying nothing, handed another three boxes to Dennis.

"I will be back in ten minutes to escort anyone who wishes . . . " Bergstrom did not finish.

"I'd like to go now, Mr. Bergstrom," broke in Lynch.

"Ah . . . come this way. Der Herr Hauptman here will guide you," Bergstrom smiled at the German as he said this. The German glared at Lynch.

Lynch moved away with the officer to the side deckhouse. Goffin was at the point of sinking his teeth into a ham sandwich. Mitchell was opening a bottle of beer from his box. Dennis was still unwrapping his box. Hannah set hers in the make-up cabinet. Perkins was spreading a large white handkerchief over his knees.

There was a sudden jolt, then a loud scraping noise. *Hoop*'s bow, underneath the Alvis, reared. The engine below sputtered and died. The ferry stopped moving. Everyone in the Alvis was thrown back by the shock. Mitchell dropped his beer bottle, Goffin swallowed half his ham sandwich, Perkins said, "I'm afraid, sir, there has been a . . . navigational mishap."

There was shouting and running on the wheelhouse deck. There was pandemonium among the other passengers. The gunboat astern stopped her engine only just in time to avoid crashing into the ferry's stern.

"What the hell?" shouted Mitchell, annoyed at losing his beer.

"She's aground, Mitch," Goffin said, as he unchoked.

Bergstrom, looking a little disheveled, came along the deck, which now sloped up toward the bow at fifteen degrees from the horizontal. He came to the window and confirmed Goffin's diagnosis of the situation. The Dutch ferry crew rushed forward to let down the ramp. They clambered to the sides of it, then they stood, speaking quietly, staring down onto the jagged iron girders of the blown-up Oude Tonge-Willemstad Bridge.

Lynch and the Hauptman made their way back to the Alvis, the German complaining loudly. Lynch grinned.

"What's got into his hair?" Goffin asked Lynch.

Dennis interjected, "He's swearing at the Alvis and us."

"The Alvis has bashed the front end of the Rumanian legation's Hispano-Suiza, squashed the fender in like a bloody ripe banana," Lynch chuckled.

"Oh dear," said Perkins, "such are the hazards of nautical progress."

"What damage do we have, Lynch?" Dennis asked.

"Little scratch on the bumper, that's all," Lynch laughed.

"Built like a tank, this bugger," observed Goffin.

Dennis was now speaking in German to the Hauptman. After an exchange of two minutes Dennis said, "I wouldn't laugh, if I were you, Lynch. He insists that we pay for the damage. The Rumanians are screaming at him. Listen!" They were silent as they listened to the shouts of the Rumanian families.

Dennis spoke again to the harassed German. When he stopped, the Hauptman turned and spoke to a large fat florid man from the Rumanian Hispano-Suiza. The Rumanian protested at first, then he listened. He protested again. He waved his arms. He shouted. He pleaded. Finally he gave the Hauptman a paper with his details. While this was going on, Dennis had written down an I.O.U. in the name of the British Ambassador to the Netherlands, for 500 pounds. He handed it to the Hauptman, who passed it to the still loudly protesting Rumanian. The fat man read it, scrutinized the letter-heading of the I.O.U., muttered, read it again, then beamed in a wide smile of complete forgiveness.

"We'll get off at high tide," said Mitchell.

"Not if it's high tide now," retorted Goffin.

Bergstrom came to Dennis' window. "Looks awkward," he said as he glanced again at the open bow door. "We are stuck high and dry, and high tide was ten minutes ago."

Dennis said, "Can't the gunboat haul us off?"

"No," explained Bergstrom. "We have run right up on top of a big bridge from Overflakee Island. It's been destroyed . . . there's a . . . "

"Span?" prompted Dennis, "fallen?"

"Span and they cannot pull us off backwards. The captain says that the, how do you call it, the highest tide . . . "

"Spring tide," Goffin interjected.

"*Ja* . . . the spring tide is not for another six days. We must stay here. There's no other way . . . until the spring tide lifts the ferry off the span. The other passengers are to be sent ahead to Antwerp, those who wish to go, but, of course, you, as enemies, must remain under the guard. I think it will be a week before you can move. I am leaving with the last of the others."

Hannah spoke, "But there are floating cranes in Rotterdam, Mr. Bergstrom."

"Nothing is allowed for civilian use," Bergstrom said. "Everything is taken over for the German military. Another three weeks, a month, maybe they would spare a crane, but I think they'd bomb the ferry and destroy it sooner than . . . " He trailed off, he had said too much already. He brightened, "But I will attempt to persuade the guard to allow you out of the car for a period each day." He turned to find the Hauptman on the dark, crowded car deck.

"Hoo-bloomin'-ray," crowed Lynch. "So 'ere we are, all nice and cozy, stuck in the middle of a river, aground on a broken bridge, under Nazi guard, in flamin' disguise. Can't get to the bog for kids . . . "

"What does *Hoop* mean, I wonder?" asked Goffin of no one in particular.

Hannah replied to the question with a smile, "It's *Hope* in English," she said.

"Blimey," countered Goffin.

"Yeah, all we need now is a bit of faith and charity," said Mitchell.

Perkins coughed quietly. He intoned, "And might I suggest, gentlemen, a little patience and good humor? I'm sure our hosts have the situation well in hand. After all, Holland is, like our own, a sea-faring nation." The butler reached down with one hand to collect his handkerchief and a trodden-on ham sandwich from the crumb-littered floor of the Alvis beneath the seat. He respread the white cloth on his knees, dusted off the sandwich with one corner of the handkerchief, and pausing before he took a bite, continued, "I do think that it is our duty, nay, our privilege, in these circumstances, to set an example to the unfortunate foreign people at the other end of this vessel. It must be distinctly more disturbing to them, coming as they do from lesser . . . ah . . . *maritime* origins." Perkins bit into the sandwich, a bland look on his round face. Hannah looked at him in amazement.

Dennis nodded. "Quite right, Mr. Perkins."

All the while, from the other end of *Hoop* there was a caterwaul of shouting, a bleating of complaint, a wailing of mothers, and a screaming of children in a half-dozen languages.

Bergstrom was quickly back at the Alvis. "The Hauptman says that you can leave the inside of the car," he said excitedly, "but you must at no time move more than one meter away from it without permission." He passed the order hurriedly, then he said, "Excuse me, the Spanish family . . . the smallest child is trapped in the ladies' toilet. The door was jammed shut by the shock. I have to help comfort the mother." Bergstrom went away toward the sound of three loudly shouting ladies and the cries of eight small children.

"Thank heavens for small mercies," Dennis prayed as he opened his door. The others stiffly disembarked from the car and stood around it to take in the chaotic scene on the ferry car deck.

Dennis addressed them, "Look men, we must have fair play. We men will take turns to sleep, one on the front seat, one on each running board, and Hannah can have the back seat."

"What if it rains, sir?" Goffin blurted. He blushed slightly at his mistake. "What if it rains, Mr. Jenkins?" he asked.

"Then two sleep underneath the car," interjected Mitchell.

"That's the idea, chaps," said Dennis.

"I rather think, sir," said Perkins, addressing Dennis, "that is a most amicable solution to the accommodation problem."

"No, it's not," Hannah was sitting on the running board, "we have let's see, the front seat, the back seat, the passenger compartment floor. We ask for two planks to put across those iron boxes. That's three, and outside, two on the running boards and one underneath . . . yes?" She looked at Dennis. "Then that makes six beds. Three sleep inside, three out. And we all take turns, three at a time, sleeping inside and sleeping outside . . . no?"

"Yes," said Lynch.

"A more equitable arrangement, if you don't mind my saying so, sir," said Perkins.

Dennis said, "Good, then that's settled, chaps . . . Whose turn to sleep in the car tonight?"

"Alphabetical order, same as in the hut," Mitchell suggested.

"That's it," said Dennis. "Good show, chaps!" as he climbed into the back of the Alvis. He turned and called quietly, "Hannah?"

She turned.

"Come in here a moment, will you? I've some things to talk about," he said. He turned to the four men outside the car. He said, "Look chaps, I want to have a little confidential talk with Hannah, while all the row and diversion is going on . . . no chance of being overheard. Be good chaps, will you, and sort of mill around the ends of the car?"

The four men moved away from the rear door. Hannah climbed in. *"Qu'est-ce que vous voulez Lieutenant?"* she asked in French. Dennis also replied in French.

"You've been on the ferry before?" he asked.

"Many times."

"The captain and the crew know you?"

Mitchell, having learned French in the trenches of Flanders, the hard way, could understand every word as he listened, poker-faced.

"Yes, they were involved in our . . . children's operation, of course. They were paid well . . . "

"Was that the only reason they helped you?" he murmured.

"Not the captain and the engineer, no. They are good men. At first they refused extra money for the passages."

"What about the three sailors?"

Hannah frowned slightly, then she said, "They know me. They were involved, too. They obey the captain, *natürlich*."

"Do you think the captain and the crew will help us if we make a run for it?"

"What, here?" she asked. "Are you mad, Lieutenant?" her voice rose slightly. *"Vous êtes fou?"*

"No, Hannah, but I've a plan in mind . . . later."

"Yes, they will help, but quietly, you understand. They have families in Rotterdam. I know they are on our side. They are . . . they have seen me, the crew, and they looked at me and looked again, but they said nothing. Yes, they will help."

"Can you go out on the deck and quietly ask one of your crewfriends to get hold of a chart for the Scheldte delta?" asked Dennis in a low voice.

She stared at him for a moment with her dark eyes. "It's crazy, Lieutenant . . . it's crazy!" She spoke in a low whisper. "They have guards onboard, they have the gunboat . . . "

Dennis did not let her finish. "They've ordered the gunboat back to Rotterdam. They're sending a guard launch out to us from Numansdorp each day with supplies, each morning, I heard them discussing it, the gunboat captain and the Hauptman."

"But this boat, she's so fragile, and now she's been damaged," Hannah said.

"It's our only chance, Hannah. They know that we are loose somewhere. After the Palace episode, they will stop every car they see. If we'd reached Terneuzen on time . . . yes, we might have got to the Swedish ship all right. Of course, she'll wait for us . . . for the others, but the alarm will be out. The Germans will be watching for a British car. If we go to Terneuzen or Antwerp we'll never get through." His voice dropped even lower. "They're not fools. They will have distributed Morgan's and Jenkins', Perkins', and Beasley's pictures around. They'll check people much more once they consolidate their hold. It's only the chaos all around that has allowed us to get this far. I mean, chaos on every side, even theirs. Look at that Hauptman, probably a railway-station master in civilian life, but once the Sicherheitdienst, the Abwehr, and the Gestapo take over, there'll be little chance of our getting through. Every road will be blocked, every face scanned. It won't take those organizations more than another week or so to set themselves up in business. You, of all people, must know that, Hannah?" he looked at her.

She nodded her head. "Yes, Dennis, of course, you're right." She moved to leave the car. "I'll ask Hank to get a map for us. You can have my ham sandwich if you are still hungry." She stood outside the car, waiting to ask for permission to go to the toilet, making as certain as she could that the captain, up on the wheelhouse bridge, and the engineer, now out on the lowered ramp, might see her face in the moonlight, and in the flashes of the searchlight beams overhead. She bent to speak to Dennis. "Lieutenant . . . "

"Yes?"

"Be careful of German railway-station masters," she said in English. "My father was also a station-master in Germany before the last war."

"Oh really?" said Dennis, "Is he still?"

"No, he, too, was a Hauptman in the old Kriegswehr. He was killed in the Battle of Verdun in 1916. My mother struggled along until 1930. Then I was left an orphan at sixteen. You see, that's why the children are so important to me, because I was alone, too. They have become my family . . . " The voice trailed off.

"I see," said Dennis, surprised at her outburst.

"I . . . I don't want to lose anyone else, Denny," she said.

He looked into her eyes. He saw tears start.

"Yes, Hannah, I know, I, too . . . " Dennis tried to say, reddening, feeling more embarrassed than he'd ever felt before.

She saw him flush, turned away for a moment, then she bent low and spoke in French again, "and be careful of Lynch."

Dennis looked at her, quizzically. "What has he said to you?" he asked.

"Not much, so far, but I, it's a strange feeling, I can't explain it. He's like a dog, an Alsatian dog my grandfather had. It was so good with everyone, with children, then suddenly one day it went absolutely crazy and attacked a baby in its carriage. Of course, the police shot it . . . dead."

"Oh, I think Lynch is all right . . . just hasn't had a fair chance in life that's all," said Dennis.

"Neither did the dog," said Hannah. "Nor the baby. It lost an arm and died before they shot the dog."

"Oh well," said Dennis cheerfully, "accidents will . . . " he stopped.

"It wasn't an accident, Denny, it was murder!" she said as she moved away.

In the morning Dennis had the ferry captain's chart of the Scheldte estuary. In muttered conversations during the next two nights a plan had been made and finalized between Dennis, Hannah, and the four desperados, for by breakfast time on the twenty-sixth of May, this is what Mr. Perkins considered himself to be. As the final details of the plan were concluded, he had intoned, "And may I be the first, sir, to take the liberty of congratulating you on a most ingenious plan, a most ingenious plan, indeed."

At their end of the tipped ferryboat, the Alvis party kept a careful eye on the tide, watching its upward creep, a little higher every day. They also watched the Hauptman, who was now living in the engineer's cabin. They checked the regular changing of the two sentries, every four hours, day and night. In between, they listened for two days to the continual yelling and screaming of the Rumanian mother and her brood, until, to everyone's relief, including the Hauptman's, they were finally taken ashore by the daily supplies launch, transferred to a Rhine steamer, and sent up river.

"Bet the Ruhr war effort will drop 20 percent when that lot steams through," commented Goffin.

They listened in the nights to the steady, continuous drumbeat of

Luftwaffe bombers passing overhead, and in the days they saw the vapor trails of the Messerschmidt 109Fs, the Focke–Wulfs, the Dorniers, and the Stukas high in the blue skies.

27th May, 1940. 8:30 A.M.
Abwehr Headquarters, Kiel

Oberleutnant Fiegler walked into the admiral's office.

Admiral Canaris looked up. "Yes, Fiegler?" he said.

"The report from Kapitan-Corvetten Ludwig is here, sir. I had it sent by hand, bearing in mind what you told me about top secrecy in the matter of . . . "

The admiral broke in, "Briefly, Fiegler, briefly, please," he sighed.

"Amsterdam. They had a Dutch prisoners' working party."

"Who did?"

"Ludwig, sir," replied Fiegler.

"Then say so, man, say so!" the admiral raised his voice.

"Ludwig had a Dutch working party dig out the passage in the Palace basement. The strong room was still shut tight. They tried to blast it open. Finally, sir, bearing in mind your thoughts on Luftwaffe interfer . . . er participation in the exercise, they contacted the naval base at Wilhelmshaven. Bruckner took eighteen tons of nitroglycerine to Amsterdam by fast naval launch."

"And?" the admiral asked, impatiently.

"They blew it open, but there was nothing there, sir, except three cases of old Royal Family documents and this note, sir." Fiegler opened the envelope in his hand and passed the contents to the admiral.

The admiral placed his spectacles on his nose and read:

FINDER'S KEEPER'S—FEATHERFINGERS

Admiral Canaris gasped a short laugh. His face recomposed itself. He ordered, "Fiegler, I want every unit of the Abwehr from here to the front to be concentrated on the Rhine and Scheldte deltas. I want every bridge, every car, every boat, every cart, every jetty, every road covered!"

"Who are we looking for, sir?" asked Fiegler.

"Two gray steel boxes, about the size of sewing machine cases, in a long black car, probably of British make, that also contains four men." He glanced at Ludwig's report, "Four men, possibly more."

"That's all, sir?" asked the adjutant.

"That's enough, Fiegler, but you can include on the order the information that I will personally recommend the finder of these two boxes to . . . I will ensure his immediate promotion two grades in rank."

"And the men, sir? . . . the men in the car?"

"Dead or alive, Fiegler. Dead or alive, that's all!"

Fiegler saluted and left the room.

The admiral again read the burglar's note. Again he scoffed a short laugh.

1st June, 1940. 8:00 A.M.
Margate Roads, Kent. Onboard sailing barge Beatrice Maud

Young-Mike spat into the green-gray water of the roadstead. "Like bloomin' Piccadilly Circus, innit?" he said.

"Henley Regatta," Josh suggested.

They had finished their breakfast and left Knocker down below in the afterflat to eat his porridge and kipper in peace. They were silent as they contemplated the scene around them.

There were craft of all shapes and sizes at anchor, at moorings and alongside the town jetties. There was *Barbara Jean*, sailing barge, right next to *Beatrice Maud* and almost twice her length, swinging to her anchor to seaward of her. Between *Beatrice Maud* and the crowded fleet of smaller vessels inshore, there was *Barbara Jean*'s sister ship *Aidi*, built at the same time, at the same place, on the foreshore at Brightlingsea, sixteen years before. Inshore of *Aidi* was *Doris*, smaller and six years older than *Beatrice*. There were *Tollesbury*, *Ena*, and *Scone*, all about seventy tons each; a little smaller than *Beatrice Maud*. Astern of them and a little out to seaward, were four 158-ton steel-hulled barges at anchor in line together, all brightly painted, all with their red sails brailed up against their yellow-painted eighty-foot steel masts. As Young-Mike turned to look at each of the bigger sailing vessels, Josh murmured their names. It was a roll call of the previous hundred years of the Thames estuarial trade . . . *Ethel Everard, Alf Everard, Will Everard, Fred Everard*.

"That's what they called me onboard the *Genesta*," observed Young-Mike.

"What's that?"

"Mike ever 'ard," Young-Mike said, dodging Josh's backhand.

Even as Young-Mike skipped three paces away from Josh, Knocker appeared at the afterhatch, wearing brass-rimmed spectacles.

"Josh," he called.

"Wazzup Knocker?"

"Did Old Mad Jack on *Prince Albert* sign a *recipe* for them bags of coal we passed him at Gravesend the other day?"

"Yes," said Josh.

"Did you see what I done with it?" implored Knocker, patting his waistcoat pockets.

"You put it inside your 'at," interjected Young-Mike.

"Oh Lord, so I did," mumbled Knocker, "so I did." He turned to go below again. He looked around as he lowered himself down the hatch. "Fine collection, eh, Josh?" he observed.

Josh followed Knocker's gaze all around the odd armada, first at the ten sailing barges, then his eyes followed along the lines of rowing boats, wherries, and cabin cruisers with their motorboat towing leaders. They stared for a while at three Royal National Lifeboat Institution rescue craft, in their red, white, and blue livery. Then Knocker and Josh gazed inshore at the town jetty, where the two biggest vessels in the fleet, Dutch coasters now wearing the Royal Navy white ensign, lay.

Josh looked at Young-Mike for a moment. Knocker waited. Josh grinned. Young-Mike stood there, in his moleskin trousers, his feet bare, his tow hair ruffling in the breeze, freckles on his snub nose, looking at both Knocker and Josh silently.

"Why should England tremble?" quoted Josh, shaking his bald head.

All three grinned widely. Knocker disappeared down to square away his bookkeeping duties in the big, brown leather-bound ledger that, apart from the Holy Bible by his bunk, was the only book onboard the vessel.

Josh went to the afterhatch. "Knocker!" he called. "What time're we moving?"

Knocker's muffled voice came from his cabin. "The tug'll be alongside in about half an hour."

"They need a tow line?" queried Josh.

"No, they're a-going to lash us alongside same as the last trip, so that Navy bloke that was onboard last night reckoned. We'd as lief keep the leeboards hoisted, Josh."

"Right, then I'll get the fenders ready, which side, Knocker?"

"Don't know yet. Just lay 'em out on deck, then we can sling 'em when the tug comes," replied the Skipper.

Josh walked aft to collect six heavy motortruck tires from *Yarmouth Roads*, the spacious afterdeck box, where all the loose deck gear was stowed.

As Josh walked aft he saw, above in the blue sunny sky, the crisscrossed vapor trails of dozens of aircraft. There was no way for him to know which were those of the RAF planes and which were those of their adversaries. At intervals he could plainly hear the spatter-rattle of distant machine-gun fire and the thumping, crumping grumbles of heavy antiaircraft guns. In the intervals there was only the creaking of the blocks and the sail hanks as the ship rolled and the mewing of the gulls as they dived for the remains of the breakfast kippers.

1st June, 1940. 8:30 A.M.
Onboard car ferry Hoop *stranded off Overflakkee Island, Havengvliet, Holland*

During the six days in which *Hoop* had been stranded, her only contact with the outside world was the daily supplies launch, a small Dutch fisherman's motorboat that had been commandeered by the Kriegsmarine, and by her captain's flash lamp that was used in only one emergency—when it urgently beseeched the jetty at Numansdorp to send out the launch on a special errand of mercy to collect the Rumanian brood.

Each day at ten A.M. precisely, the launch, steered by a German naval rating, came out with food, milk, water, and very unreliable news of the war's progress. Each day it returned to the jetty with empty bottles and water cans, empty food containers, and another group of the diplomats and relatives who left the stranded ferry to make for Antwerp by independent means, after interminable argument with Bergstrom and the Hauptman.

As the number of passengers, and particularly children, diminished, the tension onboard *Hoop* eased, greatly aided by the reassurance provided each morning as the tide crept a little higher every day. By the morning of the first of June, even the Hauptman was greeting people, and the sentries were relaxing their vigilance, when the Wehrmacht officer was not on the car deck, or when he was chatting with the Argentinians, the only two other passengers remaining.

Only between Lynch and Hannah did the tension heighten, as he sidled up to her with pleasantries ever ready, and as time after time she rebuffed him.

"Nice day, Hannah . . . "

"Not as nice as yesterday, Mister Lynch."

"Cigarette?"

"Not now, thank you, Mister Lynch."

And each time Hannah spurned Lynch's approach, another layer was peeled away from Lynch's inner self, another raw leaf was raised, exposing a little more—but only to himself so far—the dark hatred in his soul. Each time he retreated into himself, remembering his shoddy childhood, his tired mother, worn out at thirty, scrubbing floors on her knees during his father's frequent imprisonments, the visits with her to the Liverpool Public Assistance Committee office to draw little pink bread tickets after interminable waits in cold, dirty halls, the eternal dearth of money. And each time he saw again in his mind the bright blood in the small room in Rio and the poopdeck of the ocean liner—the only two times in his life when he had truly felt *free* and in control of his own destiny.

On the twenty-sixth a light southwest wind had risen, bringing with it sporadic rain showers, day and night. The Alvis party had found it impossible to sleep under the car, because of rainwater running back from the up-tilted bow. The nights of the twenty-sixth and the previous night they had all sat in the car dozing uncomfortably.

The main difficulty for the Alvis party during the six days high and dry in the middle of the wide Haringvliet estuary was keeping their clothes clean and tidy. When the sun shone, they removed their jackets, of course, but this morning everyone, except Hannah and Perkins, looked disheveled.

All the men except Perkins wore six days' beard growth. The butler, in the three minutes' allotted time each day in the ship's tiny toilet, managed to scrape his face and to quickly wash his celluloid collar. When he was escorted back to the car, Perkins brushed his own, Dennis', and Hannah's clothes. "One has to maintain appearance, sir, particularly with these . . . other . . . er . . . people about. One must set an example, sir," he murmured, eyeing the Argentinians, who grew more silent and depressed every morning.

At 8:30 on the first of June, the ferry *Hoop* moved slightly. At 9:30 the bow was rocking. At 10:30 she slid off the iron girder and, to the ringing cheers and hollers of the eight remaining passengers and the relief of the Hauptman, started up her diesel engine and moved slowly away from the wreckage of the bombed bridge wreck.

Life inside the Alvis was more comfortable now that *Hoop*'s hull was once again more or less horizontal.

"When do we go in action, sir?" asked Goffin.

"When the boat emerges from the Walcheren Canal, at Flushing," said Dennis, quietly.

Hannah interjected, "It's the last control before Antwerp, before Terneusen. They'll check us at Veere, first, when we enter the canal, and then again at Flushing."

"It's better that way," said Dennis. "Otherwise it means taking the Germans and guarding them, and even then we're not at all certain that they'd deal with the checks under gunpoint."

"Can't wait to clobber that bloomin' Jerry officer," said Lynch.

"I'm dealing with him," replied Dennis curtly, as Lynch climbed out of the car to see what he could over the bow as the ferry chugged through the Goeree Strait and on into the wide waters of the Grevelingen. It would not do to climb onto the back of the Alvis—the sentry was watching the car—instead, as the roar of bomber and fighter squadrons echoed from the sky above, he stood on tiptoe, on the running board, and peered over the ramp. Tiring of the flat sea, the flat land, he lowered himself and sat on the running board, waiting.

1st June, 1940. 3:00 P.M.
Onboard the sailing barge Beatrice Maud, *lashed alongside His Majesty's tug* Hermes, *ten miles due north of Gravelines, Pas De Calais, France*

All around the horizon were long lines of small craft, some under their own power; cabin cruisers, lifeboats, fishing boats, large sailing yachts with their sails furled, and harbor ferry launches. Around them, on either side, were the towed vessels, sailing barges and dumb lighters, also in long lines towed by large Naval tugs, which had yet another two sailing barges lashed alongside port and starboard.

On either side of the towed vessels were the bigger craft, steaming under their own power. These were paddle leisure steamers from the Isle of Wight, Southend and Brighton, the Mersey and the Clyde, a couple of Hebridean chuffys—island cargo steamers, harbor tugs from London and Southampton, Dover and Harwich and Hull, thirty-six-foot naval launches, twenty of them, in line ahead; larger pleasure yachts from Cowes, an ocean sailing vessel, two "Shell" fuel tankers, empty, a Southampton car ferry, two smart Dutch coasters, wearing the Royal Navy white ensign, four commandeered Breton trawlers, eight Lowestoft and Yarmouth drifters, an up-river Thames King's-swan-upper's launch, beautifully varnished, and the Seaman's Mission motor launch, taking a sabbatical from its task of ministering to the needs of mariners at anchor for hymns, prayers, and a library.

The vast armada of 180 vessels in a hundred different shapes and sizes was led east, at a speed of three knots, through the slow heaving, windless waters of the eastern Strait of Dover by a solitary minesweeper that rolled her chubby hull from side to side as she wallowed in the swells.

High, high above the vast array of sea and harbor craft flights of fighters, Spitfires flew round and round, every now and then breaking formation to counter the incessant parries and thrusts of the attacking Luftwaffe fighters and diver bombers.

The sounds were the sounds of desperate urgency. They were the spitting rattle of machine-gun fire, the thud-thud-thudding of the larger ship's bofors, the pop-pop! of rifle fire, the hissing sprrrrrd! of World War I Lewis guns from the yachts, the noises of 120 engines, diesel, gasoline, kerosene and steam, the sudden crump! as a Stuka bomb found its mark, the faint cries of wounded men in the sea, the cursing of skippers, mates and gunners, and the cries of frightened seabirds, as they flew away from the convoy and her guard, toward the gray headland of Cap Griz Nez, low on the southwestern horizon.

Once again the English and their Celtic cohorts, the whole people of the Islands, were fighting for their very existence as a nation. There was no show of emotion, no histrionics, but it wasn't like Henley Regatta either; it was *much* noisier.

"Young-Mike!" Knocker called, "Hoist that there for'ard fender a touch, will you?" He turned to Josh who was standing at his side watching a screaming Stuka dive, aiming for the leading minesweeper.

"Rum do, this, eh Josh?" said Knocker as he filled his pipe.

Josh turned his head to stare directly above him. Knocker followed his gaze. They saw a Stuka coming straight down at them, from a westerly direction, out of the sun's glare, a mere blur in the blaze.

"Blimey," said Josh, loudly over the bang-bang-bang! of their tug's bofor gun.

They saw the bomb leave the plane as it leveled off. The bomb hit the tug. The tug's funnel flew into the air before their eyes. The blast jolted the tug, breaking the lashings of the two barges on each side.

Knocker didn't see Young-Mike's head leave his body as it hit the outboard shroud wires. He didn't see the three-foot-long sliver of tugboat engine-room-hatch, quarter-inch steel that skewered Josh to the mizzen mast. He didn't see *Beatrice Maud* heave out of the sea, then crash down again as the tug turned over and sank.

Captain George Edward White, born 1873, was dead in the sea, blown over the portside of his ship in five pieces.

The vast convoy plodded on east, slowly, toward the smoke-heavy horizon. The little rescue boats followed. They picked up the moaning survivors; they weighted the dead, presented them respectfully to the sea, and they too moved on.

Beatrice Maud, her sprit and mainsail slowly flapping from side to side in time with her roll, was left alone with her mortally damaged, abandoned sister barge, *Doris*.

Beatrice wallowed away as *Doris* slowly filled and sank lower and lower, until *Doris* surrendered her spirit and disappeared beneath the sea, to the distant dirge of rumbling guns.

Twilight in the west was a golden streak across the sky. To the south and east the whole horizon was lit by the blood-red, pulsing glow of death and destruction.

As the golden streak on the western rim of the world gave way to the pitch black of night, a lone all-white gannet, on his evening foray, winged lazily over to *Beatrice*'s masthead. Curious, he lounged on the slight evening airs, studying the ship as she lay heaving, agonizing, as if her life were slowly leaving her. His great hooked bill moved from side to side as his head eagerly traced his night hunger, until his eyes caught the sight of Knocker's shattered, torn remains; those that yet floated on the dark, gleaming, silent swells. He dived toward the seaweedlike trail of dead flesh.

The gannet swooped until he was within five feet of the swell crests. Then, with a great backward fling of his wings, he stopped in the air. He hovered, holding his feet hard back, his breast arched in, and his wings stretched out to their very limits, his fluffy trailing feathers shivering, his head bent down, staring at his find. He remained so, very still, except for his involuntary balance glides as the zephyrs moved him slightly up and down, backward and forward. The movements of his head slowly lessened and stilled until finally it was as if the bird had been carved out of the shine of the fire glow on the base of the fog cloud. Now and then, his body shifted a touch sideways and his wings fluttered slightly, but only when there were louder explosions above the rumble in the south. He loitered, hung in space, almost as if he were sculptured out of sea and sky.

Quite suddenly the gannet beat his wings rapidly, violently, as if his soul had been quickened. Faster and faster his wings fluttered, then, with an upward thrust of his head, and gracefully, he rose again to masthead height. Again he hovered, moving his head this way and that, canting it as if he were listening carefully for something only he knew.

As the bird hovered, the weeping cries of *Beatrice*'s sheet block, the wails of her foresail hanks, the sobbing thuds of her great mainsail sprit and the teardrops from her pleading forefoot, as her bow lunged and plunged in the smooth sea swells, gradually eased.

The white bird waited for the sounds to die, then he cried out loudly and wheeled, mewing, and flew away south toward the red-glowing land, leaving *Beatrice Maud* alone with her grief and the heaving sea.

1st June, 1940. 5:50 P.M.
Onboard the car ferry Hoop, *Vlissingen*

The passage through the Graveling, between the Islands of Schouwen and Tholen, and over the six-mile-wide East Scheldt River mouth, had been smooth. The wind had dropped, and for the rest of the passage, through the Beveland Islands, the ferry had been in calm, protected waters. They had anchored for two nights and two days, waiting to pass into the Walcheren Canal.

There had been a cursory glance onboard the ship by a Feldwebel at Veere, then they had passed through the ten-mile-long canal to Vlissingen. There the inspection had been slightly more worrying to the Alvis party. Two German army officers had come onboard and talked with the Hauptman for half an hour, inspecting the papers and scanning the passengers. Finally, the German naval officers had waved them on, and *Hoop* chugged her way east into the West Scheldt estuary, with only twelve miles to go to Terneuzen, the terminal for Antwerp.

Dennis had drawn a rough map of the route from Terneuzen to Antwerp. "Of course," he said to Hannah and Mitchell with Lynch looking over their shoulders, "Terneuzen is still in Holland, in this little enclave. There is no direct road from Terneuzen to Antwerp. The convoy is supposed to go to Ghent, in Belgium, over the frontier at Zelzat, and then from Ghent to Antwerp. At our convoy speed they would expect us to arrive in Antwerp in the morning. They would not, of course, allow us to travel overnight."

"What about the checkpoint at Terneuzen?" asked Mitchell.

"That would be about the same as the place we've just passed, Flushing. It's at the Dutch-Belgian frontier. We would have had some delay, of course."

"Really?" said Lynch, grinning. Dennis frowned at Lynch.

The Hauptman was on the wheelhouse bridge, looking astern at the ferry's wake.

"Gentlemen," said Dennis quietly watching the Hauptman, "I think it's time for our move . . . all ready?"

"All ready, sir," said Goffin.

"My pleasure, if I might say so, sir," Perkins said, as he started to clamber out of the car.

Dennis held his hand up. On the other side of the Alvis so did Goffin. The German sentry who had been strolling on the car deck nodded at Goffin, toward the door of the men's toilet in the side deckhouse. Goffin ambled over. He opened the door, stepped over the high sill, and disappeared. The door closed behind him.

Suddenly, there was a cry from inside the toilet. The guard moved over to open the door and look inside. In a flash, Lynch slid the Alvis tire lever from under his jacket. He bashed the sentry on the head. The sentry fell. Lynch dragged him by the feet out of the way of the door. Goffin rushed out of the toilet, grabbed the sentry's schmeisser belt, pulled it down the sailor's arm, and pointed the gun up at the Hauptman.

Dennis and Mitchell, as soon as Lynch drew the tire lever, crouched down over the back of the Alvis, and with both hands wrapped around the butts, aimed their Enfields up at the Hauptman.

For a space of four seconds there was no noise apart from the ferry engines and the faint drone of passing bombers overhead.

Goffin broke the silence, "I wish I knew," he said to Lynch, as he glanced down at the schmeisser, "how this bastard works."

Dennis called, "Herr Hauptman!"

The German had not heard him. In the wheelhouse, the captain and a sailor gazed down at them in amazement.

"Herr Hauptman!" Dennis repeated. Still the German could not hear.

Dennis stood up, looked at the helmsman behind his glass window and jerked his finger in short jabs at the German. The captain went to the wheelhouse door and called to the Hauptman. He pointed down at the Alvis. The German turned. For a moment he did nothing. He stared at the two revolvers and the submachine gun aimed at him. His mouth opened, then closed. Slowly he raised his hands.

Lynch scrambled up the ladder to the wheelhouse bridge. He unbuckled the Hauptman's revolver. He threw it down to Mitchell, who caught it. Mitchell, in turn, threw it back to Hannah. She offered the Luger to Perkins, who declined at first, then accepted it, holding the holster in his hand.

"Christ!" shouted Lynch, "Keep him covered. I don't have a gun!"

Dennis was by now at the head of the ladder and covered the German with his revolver. Goffin was covering the captain and the helmsman from the car deck.

"Turn the ship round, head west!" ordered Dennis, opening the wheelhouse door. The captain and the helmsman nodded, expressionless. Dennis shouted down, "Mitchell, come up here and keep the wheelmen covered!"

In a moment Mitchell was on the bridge. He had his Enfield in his hand, but he did not point it at the Dutchmen. The ferry crew looked poker-faced. Mitchell shyly smiled at them, saying nothing.

"What we going to do with these Jerries?" asked Lynch. "Knock 'em off?"

"First we'll get this one down below," Dennis replied as he gestured at the Hauptman toward the ladder. "Then they can have a dose of their own medicine. Put them in one of the cars and secure them."

"Right, just up my street," said Lynch, clambering down the ladder after the German. "Still reckon we ought to top 'em, though!"

"Keep the crew covered, Goffin," ordered Dennis. "Make sure no one moves."

"Aye aye, sir," acknowledged Goffin.

Dennis told the Hauptman to call out the off-duty sentry in the captain's tiny cabin. He did so. The sentry came out to feel two Enfields poking his side, one left and one right. His hands shot up. Hannah ran into the cabin and picked up the sentry's schmeisser. She hurried over to Goffin, and, still covering the passengers, showed him how to take the safety catch off.

Dennis showed the Hauptman and the sentry the open door of the Hispano-Suiza. He ordered them to pick up the unconscious sentry and lay him on the back seat. The Hauptman and the sailor climbed into the big car and, while Dennis covered them, Lynch went into the engine room, returned with some wire cable and wired the doors shut.

"You can open the windows half-way down!" Dennis said in German. He scratched the metal side of the Hauptman's window with the muzzle of his pistol. "If it is opened any lower than that, my men will blow your brains out!"

The Hauptman nodded miserably.

Dennis turned to Goffin and Hannah, both covering the speechless crew with their schmeissers. "Now," he said quietly, "it's all or nothing."

"Shit or bust, sir," said Goffin.

"Keep everyone covered, Goffin, Hannah. I'm going up to talk with the captain for a few minutes." Dennis said as he headed for the bridge deck.

Perkins stopped him. "Excuse me, sir," he said as he stood holding the Hauptman's holster between a finger and his thumb, "what shall I do with this . . . object?"

"Put it on, Mr. Perkins. Put it on," shouted Dennis as he hurried to climb the ladder.

"Very good, sir, and please allow me to say, sir . . . " But he got no further. He saw that the lieutenant was gone. He turned to Hannah. "A remarkable young man, miss, a most remarkable young man."

As Dennis reached the wheelhouse, the captain spluttered in German, "You'll never get away with it!"

Dennis ignored the statement. "How much fuel do you have?" he asked the engineer, who was now also on the bridge.

"Four hundred gallons, about a hundred miles," the Dutch engineer replied.

"Head her out to sea and then west, Captain."

The captain stared at Dennis aghast. He cried, "But west . . . west? That's Ostende . . . the fighting goes on there!"

"We're not heading to Ostende. I mean due west," said Dennis.

"Due west?" the captain murmured," But that's . . . "

Dennis broke in, "That's right, England!"

The captain frowned. He said in a quiet voice, "But the sea, this is only a riverboat."

"There's been hardly any wind for three days, Captain. There'll be only a swell out there. Once we get out, we'll batten down the hull and plug up the gaps in the ramp sides on the bow."

"But . . . " the captain started to protest.

"No buts, please," said Dennis. "Give your men the orders immediately."

"Of course, Mr. Jenkins," said the captain.

"Lieutenant Dennis is my real name, sir, Lieutenant Dennis, Royal Engineers. Your company will, of course, be reimbursed after the war."

"Of course, Lieutenant Dennis," said the captain. He left the wheelhouse with Dennis to address the crew.

Hoop, her wheelhouse covered with the white tarpaulin, the red cross painted on it, chugged out of the Scheldte estuary, into the calm North Sea, past a Flushing-Breskens ferry loaded down with Wehrmacht troops, at the very moment when, eighty-five miles to the southwest, *Beatrice Maud* wallowed helplessly as the dying *Doris* plunged below the surface of the sea.

Once the three seamen had completed the tasks of battening down *Hoop*'s three hatches on the car deck and plugging up the forward ramp with canvas, they were confined to one of the cars. The captain and engineer were in the wheelhouse. Dennis set two-hour watches for two sentries with schmeissers, to be stationed on the wheelhouse bridge.

Dennis and Goffin kept the first two-hour watch. Then Mitchell and Perkins. Lynch and Hannah had the 4 A.M. to 6 A.M. watch.

At four-thirty, while the off-watch Alvis party was dozing as well as they could in their cars, Hannah and Lynch stood quietly talking on the wheelhouse bridge. They had both laid their machine guns down to have a smoke.

Lynch had decided to make his move. He was peering ahead of the boat, smirking to himself.

"What do you find so amusing?" asked Hannah.

"I'm thinking what a bloody joke it is . . . us taking over this Dutch boat from the Germans, to steal a load of loot that the Dutch have already stolen from their colonies . . . that the Dutch Royalty have nicked from the ordinary Dutch people—the working idiots— over the centuries and from the East Indian bloomin' sultans who'd already pinched it from their poor bloody wog minions."

"But the Queen only holds it in trust for Holland."

"Bullshit, Hannah. That's the same old story they've been telling the mugs at the bottom for centuries, *trust*! That's the same as the British aristocracy says about all their landholdings, the railways, the bleedin' coal mines." He looked at Hannah. "I'm telling you, it's pure unadulterated bullshit, to keep silly buggers like Goffin and Dennis quiet," he hesitated, "Dennis and his soppy ideas about Mitchell and me. I'm a *tea-leaf*, I was born . . . "

"What?" Hannah's face frowned in puzzlement.

"Sorry, a thief. I was born a bloody thief and I'll die a thief, and my kids will be thieves too, least they will be if they have any sense." He put his cigarette to his lips, then jerked it away in the palm of his hand. "And when Dennis' kids have what he has now, my bloody kids'll nick it off them, too, and so will Mitch's. Don't you bleedin' highbrows realize that? It's in our bones."

There was half a minute's silence.

"You interested in coming in with me, Hannah? I reckon we could grab all that loot with no trouble. It would be dead easy to turn the tables on Dennis. He's a soft bloke, thick as two planks, him and 'is

Bloomsbury bullshit. I'm telling you, Hannah, I heard it before we took the stuff in Amsterdam, there's a bleedin' fortune in those two boxes."

"What are you talking about? Are you mad?"

"I'm talking about all this lot here. What are they going to get out of this bloody war? Mitchell, he's a lad, he *knows* what *he's* going to get. Same as he got after the last lot, sweet bugger all."

"There's a lot of evil philosophy let loose in Europe, Lynch," Hannah said. "It has to be resisted . . . "

"What, you mean ordinary Jerries gettin' their fair shares of the pie, you call that evil?"

She scoffed, "Ordinary people being completely fooled by a . . . a . . . lunatic megalomaniac."

"Gets things done, don't he? The old gang don't like that, do they?"

Hannah glared at Lynch straight in the eyes. "You know, Lynch, you're nothing but a selfish, amoral scoundrel. You haven't one scruple in your body, do you? Some family you must have come from!"

"Smashing," said Lynch. "My old man was the best housebreaker in Liverpool. We got on like peas in a bloody pod . . . when he was out of the nick. This is going to be the century of us that get what we can as much as we can, *when* we can, an' if we don't—well, what d'you think Goffin's life will be like after this bleedin' war's over?"

She tossed her head toward the Alvis. "They're much more powerful than you," she said. "It doesn't matter what you might or might not be tempted to do, they will stop you."

"Bullshit!"

"They aren't after heroics," she said, her voice rising.

"Bloody victims," he scoffed.

"We all are!" she shouted.

"Maybe so, but this kiddie's going to be a flamin' *rich* victim." He threw his cigarette over the stern of the boat and picked up his schmeisser.

To the southwest of them the whole horizon was ablaze with the red glow of burning oil tanks and buildings. There was a low rumble of gunfire. Overhead plane after plane passed them, the engines beating a monotonous whoom! zoom! whoom! zoom!

Hannah glanced up. "Heinkels," she said.

At the moment Hannah turned her face up to the sky, Lynch kicked the schmeisser that had been at her feet away from her along the wheelhouse bridge.

She screamed out, "No, Lynch!"

Dennis, dozing down below, heard Hannah's scream. He rushed out of the car just in time to see Lynch point his gun at Hannah.

Dennis drew his Enfield, "Lynch!" he bawled—his hands, his whole body shaking.

Lynch turned. He fired a burst at Dennis. The first rounds passed over Dennis' head as he aimed his Enfield. The fourth bullet passed into his forehead, between the eyes, out of the back of his head and hit the steel ramp. Dennis' body dropped.

Hannah dived for her machine pistol. Even as she raised it to fire, Lynch shot her. Bullets sprayed into the Bugatti, instantly killing the two Argentinians inside. "Bloody bitch . . . shoot me, would you?" Lynch shouted in his rage.

Goffin, Mitchell, and Perkins woke at the gunfire. In a shocked stupor, they saw Dennis' body drop. They gazed petrified as the bullets hit Hannah, sending her lifeless, bleeding body spinning off the wheelhouse bridge. They heard the engines stop, as the frightened captain shouted down the voice pipe, his face horror-stricken. *Hoop* wallowed in the swell.

They heard Lynch, trembling with excitement. "Goffin! Mitchell! Perkins! Come out of the car one by one, when I tell you! Any wrong moves and everybody gets it! Come out one by one and throw your guns over the ramp!"

"The bastard!" whispered Goffin. "The bleedin' toe-rag!"

"Better do as he says, Goff," said Mitchell. "This is a topping job and he knows it."

When they had thrown their own and Dennis' Enfields over the bow ramp, into the sea, they each returned inside the car.

The three waited in silence for two minutes.

Lynch shouted again, "Mitchell!"

Mitchell stuck his head out of the window. "Right here," he called.

"You comin' in on this with me?" Lynch yelled in a high scream.

"I'll miss out on this one, Banger. It's a *toppin'* job."

Lynch cursed, "You bloody fool, Mitch. I've ordered the skipper to lower the lifeboat. All you lot are goin' in it, unless you yourself want to come fifty-fifty with me!"

"I'll take my chance in the boat!" called Mitchell.

The shaking sailors, grim-faced, lowered the nine-foot wooden rowboat over the ferry side. The first one down the lowering ropes was Goffin. He muttered, as he slid down the twisted lines, "Friggin' maniac!"

Perkins was next, clambering down hand over hand as Goffin

steadied the lines for him. He fell into the dinghy, almost overturning it.

As Mitchell grasped the hoist rope to lower himself down, Lynch called, "Sure you won't change your mind, mate?"

Mitchell didn't look at Lynch as he replied, "Not me. You'll never get away with this." He paused and looked around the horizon. "Anyway, where the hell are we? You can at least tell us that."

Lynch thumbed at the wheelhouse. "Ask him." He gestured toward the cowering captain.

Mitchell shouted, "Captain!"

The captain, frightened, opened the door.

"Ja?" he asked.

"Wo ist dieses Schiff?" asked Mitchell. It was the first and only time Goffin had heard him speak German.

The captain pointed to a darker patch in the glowing southern horizon. "Zeebrugge," he said in a shaking voice, then he repeated, "Zeebrugge."

"Danke, Kapitan, danke sehr," said Mitchell. Without looking again at Lynch, he slid down the rope, sat down in the dinghy, and cast off.

As Perkins and Goffin rowed away from the ferry they heard Lynch, standing on the dark deck above them shout, "Now Mister Bloody Banger Lynch is in charge . . . at long bleedin' last!"

Chapter 10

*   *

It's a Long Way to Tipperary

2nd–3rd June, 1940

It's a long way to Tipperary,
It's a long way to go—
It's a long way to Tipperary—
To the sweetest girl I know.
Goodbye, Piccadilly,
Farewell Leicester Square,
It's a long, long way to Tipperary,
But my heart's right there!

Chorus from the British song, World War I
Music by Jack Judge, words by Harry Williams, 1912

10.

"It's a Long Way to Tipperary"

2nd June, 1940. 5:00 A.M.
At sea, eight miles due north of Zeebrugge, Belgium

They rowed the nine-foot dinghy away from the car ferry in silence
for an hour. The dinghy rose up and down slowly in the surprisingly
bigger swell than they had supposed from the deck of *Hoop*.

"You bring the milk, Perkins?" gasped Goffin, as he pulled back
his oar. They were well clear of the ferry now.

"All four liters, like you said, Mister Goffin," panted Perkins, his
voice shaking.

Mitchell took stock of their situation. First he looked at Goffin, in
his dirty and bedraggled wing commander's get-up. He then stared at
Perkins, still in his best Sunday clothes and Homburg hat, looking
almost as immaculate as ever. He glanced at his own Royal Navy
Captain's uniform. He saw that the top gold braid ring on his right
sleeve was torn and hanging from the cloth. He ripped the braid off
and threw it over the side of the nine-foot dinghy.

Goffin grinned at him. "Should 'ave kept that on, Mitch," he said,
"now you got your own ship."

"I could have sewn that on for you, Mr. Mitchell," said Perkins.

"Ahhr, cut out the Mister, for crissake, Perkins," said Mitchell.

"Very good, but only on one condition," replied Perkins.

"What's that?" asked Mitchell.

"That you call me by my first name, too, Mister Mitchell."

"And what might your first name be?" Goffin enquired.

"Randolph," said Perkins, smiling.

"Randy!" yelled Goffin. "Randy by name, randy by nature!"

Mitchell said, "I reckon that the best way is if I relieve you after an
hour, Randy, and then you relieve Goff after an hour, then he relieves
me, and so on. We got a long way to . . . "

"*Tipperary, it's a long way to go!*" sang Goffin, shouting at the top of
his lungs.

"Shut up Goff!" Mitchell shouted. Then he lowered his voice,
"Sorry mate. It's not your singing. It's that bloody song. I hate it. I
had too long with the . . . in the trenches . . . with that bloody
lot," Mitchell pointed his arm out to the glowing red sky in the south.

"I lost too many . . . we had almost 60,000 casualties in one day
when the Somme offensive started an' they only got across three
bleedin' lines of Jerry trenches. They advanced a 'undred

214

yards . . . *60,000 in one day*! Almost a million dead in the whole war, and that was only on *our* side."

"No wonder you don't want to head for the shore, Mitch," Goffin said quietly as he pulled another oar stroke.

"That's it. I don't want none of that again, ever!" said Mitch. "I'd rather be in this boat for a month than back there in those bloody trenches for one day."

"I would like to point out at this juncture, gentlemen, that I too was present at the first Somme offensive," said Perkins.

"Really, what outfit?" said Goffin, genuinely interested.

"I was batman to Earl Haig, the commander-in-chief, a most impatient, impetuous gentleman, if I might add."

"Bloody bastard," said Mitch, "Haig—bad as that one there." He jerked his head back toward the ferry, which by now was no more than a faint shadow, alternately black and pink as it wallowed in the light of the glare from the Belgian shore. "Only difference was he was a general."

For five minutes the silence was broken only by the squeaking of the oar locks.

"What about that toe-rag back there, Mitch?" Goffin asked, nodding at the ferry.

"Banger? What about him?" murmured Mitchell.

"Well, I mean, if we get back."

"What do you mean, *IF*? We're, I'm going to row this bastard boat all the way to Blighty myself if I have to."

"Well, all right then, *when* we get back, what're you going to do?"

"I'm going to walk into the first pub I come to and knock off three pints in one swallow!" Mitchell said, his face serious. Everyone laughed softly.

Goffin said, "No, serious, though, what're you going to do, split on him?"

"Me narking? Not on your bloody nelly!" rasped Mitchell. "I've never narked yet, not even for a topping job like this one, and I'm buggered if I'm going to start now. Balls to that for a skylark!"

"What about you, Randy?" asked Goffin.

Perkins paused in his rowing for a moment. The boat's bows shot round to face Mitchell to the glowing southern sky. They all rested.

Perkins intoned, "I shall, of course, be obliged to make a report at the . . . er . . . Foreign Office Staff Department, but I shall insure that you two gentlemen are completely exonerated when the commission of the recent appalling occurrences is discussed."

Goffin screwed up his eyes. He nodded his head sideways toward

Perkins, all the while facing in Mitchell's direction, looking puzzled.

Mitchell explained quietly, "He's going to report what happened, and clear us."

"Oh," said Goffin.

They set to rowing, keeping the scarlet glow to the south on the left of Mitchell's shoulder as he sat facing forward, steering the 120 miles of treacherous North Sea to England.

2nd June, 1940. 7:00 A.M.
Abwehr Headquarters, Amsterdam

Major Von Beihlsdorf was still in his pajamas when Kapitan Ludwig arrived. He was speaking on the telephone. He gestured to Ludwig to sit down on the settee. Von Beihlsdorf listened for three minutes. He grunted a "thank you" and hung up. He turned to Ludwig. "Excuse the *déshabille*, Ludwig," he said.

"Sir," said Ludwig.

Von Beihlsdorf studied his yet unshaven face in the great looking glass over the mantelpiece as he spoke. "The reason I've sent for you is that I've had a . . . very curious telephone call from Antwerp." The major walked around to his desk chair and sat down. "It seems that a certain Herr Bergstrom, of the Swedish Red Cross, complained late last night about . . . er . . . " He looked down at the scribbled note on his desk. "Yes, *twelve* motor cars belonging to the Hague diplomatic community missing, along with the British Legation party who were on a ferryboat from Rotterdam," he continued for five minutes, recounting the adventures of *Hoop* as far as they were known to him.

"And those two damned fools in Flushing reported that the cars passed through the control there at 5:00 P.M. yesterday, but control at Terneuzen swears there hasn't seen sight nor sound of the ferry."

Ludwig said slowly, "So they've stolen the ferry?"

"Our local naval command down there in the Scheldte searched all night in the estuary, not a sight," replied Von Beihlsdorf. "Of course, the affair passed through Bohlen's desk—a sharp fellow that one—and he put two and two together. He came out with the not really surprising sum of four." The major grimaced. "Bohlen contacted me at 3:30 this morning."

"What's our next move, sir?" asked Ludwig.

"I've already received orders from Kiel. You are to fly down with three good men right away to Antwerp—they've laid a Junkers on—and pick up a car and get down to the Belgian coast." He rose.

He walked to the wall map. Ludwig followed him and studied the map as Von Biehlsdorf traced his finger over the route he was to take. "You start off at Breskens, here, and you cover every yard of that damned coast, all the way down to Calais, to Brest, if necessary."

"But the British are still holding out on the French frontier, aren't they, sir?"

Von Biehlsdorf turned and looked at Ludwig. He was silent for a half-minute. He said, "They were last night, but whether or not they will be tomorrow morning, Captain Ludwig, is another matter entirely." He smiled. "It looks extremely doubtful for them. Our tanks are already in Veurne here, and the British main rear guard at Hazebrouk has fallen back northward, toward the sea. As you know, Colonel Rommel is already in Calais. The latest information is that thousands of our erstwhile . . . " he grinned broadly, "enemies . . . are packed on the beaches on both sides of Dunkirk like rats in a trap. The trap is about to snap shut. So Ludwig, by the time you reach La Panne here on the Belgian-French frontier, there should be nothing at all to stop you continuing to drive on down the coast." He tapped Ludwig's shoulder, "All the way to Brittany, Ludwig, all the way to Brittany. All you have to do is be careful not to run over any of the prisoners!" He laughed.

"What range does the ferry have, sir?" asked Ludwig, smiling.

"We've checked that with the ferry company. When she departed Rotterdam she had enough fuel for the return trip to Antwerp and back. So when she passed through that damned control at Flushing, she had about 120 miles of fuel, if the weather holds out."

Ludwig asked quietly, "You don't think it's possible she's on the way to England?"

"These gentlemen are desperate enough to try anything, but I've sent out her details to Kesselring's No. 2 that she is carrying escaped assassins and is to be sunk at all costs if she approaches within ten miles of the English coast. If she stays near the French coast, she is to be left alone, watched, and her position is to be reported."

"And our navy, sir?" asked Ludwig.

"Impossible. They can't get within fifteen miles of the evacuation channel across the straits. The British have five destroyers on the Belgian side of the channel and continuous flights of fighter and bomber patrols by their damned Royal Air Force. From Ostende down to the Belgian frontier at sea, it's a complete no man's land. We can't risk our E-boats; the few we have we need to conserve for the invasion of England."

"Do you think we'll invade this summer, sir?"

"The simple answer to that, my dear Ludwig, is that our people are inspecting the Dutch barges already. Very good, Ludwig, you may proceed," he ordered. "By the way, there's that jump two ranks if you get it."

Ludwig smiled, sprang to attention eagerly, saluted, and left the room.

The major pulled the bell cord on the wall. His adjutant entered the room. "Bring Briggs in, will you?" requested Von Biehlsdorf. He crushed his cigarette in the hotel ashtray on the table desk.

Briggs was half-carried into the room by two detectives. His face had aged ten years in two weeks. He was still dressed in the clothes in which he had been arrested in Apeldoorn. He was brought to attention by the sergeant who thumped his shoulders.

"You are due to be executed in the morning, Briggs," announced Von Biehlsdorf. Briggs looked at the top button of the major's pajamas. He said nothing.

"The sentence was passed by the military tribunal in accordance with the Rules of War," Von Biehlsdorf said, then he added, "however, I have here a chance for you to save yourself." Briggs' eyes met his for a fleeting second. The major coughed and continued, "We know that North Pole is in operation. We are fairly certain that it's the work of Captain Van Velzor. We want to make sure. You can help us." The major paused. "Briggs!" he bawled.

Briggs looked up.

"Will you help us?" Von Biehlsdorf pleaded, quietly, menacingly.

"What do you want me to do?" whispered Briggs.

"Simple," Von Biehlsdorf smiled as he raised his voice again to conversational level. "We know where Orange is; we want you to tell Van Velzor."

"How? He must know I'm in your hands?"

"You contact him, tell him the truth . . . that you have offered to work for us in exchange for your life and that you have learned that Orange is free and where they are . . . "

Briggs mumbled, "Why do you want him? Oh, I see, you wish to monitor his broadcasts."

"Not monitor, Briggs," murmured the major, "not monitor, we wish to *dictate* his broadcasts through you. And when we've insinuated you into the North Pole organization, we shall not merely dictate, we shall originate!" He paused for a moment. "Will you do it?"

Briggs said nothing for ten seconds. He nodded his head.

"Take him out and clean him up," Von Biehlsdorf ordered the

sergeant.

Briggs interjected, "But how will I contact Van Velzor?"

The major spoke as if to a six-year-old, "Simple, my dear Briggs, telephone the Dutch Army Headquarters and ask to speak to him, now!" He ordered the sergeant, "Take him away, sergeant."

The sergeant saluted. The guards supported Briggs on his way out into the hotel passage.

2nd June, 1940. 7:15 A.M.
At sea, onboard car ferry Hoop *twelve miles due north of Ostende, Belgium*

Lynch forced the two German soldiers out of their car at pistol point as soon as daylight broke the eastern sea sky. He ordered them to heave Dennis' and Hannah's bodies, weighted, over the side. They also threw the two Argentinian corpses after them. He ordered the Hauptman out of the Hispano-Suiza.

"Over the side you go, mate," he growled, as the ferry crew, all mustered aghast and anxious on the bridge above, looked on. The Hauptman quaking, did not understand. Lynch waved his gun in the direction of the forward ramp. "Go . . . go!" he shouted.

The two German sailors, their hands held on top of their heads, moved forward. The Hauptman, his eyes pleading to Lynch, reluctantly followed the sailors.

"Go on, you bastard . . . get!" Lynch howled. "Keep Banger in a bleedin' car for a week would yer?" He fired a shot from his Walther .38 over the bow of the ship. "Get!"

The three Germans scrambled up the inboard side of the ramp. The two sailors swung themselves over. The first one dropped into the sea. The second clung to the top edge of the ramp for five seconds, then he too dropped into the bow wave. The Hauptman sat on the ramp top, his shaking body facing forward, his frightened eyes still staring at Lynch. The Englishman moved toward him, slowly, grinning. The German stared at the Walther as he slid himself carefully over the ramp edge. He clung desperately onto it. He looked up as he hung there. Lynch leaned over the ramp. He grabbed hold of one of the Hauptman's wrists, preventing him from falling. For one brief second the German imagined that Lynch was going to heave him back into the ferry. Then, as he looked into Lynch's eyes, the Englishman held the muzzle of the Walther onto his forehead and pulled the trigger.

The Hauptman's body fell. The moving bow hit it. The hull passed over it, just as it had done to the two sailors. The whizzing ferry propeller gashed it in a split second, into a dozen unrecognizable chunks of flesh that shot out of the ferry's wake, under the horrified eyes of the Dutchmen now staring aft.

"That's cleared that little lot," chortled Lynch. He climbed to the portside of the wheelhouse, being careful to keep away from the Dutchmen. "Head for the coast!" he ordered the helmsman. The sailor did not understand. "Nearer the coast!" Lynch glowered. He jabbed the Walther muzzle in the direction of the billows of smoke filling the southwestern horizon. The captain guessed he understood. He snapped an anxious order to the helmsman. The good ship *Hoop* changed course toward the smoke.

Lynch grinned, glancing quickly at the crew and then at the Alvis, where the still-loaded and cocked schmeissers sat on the back seat. He climbed down the ladder, and, watching the captain, the engineer, and the three seamen all lined up on the starboard side of the wheelhouse bridge, he tore open the Alvis luggage compartment.

Taking his time, he divested his civilian suit and donned Netherlands army working fatigues. This done he climbed back to the portside of the bridge. "Cherbourg, France!" he shouted at the helmsman. The Dutch sailor nodded, desperately afraid.

After five minutes on the bridge, Lynch slid down the ladder to the car deck again. He opened the Alvis door. He dragged both steel boxes out of the passenger compartment. He set a tiny *plastique* charge on each lock and stood well back to fire them. While the Dutchmen jumped at each retort, he blew both locks off each box. Keeping one eye on the Dutchmen he tore open the first box. It was full of papers. He snatched the securities, land titles, and the shares of the Royal Dutch Shell Oil Company, a billion pounds on paper, out of the chest, throwing them to the breeze over the car deck in disgust.

Lynch lifted the lid of the second box. He stared at the contents for five seconds. A big grin broke out on his face. He let the box lid fall. "Done the bugger!" he whooped.

Glancing at the Dutch crew above him, he hefted the second box into the Alvis. He returned to the bridge, pointing his Walther at each of the crew, one after the other, as they stood quaking on the bridge.

2nd June, 1940. 7:35 A.M.
Onboard His Majesty's Motor Fishing Vessel MFV
4203 at sea, five miles north of Gravelines, France

"Funny that there big gannet, he's been with us all the night, only bloomin' bird I've seen anywhere near the beaches," commented Petty Officer O'Brien, bending slightly to peer aloft.

"That barge over there is drifting," said Leading Seaman Lofty Willis in his New Zealand accent. As O'Brien turned, he pointed at a gray shape in the morning mist.

"We'll nip over a bit closer an' 'ave a look," murmured the P.O. skipper. "Come on in the wheelhouse, Lofty, we got a cup o' cocoa goin'."

Lofty pushed his round steel helmet back off his forehead and sipped the hot cocoa from a tin mug as they approached the sailing barge. He watched the gannet fly over to her and hover over her masthead.

"No one on deck, mate," said Petty Officer O'Brien, in a sharp cockney accent. "We'll soon see though."

He swung the MFV around the stern of the wallowing barge. They read the name on the counter *Beatrice Maud, London*. They both gazed up and forward at the flopping, loose mainsail, and the huge sprit-boom crashing back and forth across the vessel as she rolled, then they saw the body of a big, bald man pinned to the mizzenmast, his eyes bulging out of their sockets as his head lolled back and forth across his chest.

"Poor bastard," murmured O'Brien.

Lofty was already prepared to spring onboard the barge. He made a flying leap at the starboard chain plates. He clambered on the rolling ship. He went straight back aft. He held the body with his eyes shut and heaved at the steel plate. He pulled hard. It wouldn't budge. Lofty opened his eyes and saw a rag in the corpse's boiler suit pocket. Lofty wrapped it around his own hand. He jiggled the metal from side to side. He worked it up and down. It came slowly loose. It jerked out. The body fell into its own dried blood stains on the deck.

By this time Lofty's *winger*, Able Seamen Taff Crawford, a half-caste from Swansea, was at his side, his wide eyes staring in horror at the body.

"Get a nice big weight," Lofty said quietly. "That there locker should have something in it."

Taff opened the locker. He delved inside, under the jumble of scrubbing brushes and rags. In the bottom of the locker his hand encountered a great hunk of metal. He dragged out a spare mainsheet block. He turned to Lofty. "This do?"

"Right, mate. Bring some line," shouted Lofty.

He tied the iron block around the big body, gently. "Give us a hand to lift him over the side," he whispered to Taff.

The body was heavy. They were forced to lift the feet up first until the corpse's backside was on the gunwale. As they lifted the upper part of the torso the head flopped back, the chest opened; light and dark gray guts spilled out over the head. Taff heaved up his breakfast as the corpse went over the side.

"God rest his soul," murmured Lofty. "Now we'll get the towline ready. Come on, Taff, skipper wants to tow her in close. Might as well, while we're on our way in, never know, some poor blighter might know how to sail."

They first made fast one of the barge's sheet lines on the knighthead. Lofty threw the fag end of the line to O'Brien, who made it fast on the MFV. Lofty seized the sprit tang that was flogging as the great boom banged back and forth. He made it fast on the knighthead, too. The sprit was now held tight against the starboard shrouds. First Taff, gray and shaking, then Lofty jumped back onto the MFV, which moved forward, ahead of the barge. The towrope tautened, and the massive wooden bulk of the knighthead bitt creaked faintly. *Beatrice Maud* started, slowly, to move forward.

Her foresail hanks still wailed on the forestay but quieter. Her loose mainsail still fluttered a little, but her low sobbing was stifled.

Guarding the towrope on the stern of the MFV, Lofty watched the big all-white gannet, looking out for his breakfast now, head toward the barge. Lofty gazed at the delicate, slow lift and drop of the bird's wide wings as he glided gracefully over the barge's topmast on the still air of the June morning.

The masthead pennant lazily flapped in the light breeze of the barge's slow forward movement. The bird suddenly swooped, mewing, down to the level of the topmast housing. His wings swiftly spread and he turned, in a wide, sweeping circle, seeming not to move his wings, and headed for the stern of the MFV.

As the bird neared Lofty, his head, with the large hooked yellow beak, searched from side to side of the fishing boat's wake. Lofty bent down, took a slice of stale bread from the top of the galley gash bucket, and threw it up to the gannet. With an explosion of flurries and squawks the bird dropped again and caught the bread on downward curve of its trajectory into the sea.

When the MFV reached half a mile off the beach, she hove to. Lofty cast off the barge's towing line. The MFV, with a great churning of her propeller wash, got under way. The gannet moved off to watch over *Beatrice Maud* as she rolled to the roar of gunfire in the near-distance, over the land and the sea.

2nd June, 1940. 8:15 A.M.
The War Room, London

"How many now?" asked the P.M. He was tired, dead tired.

"Latest figure 340,000, or close to it," said the CIGS brightly. "We're moving them from the south coast as soon as they land."

"Risky to carry on much longer, sir," said the first sea lord. "I simply cannot lose anymore destroyers . . . four gone to date . . . if I am expected to defend the Dover Strait."

The air minister said, "Dowding is withdrawing his fighter patrols tonight, he says whether we agree or not, either that or he will resign."

The P.M. gazed at all eight men around the table, one after the other. His eyes narrowed a little when they encountered 'C''s. "Three-hundred thousand," he murmured, "beyond our wildest hopes." He sighed. "Very good, gentlemen, the evacuation by sea will cease from midnight tomorrow!"

The first sea lord stood up. "Then I'll pass . . . " He got no further.

"But," said the P.M., slowly and firmly, "any craft already on its way to the beaches will continue on its way. The dispatch of vessels from the disembarkation ports will not . . . " he glared at the first sea lord, "and I repeat, *not* cease until mid-day tomorrow!"

The men around the table nodded.

"Furthermore," the P.M. continued, "the onward dispatch of all French troops landed on our shores, back to their homeland, will continue. None will be retained here unless they request to be. There will be no withdrawals from France outside the Dunkirk enclave." He removed the spectacles on his nose. "Good day, gentlemen."

He turned to 'C'. He held one finger up. 'C' waited as the other three men left the room.

"You want to speak to me 'C'?" the P.M. asked.

"Yes, Prime Minister. Ultra reports that Hitler has told his generals, in a highly secret conference, that he has allowed the British Army to escape to avoid taking it prisoner. He told them that it would have been a major obstacle to Britain's suing for peace."

"Then that means he's going to attack Russia?"

"Yes. He told them so . . . in the spring of next year."

"Do you think the Russians know?"

"I doubt it. They don't, I believe, have Ultra."

"Can we inform them?"

"What do you think, sir?" 'C' caged.

The P.M. knitted his brows and thought for a minute. "Useless to inform them yet. Let's wait until Hitler masses his armies in the east. Once he's committed that far, there will be no turning back for him."

"Anyway," 'C' said, "I doubt if Stalin would believe us now, but with the German army forming up in Poland . . . "

"I doubt if he'll believe us even then," said the P.M. "There's only one thing he believes in . . . " he puffed his cigar.

'C' waited.

The P.M. removed his cigar. "The Marxist inevitability of events. Now, we're going to prove Marx was quite, quite mistaken," he frowned. "Sue for peace? What does this, this *Bohemian*, think we are?" he growled.

"Yes, sir, quite," said 'C'. "I've also had a message from the Dutch station, half an hour ago. It says that Orange has abducted a Dutch car ferry and is heading for England direct. My people have told the Navy and RAF, of course. They're keeping an eye out for it, but they can't spare search planes, of course. The Navy has informed all ships to watch for her."

The P.M. started suddenly, "Who can't spare search planes?"

"Coastal Command, sir."

"I'll have them detail off a flying boat. What's this car ferry look like? But tell your people to send the details to my secretary right away." The P.M. said, "See you at four," as he stalked out, into the crowded corridor.

2nd June, 1940. 9:00 A.M.
3rd Platoon of the Sixteenth Infantry Regiment of the French Army, Bergues, Pas de Calais, France

"Message from battalion, Monsieur."

Lieutenant Josef Heron donned the headphones. *Not any easy thing to do*, he thought, *when one is lying in the fiftieth ditch in eight days*. "Yes, third platoon here, Heron," he reported at the mike.

"St. Laurent here. Try to hold on there until dusk will you? Then it's *sauve qui peut*, Lieutenant. Say nothing to the men until 7:30. Try to head for the beach due north of you at Rosendam. You'll find some cover there; there's a low cliff. I'll try to rendezvous there about ten P.M., all right?"

"Right, sir," replied Heron. He shifted his spare body for more comfort, just as a shell burst a hundred yards away.

"That gives us a few hours."

"A few hours for what?" asked Heron. His dark eyes squinted.

"The evacuation ceases at midnight tomorrow. The British to the right of you have fallen back to Bourbourg, the Boche tanks will probably be behind you by dusk, but it will take time for their infantry to catch up. There's a hell of a messy chaos. Just keep your heads down and get to the beaches if you can. Over and out." The radio went dead.

Heron frowned as he laid down the headphones.

"Bad news, sir?" asked the radio man.

Heron turned to him and accepted his proffered cigarette. "What? Bad news . . . no, no . . . just a routine message. The line is still holding."

They both heard the terrifying, nerve-wracking wail-scream of a Stuka. They saw its sinister crooked wings. They grabbed their rifles and fired away, even though they both knew it was utterly useless. As the Stuka whizzed out of its dive and climbed, a plume of smoke lifted from battalion commander's trench, over to their right on a rise a quarter mile away in the distance. The earth over the battalion trench spewed up great chunks of soil, metal, and flesh. The third platoon was on its own now.

2nd June, 1940. 9:10 A.M.
In the air, eight miles due north of Neuiwport, Belgium

Hauptman Sepp Rubensdorf was Swiss. He was twenty-six years old when he had joined the German Luftwaffe in 1936. He had distinguished himself in the Condor Legion in Spain. He had flown with enthusiasm over Poland, keeping guard on the Dorniers and Heinkels while they methodically and systematically destroyed the archaic Polish biplanes on the ground, and he had watched with scientific interest as towns and villages had been pounded with high-explosive bombs.

Now he was leading *erprGr 211* group of Messerschmidt 110 fighter-bombers back to their new forward base at Bruges, Belgium.

They had been in the air since 8:30. They had flown over the beaches east of Dunkirk. Each of his twenty-five 110s had dropped a bomb on the crowded beaches; they had then stooged around for twenty minutes, shooting up the hordes of men milling around on the sand below. There had been some antiaircraft fire from the ships. They had not turned to fly back to base until the Tommies had sent in three flights of Spitfires. Rubensdorf was under orders to avoid combat with enemy fighters and so had not taken on the Spitfires.

As the fighter wing wheeled in over the coast, Rubensdorf looked down at the sea, to the southwest. Then he saw it. He peeled off from his flight and flew down toward the boat. Rubensdorf knew she could not be a German Naval vessel; none had passed Zeebrugge yet. He flew around the vessel, as it steered for the Dover Strait. He saw she seemed to be flying a white flag with a glimpse of red on it. *The Royal Navy white ensign*, he thought as his plane flashed low over the ship. He caught sight of a small black blob in the sea ahead of him. He thought it could be a boat—a rowboat. Then he banked. He went into a shallow dive until the white-flagged ship was in his gunsights. He pressed the firing button on his joy stick. The two *Rhein-metall-Borsig* machine guns on his wings blazed away for three seconds, then they stopped dead. Rubensdorf muttered a silent damn to himself as he flattened out and climbed again toward his flight companions, who were by this time almost over Bruges.

As he raced ahead to catch up with his flight, Rubensdorf was not dejected. *We've had a good start to a day's sport. There will be many more sorties today*, he comforted himself.

2nd June, 1940. 9:12 A.M.
At sea, onboard car ferry Hoop, three miles due north of Neuiwport, Belgium

They had all cringed when the Messerschmidt passed low over the ferry *Hoop*. When it made a wide circle and flew straight at them, the five Dutchmen on the starboard side of the bridge had thrown themselves flat on the steel treadway. Lynch had crouched down and aimed his Walther at the plane, but he had not fired.

Some of the German 7.92 millimeter machine-gun bullets hit the sea harmlessly, yards away from the boat, on its starboard side. Some passed over the boat into the sea on the port side. Three of the bullets pierced the thin hull. Two of them had passed through the ship's side into the engine room. One of them bounced off the inner bulkhead, harmlessly. The other had penetrated into the Bosch fuel pump of the eight-cylinder diesel engine. The fuel pump's tiny intricate helix-grooved pistons stopped a thousandth-of-a-second before the bullet exploded.

On the bridge deck the only sign they had that the German had found his mark was the engine stopping with a dull thunk! The ship's forward speed carried her a few more yards, then *Hoop* came to a halt.

For a moment, as Lynch and the helmsman craned their necks to watch the German plane fly away to the east, there was no sound until Lynch shouted, "Get the bloody engineer down there!"

As if they had understood his words, the five Dutchmen were on their feet. The engineer looked at Lynch, who prodded the Walther pistol muzzle down toward the engine compartment hatch. He hurried down the ladder and into his engine room.

They waited in silence as the ship wallowed, for two minutes. Then the engineer came out of the hatch with a lump of twisted metal. He shouted something to the captain. The captain turned to Lynch. "Mister," he said, "*Pomp . . . kaput!*"

Lynch stuck two fingers up at the captain. "Two?" he asked.

The captain shook his head. "*Een,*" he said. Lynch raised his Walther.

"*Ein,* Mister, *een!*" yelled the captain.

Lynch shot him.

The captain fell to the bridge deck, a bullet in his heart. Lynch turned to look down at the engineer. The engineer gabbled something in Dutch and dodged back into the engine room.

As Lynch turned to look at the engineer, the helmsman dove for his legs. He was too slow. Even as the sailor's fingertips encountered Lynch's trousers, a bullet lodged in his brain. Lynch jerked the gun up and fired yet again. Another sailor went down, a bullet through his left eye

The one sailor left alive on the bridge stared up at Lynch. Lynch ordered him up. The sailor stood. Lynch shot him. The bullet entered the sailor s stomach and passed through his spine. The shock knocked him over the bridge guard rail. He crashed onto the Bugatti directly below, crushing his skull on the thick metal top. Lynch scooted to the ladder. Saliva oozed from his lower lip. His eyes stared wildly. "No one is going to stop me!" he shouted.

Lynch grabbed the engine room door and fired at the engineer, aiming for his midriff. The bullet hit the spare Bosch fuel pump the engineer was holding in his shaking hands. The engineer dropped the pump. Shattered springs and washers clattered around the compartment. Lynch stared at the dropped pump body. He raised the Walther slowly with one hand. He closed one eye and aimed straight at the engineer's head.

"You lying bastard!" he shouted and squeezed the trigger.

The engineer was flung down over the warm engine like a rag doll.

Lynch turned and walked out onto the car deck. The sailor on top of the Bugatti gave a low moan. Lynch reloaded the Walther with the spare clip in his pocket. He pulled himself up, one hand inside the car, placed the Walther's hot muzzle against the sailor's ear, "Poor fellow," he murmured and put the sailor out of his agony.

He sat down then, the automatic still in his hand and stared around him for five minutes, remembering Rio, thinking about how the woman had groaned, pleading with her eyes before he gently, slowly slashed her throat, then went to the bridge. He watched as the tide slowly but surely carried the ferry closer and closer to the shore. He saw smoke everywhere over the land, and heard the noise of gunfire in the south. He went below, opened the toolbox on the running board of the Hispano-Suiza, took out a large car jack, placed it under the rear axle of the Spanish car, and started to raise it.

2nd June, 1940, 7:00 P.M.
At sea, twenty-three miles due north of Gravelines, France

The men in the dinghy were rowing more slowly now. They had pulled against the tide for six hours, though only Goffin could guess that it was against them, and he was not quite sure. Then at 4 P.M. the strong-running westerly-going tide helped by the light easterly breeze had taken them on their way to the Straits of Dover much faster than any of them could know.

As the day wore on, they sighted many ships far away on the horizon. They had waved and shouted as two fast destroyers passed them only a mile away, but the men on the destroyer's bridge had merely waved back. The two destroyers were laying a smoke screen right across the western horizon, and soon with a slight easterly breeze, they were in a dense smoke-fog. They could see nothing now beyond a matter of a hundred yards or so. They passed only scattered wreckage, dead bodies floating, bloated and obscene, face down just under the surface of the sea, and four terrifyingly loose surface mines.

As night fell, the smoke cleared for a brief hour. At six-thirty they were surrounded by a thick Channel fog. They pulled on, with the white mist swirling around them, the boat rising and falling in the long, gentle swells. They heard only the noise of the oarlocks squeaking, the heavy breathing of Perkins, who was tiring rapidly, and the distant rumble of gunfire and bombing. Each time a man was relieved, he drank half a cup of milk, marked off by Perkins in pencil scratches on the bottles.

Frequently, at odd times they stopped rowing, as the roar of a ship's engine drew closer and closer in the fog, seeing nothing, waiting for the ship to run them over at any second. Then the sound would die away again slowly. Toward 7:30 P.M. darkness was falling. Goffin crawled forward in the dinghy to relieve Mitchell. As Goffin started to row they heard the sound of a voice calling from very near. Mitchell steered toward the voice, hailing as he did so, "Right, hang on! Hello! Hello!"

They heard the voice cry back, *"Over here!"* They heard a sob nearby. *"Help me . . . I've been in since this morning!"* Mitchell turned and stared over his shoulder.

"I reckon he's over there. Right!" He shouted. "Hello! . . . Hello!" his voice echoed back from the moisture all around.

Mitchell steered the boat around. Goffin and Perkins pulled on the oars as fast as they could. Mitchell could see nothing more than two yards away through the mist. They waited.

"Over here . . . help!" The voice moaned, weaker. Mitchell looked back over his shoulder. They turned the boat around yet again. They rowed fast again in the direction of the voice. They rowed in a circle; they found nothing. They stopped rowing and sat silent, trying to stop their breathing. They listened. Nothing.

"Hello!" shouted Mitchell, peering into the thick swirl of white mist.

"Hello!" cried Goffin.

"Where are you?" hollered Perkins. They listened. Nothing but distant gunfire.

Wearily they set to, rowing again, until Goffin realized that they did not know in which direction they were heading. He said, "Okay, lads, stop rowing. We'll have to rest until this bloody fog lifts."

The two rowers dropped their heads over the oars. They listened for another half-hour in the cold misty dark, but there was no sound, only the sea lapping gently against the strakes of the dinghy sides, and the roar of war far away, seeming to come from all directions of the compass, echoing off the water droplets in suspension all around them.

"We'll sleep, if we can, lads," said Mitchell quietly, "and may God have mercy on the poor bugger's soul."

"Amen," said Perkins, as he brought his oar into the dinghy.

"Amen," murmured Goffin, then he perked up and said, "Well, at least the bloody Jerries won't see us." He went on, "I thought we'd had our chips this morning when that plane came at us."

"Might have been a neutral," Mitchell said, trying to joke.

"What, strafing the bloody Red Cross?" Goffin grinned at Mitchell.

"Perhaps he was Swiss?" suggested Perkins, joining in on the humor.

"Good old Randy," said Goffin. Then he leaned drowsily over his oar.

They heard a ship's engine close by about midnight, then nothing except the rumble of destruction and death from far away and what they thought was a cry.

"Could have been a seabird," said Goffin after they had held their breath for long minutes in the cold mist.

2nd June, 1940. 7:15 P.M.
Onboard car ferry Hoop, *one mile north of Oostduinke, Belgium*

Lynch lowered the Hispano-Suiza rear axle down again, very gently. He went to the ferry bridge again to look around the horizon. He smiled and nodded his head slowly as he took in the scene. The ferry was much nearer to the sandy beach. He could see khaki-clad figures in large groups running toward the east. *They're heading for the front line. The Germans are still being held in Belgium*, he thought.

He looked around the land horizon. There were great billows of smoke coming from behind the low rises to the southeast. He imagined that this was the battle line, as it had been in World War I. He looked to the south. The sky was fairly clear. He looked to the southwest, where there were great pillars of oily smoke reaching up into the almost still air. He said aloud, "That's the Jerries bombing Dunkirk." He gazed at the southwest sky for a minute longer. "That'll stir 'em up," he said again aloud. "That'll give them just the bloody panic I need to get through Dunkirk, and once I'm through there, Spain, here I come!" He grinned to himself. He pulled out his Walther, checked to see that the safety catch was on, and drew out the magazine clip. He counted the bullets. There were six. He snapped the magazine back into the butt of the automatic. Then he remembered he hadn't eaten. He went down the ladder to rifle the Argentinian Bugatti's glove compartment.

Lynch sat on the running board of the Bugatti for twenty minutes, eating the bologna sandwiches and drinking the milk he had found. After he had eaten, he threw the sandwich wrappings back into the Bugatti and climbed back up to the bridge. He thought that the ship had moved out from the shore again. He shook his head and looked again. Then he realized that the tide was taking the ferry out to sea. He leaned on the bridge rail and cursed until it was dark overhead. His distorted face reflected the dull orange glow all across the south horizon as he cursed on, clenching and unclenching his fists, trying to see where the shoreline was, in the darkness under the glare.

2nd June, 1940. 9:00 P.M.
Route Nationale 40, four miles west of Dunkirk, France

Lieutenant Heron woke from his half-hour nap. His platoon of nine men were in yet another ditch. They had abandoned the Bergues position at six-thirty P.M., under fire from SS tanks and heavy dive-bombing by the Luftwaffe. Crouching and running along hedgerows, they had made their way eight miles to the canal at Hondschute. There, finding no bridges left standing, they had dismantled an abandoned farm cart and used its wooden chassis as a raft to ferry them over, three at a time. Heron had waited for the third raft and crossed over last. They had then walked and scrambled three miles to the main road from Belgium to Dunkirk.

All around them vehicles on each side of the road were burning. The Luftwaffe was using the burning vehicles as beacons to strafe the road. They were coming over continually, one plane every half minute, regularly as clockwork. Each plane first dropped its bomb, then opened up with its machine guns. The road and both sides of it, for a hundred yards, were choked with men attempting to find cover and trying to cross the gauntlet of the burning highway. Many, whole groups, whole battalions even, stood around looking lost and numbed. There were British, French, and Belgians, but by far the greater number were French.

To the west Dunkirk was on fire. Great stabs of flame licked the sky. To the south the village of Ostcappel was under heavy fire from the panzers, who were only a third of a mile south of the village and the canal. To the east, Belgium was hidden under great rolling billows of fire from exploded oil depots.

To the north over the low rise of the coast cliffs, they could see the comet trails of thousands upon thousands of tracer bullets rising from the defending ships and streaming down from the attacking Luftwaffe planes.

"Like a fireworks display in hell," said Heron.

"Shall we try to cross the road, Lieutenant?" asked Sergeant Bosquet. He, like Heron, and six of the other men in the platoon, was from Rouen, only 130 miles (and, if they could only guess it, six panzer divisions) away to the southwest.

"No, sergeant," replied Heron, as another bomb burst across the highway and almost blew off his steel helmet. "We'll wait here, for a while longer, maybe the strafing will ease up as it gets more misty."

But the night didn't get more misty. The fog stayed well out to sea. Lieutenant Heron's platoon remained where they were, firing and sleeping, until five A.M. the following morning, when the Germans crossed the Veurne Canal. The Wehrmacht infantrymen advanced invincibly north. Invincibly, that is, until they came within range of the 10 percent of the Allied rear guard on the highway still capable of firing a machine gun or a rifle. Then they were stopped. So was the air strafing. There was sporadic rifle fire all night. At six A.M. the Germans brought up loudspeakers and informed the defenders that there was no sense in further resistance. The British and French navies had abandoned them, the last ship had left, they should yield honorably like good Tommies and poilus. *"You have put up a good fight,"* they bawled in French and English.

As dawn broke, with flame and fire in the sky in all directions, the bombing and machine gunning of the highway recommenced. The defenders, unable or unwilling to cross the road, stayed where they were. They continued firing at any German helmet showing itself, although they knew it was futile. Gradually, the defenders made off, some to succeed in getting north across Route Nationale 40, some to die in the fields or on the road, some to wander leaderless, east or west, dazed and in despair.

So the daylight hours of June third passed for Lieutenant Heron and his men, and as the daylight died, Europe of the League of Nations died with it.

3rd June, 1940. 10:30 A.M.
At sea, onboard the car ferry Hoop, *two miles north of Oosteduinke, Belgium*

Lynch woke with a start. He had slept fitfully on the back seat of one of the Rolls Royces. He looked around for some milk, again in the Bugatti, and finished off the bottle and a cheese sandwich. It was dry, but no worse than the thousand prison breakfasts he had scoffed in his life.

He bit into the sandwich as he climbed up to *Hoop*'s bridge. He cursed even more than he had done the previous night. The shoreline was twice as far away. The clumps of trees he could see on the rises last night were not there.

He looked to the southwest and saw that he was slowly, very slowly, approaching the rising pillars of smoke over Dunkirk.

"Well, Banger Boy," he said to himself, "the worst that can happen is that you'll drift ashore there in Dunkirk or someone may give the ferry a tow down the coast . . . all the better." He looked for an hour at the aircraft flying every which way overhead. He watched six dogfights very high above in the blue and watched two planes fall, trailing fire, then he went below again, to check his preparations of the afternoon before.

At noon, which he guessed by the sun, since his watch had stopped, he cursed himself for not stealing Dennis' watch, one of the brand-new, recently developed electric Rolex's, and looked around again. He looked to the shore. His face broke into a wide smile. Slowly but surely the boat had neared the beach again. He watched until he was sure. Then he took his shirt off and sun-bathed on the bridge deck for an hour, listening to the dull roar in the south and west. As the ferry drifted nearer and nearer to the beach, he saw trucks driving eastward along the sand. He was sure that the men in them were British. He smiled as he watched truck after truck drive slowly east. "Good old Tommy," he said to himself quietly as he watched them. "Got 'em on the run, or maybe it's just reinforcements for the front. The front must be holding like the silly mugs held it last time."

3rd June, 1940. Noon
At sea, twenty-five miles due north of Gravelines, France

"I reckon the fog's clearing now," Goffin said.

Perkins and Mitchell woke from their silent dozing. They were hungry. All the milk had been consumed.

"Let's hope so," said Mitchell.

"Couldn't 'alf do with a fag," said Goffin, shivering.

Perkins whispered hoarsely. "If it does clear, gentlemen, the first thing we must do is dry our clothes; they're soaking wet. I fear I have a cold coming on already." He sneezed, then said, "Excuse me, gentlemen, I'm sure."

They sat in silence for ten minutes, listening to the dull roar that still seemed to be all about them. Perkins cocked his head.

"I hope you don't mind my saying so, Mitch, there seems to be an engine somewhere nearby. It seems, at least to me, to be a different noise from the rest."

They listened intently, peering into the dense fog cloud all around.

"There *is* a ship coming!" cried Goffin.

They listened again as a deep-throated roar drew closer and closer.

"Let's take our shirts off—hold them on the oars. They might see us," suggested Goffin. He was already taking his wing commander's jacket off.

They all three, moving carefully so as not to capsize the small dinghy, took off their jackets and shirts. Mitchell and Perkins put their shirts on the oar blades and waited as the rumble came nearer and nearer. They sat still, listening, peering intently into the fog. The two oarsmen saw it first. Mitchell, sitting facing them, saw the looks of horror and fear on their faces. He turned to look over his shoulder.

A monstrous gray shape was coming almost straight at them, out of the fog. They shouted as they waved. The crowded destroyer missed them by no more than twenty feet. It passed too fast and too noisily for anyone at the ship's gun stations to notice them. The lookouts were too weary and exhausted, after ten days of incessant duty, to even look at the sea. His Majesty's ship *Havelock* tore past the dinghy at twenty-five knots, sending up a ten-foot, sharp-topped bow wave traveling at almost the same speed.

Before the men in the dinghy had time to do anything, the bow wave hit the dinghy. It capsized, throwing all three men into the sea. They were shocked out of their fear by the cold of the sea as they were all submerged.

Mitchell was the first to seize hold of the dinghy, which was upside down. He looked around even as Goffin grabbed the bow of the up-turned boat. "Where's Perkins?" he spluttered.

"Over here, and if I may say so, I do wish you'd call me Randy!" The sound of hoarse, fruity tones of the British Ambassador's butler made both Mitchell and Goffin laugh, even as they spluttered and cursed the ship.

Mitchell and Goffin clawed their way around the upset dinghy to Perkins, then together, with a loud, "*Heave!*" from Goffin, they righted the completely water-logged boat. Goffin started to bail it out with one hand. Mitchell saw Goffin's wing commander's cap floating nearby. He turned and swam for it.

"Got your hat, Goff. Where's mine?" he spluttered.

"Right, Mitch!" Goffin sighted Mitchell's hat. He swam to it and grabbed both it and Perkins' homburg, floating together in the misty distance.

Soon all three men were desperately bailing out the boat. It took them half an hour to clear all the water out. When they climbed in, it was still half-full of cold sea water. They were busy bailing as Goffin looked around.

"Where's the oars?" he called.

Mitchell and Perkins stopped bailing. They looked around the steaming sea. There was nothing to be seen except Mitchell's white shirt floating nearby. Goffin scrambled madly with his hands, paddling the dinghy toward the shirt. Then, seeing the boat moved slowly he jumped over the side and rescued the shirt.

"Going to look for the oars, mate," Goffin called up to Mitchell.

"Don't be a damned fool, Goff," replied Mitch. "If the fog comes down any thicker, we'll never find you." He grabbed hold of Goffin's hair.

"Okay, Mitch, okay," Goffin climbed back onboard.

The trio set to, bailing again with the caps. Suddenly Perkins looked up. "I hope you don't mind my . . . " he got no further.

Mitchell interrupted him. "If you say that once more, Randy, I'll heave . . . what is it?"

"I thought you'd like to know, there's an oar over there." Perkins held his finger out, trembling with cold and shock.

Goffin was over the side before Mitchell could stop him, swimming for the oar. He reached it and trod water, holding it over his head. "Got the bugger!" he shouted. Then his head sank. He came to the surface again and threw the oar over the dinghy gunwale.

They all three stood in the dinghy, as it heaved slowly up and down with the swell, for five minutes, then Goffin took out his knife, sat down and started to hack away at the top of the dinghy stern.

"What are you doing, Goff?" asked Mitchell, panting with effort.

"I'm making a sculling oar rollock," Goffin answered.

Mitchell grinned, "I thought for a minute you said 'bollox."

As Mitchell and Perkins steadily bailed out the dinghy, Goffin hacked away, then he passed the oar-loom over the slot he had cut, and started sculling the boat, twisting his wrist this way and that, as Mitchell continued bailing and Perkins, now coughing harshly, peered around into the fog, looking for the missing oar.

When he could bail no more with the hats Mitchell mopped out the dinghy bottom with the one remaining shirt. "At least we'll keep the boat dry," he muttered.

"And one flamin' oar is better than sod-all," responded Goffin.

They searched in the fog for an hour for the missing oar and shirts, but finally they gave up.

"Better save our energy for when the fog lifts," Goffin advised.

3rd June, 1940. 2:00 P.M.
The beach, two miles west of Dunkirk, Pas de Calais, France

Three hundred fifty French soldiers were lying and sitting under the protection of the small cliff, fifty yards up the sandy beach from the sea's edge. They hailed from a dozen different regiments. They had been split off from their units in the holocaust to the south. They had wandered, some intentionally, some not, toward the sea. The mist out to sea gave their exhausted eyes, in sunken sockets over unshaven faces, visibility of a hundred yards. They had endured a living nightmare for eight days, huddled under the cliff with little food and fresh water. They had been marshalled in a compact group by a French major the day before yesterday. He had told them to wait; a ship would come in and pick them up. They never saw him again. The only ships they saw were the seven wrecks on the hazy horizon, all with their superstructures and funnels showing above the sea, four of them still burning. They did not see the other sunken vessels within five miles of them—dozens of them.

Now they no longer heard the sounds of ships moving out in the misty haze. They heard little gunfire from out at sea. They heard now only the thudding booms of tank guns and aerial bombs inland, from the highway to the south and from the direction of Belgium in the east.

There was no rank here among them. True, there were men wearing officers' badges, and men with sergeants' and corporals' stripes on their sleeves, but there were no officers, no sergeants, no corporals. There were 350 very frightened and exhausted men under the cliff, and other mobs further along the beach. Before them, on the strip of sand that they could see, lay many dead bodies. Some were fresh from the latest spate of shelling; some the tide had washed over once. Others were just arms and knees not yet completely buried in the sandwash of two tides. The shells were bursting at intermittent intervals. The men hid their faces under their greatcoats, as they kneeled and pressed their steel helmets against the clay cliff bottom, as if they were praying in church.

In a lull between shell bursts, one of them looked out to sea. "Look, look . . . look!" he shouted, *"Regardez!"*

No one moved.

"The ship, *le bateau!*" he shouted.

A few leaned round to cast their bloodshot looks away from the cliff. They saw her. The shout was taken up by a dozen or more men. "The ship!" A couple of men started to run toward her, splashing as they waded into the water. *"Le bateau; c'est arrivé!"*

From out of the mist, as it rose for a minute, five minutes, she came slowly creeping in on the tide, closer and closer. She appeared enormous to the exhausted Frenchmen. She had great black bluff bows and a high mast, and she was coming in to the beach for them.

Another dozen scarecrows ran down to the beach, risking the shell bursts to welcome the ship. They waved their helmets. Another score broke loose from their shackling fear at the foot of the cliff. They, too, joined those in the sea, who, now up to their armpits in salt water, were holding up their helmets and waving, pleading.

Slowly, slowly, *Beatrice Maud* came to them, as if she heard their cries of anguish and terror and felt their despair. Slowly, slowly, the creeping tide carried her with it on a gentle sea. Foot by blessed foot, she seemed to know exactly where the men were and came to them.

One big, sturdy Alpine chasseur was the furthest out to sea, standing up to his chest in the water, weighted down by his boots and ammunition pouches. He reached out as her bow came forward to his giant opened hand. He beckoned her toward him with the massive paw. He grabbed her bow and he pulled her. He pulled her until the edge of her bow stem touched the sea-bottom sand softly. The chasseur bent his gaunt, tired, bearded face over to her bow and kissed her, gently. He gazed up at the boat's masthead and saw an all-white gannet hovering, beating his wings slowly, crying, as if to him.

From the beach a cheer echoed to the skies, so loud that it drowned out the sound of panzers pounding away in the west. The big chasseur held the bow while 248 of the nonwounded, less-exhausted and terrified French poilus clambered and scrambled onboard.

"Any more?" shouted the chasseur, just as a shell burst between the ship and the foot of the cliff. The blast knocked him over into the sea. The blast also blew *Beatrice Maud* five yards away from him.

The chasseur scrambled up, out of the water, cursing, and waded to her as she hesitated. He was submerged almost to his neck before he grabbed the line dangling from her bow, shook off his greatcoat and pulled himself, with a dozen of his mates encouraging and helping him, over her side. His big boots hit her deck. Streaming wet, he dropped to his knees. He slowly, reverently, bent his head and kissed her again, on her deck, three times. He heard the gannet cry again, loudly.

"No point in that," said a voice from the crowd on deck. "There's no crew."

Silence for a full minute.

"I'm an engineer," a small Parisian called. He went to search for the engine. He was soon back. The search had already been made.

"There's no engine," observed a man with stripes on his sleeve and a Midi accent.

"*Merde*," was the general mutter. "*Foûtre le camp!*" shouted a Marseillais.

"But we're safer here than over on the beach," the Midi man said. "Especially if we take shelter down below. Her sides are about a half-meter thick, and the tide might take us out to sea again."

Everybody still remaining on deck agreed. They all moved down into her hold to take shelter. It was much quieter down there, and they felt safer. They found places for themselves on the hold floor, among the coal dust, under the side decks, and were silent.

They could still hear the roar of war, but it was much more subdued down below. A few of them imagined they could hear a woman's low laugh now and again, but it was only the foresail hanks on the forestay, and a white gannet mewing as he watched the tide slowly, steadily, move her out to sea again, into the all-enfolding mist.

"I wonder what this ship is called?" asked one man with a Bordeaux accent.

"*Putain Anglaise*," replied a Marseillais. "I saw the British flag on the stern, *s'en foûtre pas mal!*"

One or two people laughed, four or five grinned weakly. The rest merely stared in misery at each other and waited, for they knew not what, landsmen whom the land wanted not and who knew not the sea.

3rd June, 1940. 6:05 P.M.
At sea, onboard the car ferry Hoop, 200 yards north of the beach a mile west of Koksjide, Belgium

Lynch had watched the ferry drift slowly in with the tide for three hours. He had unshackled the ramp door lifting chains at both ends of the boat, after substituting a rope from the after to the forward ramps. Over this rope he had slung another line and lashed it taut to the car deck shackle that held the Alvis' front wheel.

Then he had unshackled the Alvis holding chains so that the car was free to move off. He had fitted a length of flexible hose from the Alvis exhaust pipe and tied the end up to the canvas top. He then lashed both the schmeissers in place inside the Alvis, one pointing forward and one pointing behind, over the folded downtop. From the schmeisser triggers, he had rigged up wires to the driver's seat.

Now Lynch rested after pushing heavily with a long pole he had found on deck. He had done this to move the ferry around so that her forward door, in front of the Alvis, would touch the beach. He waited. She moved closer to the beach, so close that he could see the ridges on the sandy sea bed. Then he felt the flat square bow of the ferry judder slightly as it slid gently onto the hard sand. He slithered down to the Alvis. He took one last look around the deck, and grinning, waved his hand. "So long, my fine fat beauty!" he shouted as he climbed into the Alvis. He started the engine and revved it. He put his foot on the clutch and slid the handbrake to the "off" position. He reached out with the long-bladed knife he had placed on the facia board. He sawed through the ramp rope. The rope twanged and the ramps crashed down.

3rd June, 1940. 6:06 P.M.
On the beach, half a mile west of Koksjide, Belgium

They'd had a long slow drive down from Antwerp. Kapitan Ludwig had cursed for hours, as the Volkswagen had crawled along at a snail's pace behind a slow moving Wehrmacht supplies convoy that seemed to stop and snake forever. Klausen had spent all night and most of today driving at six miles per hour, most of the time, until they got to the crossroads at Bruges. From there, at three o'clock this afternoon, they had sped the Volkswagen to the coast at Het Zoute. They had not been able to follow the beaches all the way, because of deep gulleys crossing the sand down to the sea. They had dashed around the coastal roads, trying to see as much of the shore as they could in the low visibility. They had passed thousands of Belgian, French, and British troops flocking east, away from the hell of Dunkirk. Their own army was five miles inland, so far as they knew.

"Goddamned mist!" Ludwig shouted at intervals. They were driving on the beach itself now, with a clear run ahead of them all the way to the Belgian frontier with France. They had just torn through the hamlet of Koksjide. Ludwig studied the map on his knee. Hartmann was the first to see *Hoop*.

"There it is, by God, there it is!" he shouted.

They raced along the smooth sand at sixty miles an hour, towards the stranded ferry, about half a mile away. It was sitting at the water's edge, with its ramps still shut against the hull. There was no sign of life onboard. The white tarpaulin with a red cross drooped limply over the wheelhouse. They were now a quarter of a mile away. The Volkswagen speedometer showed seventy miles an hour. Then they saw the ramps suddenly open.

Chapter 11

*   *

The White Cliffs of Dover

4th–5th June, 1940

There'll be blue birds over
The white cliffs of Dover,
Tomorrow, just you wait and see;
There'll be love and laughter,
And peace ever after,
Tomorrow, when the world is free.

The shepherd will tend his sheep,
The valley will bloom again,
And Jimmy will go to sleep,
In his own little room again.

There'll be blue birds over,
The white cliffs of Dover,
Tomorrow, just you wait and see.

Pop Song, World War II
Words by Nat Burton; music by Walter Kent, 1941

11.

The White Cliffs of Dover

3rd June, 1940. 7:00 P.M.
Dover Castle, Kent, England. Room 11

Admiral Ramsey, Flag officer, Dover, sat at the head of the table. His uniform jacket hung over the back of his chair. The table was thickly littered with papers. Around the table sat twelve officers, four from each of the three services, and two women shorthand clerks.

All the men were in shirt-sleeves. Four of the officers had removed their ties and opened their collars.

The admiral stood and walked to the large open French window overlooking the harbor. Dusk was falling, but there was still enough daylight for him to see the scene below, around the harbor.

The great port, shoreward of the mile-long sea wall, was choked with ships of all sizes. Three ships were steaming out of the harbor entrance as he watched. Others were following them, towing long lines of small craft.

The admiral walked through the French w ndow out onto the terrace. He turned to look to the west. For a moment he gazed at the six thin lattice towers rising from the cliff tops in the distance. He recalled meeting the strange, scruffy professor who had *tinkered about with radio valves and things. What was his name? Watson, Watts? That was it*. He smiled to himself at the memory of the blunt elderly scientist who always seemed to forget where he had left his pipe. *Radio direction finders? What radios, which direction?* he wondered.

Sirens wailed down in the town below. The guard ship's Bofors began pop-pop-popping. Little dark puffs dotted the sky. There was the throb . . . zoom . . . throb . . . zoom . . . throb . . . zoom of Dornier engines high above. The admiral waited for the first bomb blast among the ships. He turned on his heels and returned to his seat.

"Good, gentlemen," he said. "The dispersal has started. We'll get every craft capable of moving out of here tonight." He hesitated. "The ones not earmarked for the Dover Patrol. What do we have there, Fitzroy?"

A lean, hook-nosed naval officer, who looked fifty but was thirty-three, sitting at the middle of the table, picked up a sheet of paper. "Three destroyers of the older variety," he read. "Four minesweepers and five seagoing tugs. The latter all armed," he added.

The admiral thought for a moment. Then he said, "All at sea?"

"No, sir," replied Fitzroy. "One of the destroyers has a slight engine problem. She will be slipping at midnight. All the rest are at sea in accordance with your orders, patrolling the twelve-mile area to seaward. We're getting regular reports of survivors being picked up, and, of course, wreckage and so forth."

"What was the last Naval ship in?" asked the admiral.

"*Havelock*, sir." Fitzroy glanced at another report. "She left the *Jette d'Embectage* in Dunkirk at 8:00 this morning, sir."

"That's by the channel ferry station, isn't it?" asked the admiral.

"Correct, sir, a little to the west, by the *Écluse Watier*. She was picking up bodies."

"*Bodies?*" snapped the admiral, a quizzical frown on his brow.

"Soldiers, sir, excuse me. She was picking up soldiers from the jetty as the enemy tanks were firing. The Boche had, at that time, reached the canal to the south, a quarter of a mile away. *Havelock* engaged them the whole time the troops were boarding. She reports, sir," Fitzroy looked down again, "several explosions that could have been hits."

."Not very accurate reporting," observed an army officer.

"But the aim seems to have been accurate enough," retorted the admiral, glaring at the soldier. He turned again to Fitzroy. "How many troops did she bring?"

"Five-hundred and eighty, sir . . . mostly men from the Guards regiments." He smiled. "Captain Cameron took the trouble to inform us that they all had their boots and buttons polished, and they were all shaven." There was a titter around the room. Fitzroy continued, "The rest were a hodge-podge of . . . "

"A what, Commander?" the admiral said, sternly.

"A mixture sir. British and French line regiments." Fitzroy reddened slightly. "One-hundred and sixty-two, sir. Sixteen with rifles. Fifty-three shell-shocked or wounded."

There was silence, except for the rustle of paper as the shorthand clerks turned over their scribbling sheets. Everyone looked haggard. Nobody smoked, though the ashtrays on the table were full of cigarette ends, and there was an aroma of stale tobacco smoke in the room, despite the open windows.

At last, the admiral leaned back in his chair. "Gentlemen, that's that," he said. "Operation Dynamo is completed. It only remains now for me to ask you to tidy up your paper work as quickly as you can before you all return to your various units." He smiled around the table. "And to thank you all for your efforts in . . . in . . . assisting this . . . miracle. The last figure we have arrived at, for officers and troops of all friendly armies brought back from over Dunkirk is close to 345,000." He paused for a second. "Out of 400,000. It has been a victory of sorts, over ghastly odds, but it is still the worst defeat this nation has suffered since Norman William landed twenty miles to the west of this port, 874 years ago. The enemy is now twenty-one miles away, to our south. With that thought, I'll leave you, I'm off to take over command of the Dover Patrol."

Admiral Ramsey stood, shook hands with everyone in the room, including the secretaries, and marched out.

3rd June, 1940. 7:30 P.M.
Sand dunes two miles east of Dunkirk, France

Lieutenant Heron kept the men of his platoon in a tight bunch. The beach, as far as they could see in the glare of bomb and shell bursts, was packed with men. The bottom of the low cliffs behind the beach was one long packed blur of several layers of soldiers, all trying to gain some slight shelter from the blasts of explosions. On some parts of the beach, dead bodies were stacked four and five deep.

Slowly, running fifty yards at a time, the platoon made its way west along the sands, dashing from slight cover to gulley, gulley to slight cover. They had crawled through hedge rows and ditches overland from their previous position on Highway 40. Now they were heading toward Dunkirk. Even the lieutenant didn't quite know why. He had chattered vaguely to himself about *perhaps finding a boat*, but that was only a minor consideration compared to the one big overwhelming need: find peace . . . and safety.

The heavy shelling commenced again. Again the beach, its whole length, erupted in spurts of sand, bodies, and clay. Lieutenant Heron's platoon once more clutched the bottom of the long, low sad *falaise* at the desperate edge of the fainting land of France.

3rd June, 1940. 7:35 P.M.
At sea, twenty-two miles due north of Calais, France

The fog had stayed with them all that day. Perkins remained hunched up, shivering in the stern seat. Mitchell and Goffin peered through the mist. By midnight it had cleared enough for them to see the orange glow along the horizon showing them the direction of the southeast.

They moved Perkins, gently, from his seat and laid him in the bottom of the boat, very carefully.

Goffin took their single oar. He slipped it slowly into the sculling slot. "We got to head north a bit . . . keep the fire on our starb'd quarter," he breathed, his voice thick, through swelling lips.

Then there was silence in the boat as the seaman twisted away at the oar, glancing with half-dead eyes into the sleepy face of Mitchell.

After twenty minutes Mitchell said, "Right, mate, a slope north it is."

During the night they thought they heard several ships. They actually saw one pass them a mile and a half away, its dark shadow against the gleaming black, heaving sea. They did not wave or shout. They knew that it was useless to do so; that they must save every last remaining ounce of their fast-ebbing energy.

Perkins in the bottom of the boat, was chattering his teeth, muttering unintelligibly, Mitchell covered him with their one wet shirt.

"We've got to keep moving," said Goffin, as he offered the oar to Mitchell. "Otherwise, we're for the 'ight jump, Mitch old son."

Mitchell changed places with Goffin. He sculled on, into the black void of the northwest.

"That's better, now we got a bit o' starlight," Goffin murmured, as he took the oar yet again, an hour later.

Mitchell looked up, and saw one pin-point of dim light, directly overhead, shimmering faint and dull through the thinning mist.

"That's Beetle Juice," Goffin murmured mysteriously.

Mitchell was too cold and exhausted to wonder what it meant. He closed his eyes and dozed to the murmur of the dying rumble in the southeast and the frequent loud roar of bombers overhead.

3rd June, 1940. 6:07 P.M.
On the beach a miles west of Koksjide, Belgium, ten miles east of Dunkirk, France

As the ramp doors of the car ferry crashed down, Lynch slammed his foot on the accelerator. The Alvis lurched over the still-falling ramp door. The wheels did not touch the ramp at all. They shot over the rounded iron sill, at the hinge of the ramp, and into the air. The Alvis landed its rear wheels three feet in front of the bow-ramp edge.

Its forward movement slithered it into shallow water. The Dunlop Touring tires gripped the ridged sand of the sea-bed at the high-water mark. Lynch wrenched the wheel right. There was a moment's spattering of wet sand from the rear tires as they spun half a revolution, then the Alvis, Lynch hunched at the wheel, shot forward onto the dry, hard, firm sand above the high-water mark, and away, along the shore, in the direction of Dunkirk. As the car hit the water's edge Lynch caught a glimpse of the gray Volkswagen speeding toward the ferry. He felt for the back schmeisser trigger wire with his left hand.

The Volkswagen came to a slithering halt at the ferry ramp. Lynch cursed as he watched through the rear mirror. He saw three men jump out of the Volkswagen and dash up the ferry ramp. Then he saw the Volkswagen start off again, following him. He slowed down and stopped. He flung himself over the driver's seat into the rear compartment. With one movement he climbed onto the rear seat and, straining against the securing ropes, aimed the schmeisser, carefully, at the bouncing Volkswagen.

Corporal Hans Klausen was only fifteen yards from the long black English car when a bullet through the open side window of his car took away the left side of his forehead. The Volkswagen spun violently, slid around to the right, and ran into the sea, not stopping until the water level was up to the engine distributor cap.

Lynch watched the ferry, grimacing, his mouth twitching with rage. Waiting.

Kapitan Ludwig stood on the ferryboat ramp as he paused for Hartmann and Vogel to dash round from the offside of the Volkswagen.

"After him, Klausen!" he raged as the Abwehr star driver put the gray Volkswagen into gear. "Ram him, if necessary!" He turned to gaze at the scene inside the ferry. His face changed from rage and excitement to horror and disgust. Over the top of one of the cars a blond boy was sprawled, half his head blown off. Gray brain matter and dried blood were spattered over the front windows of the Bugatti.

He glared up at the two sprawled bodies on the bridge deck. Quickly he stared along the beach just in time to see the Volkswagen slide into the sea.

"Get the nearest car!" he bawled at Hartmann. "Slip those damned holding chains off the Hispano-Suiza!" he yelled at Vogel, who was already doing so.

Hartmann looked quickly into the Spanish car. The ignition keys were in the engine switch. He jumped into the driver's seat. Vogel had the chain slip hasps on the front outside, and the rear nearside wheels released in five seconds. Ludwig ran to the Hispano-Suiza, stood on the broad, rubber-matted running board, and bent down to shout at Hartmann, "Go slow down the ramp, then let her rip, we can catch up with him before the frontier!"

Hartmann nodded as Vogel clunked his schmeisser on the floor below the front passenger seat and climbed in.

"I'll get in when you're off the ramp!" shouted Ludwig. He was upright now, holding onto the Hispano-Suiza with both hands to the inside top of the door.

Ludwig gazed forward for a split second out to the low cliff ahead. He caught a glimpse of a panzer tank coming to a halt at the top edge of the low *falaise*.

Hartmann slid the hand brake off. His left foot trod lightly on the accelerator, his right foot started to declutch.

The rear wheel slowly moved forward. The tread had moved three inches before the Bakelite box switch button was exposed and rose on its spring. Forty gallons of high-octane gasoline in the Hispano-Suiza tank spattered flame into the air. It fell back over the ferry. The explosion of the plastique sent the bodies of Hartmann and Vogel through the front window of the vehicle. Vogel landed head first on the ramp. The velocity of his flight smashed in his skull. Hartmann's body, legless, landed in the sea, eight inches below the lapping high-water mark, where he lost consciousness two minutes later— just before he died.

Kapitan-Corvetten Ludwig's body, lifeless, landed at the base of the cliff, immediately below the spot where the panzer tank was stopped.

The flaming gasoline on *Hoop's* fire-drenched car deck had all the other cars blazing in four seconds, and one by one their tanks, too, exploded. In ten seconds the ferry was a roaring inferno of flame.

The first tank commander heard and saw the first explosion. He had already aimed his gun at the ferry. He glimpsed the object flying toward him. His trigger finger jerked. The tank shell smashed right through the ferry wheelhouse, exploding on its afterside. *Hoop* blew up.

The smoke pouring from the ferry obscured the tank gunner's vision. The Panzer colonel, rolling up to the cliff edge in his own command tank, did not see the black vehicle along the beach start up and casually move off at the rate of ten sedate miles an hour, through the slowly moving clumps of Allied prisoners-to-be heading east along the beach. Neither did he see Lynch glide the Alvis in between two burned-out British Army Bedford trucks, still smoking, under the cliff a mile east of the frontier ditch. Nor, after Lynch had hidden it under the tattered remnants of the truck tarpaulins, did he see him crawl back inside the Alvis to wait for darkness to fall and for the bombing over Dunkirk to ease off. Colonel Rommel was too busy gloating over his second penetration to the coast and watching the trudge of the defeated into a possible lifetime of captivity.

As he settled back on the seat in the Alvis, Lynch thought it strange that all those Allied troops advancing into Belgium made no sound, did not sing. "Oh well, that's their bloody luck, they shouldn't have joined," he said aloud to himself.

When the sky above him turned to a darker shade of red, Lynch cleared the tarpaulin off the front of the Alvis. He jumped in, started the engine, and roared off along the sand.

On the way to the remnants of the French-Belgian frontier fence in the distance, he sent French and British soldiers flying into the sand. Three of them were dead when they hit the beach, several were severely injured. The Alvis reached one hundred miles an hour. Troops scattered out of its roaring way as it hit the nearside of the frontier ditch, eight feet deep and fifteen feet wide, soared over the top of the ditch and landed on all four wheels on the French side. It tore through the remaining section of barbed wire barrier. It slowed for ten seconds down to fifty miles an hour, then accelerated again to a hundred. The Alvis drove its deadly path through the ranks on one side of the remains of a French battalion trudging slowly east. Men scattered, silent or screaming over the beach. One soldier had the presence of mind to raise the one rifle in the battalion. He fired after the rushing shadow but the bullet passed high overhead. The Alvis screeched into burning Dunkirk.

Lynch was still hunched low over the wheel as the Alvis took the bridge over the Eastern Canal. It missed a German Panzer tank at the eastern end of the bridge by inches. Wehrmacht privates and non-commissioned officers were flung into the canal.

When the tank gunner recovered from his shock, he opened fire on the black shadow racing around the corner toward the *Maison du Marine*. He was too late. His three shells dropped into the square in front of the Harbor Master's Office. They exploded among the bodies of S.S. Sturmtruppen already smashed by the Alvis, among them officers over the rank of Sturmbahnführer.

Lynch took the left-hand corner at the edge of the *Écluse Darse I*, the main steamer dock. He sent a row of British prisoners and their

German guards flying into the waters off the dock. He smashed straight through the Waffen-S.S. machine-gun section guarding the bridge at the south center of the dock at eighty-five miles an hour.

Again the Alvis flew into the air. Again it landed on all four wheels. Lynch screeched to the right at the end of the *Darse 1*. As his eye caught the long line of Panzer tanks lined up, as if in parade fashion, on the *Chaussée de Darse*, a great wide promenade running the whole length of the five dock basins, he accelerated to 120.

The tank crews were idling around their tanks, resting after the strenuous effort of the past two weeks. Some of the crews had goggles pushed up over their tank helmets and peaked caps. Some were drinking coffee from a mobile British canteen, still with the British catering corps staff, behind its open counter, looking glum.

There was no warning. The Alvis ripped straight into the crowd of soldiers in front of the canteen. Some went flying through the air to smash into the canteen and onto the cobblestones of the *chaussée*. One Waffen-SS officer struggled to undo his pistol holster, but by the time his Luger was out, the Alvis had ploughed through the Wehrmacht sentries and French prisoners on the bridge over the western canal. It disappeared into the smoke at the north end of the *Commune Saint Pol-sur-Mer*, the Dunkirk working-class housing district. The tank at the western bridge lobbed shells in the direction of Saint Pol anyway, in the hopes of hitting *something*.

The Alvis emerged again, making eighty miles an hour, out of the rubble-strewn streets of Saint Pol. It made a right turn and was back on the beach to the west of Dunkirk.

Lynch was sweating as he whooped to himself, "Done the bugger. Spain . . . here comes Banger Boy!" He slowed down to a crawl. He drove three miles west along a body-strewn beach at ten miles an hour before he saw the German tanks blocking his way west. He realized in a flash that he was trapped. One panzer opened fire on him when he was still a quarter of a mile away. Cursing, he slid the gears into neutral. He crashed them into reverse and spun the wheel. The car's rear end reversed up the beach, backing up to the small cliff at the head of the beach. The car stopped. Lynch switched off the engine. "Bloody bastards, bloody bastards. They've blocked me off!" he sobbed.

He climbed out of the car still sobbing and emptied one of the Dutch army kit bags onto the sand.

He ripped open the rear door of the Alvis. He opened the steel box and rammed the contents into the Dutch kit bag, then he turned to look around.

A dozen haggard French poilus were staring silently at him from along the cliff. He ignored them and walked away, down the fifty yards to the water's edge. He peered around into the clearing mist and saw a lone British soldier still with his round tin hat on his head, sitting, motionless, in a tiny one-man dinghy about five yards offshore. He waded toward the dinghy.

"Hello, Tommy!" Lynch called. The soldier looked at him blankly, with unknowing, uncaring, unseeing eyes.

"Come on over, mate!" shouted Lynch. The soldier did not move. Lynch waded out further toward the dinghy, which was about eight feet long. He reached for it with one hand. He grabbed the side. Still the soldier did not move. Lynch saw that he was very young. He spun the boat around so he could grab the bow and pulled it inshore.

"There's a good fellow, eh?" Lynch murmured as he tried to pull the Tommy out of the boat. The lad resisted fiercely and moved his lips as if to shout, his blue eyes wide with shock.

"Band-boy, eh? Royal Wiltshire Regiment?" said Lynch," Well, Uncle Banger's going to make things nice and quiet."

He raised the Walther and placed it against the beardless boy's brow. The boy still stared ahead. Lynch pulled the trigger. The boy fell over. Lynch grabbed the body and heaved it out of the dinghy. He dragged the boat further toward the beach until the bow grounded. He scampered back to the Dutch kit bag, lifted it, and ran, splashing. He threw the kit bag into the dinghy and pushed off with one foot. The dinghy slid away from the shore.

Lynch heard a voice from the beach say, "You filthy *bastard*!"

A tall British guardsman was standing ten feet back from the water's edge, pointing his rifle at Lynch. The guardsman raised his rifle to his right shoulder. Lynch shot him through the stomach. The guardsman sank to the sand, moaning in agony. Lynch pulled the trigger again. Nothing happened. Lynch cursed as he realized he was out of ammunition and threw the Walther out to seaward. The thought of grabbing the guardsman's rifle flashed into his mind. He saw the Frenchmen running toward the guardsman, down the beach. He sat down, grabbed the oars, and pulled the dinghy away as fast as he could. There were two rifle shots from the group, but Lynch was already in the low mist fifty yards offshore. He turned the dinghy to follow the coastline, slowly rowing in the mist.

He had rowed for about half an hour when he saw the ship.

She was out to seaward, about 300 yards offshore. As the mist slowly moved away from her at intervals, Lynch saw that she was drifting and there was no one on deck. Excitedly, he steered with the oars toward the boat. When he reached twenty yards from the ship, he stopped rowing and looked for signs of life on deck. He saw the leeboards raised on either side and thought she might be a French fishing boat. He saw her great red sail lazily swinging to and fro. There was no sound from her except the screeching of iron rings on a wire forward.

"Hello!" he hollered. "Anybody home?"

Lynch took hold of a line that was dangling from the vessel's bow and pulled himself alongside, amidships, grabbed the kit bag, and held onto the wires that came over the ship's side and hauled himself up on deck.

Lynch stared around. He gazed up and saw a big white seabird, silent, perched atop the masthead. He went to the edge of the cargo hatch and looked down into the dark space of the hold. By the light of the red glare in the sky he saw row upon row of men with their eyes closed or silently staring at one another. He saw their French helmets, and he saw the ladder.

Here goes nothing, he thought to himself as he climbed down.

No one in the hold said anything. Lynch crept to the ship's side, stumbling over knees in the dark, and sat there, as silent as the rest, *Somebody's going to take them further down the coast*. He was confident the ship was heading for Cherbourg, or *maybe Brest*, he guessed. *Always wanted to go there . . . name like that . . . got to be some fancy khyfer."*

There was little sound from inside the boat. Now and then a soldier climbed the ladder to go on deck to relieve himself. Apart from that there was only the eerie sound of over 250 men breathing, asleep and awake, and the steadily diminishing rumbles of victory and defeat from the shore. Within an hour, Lynch fell asleep, feeling, for some reason he could not fathom, *safe*.

4th June, 1940. 1:00 A.M.
At sea, nineteen miles WNW of Calais, France, five miles southeast of Dover

The fog had wrapped itself around the dinghy again. The three men, one in the bottom of the boat and the two sitting, shirtless, chattered their teeth and shivered. The two seated men now and then waved their arms out from their sides and brought them back again across their chests. The rest of the night they sat shivering silent in the slowly rising and falling dinghy, listening to the drums and throbs of battle die away all around them. Once they heard a ship nearer than the others, but they did not bother to look around. At intervals a low groan issued from the man in the bilges as the water sloshed around him. They were three frozen wraiths in an opaque world without any dimensions; without any sound, except the dying dirge in the distance and the rumbles of imminent death overhead.

4th June, 1940. 4:00 A.M.
One mile east of Dunkirk East Pier

Lieutenant Heron's platoon had searched the beach for a boat that would float. They had come across a grounded barge, with no masts, but she was too heavy to shove off into the sea. They had seen several boats on the shore, but they all had large shell and splinter holes in them. Earlier they had seen the long, black car ploughing through the battalion of men. No one had recognized the make of car. There had been so much death, destruction, and misery in the past eight days that a few traffic casualties made no difference at all. The men stared, then shrugged and plodded slowly along. Heron looked at the slope at the head of the beach and saw a boat lying among the rough grass.

He left his men and strolled up to the boat. It was about fourteen feet long. He recognized it as an inshore fishing boat of the type common on the French channel shore from Le Havre east. He called his men. Despite the roar of the burning oil tanks nearby, to the west of them, the men heard him. They slowly slogged through the loose dry sand at the grassy verge to join him.

"A boat!" he said.

"But it's got . . . *cochon* . . . it's full of water!" said Sergeant Bosquet.

"If it will hold rainwater *in*," the lieutenant replied, "it'll hold seawater *out*!"

The indomitable logic of France won the day.

They bailed out the fishing dinghy using their helmets, until only a few inches of water was left in the bottom, then they turned it up, on its side, to empty the last water out. The oars clattered as they fell down across the bottom of the dinghy.

Working with a will now, the ten men dragged the dinghy the two hundred yards down to the water's edge. They dragged it out until they were up to their waists in water. They stood in the cold water, breathing heavily, silhouetted against the flaming scarlet sky.

"One at a time, in you go," ordered Heron.

When the ten men were all crowded into the tiny boat, it had only five inches of hull above water.

One man cried, "We'll never get far in this. It will sink!"

"We'll use it to look for a bigger boat," replied Heron, quietly.
"I've seen quite a few out there drifting around in the mist. Maybe
we'll have some luck!" Heron had seen, in the clearing mist, the shape
of a destroyer, only 400 yards offshore.

The pace of the rowers quickened, as they pulled, carefully, toward
the destroyer, now black, now gray, as the mist cleared, then pink as
it reflected the color of the sky to the west. When they were at last
alongside the ship, they found she was a complete wreck.

The men clambered out of the dinghy and clattered around the
sloping deck calling out. There was no reply. From down the hole
where the funnel had been smoke still poured. Bodies littered the
deck, distorted, mutilated, dead.

"Come on back into the dinghy," ordered Heron.

"But . . . *merde* . . . it's unsafe, sir," a voice in the dark said.
"We'll all be in the sea if we continue in that cockleshell."

Heron replied, "Get back into the dinghy!" As he gave the order,
he reached for his holster. Then he changed his mind. "Look," he
explained. "This is a complete wreck. She's been badly bombed and
shelled. Her bottom is aground. If you stay onboard her you will never
get away from the Germans. They'll come out in the morning and
either kill you off like flies or they'll take you ashore. Now where will
that get you, *hein?*"

There was no reply.

The men all silently clambered back into the dinghy. Their weight
again pushed the dinghy down into the sea until its gunwale was a
mere five inches above the level of the slowly moving swells.

They rowed on, into the mist. Heron thought to himself about the
situation. *There's little chance of reaching England in this boat. It's
forty-eight miles away by sea. Several of these men are married, with kids.
Thank God I'm not. But the weather is holding up. Now what's it to be,* he
asked himself, *A German prison camp, perhaps for years . . . ten . . . eight
. . . who knows?* He frowned, *Or a forty-eight-mile row to England in a
fourteen-foot boat with ten men onboard?* He was still frowning at his own
question when he saw the vessel.

The first thing about her that caught his attention were her drawn
up leeboards. At first, Heron thought that she was a small French
fishing boat. Then he looked up at the mast and recognized her for
what she was.

"A Thames sailing barge!" he shouted.

The soldiers with him followed the direction of his gaze, red-eyed and weary. An all-white gannet swooped out of the mist, low over their heads, then flew toward the sailing boat, to hover aloft.

Heron was transported in a quick flash of memory to the week's visit to London in 1930, when he had stood with two other French yachtsmen and had seen, to their delight, fifteen or twenty of these clumsy looking, yet graceful, gentle-moving, old-fashioned vessels.

Excitedly the rowers, with tiny strokes for lack of elbow room, pulled nearer and nearer to the ship. Soon the packed dinghy was almost alongside.

Lieutenant Heron cupped both his hands around his mouth, feeling the ten-day growth of beard, and hailed, "Anyone at home?" in English.

There was no reply. The only sound from onboard was the creaking of the sprit boom as it swayed slightly to and fro, and the squeak of the foresail hanks as the head of the sail jerked back and forth. The Frenchmen pulled alongside.

Heron saw a rope in the water alongside the ship. The men clambered onboard. Heron took the line up with him. In his twenty years of small boat sailing, he knew that lines in the water were unseamanlike and also could be dangerous.

"It could wrap around the propeller," he explained to Sergeant Bosquet, as he tied the line to the port shroud. As he spoke he heard a strange voice behind him. Heron spun around and found himself staring into the tired and haggard faces of eight poilus.

"Where the hell did you come from?" he snapped.

The poilus pointed at the hold. Heron strode over to the hatch. He looked down. He saw in the dull, early morning light the turned-up faces of almost 300 silent, frightened men.

"Where's the crew?" Heron asked the poilus. They merely shrugged.

One of the men said, "We've been onboard this boat since early yesterday afternoon, sir, most of us. A few came onboard later. There is no crew, and *merde alors*! no engine." The dirty unshaven face offered a hand to Heron. "Lieutenant Vidoq, at your service."

Heron shook the hand. He passed to the stern of the vessel. He leaned far over the counter and read the name upside down, DUAM ECIRTAEB and below that NODNOL. He repeated the name to himself aloud, *Beatrice Maud, London*. He also noticed the daylight. It was 7:00 A.M.

Heron returned to the cargo hatch. "Down below!" he shouted. "Lieutenant Heron here. I'm taking charge of you men and this vessel. Anyone with sailing experience come topside now!" He listened.

There was no sound of movement from below.

"Anyone with any experience at all with sails?" he demanded.

There was no reply.

"Anyone down there with any experience with lines and ropes and canvas?"

"Me, sir," said a voice behind him. Heron looked at where the voice had come from. A small, slim, filthy, unshaven private was standing there.

"Were you a rigger? What were you?" asked Heron.

"Acrobat, sir. One of the best in the circus business," the slim private replied. "Private Henri LeBlanc at your service, sir."

He was the first man to salute Heron that day.

Heron returned the salute with a half-grin, half-groan.

"Right LeBlanc. You're the first mate!"

"*Oui, mon Capitaine,*" said LeBlanc, smiling widely in the pale morning light.

Heron turned to shout yet again down into the hold. "Has any man down there ever been to sea?"

"*Oui, M'sieur,*" came a voice from the depths. Heron heard the single call and moaned audibly, "*Mon Dieu!*"

The man clambered up the ladder. He saluted Heron. He introduced himself, "Private Fouchet, Ex-Marine, sir . . . did a year."

Heron asked him, "Then you know which is port and which is starboard, Fouchet?"

"Mais certainment, M'sieur." *Anything to stay out of that cochonerie . . . that pig-sty . . . down below,* thought Fouchet. He studied Heron. *Il est débrouillard, a lively one, this,*" he thought.

"Good, then you can be second mate."

Heron turned to the men on deck. He shouted, "All except Sergeant Bosquet and Lieutenant Vidoq, go below and stay there. Do not return to the deck without permission!"

Most of the small crowd who had gathered about him, making sounds of relief, clambered down the ladder.

The river yachtsman-cum-lieutenant, the circus acrobat, and the ex-Marine-with-one-return-passage-to-Martinique-in-a-battleship set to, first to explore the ropes and rigging, then to set up the forestay sheet again. When all was basically shipshape, Heron ordered the acrobat to haul in the main sheet.

Even as Heron passed the order, they heard the whizz of a shell overhead. They looked to landward. There were a dozen panzer tanks rapidly approaching the spot on the beach nearest to them. Another shell whizzed through the mainsail as the slight breeze caught it. It left a neat round hole in the sail, and passed harmlessly into the sea on the starboard side of *Beatrice Maud*.

She, it seemed to Heron, willingly, joyfully, picked up speed and sailed into the mist. In a moment they could see nothing of the beach or the tanks, or anything else. Heron headed for what he guessed was the seaward direction for five, ten, fifteen minutes. Then, the boat came to a gentle halt.

Heron realized that they had run aground. He quickly released the mainsheet. In the distance, at about a hundred yards on either side in the swirling mist, he made out the shapes of two big cargo steamers, also aground on the same sandbank.

Heron knew that they had pushed out the fishing dinghy at almost dead low tide, and, with a yachtsman's eye, he had noticed that the tide was rising.

When *Beatrice Maud* ran onto the sandbank, she was moving so gently that no one down below in the hold realized that she had gone aground. A half an hour after she touched the sandbank the sea supported her again. She slid off, over the sandbank and out into the open sea, with Lieutenant Heron holding his breath at the wheel, the circus acrobat on the mainsheet, the marine on the headsail sheets, and Sergeant Bosquet keeping an eye on the men in the hold.

Heron glanced at his watch. It was 10:00 A.M.

The breeze was light southwest. At first, Heron steered *Beatrice* into the wind, on a close reach. The barge, he saw, was moving very slowly in the light breeze, and the mist was clearing.

Ten times they sighted overloaded rowing boats making for England. Ten times Heron hove to, letting the mainsheet flap in the freshening breeze as the exhausted rowers pulled over and were heaved onboard by the deck guard and sent or carried below.

By mid-day Heron, although weary from the efforts of the past two weeks, was actually enjoying the feel of the wheel under his grubby fist as the breeze freshened. It took him back to his sailing holidays at Bordeaux and Aberwrach, and he remembered the weeklong visit to Southampton, when he and three friends had crossed and recrossed the English Channel (though to him, it was, of course, La Manche). He patted the wheel as Bosquet looked at his transformed face.

"She's a beautiful, sweet English lady!" Heron grinned.

Bosquet laughed; it was the first time he had ever come close to understanding Heron's eternal chatter about sailing boats and the sea.

As the afternoon wore on, they sighted many upturned boats, many bodies floating upside down. The deck crew, all four of them, as well as Heron, kept a careful lookout, on the lieutenant's instructions, for swimmers who might be alive. They saw nothing but sad wreckage as *Beatrice Maud*, now with the wind blowing stronger, danced and played her gentle calliope toward the English shore.

Heron looked up at the eighty-foot-high mast. Knocker's pennant on top was gaily fluttering its tail-end in the breeze. The dirty, almost black, ensign back on the stern frapped its fly to the seagulls searching *Beatrice*'s wake. He looked up again.

A lone gannet, all-white, with a tremendous wing spread, was gliding on the breeze, above the masthead, turning his hook-billed head this way and that, calling and squawking as he dodged the rocking truck of the mast. The foresail hanks zizzed on the forestay as the wind filled the beautiful balloon of ochre canvas, and the sun cast a dark orange shadow over the sail's luff at the forward end of its graceful inner curve.

Heron leaned over the gunwale for a brief moment, on the port sunny side, watching the sparkling white bone in the teeth of the great dancing bows. Then he saw the sandbank—dead ahead.

Heron dashed to the wheel and spun it around. The ship, slowly at first, then swiftly, turned in her tracks. As they brought the sun and the breeze onto the starboard side of the ship and the dark sabers of shade onto the portside, the great sprit boom swung across the sky over the hold with a mighty *crash*! that brought fifteen soldiers scurrying out of the guts of her, to be tongue-lashed back below again by the sergeant. *Beatrice* leaned slightly over to port and pushed another gleaming white foot-high bow wave ahead of her, this time south, back along her track.

Heron, although happier than he had dreamed he would ever be again, was almost falling asleep on his feet when he saw the sunken lightship. He stared at the ghostly hulk as *Beatrice* charged past her. He tried to read the name painted in great white letters on her side, but the mist dropped again, hiding the shame of the faithful guardian's killers. "I think it's the *Goodwin Sands*, he commented to a mystified Bosquet.

After an hour, Heron guessed he should be clear of the sandbank danger. He changed the course again to the southwest.

As *Beatrice* turned to obey his command, seeming to scrape the whole southern, smoking horizon as her bowsprit swung through the wind, the great sprit boom clanged across. The head sails flogged for a moment, then, with a mighty thud, they were lovely and curved and full of the breeze once more.

Beatrice Maud gently leaned her starboard side into the sea, and was off again, to the southwest. Heron checked his watch. It was seven o'clock in the evening.

The thump of the long thirty-foot sprit had shocked Heron and his deck crew wide awake. He and they, at the same moment, saw the armed trawler emerge from a fog patch. She was steaming straight for *Beatrice*'s future path in the now-jagged chop of the Channel, while the all-white gannet, lazily beating his wide wings, glided in glad cycles over the spot where the two ships would meet.

4th June, 1940. Noon
Three miles south of Dover

The mist had started to clear at ten A.M. Goffin was the first to see the land. He pointed it out to Mitchell in a loud shout. "Land, Mitch—I've seen the bastard!"

A darker gray, a slight suspicion of a shade.

When Mitchell looked in the direction to which Goffin was now sculling, he could see nothing. Then, as the rising breeze swirled the mist away he croaked, "It's there, mate . . . bleedin' Blighty!"

By noon they realized that they were battling against the outcoming tide. Mitchell had an ineffective spell at the sculling oar; Goffin's efforts were much weaker.

At 2 P.M. they sighted the trawler. Goffin waved the oar. Slowly the trawler made her way closer to them, then she sent a whaler over to tow them alongside her gently pitching side.

As the trawler's whaler approached they saw the helmsman, with three red stripes and an anchor on his arm, cup his hand, and they heard him shout, "Hello! What's all this, then, lads?"

"Come on then, mate, it's three hours past tot-time!" bellowed Goffin. "We've been adrift two and a half days."

With a scraping noise the whaler came alongside the dinghy. The leading seaman in the whaler stared at Goffin in his air force officer's trousers, then at Mitchell in his naval pants, then down at Perkins, chattering, supine in the bottom of the dinghy.

"What's all this, then?" the killick helmsman called. His voice dropped a little. He shouted to his bowman, "O.K. mate, pass 'em a line." He turned to Goffin. "Make it fast on the seat, eh, sir?" he ordered him.

"Who're you sirring, Hooky?" Goffin sang out.

In ten minutes they were onboard His Majesty's Trawler *Lily*, enjoying a cup of steaming tea, wrapped in blankets, with Perkins on the settee in the skipper's cabin.

The skipper, who looked about sixty, was a lieutenant of the Royal Naval Reserve. "We got another six hours of patrol yet, afore we goes in," he said in a broad East Anglian dialect. "Soo maike yoorselves at'ome, lads, whilst we looks for your mates." The skipper turned to the signal man behind him. "Sparky," he ordered, "take their details down, will you, an' send 'em in to the Dover Command. All names, addresses, next o'kin. You knows the routine."

He turned to go back on the bridge, back to his grim harvesting.

4th June, 1940. 4:00 P.M.
The Circus, London

Margot entered the office without knocking. She had a notepad in her hand.

'C' was speaking on the telephone. He nodded to her, listened for a moment, then hung up.

"I think you ought to know about this," she said. "The Foreign Office has been on the phone to Edwards at Langley Road. They're playing hell."

'C' looked at her. "What?" he murmured. "What about now?"

"It seems that one of their chaps, one of their domestic staff, the butler from the Hague, has been picked up at sea in a boat somewhere. The poor chap's in a dreadful state, but that's not what worries them. It seems that one of the other two chaps picked up with him blurted out the Langley Road address."

"Dennis?" 'C' asked, trying not to appear startled.

"It seems to be Mitchell. He claims he's a civilian, anyway. Gave Langley Road as his home address. It seems that Dennis is . . . missing . . . it's all a bit garbled."

"Lynch?"

"Could be," she replied noncommittally,

"What is the FO complaining about?" 'C' frowned.

"The loss of the butler's private effects. They want to know who's going to reimburse him . . . " she got no further.

"Where are they?"

"Coming into Dover, onboard the naval trawler *Lily*. They think about eight o'clock," she said.

'C' said, "Get hold of Myers and Philips. I don't care what they're doing. I don't care if they are trailing every damned German in the Strand Palace Hotel. Get hold of them and send them down to Dover immediately. If there's any delay get the army air service to fly them down . . .whatever happens, I want Myers and Philips on the Dover docks by 8 P.M., and let Colonel Tarrant know, will you? Might be useful. Can't have chaps like that loose, bad form! Never know what they'll be up to next. Arrange for Superintendent Golightly to be there, too."

4th June, 1940. 7:15 P.M.
One mile due south of Dover

During a short break from steering, Heron had found Knocker's signal flag racks, just inside the doorway of the skipper's cabin. Now he pulled the "T" flag out of his pocket. This is the international code sign for *Do Not Cross My Bows*. It was also red, white, and blue stripes, the blue stripe on the fly, the reverse of the French tricolor. Heron excitedly hoisted the flag after letting the mainsheet fly. *Beatrice*'s way was carrying her still, and she passed under the bows of the trawler. A startled British sailor stared at them, silently.

Heron cupped his hands again around his mouth and bellowed, "Where is the nearest port? What port is it?"

From the trawler bridge came the reply, shouted through hand megaphone. "One mile—Dover!"

Heron stared as the trawler skipper dropped his megaphone and pointed north into the mist. Then he almost fell from exhaustion. "*Merci au bon Dieu!*" he murmured," "*et a la Beatrice Maud!*"

"*Amen*," murmured the men around him, as they glared, with red-shot eyes, into the fog ahead.

"Where in the name of Christ did she come from?" the skipper of His Majesty's trawler *Lily* asked the trawler mate. Goffin and Mitchell looked on, listening, now dressed in borrowed shirts and duffle coats, with steel helmets pushed back on their heads.

"Blowed if I know, sir," replied the young sublieutenant.

"The last ship came in from Dunkirk last night, for the love of Jesus." The skipper stared after *Beatrice Maud*, a puzzled frown on his face. "Yester-bloody-day afternoon!" he corrected himself.

"Well, there she is, sir," said the Subby. He read the barge's name in an awed voice, *Beatrice Maud of London*.

The skipper looked out to seaward, south again, into the fog bank.

"There can't be any more, sir . . . not now," said the sublieutenant.

"No," the skipper quietly replied, "the curtain's down now all right, son. You just remember in forty years' time that you saw the last ship come back from Dunkirk . . . the very last." The skipper thought for a moment, staring at the mist on the southern horizon. He said in what was almost a whisper, "The end of an age . . .so help me God . . . the end of the old Europe, an' it's a bloody old sailin' barge that was last in from hell."

"Not the end of England, sir," observed the young man.

A large white gannet beat directly past the bridge, only feet away from the men.

"Britain, you mean, son. What, with boats like that one around? Why, Mister, she's bloody indomitable! Heart o' oak!" he repeated loudly, *"Heart o' bloody oak!"*

The helmsman looked at the skipper who turned his face away from the AB's gaze, slightly embarrassed. "Steer after *Beatrice Maud*!" he ordered. "Let's stop playing silly buggers . . . got a job to do . . . "

The helmsman obeyed. The trawler steamed slowly into yet another fog patch, churning the cold gray water astern of her, under the close inspection of the all-white gannet.

They found *Beatrice Maud* fifteen minutes later, when the fog cleared a little. She was wallowing at anchor. The acrobat and Heron were brailing her mainsail. The sea was kicking up two-foot waves by now. *Beatrice Maud* rolled from side to side, as if she were laughing, revelling in her return.

The soldiers onboard became sicker and sicker. Soon the hold was almost awash in vomit mixed with coal dust. For Lynch the smell was almost unbearable. He knew they'd gone to anchor and was hugging both the kit bag and the thought that he would soon be ashore in France and on his way to Spain.

The men in the hold were noisy now, moaning, talking, shouting, and making loud noises as they vomited. Lynch could not hear the English being shouted above on th bow and stern.

"Weigh your anchor!" shouted the trawler skipper.

Heron shrugged his shoulders. They had tried, but it was much too heavy for the men on deck watch, even though there were seven of them now. The trawler scraped alongside. An able seaman jumped onto *Beatrice*'s deck. He, too, tried to haul her anchor, using the hand windlass but could not budge it. The trawler passed them a hand hacksaw. The acrobat bent to the anchor chain. It took him ten minutes to saw the cable link. The cut link opened as *Beatrice* heaved with the sea, and the chain rattled rustily overboard. As the mist cleared, revealing the great white cliffs only fifty yards away from her, *Beatrice Maud* jiggled and danced, shivered and trembled.

Lily's seamen made fast a line onto *Beatrice*'s bow, and the trawler hauled her into the port of Dover. Most of the cargo men now crowded *Beatrice*'s deck, watching the waiting crowd of waving sailors, soldiers, and dockworkers on the jetty. As the two vessels slowly passed through the mole entrance, the mist cleared, the great Union Jack above the Castle on the cliffs snapped and crackled in the passing breeze, and Knocker's house pennant, atop the eighty-foot mast, shimmered as if in reply to a salute.

The white gannet, on the shoulders of the breeze, flew to his mate on the cliffs. She, sitting anxiously with her brood, mewed an impatient welcome as he fluttered to her side on the safe cliff.

"Not one blasted Englishman among the lot," remarked the pier-master colonel as he gazed at *Beatrice*'s deck.
"I suppose this is the first time ever the French have returned to us a sailing prize-of-war, sir?" remarked the adjutant.
"Don't be damned supercilious!" retorted the colonel.

As she pulled *Beatrice* in close to the jetty, *Lily*'s siren screamed repeatedly, *Whoops! whoops!* The chorus was taken up by all the other ships in the harbor. The tugs screeched in a screaming tenor, the fishing boats piped their jaunty whistles, the paddle steamers burped, and the bigger coasters bellowed their bass descants of stern approbation.
Once inside the harbor, *Lily* cast off *Beatrice*'s tow line. Heron steered the barge, carried forward by momentum, for the jetty, and *Beatrice Maud* came alongside the crowded dock with a *bump* that almost sent the crowded poilus on deck flat on their faces.
Lily, her siren still whooping, steamed round in a wide circle, to rest herself against the outboard side of *Beatrice Maud*, as if she wished to pin her new-found stray to the jetty, to dowse her wayward ways.
Mitchell and Goffin were on *Lily*'s deck amidships, taking in all the sights and sounds of the welcome for *Beatrice Maud*. Mitchell was turning around to go into the trawler's galley when with a start he recognized the dirty Dutch army fatigues worn by one of the men on deck. He realized that he was staring at the back of Banger Lynch's head. His jaw tightened.

A fancy gangway with stanchions and ropes to hold onto was passed onto *Beatrice Maud*'s deck. It was the fanciest gangway she had ever had, or would ever have again.

Heron was among the first to go ashore, with Sergeant Bosquet still at his side. He raised a tired salute at the British colonel who met him at the bottom of the gangway.

"Welcome Lieutenant, always room for heroes, you know!" said the affable pier-master.

Heron mumbled something in reply and turned to watch the poilus stagger down the gangway.

"Que'est-ce qu'il a dit?" asked Bosquet.

"Il avait dit que nous sommes des heroes," replied Heron.

"Et?"

"Et j'ai dit que nous ne sommes pas des heroes; nous sommes des victimes."

"Victimes, M'sieur?"

"Oui, Sergeant, victimes d'une heroine." Heron gestured at *Beatrice Maud*. *"Nous sommes les victimes d'une grande dame anglaise, mais une dame charmante et heureuse."* Heron said in English, "We are merely victims. She's a heroine."

Heron watched as the poilus staggered down the gangway and as the crowd on the jetty pressed forward to shake their hands and slap their shoulders.

A women's voluntary service mobile canteen pulled up. Soon 200 Frenchmen were standing around it, wolfing down hot meals of English pork sausages and mashed potatoes . . . and tea.

"Toujours le the!" said Heron, smiling through his ten days' beard and dirt.

Bosquet grinned as he raised his steaming mug. *"Le the!"*

Mitchell turned and walked around *Lily*'s deck to the other side of the trawler.

Goffin saw Lynch a moment after Mitchell disappeared. He finished pouring the tea in his mug and passed out of the galley door on the outer side of *Lily*. He almost collided with Mitchell.

They glanced at each other, the soldier and the sailor. There was a silence for ten seconds, then Goffin turned to Mitchell, who was gazing up at the swirling clouds about the castle on the hill over the harbor. He desperately wanted to tell Mitchell about Lynch. He murmured, "I could swear I've seen . . . "

Mitchell broke in, *"You have, mate. So have I . . . Beatrice Maud . . . She passed your old Havelock when we were waiting at anchor in Sheerness Roads, before we went to tulip-land. I didn't see her name first time . . . in Sheerness . . . but I'm sure it's her."*

"Oh, that's where it was," replied Goffin quietly. *"Now I remember."*

Lynch heard the English voices as he reached the top of the hold ladder. His mind raced. He knew he had a good chance of passing through the gate control in his filthy khaki fatigues. He knew there was a reasonable chance he could probably travel on with the Frenchmen, back to France. He shouldered the kit bag. He pressed himself forward with the line of weary men passing slowly ashore. People smiled at him. Some grabbed at his fatigues' sleeve.

"Well done!"

"*Merci*," he mumbled. *Jesus Christ*! he thought, as he glimpsed the castle on the hill.

"Good show!" said one voice.

"*Merci!*" *Steady on, Lynchy-boy, only a few yards to go.*

"Poor fellow looks dead beat!" said another.

Lynch did not hang around by the WVS canteen, as hungry as he was. He ambled with the crowd through the gate. The four gate policemen did not even bother to look at his fatigues or his face. He came to a British Army five-ton truck with a dozen quiet Frenchmen sitting inside, their eyes closed. He threw the kit bag into the truck. He held onto the tailgate and braced himself to clamber into the truck. The voice behind him was gentle, courteous and terribly, terribly British.

"Excuse me, sir . . . Mister Lynch?"

There was a quiet, almost humble politeness in the voice. It was the apologetic tone that is heard when a sharp umbrella spike is jabbed into some clumsy one's calf on a crowded London tube train.

Lynch froze.

The question was repeated, "*Excuse me, sir, Mister Lynch?*"

The five innocent-sounding words had in them the rustle before the bagpipe skirl, the backward jerk of the eighteen-inch bayonet before it is plunged to taste blood, the last testing tug on the seven-coiled knot before the spring-loaded trap door lever is pulled. It was the same level, dry tone that had been spoken while the fire iron, white-hot was slowly rammed into the bowels of King Edward II (his Norman scream was heard eight miles away), in an age less forgiving of mortal sins.

Lynch glared around. He saw, at first, only a small man in a bowler hat. Then he recognized with a heart-jolting start. *The man who followed me to Soho, and Christ! Golightly of the Yard.*

Lynch darted his head around from side to side. He jumped to reach inside the truck for the kit bag. The four gate policemen were on top of him like a ton of bricks, pinning him down prone on the road.

"You got nothing on me!" Lynch shouted. "I only wanted to get back quietly!"

The big man at Myers' side introduced himself. "Chief Superintendent Golightly, New Scotland Yard." His voice went on in the same, flat, even tone. "We do, indeed, have something on you, Mister Lynch. There's a little matter of an allegation of your unlawfully taking five pounds from the . . . er . . . place of . . . er . . . business of Miss Florence Smith at number 18, Croft's Alley, London, WC1 at approximately 5:00 P.M. on tenth May, 1940, thus breaking the terms of your parole from Wormwood Scrubs prison. I am taking you into custody for the said offense, and I must warn you that anything you say may be taken down and used in evidence at your appearance before the magistrates at Bow Street tomorrow morning." Golightly paused. "Now, Lynch, how do you answer?"

"Florence?"

"Effie . . . her working name is Birgitte."

"Get stuffed!" bawled Lynch, his face distorted with rage.

Two stalwarts of the Kent County Police Force clapped the handcuffs onto his wrists.

"Bleedin rozzers!" bellowed Lynch.

Myers reached up inside the truck, grabbed the kit bag, opened it, peered inside, and closed it. As he walked to the police car, with Lynch in the charge of Golightly and another burly rozzer, Myers closed his eyes, wagged his head, and made a tut-tutting sound.

Mitchell said, "I s'pose we'll have to wait until that foreign office bloke has finished with Randy?"

"S'pose so," said Goffin. They went together into the ship's galley, saying nothing.

Minutes later, still in silence, they followed Perkins' stretcher to the dockside. A group of people were gathered around the ambulance doors. Goffin noticed the French lieutenant who had been at the wheel of *Beatrice Maud* hungrily eating sausages and potatoes. For a second their eyes met, then Goffin turned to see Mitchell gently pushing Perkins safely into the ambulance. The butler was conscious and smiling at them. "Farewell, Mitch . . . Goff. It has, if you don't mind my saying so, been a most interesting journey!"

As the ambulance doors closed, a hand tapped Mitchell's shoulder. He turned around, startled.

"Mr. Paul Mitchell?" He saw an elderly, thin man in a blue trilby, a grubby mackintosh, and dirty brown shoes.

"What?" Mitchell started to say.

"Colonel Tarrant would like to have a word with you, sir, when you arrive in London. Of course, we realize this . . . outing has been quite unusual. The colonel wants you to have his phone number. He asked me to mention it when you arrived."

"Who did you say?" Mitchell asked the mackintosh.

"Colonel Tarrant, sir," replied Philips.

"Bollox to Colonel Tarrant!" Mitchell shouted.

"Very good, sir, I shall pass your message on to him, but please be so kind as to keep this paper; it has his telephone number," Philips insisted.

"Oh all bloody right then, give it to me." Mitchell put the paper in the pocket of the naval overcoat he was wearing "on loan." He turned to Goffin, "Where you off to from here, Goff?"

"Got to look up the jaunty at the naval police office . . . get a warrant to wherever the ship is . . . s'pose she's in Scapa Flow by now."

"Well," Mitchell held his hand out to Goffin. "See you, tosh, don't forget to look me up. You got that address I gave you?"

"I memorized it, 89, Stanton Road, North Kensington," said Goffin.

"Right, cheers then, mate, get a bit for me up in Haggisland!" called Mitchell as Goffin rolled away along the quay.

Goffin stopped. He turned around. "Whatcha want, Mitch, long-horn or crossed merino?" He waved, grinning, and disappeared behind the crowd of Frenchmen at the mobile canteen.

Philips was still waiting. Mitchell glowered at him. "Ain't you got no bloody home to go to, mate?" he said.

"I do, Mr. Mitchell. I also have your railway warrant to London and traveling expenses." He handed an envelope to Mitchell.

"What about back pay?" asked Mitchell.

"I'm sure you will receive it in the very near future, sir," said the macintosh, "from Colonel Tarrant . . . be sure to call him."

Mitchell walked away as the sirens started to wail. He made his way to the waiting train as the bofors guns opened up, feeling the red clothes peg, still in his pocket, remembering the other colonel.

Beatrice Maud was alone again, but silent, deprived of all her treasures. Two gannets, one gray-white, the other all white, hovered on the wind over her masthead for a brief, quiet moment before the guns barked. They then glided back to the cliff ledge, together, and left her with only the love and remembrance of the men who had known her.

4th June, 1940. 11:30 P.M.
Stanton Road, North Kensington, London

Mitchell stared out of the taxi window. There was nothing there. All he could see in the dim searchlight casts and the flashes of the antiaircraft guns, where five houses had been on either side of No. 89, was rubble and the backs of the houses in the next street, with half of their walls blasted down.

"I'm as sorry as you are, sir," said the air raid warden, an elderly man of sixty-five. "It was quick . . . at least it was quick."

"All of them?"

"No sir. The older lady and the little boy were taken to Praed Street Hospital, but the young lady, well, sir, they didn't find her for twenty-four hours. It was the twenty-fourth of May, sir, about midnight."

Mitchell, his voice small and strained, said, "Driver, take me to Praed Street Hospital, please."

Half an hour later he was on the hospital telephone, speaking to Colonel Tarrant, writing down a time and place for an appointment in the morning.

5th June, 1940. 9:00 A.M.
The Circus, London

'C' gazed at the filthy Dutch kit bag lying on his desk. He looked up at Margot. "Thank Myers for me, will you?"

"Yes," Margot said.

"And Philips, too, of course."

"His expense account is rather high again . . . two motor garage bills, one for three shillings and fourpence . . . "

'C' broke in, "Damned motor cars. Never did like the things, noisy and smelly. Tarrant phone yet?"

"Yes, about half an hour ago."

"Mitchell's agreed?"

"Yes."

"Good. Er . . . get me the Scheherazade file and the map of Persia."

"Iran."

"All right, whatever the place calls itself these days. Then get me the ABC 1 file—"plan of concerted action to be taken by the U.S. and British forces should the United States enter the war." 'C' picked up the phone. As he waited, a smile dawned. "Get me the Bank of England, the governor, will you?"

Chapter 12

*   *

Epilogue

Land of Hope and Glory—
Mother of the free,
How can we extoll thee—
Who are born of thee?
Wider still and wider,
Shall thy bounds be set—
God who made thee mighty,
Make thee mightier yet—
God who made thee mighty,
Make thee mightier yet!

Chorus of a British hymn set to the tune of Sir Edward Elgar's "Pomp and Circumstance" March. It is sung in the Albert Hall after the performance on Prom nights.

The working-class Britons whom I have heard discuss the subject thought that this hymn should replace the national anthem, which was, they claimed, "too bloody dreary."

In the United States, the "Pomp and Circumstance" march is played at college graduation ceremonies, as slow-marching, serious-faced, begowned young graduates wonder what the future holds in store for them.

12.

Epilogue

Lynch was arraigned before the magistrates at Clerkenwell Road Court—Bow Street Court's windows were being blast-proofed.

The magistrates found the case for Miss Smith to be answerable. They remanded Lynch in custody for one week. They also took into consideration the Crown's case that Lynch had broken the terms of his parole and "directed that he be confined in custody for the four-year remainder of his original sentence of seven years' hard labor on the charge of breaking and entering the strong room of the vessel *Mauretania* (said vessel being the property of the Cunard Steamship and the Royal Mail Steamship Companies)."

It took the Metropolitan Police Special Branch detectives two days to piece together Randolph Perkins' croaked story. It took them another two days to trace the whereabouts of Able Seaman Goffin. With the assistance of the Kent County constabulary, they eventually located Goffin at his *party's* parents' Council house on the outskirts of Gillingham.

The whereabouts of Paul Mitchell was ascertained as being *somewhere in the Middle East on His Majesty's Service*. With the evidence already in hand, the chief commissioner of New Scotland Yard did not feel that Mitchell's presence at the trial would justify the costs of his return to the United Kingdom.

One week from the day he was arrested at Dover, Lynch was remanded by the same magistrates yet again on the charge "that he did unlawfully steal the sum of five pounds being the property of . . . "

The day after, in his cell in Wormwood Scrubs prison, Lynch was charged by Chief Superintendent Fred Coggins of the Scotland Yard Criminal Investigation Department Murder Squad, with "the wilful murder of Lieutenant Aubrey Fowler Dennis, late of His Majesty's Regiment of Royal Engineers." From that moment on, the prisoner Lynch was lodged in solitary confinement.

Lynch's trial was held *in camera* at the Old Bailey on September 2, 1940, before the Lord Chief Justice Rowpusher. There were two witnesses for the Crown: Perkins and Goffin. There were no witnesses for the defense. The twelve-man jury was composed entirely of British army officers above the rank of captain.

The verdict of the court was "guilty of wilful murder." My Lord Chief Justice Rowpusher, as he sat in his red robes on the high bench under the great golden Royal Coat-of-Arms, showed no emotion on his eighty-eight-year-old face. He gently raised the little square black cloth and lowered it onto the top of his shoulder-length wig. He intoned the dread sentence . . . "of this court is that you shall be taken from here to the place from whence you came, and there, on a date to be decided by the appropriate authority under the Crown's justice, you shall be hanged by the neck until you are dead, and may God have mercy upon your soul!"

Lynch was not hanged in Wormwood Scrubs prison, nor, as he had at first secretly hoped on his arrest in Dover, was he shot for treason in the Tower of London.

The public hangman was demanding danger money for attendances in the heavily bombed London area. The accountants at the Home Office calculated that it would be cheaper, by thirty-two shillings and six-pence-halfpenny, to have two prison warders escort Lynch to Manchester than it would be to bring the public hangman and his assistants to London.

The ceremony was, therefore, held in the unheated, smoky brick tower of Strangeways Prison, Manchester.

Lynch's last words, spoken through the canvas head cover, were yelled at the officiating Church of England clergyman.

"If I'd only knocked off Jerries, I'd be a bleedin' hero!"

The spring-loaded trapdoors opened under Lynch's feet at precisely 8 A.M. on December 7, 1940. It was exactly a year to the day before the P.M. at last, got a good night's sleep.

Lynch's body was buried quietly in unconsecrated ground outside Strangeways Prison. Today the site is overlooked by the largest private war-weapons warehouse on earth. It is American-owned.

Beatrice Maud, a real ship, spent the war years June 1940–June 1946 under the control of the admiralty, working mainly off the Bristol Channel. After World War II, she was returned to her old owners and took up her old trade. In 1960, she was converted to a barge-yacht. She is rigged almost the same now (1979) as she was at Dunkirk. She spends her time quietly cruising the waters around the Thames estuary in the summer, and in a peaceful, cozy berth during the sharp, cold winters.